Praise for Stephanie Grace Whitson

A CAPTAIN FOR LAURA ROSE

"An entertaining historical tale of faith, action, and romance."
—*Publishers Weekly*

"This stand-alone novel has all the makings of a great romance: love, intrigue, mystery, and unforgettable characters. Whitson's historical details on female riverboat captains are incredible."
—*RT Book Reviews*

"*A Captain for Laura Rose* is a novel rich with exciting details of riverboat life during the nineteenth century, and the well-drawn characters will steal your heart. Don't miss this exceptional read."
—Judith Miller, award-winning author of the Home to Amana series

"As usual, Stephanie Grace Whitson skillfully weaves unforgettable characters with an unforgettable time in history. Step aboard the *Laura Rose*. You will definitely enjoy the ride!"
—Nancy Moser, bestselling author of *The Journey of Josephine* and *Mozart's Sister*

"Whitson has a wonderful knack of storytelling...I highly recommend *A Captain for Laura Rose*. It is wonderfully crafted and thoughtfully written."
—RadiantLit.com

ALSO BY STEPHANIE GRACE WHITSON

A Captain for Laura Rose

Available from FaithWords
wherever books are sold.

Daughter
of the
REGIMENT

a novel

———— ❧ ————

STEPHANIE GRACE WHITSON

FaithWords

New York • Boston • Nashville

The Author is represented by Books & Such Literary Agency, Inc., 52 Mission Circle, Suite 122, PMB 170, Santa Rosa, CA 95409 www.booksandsuch.com

FaithWords
Hachette Book Group
1290 Avenue of the Americas
New York, NY 10104

www.faithwords.com

Printed in the United States of America

RRD-C

First edition: March 2015
10 9 8 7 6 5 4 3 2 1

FaithWords is a division of Hachette Book Group, Inc.
The FaithWords name and logo are trademarks of Hachette Book Group, Inc.

The Hachette Speakers Bureau provides a wide range of authors for speaking events. To find out more, go to www.hachettespeakersbureau.com or call (866) 376-6591.

The publisher is not responsible for websites (or their content) that are not owned by the publisher.

Library of Congress Cataloging-in-Publication Data

Whitson, Stephanie Grace.
   Daughter of the regiment : a novel / Stephanie Grace Whitson. — First edition.
      pages ; cm
   ISBN 978-1-4555-2903-2 (pbk.) — ISBN 978-1-4555-2904-9 (ebook)
   I. Title.
   PS3573.H555D38 2015
   813'.54—dc23
                                    2014045985

Dedicated to the memory of these
Daughters of the Regiment
and the heroines who served with them

Kady Brownell, 1st and 5th Rhode Island

Lucy Ann Cox, 13th Virginia

Bridget Divers, 1st Michigan

Annie Etheridge, 3rd and 5th Michigan

Hannah Ewbank, 7th Wisconsin

Jane Claudia Johnson, 1st Maryland

Lizzie Clawson Jones, 6th Massachusetts

Arabella "Belle" Reynolds, 17th Illinois

Rose Quinn Rooney, 15th Louisiana

Sarah Taylor, 1st Tennessee

Nadine Turchin, 19th Illinois

Eliza Wilson, 5th Wisconsin

ACKNOWLEDGMENTS

Thank you, Christina Boys, for believing in this story. Thank you for the long, brainstorming phone calls and for blessing me with the uncanny knack you have for guiding me to a far better version of each story. As author Anna Quindlen recently said of her editor: "It's like invisible ink, what a great editor does; the notes fade, and all that is left feels as though it belongs to you alone. But we [authors] know the truth." And I do.

Thank you, Daniel, for embracing the writing life, for understanding the long hours, for tramping through old cemeteries and haunting libraries, for willingly touring obscure museums, and for allowing my imaginary friends to become your friends, too.

Thank you, Janet Kobobel Grant, for championing my writing. Thank you for persevering when the answer was *no*, for never giving up on me, and for rejoicing when you found the way to a *yes*. I can't imagine doing this job without you to guide my career.

Thank you, Judith Miller and Nancy Moser, for bringing so much joy to this journey. Thank you for your listening ears, your honest critiques, your unfailing support and prayers, and for being everything a sister in Christ should be. I treasure your friendship more than words can say.

We have not seen a woman for a fortnight, with the exception of the Daughter of the Regiment who is with us in storm and sunshine. It would do you good to see her trudging along, with or after the regiment, her dark brown frock buttoned tightly around her waist...her hat and feather set jauntily on one side, her step firm and assured, for she knows that every arm in our ranks would protect her. Never pouting or passionate, with a kind word for everyone, and every one a kind word for her.

—A soldier's letter home, June 1862

I hope you will get your reward in heaven when your campaigns and battles in this life are ended. For no one on this earth can recompense you for the good you have done in your four years' service for the boys in blue, in the heat of battle, on the wearied marches, and in the hospitals and camps.

—Union soldier Daniel G. Crotty, 1874,
writing about Annie Etheridge, 3rd & 5th Michigan

Daughter
of the
REGIMENT

Chapter 1

———— ✦ ————

Little Dixie, Missouri
May 14, 1861

Given the choice between facing down a pack of wolves or half a dozen plantation belles, Maggie Malone would choose the wolves. With Kerry-boy at her side and Da's hunting rifle in hand, she'd do just fine against wolves—had, in fact, proven just that when half a dozen had come too close to the chicken coop last winter. But winter was over, and Maggie was alone at Barnabas Irving's mercantile counter, waiting while Mr. Irving weighed out the butter and counted the eggs she'd brought into town. Kerry-boy, the Malones' Irish wolfhound, was with her brothers, Jack and Seamus, and her Uncle Paddy. And here came half a dozen tiny-waisted, elegantly dressed plantation ladies, tittering their way across the threshold of the expansive mercantile.

Maggie had intended to trade for coffee and two yards of a lovely blue-and-white-checked cotton for a new apron, but she wasn't about to shop for anything remotely personal now. She glanced behind her. And quickly looked away. Where was Mr. Irving, anyway? How long did it take to count three dozen eggs and weigh five pounds of butter? And why, oh why hadn't Maggie had the good sense to take her wares around to the back door? She could have easily made her escape from there and sent Jack back for the coffee.

The Southern belles *liked* Jack. They made Maggie feel like a circus freak. She was neither deaf nor immune to the glances cast her way over the tops of those painted, gilt-edged fans, and no matter what Jack said, they *did* whisper about her. As if they'd never seen a six-foot-tall woman who farmed alongside the men in the family; a woman who could out-shoot most of the men in Lafayette County. Not that Maggie had ever been allowed to prove it. Ladies weren't allowed to compete at shooting events. *Ladies.* She took a deep breath to steady her nerves. Why'd they have to pick today to come to town?

The sound of another carriage rattling up to the mer-cantile door caused a fresh wave of conversation among the newly arrived belles. Maggie looked toward the street. All she could see of the female passenger in the carriage was an ele-gant parasol, but Maggie didn't have to see the face to know that Miss Elizabeth Blair of Wildwood Grove Plantation was about to grace Barnabas Irving's mercantile with her pres-ence. Everyone in Lafayette County knew that carriage. And the high-stepping horse. And Malachi, the driver, who always sported a black top hat and a red cravat.

As Miss Blair rose to descend from her carriage, Serena Ellerbe and company swept out of the store like so many worker bees hurrying to cluster around a particularly promis-ing blossom. Maggie smiled at the thought, for although she had about as much in common with the plantation belles as Kerry-boy did with a poodle, she could not deny Miss Blair's beauty. She'd once heard the sheriff say Miss Blair was every bit as pretty as a newly opened rose. *And probably just as use-less*, Maggie thought.

"Here, now."

At the sound of Mr. Irving's voice, Maggie whirled back around.

The storekeeper pointed to a number he'd just noted on the Malones' page in his ledger. "A very nice credit balance, Miss Malone." He set the ledger down, smiling as he reached for the bolt of blue and white fabric. "Was this the one?"

Maggie ran her palm across the smooth surface of the bolt of cotton cloth. Maybe there was time to indulge herself, after all. But just as she was about to request that Mr. Irving cut two yards, Serena Ellerbe led the group of ladies back inside.

Maggie snatched her hand away. Shook her head. "Not today. I'll—think about it." Feeling her cheeks grow warm with a blush, she reached for the now empty crate she'd used to carry her eggs and butter into the store. She would have made her escape if not for Jack, who came storming through the mercantile door and very nearly knocked Miss Ellerbe off her feet. Or so she made it seem.

"Goodness!" the young lady exclaimed and stepped back—so far that she bumped into Miss Blair.

An apology on his lips, Jack reached out to steady Miss Ellerbe.

Miss Ellerbe blushed as she looked up at Jack, put one gloved hand on his arm and then pretended to feel faint. Jack guided her to the bench just this side of the mercantile display window, seemingly oblivious to the satisfied little smile of triumph that accompanied Miss Ellerbe's syrupy-sweet *I declare*'s.

Maggie barely managed to keep from laughing out loud. Just because she didn't personally participate in the "courting dance" didn't mean she didn't recognize it. After all, she'd seen Miss Ellerbe and her circle of empty-headed friends move through the steps before, both here in the mercantile and on the board walkway just outside. Or anywhere Jack and Seamus encountered pretty girls. The ones who found boisterous Jack's broad shoulders and flashing blue eyes overpowering merely turned their charms on Seamus, "the quiet one" with the easy smile. Plenty of emotion smoldered beneath those warm, hazel eyes, and the feminine population of Littleton seemed to sense it. How they did that remained a mystery Maggie did not expect to ever solve.

The snap of a fan being closed drew Maggie's gaze away from Jack and Miss Ellerbe to where Miss Blair was standing. Was it her imagination, or was Miss Blair equally disenchanted with Miss Ellerbe's obvious flirting? Miss Blair seemed about to say something, but then Seamus and Uncle Paddy and a group of men charged into the mercantile and, with much bowing and tipping of hats, hurried past the ladies, past the display counters, and up the stairway at the back of the store that led to the second-floor meeting room.

Maggie caught only snatches of what was going on, but it was enough to make her personal feelings about uppity plantation belles seem insignificant. There was more war news, and this time it wasn't about the secession of some distant state or President Lincoln's response to the rebels' firing on an East Coast fort. Something had happened in St. Louis, a place that could be reached by steamboat in only a few hours.

Dread washed over Maggie as she realized that what Uncle Paddy had been saying in recent weeks might be coming true. He'd said that the uneasy peace in Missouri wouldn't last; the state might not have joined the Confederacy, but with the governor planted firmly in the secessionist camp and many of the state's citizens either neutral or determined Unionists, trouble was on the horizon. It was inevitable, Uncle Paddy insisted. Had his prediction just come true?

As the men clomped up the stairs, Jack, ever the gentleman, turned back to Miss Ellerbe. "You're certain you're all right?"

"Fit as a fiddle." The girl rose from the bench and gazed after the men who'd just gone upstairs.

Jack had just put his hat back on and taken a step toward Maggie when a commanding voice sounded from the doorway.

"Elizabeth." Miss Blair's older brother, Walker, removed his top hat as he stepped across the threshold and into the store. He nodded at the group. "Ladies. Mr. Malone." He spoke to his sister. "I've directed that Malachi drive you home. If you wish to invite your friends to tea, you have my permission, but news of events in St. Louis requires my immediate attention."

"But, Walker, I just—"

Blair cut his sister off in mid-protest. He didn't raise his voice, but there was an edge to his tone as he said, "I must insist, Elizabeth, that you proceed back to Wildwood Grove immediately."

For a moment, all was silent in the mercantile. The fact that Miss Blair didn't want to go home was evident in the lift of her chin. But when Mr. Blair arched one eyebrow and tilted his head, Miss Blair lowered her gaze and murmured, "Yes, Walker."

Jack spoke next, bidding the ladies farewell, crossing the length of the store to where Maggie waited, and motioning for her to follow him up the stairs to the meeting room. Maggie heard Serena Ellerbe give an exclamation of joy over being invited to tea at Wildwood Grove. Mr. Irving told Jack that it was fine for them to leave their empty crate in the back room, and together Maggie and Jack headed up the stairs to join the meeting. She paused to watch as the belles fluttered out of the store, wondering at Miss Ellerbe's excitement over having tea in a fancy parlor. Maggie could not imagine anything more boring. Nor could she imagine any of the men in her life ordering her about the way Walker Blair had just done his sister. She suppressed a smile as she imagined what would happen if they tried. Bowing her head and murmuring a submissive *yes* didn't come to mind.

An uneasy silence reigned over the meeting at the top of the stairs. Mr. Edward Markum, the editor of the *Littleton Leader*, was talking about something that had happened in St. Louis the previous Friday. Maggie and Jack slipped into the chairs Uncle Paddy and Seamus had saved for them in the back row. When a man sitting in front of Jack glanced Maggie's way, frowned, nudged his neighbor, and whispered something, Maggie pretended not to notice and gave her attention to Mr. Markum as he introduced one of Littleton's physicians, Dr. Duncan Feeny.

"...and so, since he has just this morning returned from St. Louis, and since he was present in the city to witness what happened there, I've asked him to provide a firsthand account of the situation as he sees it."

Dr. Feeny had a copy of a St. Louis newspaper with him, and he began by reading a verbatim account of what was being called the "Camp Jackson Affair." Apparently Missouri's own governor had written to Confederate President Jefferson Davis asking for heavy artillery to breach the walls of the St. Louis arsenal. Next, he'd called up part of the Missouri Volunteer Militia, who set up "Camp Jackson" about four and a half miles northwest of the arsenal. When Captain Nathaniel Lyon led Union troops to surround "Camp Jackson" and force their surrender, the Confederates refused to take an oath of allegiance to the United States. Lyon placed them under arrest, but as the rebel troops were being marched away, angry secessionists in a crowd of civilians began to throw rocks at the Union troops. Gunfire broke out, and in the ensuing melee, over two dozen people died—among them women and children. The disturbance in the city was ended only by the imposing of martial law.

"I fear," Dr. Feeny said, "that the days when a Missourian could remain neutral have ended. A Confederate flag has been raised on the bluff immediately east of the governor's mansion in Jefferson City." He read from the newspaper that Southern sympathizers were calling upon Missourians to "fight for the liberties of 1776," calling the Stars and Bars "the ensign of Southern rights" and encouraging "a union of all hearts and hands to repel the invaders."

Invaders. Maggie looked about her. Had it come to that, then? Even here in Missouri, would one group of Americans turn on another? The longer Dr. Feeny spoke, the more restive the men in the room became. Some shook their heads. Others muttered in angry tones. Unable to sit still, Maggie thrust one hand into her apron pocket and worried the crocheted edge of the handkerchief tucked inside. Fear clutched at her midsection. What would it mean for the Malones?

Governor Jackson himself had called Federal troops "Goths and Vandals." He was predicting that the South would, before long, "have Washington City for its capital." At mention of the South overtaking the nation's capital, the men in the room leaped from their seats as one, stomping and shouting against the "traitors" and vowing to "fight to the death" to ensure that Missouri would know "true liberty."

As shouts and curses echoed through the room, Seamus moved his chair out of the way and motioned for Maggie to follow him toward the door. Relieved, she did so, but her relief was short lived when she realized that both Jack and Uncle Paddy were going to stay behind. Together, she and Seamus made their way up the street to where the wagon was still hitched just outside the newspaper office.

"It'll be all right, Maggie-girl," Seamus said as she climbed up to the wagon seat.

Kerry-boy, who'd been waiting in the wagon bed, nudged her with his huge, wheaten-colored head, demanding attention. Maggie ruffled the dog's wiry fur absentmindedly. She said nothing. It was not her way to make dire predictions and had never been her way to fear the future. And yet as Seamus unhitched the team and climbed up beside her, Maggie could not still her sense of dread. Uncle Paddy had been right all along. The war had come to Missouri, and while Uncle Paddy might be too old to fight, twenty-year-old Jack and nineteen-year-old Seamus were not. Things were not going to be "all right" again for a very long time.

The meeting at the mercantile finally ended, and the Malones returned home to the farm that lay about ten miles outside Littleton. As Maggie had feared, talk of the war continued for all of the drive back to the farm and over every meal in the days that followed. She tried very hard not to resent Uncle Paddy for fanning the flames. It was as if he'd signed the very constitution that had created the United States for all he had to say about the current situation. Time and time again, as the men talked into the night, it was all Maggie could do to keep from shouting at Uncle Paddy to hush. Didn't he realize that the same people who put those NO IRISH NEED APPLY signs in their windows and drew cartoons giving the Irish the same exaggerated features as slaves and freedmen would surely not hesitate to send the Irish into battle first?

Cannon fodder. That's what the boys would be if they fought in the Americans' war.

If it was the very last thing Maggie did, she would keep her brothers from joining in the fight. Let the "Americans born and bred" settle things in regards to states' rights and slavery and any other of a dozen problems that could be traced to the days long before the Malones crossed over the ocean and set foot on American soil.

For the first week after the Camp Jackson Affair, Maggie did a masterful job of keeping Jack and Seamus focused on the things that mattered—like planting, tending livestock, repairing the roof on the smokehouse, and keeping the boar away from the sow lest he kill the dozen recently farrowed shoats. She kept them so busy, in fact, that they didn't so much as broach the topic of even going to town. And then, exactly eight days after the town meeting, Dr. Feeny drove out with news that changed everything.

Maggie was hard at work turning over the earth to create a flower bed the length of the front porch when she saw Dr. Feeny. Instead of stopping at the house, he waved and kept on going, down the hill, past the barn, and out to the edge of the field where the boys and Uncle Paddy were planting the last few rows of corn.

Maggie didn't really know why the doctor's arrival made her wary, but as she watched him climb down and hurry to the edge of the field, as she saw first Paddy and then the boys trot over to speak with him, as she left off digging her flower beds and headed inside to heat water for tea, her hands trembled. It wasn't long before she knew why.

Jack stepped up to the back door while the others washed up at the well in the backyard. "There's an Irish Brigade forming in St. Louis." With a glance over his shoulder, he stepped into the room. "You'll be fine. You've Paddy to help with the chores, the planting is nearly done, and the neighbors will help with the harvest if we aren't back. It's almost perfect timing, when you think about it."

Maggie sputtered a protest. "There's nothing 'perfect' about it."

Jack refused to argue. "Dr. Feeny's seen the brigade flag. Green silk, with a gold harp that harkens back to our own Cuchlainn," Jack said. "Wouldn't Da have loved to see an Irish warrior honored that way?"

"Don't you be bringing Da into it, may the good Lord rest his soul. As if he'd like seeing his sons march off to—to who knows what."

Jack poured himself a cup of tea and settled at the table. "One man buyin' and sellin' another is wrong, Maggie."

"No one's sayin' otherwise, but it's someone else's quarrel. Let the Americans settle it and leave us be, that's what I say."

Jack's blue eyes flashed with emotion as he said, "*I'm* an American now, Maggie-girl, and if I'm to fight, I'll be on the side I choose. As will Seamus."

Maggie snatched the basket of leftover breakfast biscuits from atop the stove and plopped it onto the table. "Are you tellin' me I've nothing to say in the matter?"

"You've said plenty, Maggie-girl," Jack said gently, "and we've listened. To every word. And now we're going to do our duty."

Maggie swallowed. She looked toward the back door,

where Seamus and Dr. Feeny stood, with Uncle Paddy barely visible just behind them. "Well, don't just be standin' there. I've hot tea and biscuits and I suppose the lot of ya will be talkin' half the night." She motioned them into the room and toward the table. "Get on with it, then." She glanced Dr. Feeny's way. "There's stew in the soup pot and you're welcome to share our supper, such as it is. I've a cow to milk down at the barn. If you all get hungry before I'm back, help yourselves."

"It's early yet," Uncle Paddy protested. "There's no need—"

Maggie didn't wait to hear what he said. She made her escape just as the first tear leaked out. She swiped it away with the back of one hand and trudged down the hill to the barn, where she could be safely out of sight before any more tears dared make their appearance.

Chapter 2

So this is what it feels like when your heart breaks. Maggie pressed one palm to her chest in a vain attempt to relieve the pain as she watched Jack and Seamus march away, up the road and toward the distant ridge, with Kerry-boy padding along at their side. Not until she caught the last glimpse of Jack's broad shoulders and Seamus's narrow ones did Maggie turn away.

Just at that moment, the sun lost the battle it had been fighting with gathering clouds all day. As Maggie retreated through the gate leading into the farm yard and hurried onto the front porch of the family's log house, great drops of rain began to fall, rattling the dry leaves still lying at the base of the oak trees in the pasture just east of the house. Sheltered from the rain, she glanced after the boys again, and then toward Uncle Paddy's unpainted two-room shack south of the barn.

Paddy was probably in the barn. He tended to work things off by polishing harness and mucking out stalls. If that didn't work, he'd grab a currycomb and go over the Belgian team's already-gleaming coats. Babe and Banner more than earned their keep, but thanks to Paddy Devlin, they also knew a more pampered life than most of the humans in nearby Littleton.

As rain began to fall in earnest, Maggie lingered on the porch, wishing with everything in her that she'd made good on her threat in recent days to tie the boys to their respective bedposts—if that was what it took to keep them home. "Should have put collars on the both of them," she muttered, and then winced at the memory of the first time she'd seen a collar used to control a man. *Men.* Three of them, connected by a chain and shuffling their way off a steamboat under the watchful eye of an auctioneer bringing "new stock" for a spring auction in nearby Lexington. The memory made her shudder.

Stepping to the edge of the porch, Maggie extended her hand out into the storm, cupping her palm upward as the rain fell. Absent the narrow fringe of lace at the edge of her sleeve, it would be easy to mistake that hand for a man's. *You'll be all right*, Jack had said, confident that between the two of them his sister and uncle could keep the farm going. She supposed he was right, but that didn't make it any easier to see them leave. Pulling her hand back out of the rain, Maggie flicked the moisture away and swiped her palm against her apron.

Finally, the rain began to let up. The clouds broke, dappling her new flower bed with pale sunlight. Maggie stepped down and began to pull weeds, inhaling the pungent aroma of fresh-washed earth. While she worked, she relived the final argument she'd had with Jack and Seamus, thankful that she'd finally relented and made peace with her brothers. She'd sat up half the night making Seamus his own mending kit—a replica of the one a teary-eyed Bridget Feeny had presented to Jack yesterday afternoon. The soldiers called them *housewives*, Bridget said. Making one for Seamus had given Maggie something productive to do last night, when sleep simply would not come.

She would cherish the memory of Seamus's smile when he'd found his own "housewife" waiting on his breakfast plate this morning. They'd joked the next few moments away, almost as if the day were like any other, and Maggie was grateful. She could never stay angry with either of her brothers for long. They'd been good boys and they'd grown into good men. She'd die for them if it came to it.

There it was again. That word *dying*. Sniffing as she pulled yet another handful of weeds, Maggie stood up and headed inside. Reaching into her apron pocket, she withdrew a kerchief and blew her nose. Just as she stepped across the threshold, she thought she heard a distant bark.

Wheeling about, she saw the dog just as he bounded into view from the direction the boys had taken only moments ago. *Dog*. Kerry-boy was nearly the size of a pony. Thanks to the rain, his wiry, wheat-colored fur stuck out in all directions. Dark whiskers made it look as though he'd shoved his face in a pile of ashes. *Were they coming back, then?* Joy surged through her as Maggie called out, "Kerry-boy! Here, boy!"

At the sound of her voice, the dog skidded to a halt in the middle of the road. He gazed back the way he'd come, waiting. Or...not waiting. Just...wishing. When the dog finally turned about and padded to her side, Maggie placed one broad hand atop his massive head and muttered, "Sent you home, did they."

Kerry-boy snorted.

"I know," Maggie said. "I'm of the same mind. I'd have gone with them myself, if it weren't for the farm." Of course it was a ridiculous notion, two brothers going off to war with a sister in tow. Who ever heard of such a thing?

Slapping her thigh to encourage Kerry-boy to follow her, Maggie made her way toward the well at the back of the house, intent on drawing a bucket of water, both to give Kerry-boy a drink and to wash her hands. Maybe the boys were right. Maybe they'd be home in a few weeks—home, with grandiose tales of bravery in battle and oh, please God, whole in body and in spirit. They both seemed to think that going off to war was a grand adventure. As if marching across a field in the face of cannon and artillery fire were nothing more than a lark.

With a crash and a flash, the skies opened again. Maggie dashed in the back door with Kerry-boy at her heels, hoping the boys were already on board the steamboat they'd be riding downriver to St. Louis, warm and dry and safe. *Safe. Dear, sweet Lord in heaven . . . keep them safe.* She looked about her at the empty house. And then, sinking into the rocking chair by the fireplace, Maggie hid her face in her hands and wept.

⁓

In the days after Jack and Seamus left, Maggie plunged into the work of the farm at a feverish pace. Hating the way her footsteps echoed in the empty house, she spent most of her time in the garden, in the barn, in the pasture—anywhere but inside. She cleaned out the chicken coop and reinforced the wire fence about the chicken yard to the point that Uncle Paddy asked if she was expecting an entire army of raccoons to attack some night.

"Well, if it were to happen," Maggie said, grinning, "we wouldn't lose a feather."

She didn't know when she first noticed the change about Paddy, but it dawned on her toward the end of the first week of life without the boys that whenever she saw him, Paddy's old musket was either cradled in his arms or leaning against a nearby fencepost or barn wall. When she teased him about it, all Paddy did was shrug and mutter something to the effect that it didn't hurt to be prepared.

"Prepared for what?" Maggie asked.

"I promised your brothers I'd mind the place 'til they returned." He paused. "And watch over their sister."

Maggie snorted. She didn't need watching over, and surely Jack and Seamus knew it.

Paddy read her mind. "Now, don't raise your hackles over it, Mary Margaret. The boys promised your father and I promised them, and a young lady should be grateful for family that loves her as much as do your brothers and myself." The sprightly old man who rarely spoke without some teasing remark or a twinkle in his eye was suddenly serious. "Much as I hate to give breath to it, dearie, I believe we are in for some difficult times. 'Tis best to be prepared. And I'm not speakin' of reinforcing the chicken coop against a regiment of raccoons."

Something about Paddy's tone washed the spunk right out of Maggie's attitude. "What else do you think needs doing?"

Paddy tugged on his grizzled beard. "Do ya really want to know?"

"I do."

He looked about the place, considering. "We should take care to lock the barn at sundown. When you retire, you must be certain to lower the bars across both doors—front and back." He paused. "It wouldn't hurt if you took the old Plains Rifle down from over the hearth and kept it where you could get to it if the need arose. And if I had my way, you'd get your da's pocket pistol out of his trunk. I can show you how to clean it. And maybe a little practice shooting at some bottles out in the yard for a few evenings."

Maggie frowned. "I'm the best shot in the family."

"Not with that pistol you aren't," Paddy said. "Not yet,

anyway. But I've no doubt that you would be, were you to take my advice."

He was truly concerned. Maggie asked him why.

Paddy shrugged. "There's a certain kind of snake that slithers about in times of strife."

Mention of snakes made Maggie think back to the morning after the boys left, when she'd seen Walker Blair talking to Paddy across the garden fence. "Did Mr. Blair say something worrying?"

"It's not so much what he said, Mary Margaret, as what he didn't say."

Maggie frowned. "So then. What *didn't* the man say?"

"He didn't say he'd be praying for the good Lord to bring our boys back to home safely. And when I asked about news from town, he didn't say much—beyond a grumble regardin' a meeting at Turner Hall. Apparently the Unionists have outgrown the room above Irving's mercantile."

Maggie had been surprised to see Blair's gleaming carriage parked in the road that day, the driver waiting patiently while his owner talked to Uncle Paddy. Save for the girls who flirted with Jack and Seamus, neither the planters nor their families paid the Malones any mind. And why would they? The only thing they had in common was that they happened to populate the same Missouri county. Any resemblance ended there.

The Malone men had felled trees and built the log house and every other building on their farm with their own hands. Walker Blair had arrived in Littleton with money to spare and enough slaves to clear his land, plant his hemp, and fire the bricks needed to raise a two-story mansion. The Malones socialized with other farmers at barn dances and box suppers, while the planters hosted cotillions and barbeques. The divide between the two classes of citizens had already been wide when Southern states began to secede from the Union, but it had been peaceable—at least on the surface.

Maggie thought back to that day a few weeks ago, before the boys had left for St. Louis, and how trapped she'd felt when Serena Ellerbe and her friends came mincing into the mercantile. When Maggie had commented on the ride home how Serena had feigned a bout of the vapors, Jack had only laughed.

"'Tis a game, Maggie, and a harmless one at that. I've no doubt that every one of them will be betrothed to a planter's son within the year." He winked. "Or, perhaps, a Virginia cousin. In the meantime, they're adventuring a bit of a flirtation with an Irishman, in the hopes it will rile their parents. Which it will. They're spoiled children playing at life."

If Paddy's instincts were right, things had changed, now that the war had come to Missouri. No one was "playing at life" now. She remembered the anger in that room above the store when they met that day, the epithets sworn against the rebels and anyone who supported their cause. It only made sense that the planters would be just as firm in their beliefs. Did Walker Blair and the rest of the Lafayette County planters think of the Malones as "the enemy" now? The notion sent a chill up her spine.

"Did ya hear what I said, Mary Margaret?" Paddy's voice called her out of the fog and back to the moment.

"Da's pistol. You want me to carry it," she said.

"Aye. Does it frighten ya to hear me speak of it?"

Maggie shook her head.

"This evenin', then, for the cleanin' and such. I'll retrieve some bottles and cans and set us up for a shootin' match in the mornin'." Paddy headed back to the middle of the garden, uprooting weeds with the hoe as he walked.

Maggie retreated to the house for a basket and returned to the garden to harvest green beans. After dousing the mess of beans in a bucket of clean well water, she carried them inside, then took time to swing the soup pot over the fire, where its contents would simmer until she and Paddy came in to supper. She strung green beans to hang from the hooks Seamus had placed at intervals along the bare rafters of the room that took up the entire west side of the cabin. Once they were dried, she'd take them down and store them in the cellar. And all the while, she wondered about Jack and Seamus and worried over what Walker Blair's talking to Paddy might mean. She wondered when Jack and Seamus would write and wished they hadn't gone in the first place. She pondered Paddy's thinking she needed a weapon and that they should lock the barn and bar the door and—*ouch*.

With a mild curse, she looked down at the drop of blood emerging from where the needle had plunged into the tip of her finger. Taking a deep breath, she set the project aside. She could string beans after the sun went down. At the moment, she needed to do something else. Something outside. She needed fresh air and hard work. The kind of work that would make her too tired to worry.

Taking the old rifle and powder horn down from where they hung over the fireplace, she retrieved ammunition and patch, then stepped outside to call Kerry-boy. "Let's see if we can scare up a rabbit or two," she said, and set off in the direction of the field beyond the barn where Uncle Paddy was planting the last of the corn.

"Hunting!" Uncle Paddy exclaimed when she told him what she had in mind. "Just when I've said we need to be careful?"

"And aren't I being careful?" she argued. "I've a massive

dog that would be at the throat of anyone who dared try to hurt me—not to mention a rifle. And I can shoot the ears off a rabbit at fifty yards." She thought Paddy might be weakening, and so she added a promise to stay off the road and on Malone property. "I won't stay away long," she said. "I just need—I'm as nervous as a colt who's just been separated from his dam. I need to walk it off."

"All right," Paddy said. "But you be back long before sundown or I'll be settin' out after ya." As she marched away, he called after her, "Keep yer wits about ya, and remember what I said about snakes."

Maggie raised her hand to let him know she'd heard what he said. She already felt better.

⁂

"Good dog," Maggie said as she grabbed the rabbit she'd just shot by the hind leg and held it up for inspection. Kerry-boy whimpered a request. "Not until we get home, boy-o," Maggie said. Kerry-boy shook his head in what Maggie took to be disdain. It made her laugh. How good it felt to laugh.

As she made her way home, she reveled in the sound of her own sturdy boots stepping along through the tall grass and the whisper of breeze tickling the back of her neck and making the blooming wildflowers bob and sway. She paused before topping the last hill toward home and spoke sternly to the dog. "Now, I'm going to lay this rabbit down while I make myself decent." She lowered the rifle to the earth first and waggled her finger at the dog, whose golden eyes flicked from the rabbit to her eyes and back again. "I mean it, Kerry-boy. *No.*"

The dog sat a respectable distance away while Maggie put the rabbit down at her feet and pulled the hem of her plaid skirt down from where she'd tucked it into her belt. Smoothing it into place, she spoke again to the dog. "There, now. The huntress no more." She'd just picked up the rabbit and the rifle when shots rang out. Kerry-boy leaped to his feet and disappeared over the hill. She heard him snarl. Dropping the rabbit and clutching the rifle in both hands, she broke into a run, but with the first step, her booted foot tangled with the hem of her skirt and she went down on her knees, then fell forward.

Scrabbling her way up to the top of the hill, she peered over the ridge just in time to see Kerry-boy launch himself at a man sitting astride a sway-backed bay down by the barn. The force of the dog's charge not only knocked the man out of the saddle, but carried him across the bay's body and at a second rider, who barely had time to turn in the saddle before he, too, was knocked to the ground. Four other riderless horses strained to get free from where they were tied to the barnyard fence. The two men Kerry-boy had attacked now faced a very real danger of being trampled in addition to being torn to pieces by the wolfhound.

As she stuffed the hem of her skirt back into her belt so that she could run unimpeded, Maggie finally saw the other men. Her heart sank at the sight of two of them dragging a seemingly unconscious Paddy Devlin out of the barn. The owners of the remaining two horses must have gone into the house, for as Maggie grasped the rifle and rose to her feet, someone launched her rocking chair out the back door.

Pulling the stopper out of the powder horn with her teeth, she planted the butt of the rifle on the ground and poured in powder. Next came the patch. She placed a ball atop it, thumbed patch and ball into the barrel, and ramrodded it into place, then charged down the hill, yelling at the top of her lungs. The two men carrying Paddy dropped him in the dirt and tried to wrest their guns from their holsters.

When one of them got off a wild shot, Kerry-boy charged him. Seeing his partner dragged down by the snarling wolf-hound, the other man yelled, dove through the two rails that formed the corral fence, jerked the reins of his horse free, mounted up, and took off. As their partner fled, the two men Kerry-boy had knocked off their horses began to fire at the dog. Her heart racing, Maggie stopped running, took aim, and fired. She didn't hit anything, but with a glance in her direction, two more men scrambled aboard their horses and charged into the woods and out of sight.

Maggie worked to reload and take up the fight against the lone bandit left down by the barn, screaming as she ran. Her lungs burning, she didn't falter as she once again cocked the rifle. This time, though, she hesitated. Was it her imagination, or had Paddy moved? He must have, for Kerry-boy hesitated for a split second and looked over at him. The hesitation gave the lone man near the barn the chance to take aim.

Her heart thumping, Maggie took aim herself and fired again. This time, she didn't miss. The man screamed, dropped his weapon, and clutched his arm. Instead of attacking, Kerry-boy trotted to Paddy's side, lowered his head to snuffle at his still form, and then stood over him, protecting Paddy. The injured bandit fumbled to pick up his gun, shoving it back into its holster while he charged to his horse. Flinging himself into the saddle, he hightailed it after the other three.

Maggie looked toward the house. The men inside had stopped launching things out the back door. Crouching down, Maggie scrabbled her way to the well and ducked behind it, listening as she loaded the rifle, willing herself to breathe evenly, ignoring the terror clawing at her midsection. A scraping sound lured her to peer out from behind the well just in time to see the back door close. She heard the bar drop over it.

Footsteps sounded as the two men—ran? Out the front! Half cocking the rifle this time, she charged right, rounded the front corner of the house, and jumped onto the porch, just in time to see a flash of gray as the two men disappeared in the direction of the barn. She was headed after them, but a flicker of yellow light made her look into the house. Fire! They'd raked the embers out of the fireplace, and flames had begun to lick at the floorboards near the hearth. Uncocking the rifle, Maggie charged inside.

The interior of the house had been ransacked. The cream pitcher she treasured as the only thing she had of her mother's lay in pieces on the floor. Setting the rifle just inside the door, she snatched up the quilt that was usually draped across the back of her rocker and threw it over the embers, smothering the flames as best she could. Snatching up the rifle, she darted back outside and chased after the two remaining gunmen. In their frenzy to escape, they hadn't taken time to shoot at anything more. All Maggie saw was a flash of pale slouch hats and two dark bay rumps, as the last two men spurred their horses into the woods beyond the barnyard fence.

Dropping her rifle, Maggie dove between the fence rails. When her skirt caught on the bottom rung, she ripped it free and sank to the earth beside Paddy's still form. Kerryboy stepped aside and sank down onto his haunches. She was shaking so, she could hardly manage to support herself with her arms as she leaned close, listening, praying to feel even the faintest whisper of a breath. Tears streaming down her face, she called the old man's name, but in vain.

Kerry-boy gave a soft woof. Stretching out his great head, he touched the tip of his tongue to Paddy's cheek. When Paddy didn't move, Kerry-boy gave the cheek a bigger swipe. His tail thumped. Just once.

Maggie took up one of the old man's still, battered hands and held it to her cheek, sobbing. And then the miraculous happened. A moan. A tremulous cough, followed by a louder moan.

Kerry-boy rose to his feet and began licking Paddy's swollen face in earnest, pausing from time to time to let out a bark. His tail never stopped wagging.

"All right, Kerry-boy," Maggie sobbed. "All right." She looked down at Paddy. "I'm going to get the team hitched up and get you to Doc Feeny," she said. "Do you hear me, Paddy? You're going to be all right."

She rose to her feet and saw stars. Squeezing her eyes shut, she brushed her forehead with the back of one hand. Taking a deep breath, she opened her eyes again. For the first time, she noticed the milk cow. Dead, up along the tree line.

The horses! The team! What if—she staggered toward the barn, relieved when two golden heads appeared over the tops of the stalls. She glanced over her shoulder at Paddy. He must have put himself between the bandits and the team. And nearly died for it.

"You old fool," Maggie muttered as she raced to harness the team and hitch them to the farm wagon. "You wonderful... stupid...brave...ridiculous..." As the words tumbled out, so did her tears. She mumbled and fumbled her way to being ready to drive Paddy to town, running back to the house only long enough to gather more blankets and quilts to cushion the ride as much as possible.

Lowering the back gate of the wagon, she bent to pick the wiry little man up and transfer him to the pallet in the back of the wagon. She just managed it, albeit not without a few decidedly not-feminine grunts. Kerry-boy leaped up beside Paddy, and Maggie lifted the tail gate and bolted it in place. As she laid Paddy's musket next to him, she said, "Don't you so much as consider the possibility of slippin' from this earth, Paddy Devlin."

Paddy grimaced as he raised one hand from the pallet. It wasn't much, but it would do. Hurrying to the wagon seat, Maggie shoved Da's rifle beneath it and climbed aboard. For the first time in her life, she was grateful that God had made her as she was. A fine lady would never have been able to lift Paddy into a wagon. Nor would she have torn down that hill, screaming while she loaded a rifle. What a sight it must have been. She supposed she should be embarrassed to think on it, but she was not embarrassed. She was proud. And furious.

Maggie grasped the reins with her fine, strong hands and, bracing her feet against the footrail before her, leaned forward and urged the team into a barely controlled gallop. She could only imagine the pain Paddy was enduring as the wagon bumped along the rutted country road. Even poor Kerry-boy yelped from time to time as he was tossed this way or that. But, Lord bless him, he didn't leave Paddy's side.

Terrified at the thought that at every turn she might encounter the bandits returning to finish what they'd started, wondering if she'd managed to put the house fire out or if a smoldering ember would reignite the pine floor surrounding the stone hearth, Maggie felt the effects of cold terror begin to wrap its way around her until she thought she might not be able to draw breath.

Finally, gathering every ounce of her failing strength, Maggie shouted over her shoulder, "They haven't beaten us yet, Paddy! Hang on!" She began to sing a tune that Da had learned from his father, who'd fought alongside Protestants in a rebellion against the British in 1798. She didn't know the full meaning of the words, but shouting at the top of her lungs about warriors and "brave, warlike bands," gave her courage.

Chapter 3

Malachi's amber eyes were warm with sympathy, even as he refused to obey the mistress of Wildwood Grove. "I'm sorry, Miss Libbie, but Mastah Blair said you wasn't to ride until the Home Guard has a chance to make the county safe again. He jus' left with Sheriff Green. Don't know what that was all about, but the sheriff came charging up on that big white horse of his and fairly ran in the house and it wasn't five minutes that here come Mastah Blair out to have me saddle Highboy. They rode off together and left me to tell ya. Mastah said he couldn't find you."

Libbie looked toward the house. She'd been helping Annabelle hang herbs to dry on a rack in the keeping room. If Walker had made any effort at all, he could easily have found her. She would have heard him if he'd so much as stepped out the back door of the house and called her name.

Malachi must have misunderstood Libbie's silence, for his tone was placating as he said, "You know I got to obey, Miss Libbie. I shore am sorry."

"I do know, Malachi. Thank you." Libbie looked past Malachi to the long row of stalls. Her chestnut gelding had heard her voice and thrust his fine head over the half door to his stall. He was looking her way, his ears alert.

Malachi had been polishing the carriage when Libbie came out to the stable, expecting to take the ride she'd taken every afternoon since Walker had given her Pilot. She was so predictable about it that, once she was in the saddle, the horse scarcely needed to be guided. They would ride down to the river, following it for several miles, and then climb up to where the combination of a concave rock wall and the flat clearing at its base created a natural shelter that not only offered an expansive view of the river but also kept anyone resting there out of sight of anyone who might be riding along the ridge above. Pilot would drink from the natural spring bubbling out of the earth nearby, and then wait quietly while Libbie savored the time alone.

Libbie looked back at poor Malachi, fidgeting with the polishing cloth, rubbing a corner of it between thumb and forefinger while he waited, no doubt expecting her to rain fire and brimstone down upon his head. After all, that's what Walker did when things didn't go according to his liking. Taking a deep breath, Libbie looked across the well-manicured lawn, past the house, and toward the ever-changing river. *This, too, will pass. Let it flow on by. It's just one more "Walker."*

Libbie sighed. She supposed she could deal with *one more Walker.* After all, she'd been dealing with the difficulties that characterized life with her older brother for so long that she'd given them his name. *Walkers* were things ridiculous, things unreasonable, and—on occasion—things downright mean and ugly that no gentleman would want known among his gentlemen friends. Unless, of course, they were all smoking cigars together after withdrawing after supper, at which point Libbie supposed they commiserated over the silliness of the women in their lives so that they could feel absolved for the sins involved with their own *Walkers.*

Malachi cleared his throat. "I know that color on your

cheek blooms best when you is upset, but I can't help what I got to do. Please don't be angry with me, Miss Libbie."

Libbie smiled at him. "I know it's not your fault. It's just that I was looking forward to my ride."

"I know you was," Malachi said and nodded at the horse. "And so was Pilot."

At the sound of his name, the horse whickered. That made Libbie smile. Waving Malachi back to his polishing, she stepped inside the open stable door and proceeded to the tack room. Laying her riding crop aside, she retrieved a curry-comb, a brush, and a rope lead. At Pilot's stall, she snapped the lead to his halter and led the leggy gelding out into the wide passageway. He didn't really need grooming, but it was as good an excuse as any to spend time with him, and a better excuse than most to avoid going back up to the house before she'd had time to mitigate her frustration with her brother's tyrannical rule over her life.

If only Mama and Papa hadn't succumbed to the cholera. If only there'd been anywhere else for Libbie to go. Of course, she could have married and remained in Tennessee, but that would have meant waking up every morning in bed with Lorenzo Cadwalader, and even eight years into life here on the Missouri River, that notion still made her shudder with revulsion. Life as Walker's hostess might not be perfect, but it was far better than taking the name *Cadwalader*.

Walker hadn't wanted her at first, but that had changed, once he set his eyes on a political office. When he realized the benefit of having a beautiful hostess, there had been rewards for being in his good graces. Pilot was one of those rewards. Walker had presented the horse after a particularly wonderful barbeque here at Wildwood Grove. He'd called it an early birthday present, but Libbie had learned the real reason for Walker's unusual display of generosity from Sheriff Isham Green the first time she rode Pilot into Littleton. Apparently someone powerful had complimented the fine food and "the lovely hostess" just before uttering the words *governor* and *Walker Blair* in the same sentence.

Walker was nothing if not a man who made it his business to protect his assets, and apparently "his lovely hostess" was a valuable one. Which was probably why, Libbie realized, as she brushed Pilot's already gleaming coat, Walker had told Malachi that Miss Libbie was not to be allowed to ride "until the Home Guard had made things safe again." Heaven only knew exactly what that meant.

As far as Libbie knew, the unpleasantness in the East had yet to affect Lafayette County—at least directly. Some of the local boys were rattling their sabers and heading off to join Governor Jackson's Missouri Volunteers, but other than Billy Ellerbe, no one Libbie knew personally had done so. She only knew about Billy because Serena had driven over the day he left and made quite a dramatic scene of weeping and wailing.

Malachi was humming a familiar hymn while he polished the carriage. When he stopped mid-verse, Libbie stood on tiptoe and gazed across Pilot's broad back toward the house. Walker and Sheriff Green had returned. Both men were tying their horses to the hitching posts that bordered the curved drive behind the house, but instead of going on into the house, they were heading toward the stable.

Libbie grimaced. If only she'd left Pilot in his stall and worked on him there. She might have had a chance to scoot out the side door. There was no chance of that now. The brilliant late afternoon sunlight behind the two men had obscured the details, but as they came closer, Libbie realized that Sheriff Green had donned a uniform. Malachi hadn't said anything about it when he'd mentioned seeing the sheriff earlier. Then again, Libbie knew that the servants chose their words very carefully when speaking to or about white people.

Libbie couldn't decide if Green looked dashing or ridiculous, but when she caught sight of the exceedingly long ostrich feather tucked into the hatband of his pale gray hat and his thigh-high black leather boots, she was inclined to think the latter. Two rows of gold buttons accented his double-breasted gray frock coat. He'd tucked both sides of the coat out of the way in a rather obvious attempt to display the brown holster on the right and the glittering new cavalry sword on the left, each one held in place by a black belt fastened with a polished brass buckle. If there'd been any doubt as to where Isham Green's loyalties lay, it was laid to rest by the letters C and S on the oval buckle.

Green spoke first, sweeping the hat off his head and exclaiming, "I understood that Walker said you weren't to go riding."

Libbie smiled at him. "Good afternoon to you, too, Sheriff Green." She glanced down at the braid on his sleeve. "Or is it already General Green? I have no idea how to interpret all this finery—beyond the obvious, which is that you are goin' to war. And as to my brother's dictum, I have obeyed it." She smiled at Walker.

Walker smiled back—rather distractedly, Libbie thought—then said, "Recent events have made it clear that if we are to protect our way of life, we must all make sacrifices. I have decided to heed the call, Elizabeth." With a little flourish, he indicated Sheriff Green. "Isham has accepted the appointment as my major." He straightened a bit and lifted his chin. "I'm to be Colonel Walker Blair of the Wildwood Guard."

Taken by surprise, Libbie blurted out the first thing that came to mind at the ridiculous notion of Walker as a soldier. "You're—but Walker, you're nearly middle-aged. Surely you can't intend—"

Sheriff Green interrupted. "It's an honorary position, Miss Walker. No one expects your brother to actually take up arms and fight. That part of the battle is for younger men. But there is much that a man of your brother's standing can offer to our valiant cause."

Ah. Suddenly, Libbie understood. She glanced at Walker. "They want your money." The moment she'd said the words, she realized she'd made a terrible mistake. Walker would not appreciate her tone of voice. Even if she'd only said it in front of the servants, he would have been angry for days. He'd locked her in her room for lesser offenses. But for her to blurt out something like that in front of Isham Green?

Libbie's heartbeat ratcheted up as she wondered what Walker might do after the sheriff left. She began to rake her fingers through Pilot's mane in an effort to camouflage the fact that she'd begun to tremble. "Of course I'm only a silly woman," she said. "I don't understand such things." She took a deep breath. "I do suppose it takes money to fight a war, doesn't it? And a great deal of it, at that." She swallowed. "We must all make sacrifices, I suppose."

Sheriff Green nodded. "Your brother has made a much more personal sacrifice than money. Just now, in a meeting with several key men, he offered up his dearest possession for the sake of our glorious cause."

With a smug smile, Walker explained, "I've offered the Grove as headquarters for the regiment. The officers— including Major Green—will be our guests for the foreseeable future."

Hence, the *Wildwood* Guard. Of course. Libbie nodded. "I see."

"I've already put Asa James to work makin' arrangements to move some of the livestock in preparation for the encampment—and a parade ground, of course," Walker said. "In due course, I expect we'll be able to see the light of a hundred campfires from our upstairs balcony." His expression changed as he added, "And God help any Federal regiment that threatens Wildwood Grove—or its inhabitants."

"Whatever may happen in coming days," the sheriff said, "you will be safe, Miss Libbie."

Libbie dared a question. "Isn't allowing an encampment here the equivalent of inviting a battle?"

Walker sounded like a schoolteacher drilling his less promising students as he said, "Our home is known far and wide as the finest house in the county, Elizabeth. It's obvious that any commander in his right mind would want to procure the Grove as their headquarters. Our little hilltop is the perfect place from which to monitor river traffic, and control of the river is a key to securing the state for the Confederacy." He paused. "Organizing a regiment is not just about defending our home. It's also a strategic decision. The presence of the Guard here will ensure that our levee becomes a beacon to our brothers north of the river who wish to cross over and join in defending our way of life. The battle will come to us in due time, no matter what we do. I have taken precautions to assure that we are not only ready but also well defended."

Half a dozen men galloped into view. Hitching their mounts near Sheriff Green's, they headed for the house. The sheriff took his leave and went to greet them, but Walker lingered. "We'll be convening in the library. Inform Annabelle that we will require a late supper for a dozen." He paused.

"And you might encourage her to enlist help. Tell her the next few weeks will be trying for us all. We must adapt. She'll be cooking meals for at least a dozen extra men for the foreseeable future." He cleared his throat. "I've discouraged the officers' wives from joining us, but there may be occasions where I fail to get my way. Should that occur, I will expect you to welcome them in your usual gracious manner."

Libbie could only nod. "Of course, Walker. I—I just—it's a shock, that's all." He really did mean to transform Wildwood Grove into a military camp.

"I realize that what I am asking is not a simple thing, but in time you will be glad for your role in serving the Wildwood Guard." He paused. Cleared his throat. "I know that you have strong feelings against Isham," he said. "But I am asking that you set those aside for the good of the cause."

Libbie frowned. "I'm not sure I know what you mean."

Walker took a deep breath. "You have spurned his attentions in the past, but he is an officer in my regiment now, and it would be to your advantage to see that he has nothing to complain about while he is our guest."

With a quick intake of breath, Libbie looked away. She was going to be sick. He couldn't mean what she thought he meant.

Walker scolded mildly. "Just be cordial, Elizabeth. If he should ask you to take an evening stroll, accommodate the man. That's all I ask. I know he has his failings, but he also has a great many friends in high places—friends who could be very helpful to us in the future."

"What 'future' are you talking about?" She suspected she knew, but she wanted him to explain himself to her—for once—in no uncertain terms.

Walker sighed. "I suppose that's my fault. I do have a habit of keeping you in the dark about my plans." Sweeping his hat off his head, he raked his fingers through his graying hair. "When all is said and done, the people of our great state are going to want a leader who was at the heart of the action. Someone who showed himself to be a man of courage and purpose. A true son of the South who proved his loyalty by making sacrifices when sacrifice counted." He paused. "I know that giving up your daily rides and some of the freedoms that you've enjoyed will be hard on you, but if you can be patient, you will share in the reward." He smiled at her. "They are goin' to love you in Jefferson City, Libbie."

Libbie. Walker never called her that. He was, in fact, very careful not to use her childhood nickname. As to Jefferson City—mention of the state capital verified what Libbie suspected. The real reason behind Walker's founding a regiment, making the sheriff an officer, and transforming Wildwood Grove had little to do with patriotic fervor. It was all intended to be a stepping-stone to the governor's mansion.

Libbie barely managed to squelch an audible sigh. If Walker thought the idea of becoming the leading hostess in the state appealed to her—well. They'd never been close, but now it was even more obvious that her brother didn't know her at all. The idea that he assumed she shared his political ambition made her feel lonelier than ever.

"You'll be right there beside me." Walker took her hand and drew it beneath his arm, holding it firmly in place as he said, "Now leave Pilot to Malachi and come inside."

She couldn't resist without creating a scene, and Libbie knew better than to do anything of the sort. As Walker led her up the path from the stable, past the garden and the ice house and, finally, to the edge of the porch that ran the entire length of the back of the house, he explained more about both his reasoning and his expectations.

"There is another reason I'm inviting the regiment onto our property. I haven't wanted to frighten you, but with war comes lawlessness, and it is already on the rise. I have just this afternoon received word that someone has attacked one of the farms east of Littleton. Hearing about the destruction rained down upon the Malones has only strengthened my resolve to protect the Grove. And you."

Malone. She knew that name. "Was anyone hurt?"

"Now, now." Walker patted her hand. "I'm only telling you so that when volunteers begin to filter onto the place in coming days, you'll be grateful for the brave men who have come to defend your home."

"But—the Malones. Shouldn't we help them?" Finally, she remembered. "Isn't that family who owns the team of Belgians you tried to buy last year?"

Walker cleared his throat. "You do have an excellent memory when it comes to my failed business dealings, Elizabeth. The answer is yes, the Malones own a fine team of Belgians, and they declined my most generous offer to buy them. But I hold no grudge. As a matter of fact, I plan to offer our assistance, should it be required—and I assume it will be, since the Malone brothers have gone off and joined some Irish brigade forming in St. Louis."

The Malone brothers. Libbie didn't remember much about the younger brother beyond reddish hair and a nice smile. Jack Malone, on the other hand, was another matter entirely. A woman only had to see Jack Malone once to understand why his name was so often on Serena Ellerbe's tongue. Libbie remembered broad shoulders, thick blond hair, blue eyes, and a smile—ah, yes. A smile to give a woman something to ponder on a dark night.

Libbie chose her next words carefully. "The Irish Brigade," she said. "That's not—"

"No," Walker interrupted. "It isn't the right side of things. But they are our neighbors, and just because Miss Malone's brothers have made an ill-advised decision does not mean that we should tolerate lawlessness."

He was saying the right words, but simmering resentment colored those words, and with a little shudder, Libbie changed the subject to less inflammatory topics. "I'm certain Miss Malone will appreciate your kindness," she said, rushing to add, "and now I'll leave you here and speak with Annabelle about the increased workload. I'm certain she'll be able to make helpful suggestions about enlarging the house staff."

Walker nodded. "Reassure her that there is no need to be afraid. Gallant men will keep us all safe." He smiled and leaned closer, as if sharing a secret. "Annabelle doesn't need to know this, but when you hear a steamboat whistle this evening, take it as proof of my keeping my promise to defend our home." He winked. "A Mr. Henry is expected to disembark, long about sunset."

Henry. Libbie had heard enough discussion of hunting rifles and dueling pistols and the like to know what that meant. She didn't hide her surprise. "You're smuggling arms past the Federals?"

Walker sniffed. "I am providing the means to protect my property." He chucked her beneath the chin, thereby forcing her to look him in the eye. "There's more than just Henrys to be unloaded, my dear. Plenty of sympathetic friends will be sending provisions for the men. Our little levee is going to be busier than ever in coming days. But you, my dear, needn't worry your little head about anything beyond managing the kitchen and entertaining the officers." He kissed her on the cheek and headed inside.

Libbie stood for a moment, her mind reeling, her nerves jangled. She could not shake the image of bandits taking advantage of the absence of Miss Malone's brothers. She hoped that nothing outrageous had been done to the poor woman who lived there. What was her name? Libbie remembered nothing beyond unusual height and a rather brusque manner that had on occasion made the woman the brunt of some very unkind words on the part of Serena Ellerbe. *Maggie*. That was it.

The last time she'd seen her was nearly a month ago at the mercantile, when she'd come to town with her brothers. Libbie recalled how Jack Malone's sister had barely managed to hide her distaste that day as she watched Serena's little drama play out. Given the chance to get to know her, Libbie thought she would probably like the tall, hardworking Irishwoman.

Chapter 4

The late afternoon sun had just dipped behind the trees as Maggie hauled on the reins to slow Babe and Banner to a brisk trot at the edge of town. She drove them up the main street of town, past Turner Hall and the newspaper office and finally to the Feenys', where the doctor conducted a busy medical practice from a small frame building behind the family's two-story brick home.

When the team pulled up alongside the Feenys' back lawn, they were trembling, the white crust of their own sweat staining the harness, their breath coming hard. Maggie tied off the reins. Flinging herself down from the wagon seat, she charged across the yard and up the steps of the Feenys' back porch to bang on the door. Sally, the Feenys' Negro cook, came to the door. One look at Maggie, and she fetched the doctor.

"Bandits," Maggie blustered. "Trying to take the team. Paddy wouldn't let them—I was gone—" She babbled as she followed Dr. Feeny to the wagon, where he climbed up beside Paddy, running his hands down the unconscious man's arms and legs, putting his palm to Paddy's forehead, raising his eyelids to look for—what, Maggie didn't know.

Sally and the doctor's daughter, Bridget, had followed them to the wagon. The doctor spoke to the cook first, his tone sure, his voice calm. "Would you kindly fetch Dix? I need his help to transfer Mr. Devlin into the clinic."

"I can do it," Maggie said.

The doctor shook his head. "You've done enough for now. Try to calm yourself. Dix won't be long."

Maggie took hold of the edge of the wagon with both hands and, bowing her head, took a deep breath. And another. Sally had trotted across the grassy yard spanning the space between the residence and the clinic and ducked beneath a low trellis. She returned with her husband, a square-jawed, broad-shouldered freedman.

Expecting Kerry-boy's hackles to rise at the sight of the hulking stranger, Maggie was about to speak peace to the dog when, to her surprise, the wolfhound rose and, tail wagging, thrust his head Dix's way for what was obviously an expected pat. Dix swept a beefy palm across Kerry-boy's head while he took instruction from Dr. Feeny, who'd retrieved a canvas litter from his office while Sally fetched Dix.

Together, the men climbed into the wagon bed, unrolling the litter between Paddy and the wagon seat. With Dix on one side of the quilt where Paddy lay and Dr. Feeny on the other, the men slid the patient, pallet and all, onto the litter.

Sally ran ahead to the clinic and opened doors for the men, while Maggie and Bridget followed. Once inside, as if waking from a dream, Maggie remembered the team. "I've got to tend the horses," she said. "Paddy would never forgive me if I didn't see to cooling them down and—"

"I'll see to it, Miss Maggie." Dix's rumbling voice reminded Maggie of distant thunder.

"Dix is good with horses," Sally offered.

"I'll walk 'em out, cool 'em down, see they watered and fed proper—so as not to have any chilblains and such." He smiled. "I know them horses. Mr. Devlin, he spoil 'em something terrible. So will I. Give 'em a nice molasses mash after they settle down. They be ready to take you home when the time comes, none the worse for the run."

"Thank you," Maggie said. Grateful for the support when Kerry-boy pressed against her, she put her hand on the dog's head, suddenly aware of the fact that she was trembling again, and this time she could not stop.

"You best be sittin' down now," Sally said. Taking Maggie's arm, she guided her to a chair by the door. "Don't you worry for the team, Miss Maggie. Dix knows what he doin' with horses. I'm goin' get you a glass of lemonade and maybe"—she looked to Bridget for agreement—"maybe a tiny bit of somethin' stronger?" Bridget nodded. "Bet this old monster you call a dog wouldn't mind a little somethin', neither," Sally said.

"I'd give him the best cut of meat in the smokehouse if I could." Maggie stroked Kerry-boy's side. "You're a good boy, Kerry. A very good boy." The dog chuffed softly and nuzzled her hand, but when Sally left and called him to follow her, he did so willingly.

When Sally came back bearing a tray with a pitcher of lemonade, two glasses, and, Lord bless her, a decanter of raspberry cordial and two small glasses, Maggie gulped the lemonade like a woman who'd been wandering a desert for days.

Bridget poured raspberry cordial. Maggie took a sip, and then decided she preferred the lemonade. For a few minutes more, the two young women sat quietly, sipping lemonade and occasionally glancing toward the next room, where Dr. Feeny attended Paddy Devlin.

Presently, Maggie took a deep breath and set her glass back on the tray. "Thank you for waiting with me," she said to Bridget. "I thought—well"—she laughed an embarrassed little laugh—"for a moment there, I thought I might faint."

Libbie was halfway across the backyard to the kitchen when the door opened and a skinny, dark-skinned child emerged. He'd just opened his mouth to greet Libbie when the cook's voice filtered out the door. "...and don't you be telling me they's no more peaches in the fruit cellar. I saw at least half a dozen quarts myself jus' las' week."

"Hello, Cooper," Libbie said.

"Afternoon, Miss Libbie," the child said, and scampered off toward the fruit cellar. Libbie crossed the yard and stepped inside the door of the brick kitchen that took up the entire ground floor of a fourteen-foot-square, two-story building behind the dining room. Both stories connected to the house by only a breezeway, and both admitted servants to the house via back doors, one leading directly into the dining room, the other leading into a second-story combination closet and storage room and, from there, into the upstairs hall and the bedrooms. Annabelle, the cook, and Malachi shared half the space above the kitchen. Another couple, Walker's man, Robert, and his wife, Betty, the only housemaid, occupied the other half. Cooper was Robert and Betty's only child.

Libbie stepped into the kitchen, where Annabelle was standing at a table, kneading a massive pile of dough. "Mr. Blair has formed a regiment or a company or—well, I don't really know which, but he's calling it the Wildwood Guard, and he's invited them to camp here at the Grove. He's just informed me that several officers will be our guests for some time to come." She paused. "He says provisions are to be delivered by way of the river. Still, it's going to mean a lot of work. Is there someone you might want to bring up from the quarters? I'd think you'd want at least two more to help with all the extra cooking and housekeeping."

Annabelle brushed a strand of gray hair back off her forehead with the back of one large hand, then went back to kneading as she talked. "Where the new ones gonna sleep? We got to share the upstairs?"

Libbie hadn't thought about it and said so. "Mr. Blair only just told me about it all. Do you have any ideas?" Annabelle looked out the kitchen window toward the small brick building near the garden. Libbie nodded. "Of course. That should work. I'll ask Malachi to move the old spinning wheel and such into the other room next to the loom." She paused. "Will you be asking anyone with a baby? The old nanny rocker is in the attic. I could have that brought down."

Annabelle shrugged. "Can't say yes or no, Miss Libbie. I be thinkin' on it and let you know. Need to see what Betty thinks 'bout housemaids. If you gonna be presiding over meals every day, you gonna need extra help, too." Libbie had always resisted the idea of a personal servant. Annabelle knew about it and spoke to it now. "I knows you never wanted your own personal slave since old Mariah died, but the truth is, if Betty don't have to worry over lacing up corsets and pressing lace collars and such, she'd have considerable more time for housework. She'll be needin' it, too, with all those gentlemens staying here. Her sister got a girl, name of Ora Lee. I think she might do."

Mariah had raised Libbie and survived the cholera in Tennessee only to die here at Wildwood Grove only a few weeks after they arrived. To this day, a framed photograph of the beloved nanny holding a nearly bald baby Elizabeth held a place of honor on Libbie's dressing table. No one could possibly replace Mariah. On the other hand, it was wrong to make Betty suffer just because Libbie felt that way.

"Tell me about Ora Lee," she said.

"She'd have to learn about the silks and all, but Betty can teach her everything she needs to know." Annabelle punched the dough with extra force as she said, "She's a good girl. Works hard. You bring her up to the house, that girl gonna be so grateful, you will have the loyalest slave you ever had."

"Well, I'll certainly consider it," Libbie said. "But I'll need to consult Mr. James. He's not going to appreciate my plundering the row to shore up things here at the house."

Annabelle slapped the dough again. Punched it. Tore off a hunk and began to shape it. "I don't want to cause trouble for nobody, Miss Libbie, but Mr. James might not give a good report if he thinks he'll lose Ora Lee." She cleared her throat. "She growing into a real beautiful woman."

Far back in Libbie's mind an alarm bell rang when Annabelle mentioned Ora Lee's appearance and Asa James. It resurrected the memory of an incident that had occurred not long after Libbie arrived at the Grove. Another beautiful woman down at the quarters had been forever scarred in a late-night accident witnessed only by Asa James. When Libbie took an interest, Walker ordered her to mind her own business. Remembering it just now made her feel ill. "I'll send Malachi down to the quarters right away," she said. "Ora Lee can help me clean out the new room. We'll get acquainted that way. If Betty's willing to teach her, and if she's all you say, I won't mind giving her a little time to learn."

"You won't be sorry, Miss Libbie."

No, Libbie thought. She didn't think she would. "As soon as you know who else you want, let Malachi know. It's going to be a rush to do it, but let's try to get everyone moved up here before nightfall." She paused, emphasizing the words as she said, "Whoever you want, Annabelle. You know the people down in the quarters. You make the choices."

Libbie left the kitchen to go up to the house and change into work clothes. She'd just stepped onto the back porch when Annabelle called to her from the kitchen doorway. "God bless you, Miss Libbie."

Annabelle wasn't expecting a response, and Libbie didn't have one. She didn't want to think about Asa James and the young girl named Ora Lee. She had to think about cleaning out the spinning room in time to preside over supper, lest Walker be upset. She would wear the simple red gingham dress and tie her hair up with a kerchief. Perhaps she would even leave the hoops hanging in her closet so that she could actually do some real work for a change.

Intending to head into the front hall and up the main stairs to her room, she stopped just inside the back door. When she heard rumbling male voices spilling out into the wide hall— among them, she thought, that of Asa James—she backpedaled. Instead of taking the main stairs, she opted for the steep flight intended for the servants.

Red gingham. Kerchief. Spinning room. Broom. She repeated the words to herself as a litany until, finally, the specter of Asa James faded.

❧

Maggie had sunk into a numb stupor when hurried footsteps sounding on the board porch just outside Dr. Feeny's waiting room made her start and jump up to greet whoever it was. It was the sheriff. He'd donned some kind of uniform. *Confederate*, Maggie realized.

Sheriff Green had no opportunity to give more than a

greeting before Dr. Feeny appeared in the doorway that led into his examination room.

Again, the clutching fear returned, as Maggie tried to interpret the doctor's expression.

"It will take some time," the doctor said, "but he's going to be all right."

Relief flooded in, and Maggie sank back onto the chair where she'd been sitting. Dr. Feeny greeted the sheriff before sending Bridget to fetch Dix again. "I'd like his help with transferring Mr. Devlin to one of the cots in the infirmary." He nodded at Maggie. "If you'll follow me." And then to the sheriff, "We should only be a moment."

Still trembling, Maggie followed Dr. Feeny into the examination room where Paddy lay, still as death, his face pale beneath the bruises beginning to show around both eyes, one of which was already swollen shut. Maggie pressed the back of one hand against her lips to keep from crying out in protest.

"They dislocated his shoulder," Dr. Feeny said. "I'm not certain, but I think the collarbone on that side may have been fractured." He paused. "I've put the shoulder back in place, but it's going to have to be immobilized for at least a couple of weeks. From the bruising on his torso, he's been kicked. I'm suspecting at least three fractured ribs—unfortunately, on the opposite side of the shoulder injury. He's going to be in a lot of pain."

Maggie nodded, hardly able to take in all the things Dr. Feeny suspected might be wrong. Paddy hadn't moved since she'd come into the room. "He—how long—" Her voice wavered. Finally, she managed to croak out a question as to when he might wake up.

"Hopefully not until tomorrow. I gave him a hefty dose of laudanum. Sleep is the best thing for him right now."

"He—he isn't unconscious?"

Dr. Feeny shook his head. "He felt his injuries in all their infernal glory—until the laudanum took effect."

Maggie frowned. "But he didn't cry out."

"Toughest little man I've ever seen," Dr. Feeny said. "He was more worried about you than himself. I reassured him that you're fine."

The sheriff had been standing in the doorway listening. "I wish you'd let me question him before you put him under," he said.

Dr. Feeny didn't hide his indignation at the implication that he'd done something wrong. "And I wish you'd come running the minute Miss Malone's team charged past the jail. It had to be obvious there was something wrong."

"As it happens," the sheriff retorted, "I was not at the jail this evening." He pointed to the braid on one sleeve of his gray jacket. "As you can see, there's to be a change in the office of the county sheriff."

"Then why isn't whoever is taking your place here with you?" Dr. Feeny asked.

"I'll be sure my replacement is fully apprised of the situation," the sheriff said. "As soon as I know what the situation *is*." He turned pointedly to Maggie. "Miss Malone? All I know is that when I was returning to Littleton from Wildwood Grove just now, it was obvious something terrible had taken place on your farm—and equally obvious that there was no one there. Barnabas Irving saw me ride into town and hurried over to tell me about seeing you race by with the team." He glanced over at the doctor. "I did not so much as get off my horse, but came here immediately."

Bridget returned with Dix. Dr. Feeny ordered her to sit with Maggie again, while Dix helped him move Paddy. "I've a couple of cots in the infirmary," he said to Maggie. "And I'll expect you to occupy one tonight. You've had a shock, and you need rest almost as much as Paddy. Sally will let you know when supper is ready, and I'll expect you to eat in the house with Bridget and me." Next, he spoke to the sheriff. "I'll thank you to wait until we've returned from transferring Paddy to speak further with Miss Malone. I may be able to offer helpful information for your investigation. Paddy was quite talkative until I administered the laudanum."

The sheriff cocked an eyebrow. "And?"

"And we'll speak of it after Miss Malone has a moment to gather her thoughts." Without another word, Dr. Feeny and Dix left the waiting room. The sheriff stepped back outside, where Maggie could hear him pacing back and forth beneath the overhang, clearly unhappy at being ordered about by Dr. Feeny.

After what felt like an eternity, Dr. Feeny emerged from the infirmary, crossed to the waiting room door, and summoned the sheriff back inside. "Paddy's resting. Dix will stay with him until we're finished here."

Clearing his throat, the sheriff directed his first question at Dr. Feeny. "You said you talked to Mr. Devlin while you were tending him?"

The doctor nodded. "He didn't recognize anyone. Said he thought they were outsiders. Rebels, he said."

The sheriff grunted. "How could he possibly know that?"

"One said something about making General Price proud," the doctor said. "And a couple of them had accents. Deep South."

"Not soldiers," the sheriff said. "True soldiers would never attack the defenseless in such a cowardly manner. Bush-whackers, more than likely." He shook his head. "I'd hoped all that nonsense would stay upriver where it started." With a sigh, he pulled up a chair and sat opposite Maggie. "Tell me everything you can remember—and I do mean everything. Every detail. Something you think unimportant could be just the thing that helps us find them." He looked away for a moment. Cleared his throat. "They didn't...um...hurt you, did they?"

"As you can see, I'm fine."

"Of course." The sheriff hesitated. "I merely wanted to make certain that no outrage was committed against you... personally."

It took a moment for Maggie to comprehend the meaning. When she did, she felt her face flush bright red. "No." Just the thought renewed her fierce regret that she had only managed to wound one of the six men. "I wasn't even there at first. I'd taken Kerry-boy and gone hunting."

She thought of the lone rabbit she'd dropped just over the hill. The dead cow. The mayhem inside the house. And finally, the burlap bag tied to one of the men's saddle horns. *Chickens*. She swore softly.

"Ma'am?"

"My chickens," Maggie said. "One of those sons of—one of them had a burlap bag tied to the saddle horn. I just realized it was probably full of chickens."

"You were going to tell me exactly what happened. You'd gone hunting?"

With a nod, Maggie recounted everything she could remember about the incident, beginning with Kerry-boy sounding the alarm.

"And you're certain that you didn't recognize anyone. A voice? A limp? Anything at all?"

Maggie shook her head. "The horses were—poor. Bays,

mostly—but—" She paused, trying to remember. Something about the horses. "When the last one reined his horse about... there was white...almost as if someone had splashed it with whitewash on the off side." She frowned. "Only the neck—I think." She frowned. "Maybe a splotch on its flanks. I'm not sure."

"Anything else? What about hair color? Did they have beards or mustaches?"

"I—I'm sorry. I was too—it all happened so fast. Some had beards, I think. But it's—it's just a blur."

"Were they white?"

"Yes. At least two of them probably have bite marks or slashes on their hands or arms from Kerry-boy. From the way one of them yelped, I think I might have hit him. Well enough to make him drop his weapon, at least. But it probably isn't serious. He grabbed the gun back up before he ran." She looked away for a moment, murmuring, "Uncle Paddy wanted me to get Da's pistol out." She glanced toward the doorway that led into Dr. Feeny's examination room again. "We were going to do some practice shooting with it tomorrow." Her voice wavered. Pressing her lips together, Maggie willed her tears away. Anger flared up, and she fanned the flames, not only with the memory of Paddy's still form lying in the middle of the corral, but also with images of the dead cow...her rocking chair sailing out the back door of the house...Mam's cream pitcher, shattered...flames licking at the floor just beyond the hearth. And suddenly, the memory of Walker Blair talking to Paddy over the garden fence. She blurted it out. "Walker Blair might know something."

The sheriff seemed to stiffen. He cleared his throat. "Now, ma'am. That's a mighty serious accusation."

Maggie lifted her chin. "He and Uncle Paddy had what

seemed to be a very serious conversation across the garden fence one morning not long ago." She paused. She'd been about to mention how Paddy had started carrying his old musket with him everywhere he went not long after that, but the sheriff's new uniform made her hold back. That and the knowledge that he'd just said he'd been "visiting" at Wildwood Grove. She chose her next words carefully. "I'm not accusing him of anything. I only wonder if he might have knowledge of resentments brewing. Things he might have mentioned to Uncle Paddy—by way of being neighborly."

The sheriff took a deep breath. He nodded and got back to his feet. "All right, then. I'll ride out to the Grove first thing in the morning and see if Walker—uh, Mr. Blair— might know anything." He put his hat back on, pausing at the door just long enough to say, "I am very sorry for what you've endured, Miss Malone. It is an unfortunate reality that men of low moral character often take advantage of troubled times." With a little jerk on the brim of his hat by way of a salute, the sheriff took his leave.

Chapter 5

———— ❦ ————

The sound of someone muttering her name brought Maggie back to the land of the living. She jerked awake and glanced outside. *Gray light.* She hadn't thought she would sleep at all, and here she'd slept the night away. She hadn't even heard Dr. Feeny coming and going. A hoarse voice spoke her name again. Paddy had opened his eyes and was looking over at her. She sat up. He grimaced and tried to raise his head.

Rising to her feet, she stepped to Paddy's cot and put her hand on his forearm. "Don't try to get up. Dr. Feeny wants to keep you here for a few days, but you're going to be all right."

Paddy frowned. Cleared his throat and croaked one word. "You?"

"I'm fine. I—we—Kerry-boy and I chased them off."

Paddy gave a soft grunt. "Amazing. You."

"I'm not," she protested. "I only managed to get two shots off. They got away."

He grimaced. "The place?"

"We'll have it back to normal in no time," Maggie lied. Paddy didn't need to hear about the dead cow. He didn't need to worry over the churned-up garden or the missing chickens or the scorched floorboards. For a long while, Maggie thought he might have fallen back to sleep, but when she took a step toward the door with the intention of going to the well for water, he stirred.

"Jack. Seamus," he croaked. "Get them home." He took another shuddering breath. "I'm useless," he said. "You... alone...not safe."

"Don't you be worrying over me or anything else." Maggie forced confidence into her voice. "Dix saw to Banner and Babe. They're rested and well fed. Kerry-boy and I will be heading home soon."

Paddy protested. "Not alone."

"Well, of course not alone. I'm not an idgit, to be venturing out there alone in the wake of bushwhackers. Sally's to sit with you, and Dr. Feeny and Dix will go with me to reconnoiter. After we see what's to be seen, we'll make a plan."

For a moment she thought Paddy had fallen back to sleep, but then he said he had something important for her to do. He told her in bursts of language and then made her repeat it. "Four boards from the knothole beneath the front window. A key, wrapped in a rag. Next, pry up the board beneath the rag rug I made. Another board with a knothole in it. And bring you the black metal box."

Paddy nodded. "Put it in the bag. Leather. By the door."

"I'll see to it," Maggie promised, "and bring it to you."

The deep creases across Paddy's forehead relaxed. Maggie looked up as Dr. Feeny entered the clinic by way of the back door. "Here's Dr. Feeny now, come to check on you." She bent to kiss the old man's weathered cheek. "I'll give you a full accounting by this afternoon—and, hopefully, news that the sheriff has identified the varmints responsible and set out after them."

Doubt sounded in the tone of Paddy's grunted response— doubt that Maggie was inclined to share, especially now that Sheriff Green had donned a uniform. But Paddy didn't need to worry about any of that. He just needed to heal. While he healed, Maggie would take care of everything.

It was mid-morning by the time Dr. Feeny and Dix were ready to accompany Maggie back to the farm. While he was doing his best to appear relaxed, Maggie noticed that the doctor kept his grip firm on the rifle cradled in his arms and his gaze fixed on the horizon. Kerry-boy and Dix rode behind them in the wagon bed.

When movement rustled a stand of tall grass just ahead of them, Dr. Feeny took aim. Dix grabbed a handful of Kerry-boy's fur, forcing him to stay in the wagon. A massive hog stepped out of the tangle of grass into the road, and Maggie laughed with relief. "It's only Hermione," she said. "She's Uncle Paddy's prize sow." She shifted in the seat, looking past Hermione and into the tall grass. "She had a dozen shoats. I wonder where they are." Had the rest of the bushwhackers had burlap bags, too? A man could easily carry a shoat that way.

Dix nodded at Hermione. "She mean?"

Maggie shook her head. "Practically a pet."

"Then you just hold up a minute and I'll load her in the back."

Maggie was doubtful. Hermione probably weighed nearly three hundred pounds.

"Leastways let me try," Dix said, staring toward the woods. "I'd drive her home, but we ain't sure them bushwhackers is all the way gone."

Maggie pulled the wagon alongside Hermione. Dix jumped down and dropped the tailgate. Leaning over the sow, he clasped his hands beneath her belly and hoisted her into the wagon bed. She barely had time to squeal a protest before he had the tailgate back in place.

With a sharp bark and a snarl, Kerry-boy jumped down and tore off in the direction of home. At Maggie's side, Dr. Feeny again readied the rifle. Dix rummaged in the toolbox they'd brought along to make repairs easy, and when Maggie glanced back, he was standing tall, a hammer clenched in his fist.

Three riders came into view. Maggie recognized Sheriff Green's white horse. Or was it *former* Sheriff Green by now? She kept the team moving, pulling them up only when the sheriff and the other two riders—who proved to be Walker Blair and a man Maggie recognized but whose name she couldn't recall—got within earshot.

"What happened back there," Mr. Blair said before the sheriff could speak, "is unconscionable." He removed his hat and nodded at Maggie. "May I offer the services of some of my boys to help you put things to right?"

At mention of "boys" Maggie thought *slaves*, and then she realized who the other man was. Asa James, Blair's plantation overseer. Was Blair offering to send slaves onto her place? Newly aware of Dix's presence in the wagon bed behind her and feeling self-conscious and strangely rankled by the man's genteel tone of voice, Maggie said, "Thank you, but we'll see to things." She shifted her attention to the sheriff. "Did you find anything to suggest who they were?"

Green shook his head. "That doesn't mean we won't." He glanced over at Mr. Blair. "We're on our way into Littleton right now to settle the matter of who's to take over the office now that I'm serving with the Wildwood Guard."

"For your own safety," Blair interjected, "I do hope you'll agree to seek rooms in Littleton, Miss Malone. At the very least until your brothers can be contacted." He paused. "They will surely wish to return home when they realize that their absence has put you at risk."

"Bushwhackers put me at risk," Maggie snapped. Jack and Seamus hadn't done anything wrong. She wanted them home, but not because she couldn't manage without them. "I can't be begging my brothers to run home, just because there's been a bit of trouble."

Blair and the sheriff exchanged looks. The sheriff took over. "All due respect, Miss Malone"—he nodded over his shoulder in the direction of the farm—"that's more than just 'a bit of trouble.'" He turned his gaze on Dr. Feeny. "You'll help her see reason, I hope. No woman should be alone in times like these. It's a wonder worse didn't happen."

The overseer spoke up. "If y'all will excuse me, it's time I was getting back to attend to things at the Grove." The man barely glanced at Maggie, but the look in the glittering eyes visible just above his thick, dark beard made her uncomfortable. Her gaze slid to the neck of his horse. She half expected to see a splash of white.

Mr. Blair spoke again. "Please let me know if you decide to accept our assistance. Neighbors must support one another in times like these." He paused. "I am truly sorry that the fears I expressed to your uncle the other day have been realized. I was afraid somethin' like this would happen when Mr. Devlin told me your brothers had volunteered with the Irish."

Dr. Feeny broke in. "If you'll excuse us, we need to be getting to the business of taking an accounting of things at the Malones'."

Maggie chirruped to the team and got the wagon moving again. She looked over at Dr. Feeny. "What did he mean, the 'Wildwood Guard'?"

"Another volunteer militia, this one probably funded by Walker Blair, since it's taken the plantation name." The farm came into view, and he muttered a low curse.

Things were worse than Maggie remembered. Intending to pull as close to the barn as possible so that Dix could get Hermione into a stall without too much trouble, she drove the wagon past what had been a thriving garden. It was as if someone had walked the rows with the sole purpose of uprooting every plant. Maggie circled the corral and pulled up at the back of the barn.

Dix jumped down to open the wide double barn doors. As the pulleys and gears creaked and the doors opened, Maggie looked toward the hog pen. Her heart sank. Seamus's magnificent boar lay dead in the tall grass, shot in the head, already beginning to bloat in the summer sun.

As she and Dr. Feeny climbed down from the wagon seat, Maggie heard rather than saw Dix get Hermione penned up in one of the stalls. When Dix exited the barn door, Maggie thanked him and glanced off toward the woods. The cow lay dead up there. Why wasn't the calf bawling? While she and the doctor trudged past Uncle Paddy's cabin toward the house, Dix trotted off to see if he could find the calf.

At the back of the house, Dr. Feeny reached for a chair and pulled it off the top of the pile of furniture that had been tossed out the back door, grimacing as he swore. "They were planning a bonfire. I smell kerosene."

"At least they didn't break it all up," Maggie said. Still, her heart sank. How would she ever get rid of the smell?

Crossing to the open back door, she paused at the threshold and took a deep breath before stepping inside. Bits of broken crockery littered the floor. The ruined quilt she'd used to put out flames lay crumpled atop the blackened floor-boards bordering the stone hearth. The bushwhackers had even ripped the green beans down from the rafters.

As Dr. Feeny helped her right the overturned kitchen table, Dix appeared at the back door. He'd found the calf not far from the cow. "I think it was coyotes," he said. "At least your uncle's place don't look bad. They must not-a had time to git to it."

A burst of cool air drew Maggie's attention to the windows. Da had been so proud when he could replace oiled paper with real glass. The bushwhackers had broken every single cherished pane. The stew she'd left simmering when she went hunting had been poured all over Jack's bed. Only two square panes of glass in the upper corners of the bedroom window had survived.

In Maggie's room, the bushwhackers had pulled Da's small trunk out from beneath her bed, ripped the lid off, and scattered the contents. Pages from Mam's prayer book lay strewn about the room among the broken bits of her rosary. At the sight of Mam's torn wedding handkerchief, Maggie groaned *oh no* and began a frantic search for the coin that had been tied in one corner.

"What is it?" Dr. Feeny asked.

Maggie choked out a reply. "An ancient coin that Da dug up when he was a boy. It was the first thing he gave Mam. She had it t-tied—" Her voice gave out. Mam had carried the handkerchief with the coin tied in one corner tucked in her sleeve on her wedding day.

Why, of all the things in the house, would a man steal an ancient, discolored coin? It made no sense.

Slumping to the floor, Maggie braced her back against the wall, hid her face in her hands, and gave vent to everything—

to fear, to anger, to the sense of loss, and to the longing for things to be as they had been. Kerry-boy padded into the room. Stretching out next to her, he forced his giant head beneath one arm and rested it in her lap while she cried.

Dr. Feeny handed her a clean handkerchief. "You're a brave girl, and you've earned a good cry, Maggie. I'll be out back if you need me."

The sound of sweeping in the main room finally got her attention. With a last sniff, she moved to get up. Kerry-boy rose with her. Dix kept sweeping. Dr. Feeny was drawing a bucket of water out back. Setting it on the ground, he dipped a brush in it and began to scrub Maggie's rocking chair.

Defeat washed over her. Paddy wouldn't be able to help for weeks, and while Dr. Feeny was being kind to help, he had patients to attend to. Crossing to the back door, she called to Dr. Feeny. "It's too much for us to handle," she said. "I've something to do for Paddy down at his cabin, and then we can head back into town." She looked about her. Shook her head. "I just—I need some time to think."

As she trudged down the hill toward Uncle Paddy's cabin, Maggie's gaze roved back and forth between the distant ridge and the edge of the woods to the east. When a hawk took flight from the top of one of the trees, the sudden movement made goose bumps rise on her arms. The truth was, she might don a courageous mask, but she didn't want to stay out here by herself—not even with a rifle and Da's pistol and Kerry-boy—*Da's pistol*. Perhaps the bushwhackers had stolen something besides Mam's wedding coin, after all.

෴

The leather satchel was right where Uncle Paddy had said it would be, hanging just to the right of his front door. Maggie counted boards and knotholes and retrieved first the key and then a metal box, both of which she thrust into the leather satchel. She paused to look around her before stepping back outside. The bushwhackers hadn't bothered things here. Surely they'd intended to. Maybe she and Kerry-boy had managed to save something, after all.

When Maggie stepped back outside, Dr. Feeny was driving the team in a wide semicircle to get the wagon turned around. Dix came trotting out of the barn—he'd said he would see that Hermione had water—smiling. He held up Da's pistol. "Hermione found it," he said. "Rutted it out of the straw in that stall where I put her."

Learning how Da's pistol had ended up in the barn would have to wait until Paddy was well enough to tell her. For now, though, Maggie was grateful for the feel of the grip in her palm. She thrust it into her skirt pocket, then handed Paddy's leather bag to Dix and climbed up beside Dr. Feeny. Kerry-boy and Dix climbed into the wagon bed and they were on their way. As the wagon turned into the road, Maggie gazed back at the ruined garden, which looked like so many piles of wilted weeds just waiting to be gathered and burned.

Again, uncertainty swept over her. She was not one to cower in the face of a challenge, but she couldn't help feeling overwhelmed by the task that lay before her. What if the attack on the farm was only the beginning of trouble in Lafayette County?

✑

In the week after the bushwhackers attacked the farm, it seemed to Maggie that some new bit of gossip or news was forever drawing the men of Littleton out of their homes and into the streets, where they milled about outside the news-paper office, smoking and swearing as they resolved to "fight tyranny" and "preserve liberty at all costs." The definitions of words changed, depending on who spoke them and whether they sympathized with the North or the South.

For all his initial reassurances about finding the men responsible for the attack, Sheriff Green did nothing beyond resigning his post and taking up residence at Wildwood Grove as an officer in the Wildwood Guard. He clearly had no intention of "pursuing justice" for the Irish. In the wake of the mounting unrest, Maggie's neighbors also proved reluctant to help her. She could not blame them. After all, with the former sheriff in the Southern militia and no new sheriff taking the office, wasn't everyone who flew the Stars and Stripes vulnerable to something similar?

In the midst of all the turmoil, Maggie did what she could at the farm. With Dix's help, she swept out the house, scrubbed the kerosene-drenched furniture with lye soap, and hauled bedding and clothes back to town, where together, she and Sally did laundry and mended what they could. By Friday of the week after the attack, the house itself was habitable again, but Dr. Feeny insisted that Maggie could not live there alone—and that Uncle Paddy needed a few more days of recuperation before the two of them returned to the farm.

Maggie didn't argue. She wouldn't have admitted it aloud, but she was grateful for the delay. Confederate and Union militias had taken to marching the streets of Littleton. Thus far, they seemed willing to organize things so that they didn't meet face to face. Still, things were growing increasingly tense.

When Paddy developed a rattle in his chest and a wheez-
ing cough that caused him agonizing pain, Dr. Feeny and Dix
fetched Hermione into town and Maggie gave up going to the
farm. She and Sally took turns sitting with Uncle Paddy, wiping his brow, spooning broth into his mouth, and running for
the doctor more than once when it seemed that death had a
stranglehold on the wiry little Irishman.

And still, there was no word from either Jack or Seamus.

Chapter 6

———————— ✧ ————————

Twenty-two days. Maggie stood at the infirmary window looking toward the east as the night sky gave way to the dawn. Jack and Seamus had left twenty-two days ago and she had not heard a word from either one. Paddy had been near death's door for part of that time, and all told, it had been the worst twenty-two days of her life. But thanks be to the dear Lord, Paddy's fever had broken in the night.

"As I said when you first brought him in," Dr. Feeny had said, "he's the toughest little man I've ever seen." He'd put his hand on Maggie's shoulder and given it a pat as he ordered her to get some sleep—lest he have another patient made ill from sheer exhaustion.

She had slept—for a while. Now, though, as Maggie watched the sky and listened to the morning cries of the songbirds nesting in the trees across the way, she determined that today she would finally write the boys and tell them what had happened out at the farm. Paddy had been very ill. He was going to live, but the farm—Maggie couldn't handle everything on her own. She needed help and they could decide which of them would give it, but one of them must try to come home. She hated admitting that she needed help, but it was the truth and she supposed there was no shame in telling the truth, even if it did mean she had to admit a weakness.

Startled by noise out in the street, Maggie slipped out the

door and stood, listening. Flickering lamps caught her eye. When she looked toward Main Street, she realized that a good-sized crowd of townsfolk were making their way by lamplight toward the east. She heard the back door of Dr. Feeny's house open and close, and the doctor came to her side.

"Is the patient still sleeping?"

Maggie nodded. "Snoring, in fact—the first natural sleep I think he's had since he was hurt."

The doctor nodded. "That's good. I'm going to follow those folks and see what I can find out. I'll be back directly."

At first light, Sally crossed the yard from the direction of the cabin where she and Dix lived, just the other side of Dr. Feeny's barn. She brought a tray out to the clinic, and it wasn't long before Bridget came in search of her father. Hearing that he'd gone up the street to learn the news, she went after him. Both returned shortly thereafter.

One look at the pair, and Maggie knew the news was bad. Bridget was clinging to her father's arm while she sobbed into a handkerchief. The minute she saw Maggie, she wailed, "It's Jack. There's been a battle at Boonville and the newspaper has the list and he's on it."

"What list?" Maggie almost barked the question. Was Jack wounded or—please, Father in heaven, Mother Mary, and all the saints—please, not dead.

"Wounded," Dr. Feeny said quickly, grasping Bridget about the shoulders and giving her a little shake. "Hysterics are of no help, daughter. Get hold of yourself."

Relief so strong that it made her ache flooded through Maggie. *Not dead.* Something to cling to. Something to hope in. Her weariness forgotten, Maggie asked Sally to stay with Paddy, then lifted her skirts and ran for the newspaper office herself, only vaguely aware that Kerry-boy was at her side.

Snatches of conversation among those gathered on the street told her nothing about Jack. If only she'd paid more attention to Paddy's and the boys' conversations. If she had, maybe terms like *untrained Home Guard* and *howitzer, picket fire*, and *retreat* would do more than just fray her nerves.

Thankfully, Dr. Feeny was soon back at her side, and in the next few moments he'd learned enough to explain what had happened. "You already know about the Camp Jackson Affair in St. Louis," Dr. Feeny said.

Maggie nodded. "Fighting in the streets. A Captain... *Lyon*, I think his name was...led Union soldiers to roust secessionist troops from an encampment. He was worried they were planning to march on the arsenal."

"That's right. Since then, Captain Lyon has been promoted. He's now General Lyon. A week ago, there was a meeting in St. Louis—an attempt to mitigate hostilities between the two sides. It went badly. General Lyon stormed out, but not before saying, 'This means war.' Governor Jackson and General Price fled St. Louis and headed for Jefferson City, intending to 'protect' the state capital from what they consider an 'invasion' by Union troops. General Lyon took two volunteer regiments—Jack and Seamus's Irish Brigade would have been with them—and went after them, intent on securing the capital and dispersing the rebel troops.

"Governor Jackson is no fool. He realized that he and his volunteer militia were outnumbered, ordered the bridges on the main rail lines burned, and withdrew fifty miles upriver from Jefferson City to Boonville. When the two sides met, Lyon not only had superior numbers, but many of them were well-trained regular army—and they were supported by a howitzer mounted aboard the steamer *McDowell*.

"It was more of a skirmish than a battle. Word is that the

state's secessionist government is in flight, with Governor Jackson and his supporters retreating toward the southwest in concert with Major General Price and the Missouri State Guard which, by all accounts, is growing as they march south and are joined by secessionist sympathizers bent on 'saving Missouri from tyranny.'"

"If the Southerners mean to join up with their men in the southwest," Maggie asked, "doesn't that mean the Wildwood Guard will go, too, and leave us in peace?"

Dr. Feeny pondered the idea. "I don't know, but—there's sure to be a struggle for control of the river, because that represents communication and supply lines. A Union-controlled river would also be a natural barrier to rebels trying to cross over from the northern part of the state and join up with the enemy."

The enemy. To General Lyon's men, the Wildwood Guard was the enemy.

Dr. Feeny put a comforting hand on her shoulder. "As I said, it was more of a skirmish than a battle. Only three of the wounded are local boys."

Three. Maggie hadn't even thought there might be others and felt guilty for it. "Who else?"

"Edgar James and Dick Green—both with the Guard."

With the Guard. The Rebels. Dick Green was the sheriff's brother.

When Maggie said it aloud, Dr. Feeny nodded. "You know Edgar's brother, as well. He's the overseer at Wildwood Grove."

Maggie just shook her head. The men who should be chasing down the bushwhackers were more than just "sympathetic" to the Confederacy. They had family in the fight. Family who'd shot at Jack and Seamus...who'd tried to *kill* them. She blurted out a question. "What will they do with the wounded?"

"Army surgeons will have already tended to Jack," Dr.

Feeny said. "If his injuries are slight, he might remain with the regiment while he heals. He could be given light duty in camp—depending, of course, on whether they remain in camp. They could be charged with holding Boonville, or they could be sent elsewhere. No one believes that one skirmish is going to settle things in Missouri."

War. Battles. Skirmishes. Was anyone safe? "And if his injuries aren't slight?"

"Then he'll probably be sent downriver to the military hospital at St. Louis. By steamboat or a combination of steamboat and railcar—assuming the track from Jefferson City to St. Louis hasn't been entirely destroyed."

Destroyed. Train track destroyed, steamboats armed with howitzers...it made what had happened at the farm pale in comparison. How long would things go on? How much more would be destroyed...how many lives...Maggie and Dr. Feeny had been walking back toward the clinic while they talked. It was going to be a fine day with bright blue skies and brilliant sunshine, but as Maggie contemplated the future, she clutched her shawl about her in a vain attempt to cast off a bone-deep chill.

⚭

Maggie had never paid much attention to the steamboat whistles that drifted up from the levee when she was in Littleton, but once she knew that Jack was hurt, every signal roused her. What if, at this very moment, he was hearing arrivals and departures sounded downriver at the Boonville levee? Who was tending him? What if he needed extra care? Was there anyone to ease his pain? What, exactly, had happened to him?

Her imagination sketched horrible things against the backdrop of the day's activities. Round and round her thoughts went, while Paddy alternately sipped broth and slept like the dead—a healing sleep, Dr. Feeny declared it. Maggie allowed a little smile at the notion that Paddy's snoring meant he was returning to himself. His horrific snore had inspired the construction of his cabin. Da had tried to save Paddy's feelings by saying that Paddy had more than earned a place of his own, but they all knew the real reason—and here it was, loud enough to raise the rafters and rattle the windows.

The day dragged on, with Maggie walking back and forth to the newspaper office several times, hoping for more news or a miracle in the form of a letter from Jack or Seamus. With the sun setting and the last steamboat whistle of the day sounding, she shrugged into her shawl and stepped outside to look up at the evening sky. If Jack had a fever, would anyone sit by his cot and sponge his forehead? Would anyone spoon broth into his mouth and help him regain his strength?

With a glance behind her and a murmured "come along" to Kerry-boy, Maggie hurried back to the newspaper office. Boonville was only a few steamboat stops downriver. Whatever had happened to Jack, not knowing was causing her more suffering than anything she might discover by going to him. If she left in the morning, she could be there by sunset—maybe sooner if she managed to board a lightly loaded packet piloted by a captain bent on speed. Paddy was on the mend and in good hands. As for the farm, it would have to wait. In the grand and horrible scheme of her boys being caught up in a war and one of them wounded, wandering pigs and broken windows didn't really matter that much.

Once at the newspaper office, Maggie peered up at the riverboat schedule posted on a board just outside the door. The *Nellie Magee* was expected tomorrow, her destination St. Louis by way of Lexington, Glasgow, Boonville, and a long list of other stops that didn't matter, because Maggie wasn't going beyond Boonville—unless Jack had been sent to the military hospital at St. Louis.

She would need money. Would Dr. Feeny make a loan? She would offer to work it off washing windows or cleaning the clinic. She'd offer him Hermione. If he refused, she'd talk to Mr. Irving and ask him to make a loan against the credit balance they had at the mercantile.

She'd do whatever it took to get to Jack.

Uncle Paddy was sleeping soundly when she returned to the clinic. After Dr. Feeny made his last check for the evening, she followed him outside. Her voice lowered, she told him what she wanted to do and then, swallowing, asked him to loan her the money.

Dr. Feeny's response was not what she had expected. "I'm sorry, Maggie, but I cannot agree to it. No gentleman in his right mind would allow a lady to undertake such a journey alone."

"It's a short steamboat ride downriver. I've done it dozens of times with Da or the boys."

"The key part of that being 'with Da or the boys,'" the doctor said.

"It's only to Boonville."

"Not if Jack's wounds have required he be taken to the military hospital in St. Louis. I know you, Maggie. Once you set out, you won't give up until you've found both your brothers—no matter what that involves."

"If you know me," Maggie said, her voice trembling, "then you know I will find a way to go." Tears threatened. "Please, Dr. Feeny."

He put a fatherly hand on her shoulder and gave it a light squeeze. "You are a brave woman and a devoted sister and niece. But I must decline. You're needed here." He paused. "I've a friend attached to the medical department in St. Louis," he said. "I'll send a telegram tomorrow, asking him to look into Jack's situation."

It took all of her self-control for Maggie not to argue. Somehow, she managed to mutter a terse *thank you*. She retreated back inside. She would speak with Mr. Irving first thing in the morning. There had to be a way to get to Boonville, and she would find it. She had taken down her hair and was brushing through it in preparation to retire, when Paddy stirred and croaked her name.

"I'm sorry, Uncle Paddy. I didn't mean to disturb you."

Paddy dismissed the apology with a wave of his hand. "What disturbs me is knowing you've been keeping things from me. I heard you just now, and I'll thank you to tell me what's happened to our boy. All of it, if you please."

Maggie told him.

Paddy was quiet for a while, and then he said, "And now, about the farm. How bad is it?"

"Not so bad as it could be," Maggie said. She could feel him peering at her. She sighed. "Bad enough."

"Tell me true, Mary Margaret. All of it." Maggie told him everything, from broken windows to dead livestock to ruined garden and on through to the fact that people seemed afraid to leave their own places long enough to help with the cleanup.

Finally, he cleared his throat and said, "Did you bring what I asked for from me cabin, Maggie-girl?"

"It's right here," Maggie said. "Dix helped me load Da's trunk and bring it to town for safekeeping, and I put your satchel inside."

"Open it."

Moments later, Maggie sat on her cot staring in disbelief at the contents of Uncle Paddy's cash box. How on earth had he managed to save so much?

The old man chuckled. "You won't be needing it all, but be sure you take enough. Enough to bring Jack home or feed him at hospital or do whatever is necessary. And allow plenty for postage. *You'll* want to write so as not to leave me wondering as the both of us have been these long weeks since our boys left us."

With trembling hands, Maggie counted out what Paddy said she should take with her.

"Don't keep it all in the same place," Uncle Paddy said. "'Twould be best to stitch the most of it inside a hem or two."

"Dr. Feeny won't be pleased," Maggie said as she lit a lamp and got to work, snipping at hems, inserting a bill or a few coins, and then stitching them back up.

"He's a good man," Uncle Paddy said, "but he doesn't realize there's a world of difference between his daughter and Keagan Malone's."

Maggie snorted. "In more ways than one."

"In all ways that matter for a time such as this," Paddy said. "I only wish we'd had time for that target practice. But you keep Keagan's pistol with you just the same." He closed his eyes. "And don't you dare depart without myself saying a prayer over you."

<hr />

As the steamboat *Clara* edged away from the Littleton levee, Maggie steadied herself by bracing one knee against the crate that served as a barrier between her and the edge of the freight deck. When the final whistle sounded, she raised one hand, signaling good-bye to Dr. Feeny and Bridget.

Dear Dr. Feeny. She'd been right when she told Paddy that the doctor wouldn't be happy about her leaving. But he'd finally relented and insisted that he and Bridget would see her off. As the packet moved into the channel, Kerry-boy charged along the riverbank. Maggie held her breath, willing the dog to go back, when he launched himself into the river and attempted to catch up. Finally, as the *Clara* picked up speed, Kerry-boy relented and returned to shore. Shaking himself off, he let out a final, sharp bark of disapproval and loped back to where Dr. Feeny and Bridget stood.

As the Littleton levee slipped out of sight, Maggie watched the shoreline slide past, willing the packet to go faster. She'd spoken to no one on board, keeping a promise to Uncle Paddy to "watch out for the snakes, and should anyone try to take liberties, thump them alongside the head with me satchel." Thinking on it now, Maggie slipped her hand into her left pocket, where she'd secreted the broken bits of Mam's rosary and a small cake of lavender soap. "Lavender soap and a broken rosary," she muttered. "You're a sentimental fool, Mary Margaret Malone." The incongruity of feminine things in one pocket and Da's pistol in the other made her laugh at herself.

She was surprised when the *Clara* stopped at the Wildwood Grove landing, and even more surprised by the number of crates the deckhands unloaded—among them, the one she'd been using for her perch. Even more surprising—and unsettling—was the fact that the men receiving the freight onshore wore uniforms. Apparently, at least part of the Wildwood Guard was staying put in Lafayette County.

The *Clara* continued downriver, past the mouth of the Grand River and finally on to the Brunswick levee, piled high with barrels and freight—most of it apparently intended for destinations upriver, for the *Clara* took on only a few crates and passengers before sliding back into the channel. Maggie found another perch on another crate and had just eaten the bit of bread and cheese she'd brought along when the *Clara* put in at Boonville. Her heart pounding, she disembarked and crossed the levee, hesitating just long enough to gain the unwanted attention of a ragged mulatto boy, who offered unsolicited advice on everything from where to find good lodging to which livery offered the best prices if a lady wanted to hire a buggy.

"You seem to know everything about Boonville," Maggie said.

"Nobody knows everything about anything," the boy said, and then he grinned up at her from beneath the brim of his battered straw hat. "But I know more'n most and charge less."

"You charge for information?"

The boy shrugged. "A feller's got to make a livin' somehow. Can't live on catfish. A body gets tired of catfish. Hankers for a taste of pie now and again."

Behind them, the *Clara* sounded her departure and, with a clattering and clanking, pulled away from the levee and into the channel. Another shrill whistle, and the paddlewheel reversed direction and, with the help of the river current, swept the steamboat downriver.

The boy was still there, and when the noise died down, he tilted his head and asked, "You looking to find the Irish?"

"And why would you think such a thing?"

The boy put his hand to his heart as he said, with the perfect inflection of a newly arrived immigrant, "Because me heart lep into me throat the minute I heard ye speak. 'Noah,' I says to meself, 'did ya ever hear the likes of it?'"

Maggie laughed. It couldn't be this easy, could it?

Chapter 7

As Sergeant John "Colt" Coulter of the Irish Brigade approached Captain Quinn's tent, he kept a wary eye on the dog curled up next to the captain's camp seat. Colt was still a good distance away when the mostly white, medium-sized dog raised its head and looked his way. Colt slowed down a bit when the dog sat up, his brown-tipped ears alert. Captain Quinn, who'd been working at the portable desk positioned just inside his tent, looked first in Colt's direction and then down at his dog.

Once he was within earshot, Colt patted the sling the surgeon insisted he wear. "What? No welcoming snarls? Don't let this fool you. I'm still the man you love to hate."

Hero tilted his head, but he didn't growl. In fact, he whined and thumped his tail.

"What's this? Sympathy?"

The dog chuffed softly and ambled toward him.

"Oh, no you don't," Colt said, and backed away. "I may not be hurt badly, but this arm makes it a challenge to clean my boots. I haven't forgotten what you did to them the first time we met. You just keep away."

The dog sat. Tilted his head. Whined again.

"That's pathetic."

"I think it might be sincere," the captain said. "He has a soft spot for the wounded."

"Really." Colt looked back at the dog. "Is that true, old man?"

Hero's tail thumped the grass. He lifted his chin and gave a little yelp, then rose up on all fours and spun about.

When Colt knelt down, the dog trotted over. First, he nuzzled the sling. Then, he licked Colt's hand, and finally, he circled him, yapping and generally making such a scene that Colt had to laugh. A sudden surge of relief and gratefulness that he was alive clouded his eyes with tears.

When Captain Quinn rose from his camp chair, Colt jumped to his feet and saluted. "Sergeant Coulter, reporting for duty, sir."

Quinn returned the salute. "Thank God," he said, motioning toward the desk just inside the tent. "I'm drowning in reports. But you'd better check in with your horse before I put you to work. From what I hear, even Fish can't get him to eat."

Colt grimaced. "I...um...actually, sir—"

"You checked on the horse before you came here."

"Yes, sir."

Quinn chuckled. "And I would have done the same. So tell me, did you get him to eat?"

"Yes, sir. Had a feed bag strapped on when I left."

"That's good." The captain pointed to the sling. "You were lucky."

"Yes, sir." Thinking about his arm made him flex it—which hurt, but the wound was healing. Colt had been charging across an open field past a farmhouse—which he'd suspected might house a rebel sharpshooter—when a bullet sliced across the outside of his upper arm, leaving a finger-sized gouge. Thanks to Jack Malone's answering shot, the rebel sharpshooter didn't get a second chance to fire. "The sling is just to remind me not to move around too much and rip the stitches. It's really not serious." He expected to be back at full strength within the week. "I only wish Private Malone could say the same."

At that moment, Hero barked sharply and was off like a shot, tearing across the earth and then launching himself into the air and into Fish's arms. The gangly quartermaster was nearly bowled over by the force of the dog's landing against his chest. But it wasn't Fish who caught Colt's attention. It was the woman with him.

She was taller than Fish—taller than any woman Colt had ever seen. She wore a dark blue cape and an outmoded bonnet that reminded him of something his mother might have donated to a missionary barrel. Whoever this was, she wasn't anyone of means. Captain Quinn must have made the same assumption, for he muttered *oh no* as she approached. Colt almost felt sorry for the woman, knowing what was about to happen. Captain Quinn did not tolerate "camp followers." Whoever she was and no matter how sad her story, this woman was about to be summarily escorted out of camp with orders to return whence she came and to stay there.

The closer she got, the more Colt thought she looked familiar. Which was impossible. And yet there was something about those blue eyes and that firm jaw. She was not going to be easily run off. She had a firm grip on the battered leather bag in one hand, and she walked with a confident stride that almost reminded Colt of a soldier on parade. Not very feminine, now that he thought about it. But not unattractive, either. How was that possible?

Fish set Hero down. "Captain Quinn, may I present—"

The woman didn't wait for Fish to finish. "I've come to fetch me brother home. *He*"—she indicated Fish with the flick of her wrist—"won't tell me where the infirmary is."

When she looked past the captain toward the other tents, Colt thought her expression almost wistful. Or maybe she was just nervous. The wind shifted, treating them all to a heavy dose of the stench from the latrines. The woman reached for the handkerchief tucked in her sleeve. When she withdrew it and shook it out, Hero snarled and charged her. Instead of backing away, the woman made a strange hissing sound and stepped forward, then uttered a firm "No. Stop that."

Hero hesitated.

The woman held out the handkerchief as she said, "Such a show of nonsense over a bit of white cloth, and you a fine, intelligent dog. Quit playin' the fool and behave while I speak with the sergeant." She didn't wait to see if Hero would respond. She obviously expected to be obeyed, and she was. Hero sat down and the woman turned to Captain Quinn. "Now, Sergeant—"

"How did you do that?" Captain Quinn didn't even bother to correct her regarding his rank.

"Do what?"

"My dog. He doesn't like strangers."

"I didn't ask him to *like* me. I demanded he behave himself."

"But—Hero doesn't do that."

The woman frowned. "He doesn't obey? A big, strapping man like yerself—an officer in the army—what cannot get his own dog to obey?" She waved the handkerchief toward the rows of tents just beyond an expanse of pasture. "How is it that you command men?"

The captain shot back, "How is it that you weren't afraid of being bitten?"

The woman glanced at Hero. "By that? That's scarcely a dog compared to my Kerry-boy."

Kerry-boy. Suddenly, Colt knew why the woman looked so familiar. "You're Maggie," he blurted out. "Maggie Malone." When the woman turned to look at him, Colt said, "You're here about Jack."

"You know my brother?"

Colt put his free hand to the sling. "He saved my life."

Miss Malone looked back at the rows of tents in the distance. "Can you take me to him?" Again, she looked at the captain. Her voice wavered. "Please, sir. I—we—we only saw his name on the list. Is he—is it bad? Littleton's not so far, sir. I thought I could take him home and care for him there. If he was—is—able." Again, her voice wavered. "I'm hoping Seamus might be given leave to help me get him home?"

Captain Quinn scowled. "You haven't heard from *either* of your brothers?"

"No, sir." The woman's face paled. The hand that clutched the handkerchief went to her chest. "Don't tell me—is Seamus hurt, too? His name wasn't on the list."

"Seamus is fine," the captain said quickly. "As for Jack—he's something of a hero—just ask Sergeant Coulter, here. And yes, he was wounded—as you can see from the sergeant's sling, they both were. But neither one was hurt badly enough to need medical leave."

"It isn't s-serious, then?" She swallowed and looked away, clearly having difficulty controlling her tears.

The captain nodded at Colt. "Sergeant. Escort Miss Malone to her brothers' tent." His smile was kind as he said, "You can see for yourself. And don't think I won't have a 'word' with them both for worrying you."

"As will I," she said. Her expression transformed, and Colt was glad that he wasn't going to be on the receiving end of that temper. She glanced down at Hero. "He's a fine fellow when he behaves himself. Looks like something of a soldier himself, sitting there at attention."

The captain agreed with a laugh. He returned Colt's salute and sent them on their way.

Colt led the way to the tent Jack shared with his brother Seamus and four others, all of them gathered around a chess-board sitting atop a tree stump. Jack had his back to them, and so it was Seamus who saw his sister first. His mouth fell open. He stared.

"Quit stalling," Jack said, gesturing at the board.

"It's M-Maggie," he stuttered. Still, he didn't move.

Miss Malone stopped. She set her bag down and waited. A muscle in her jaw twitched.

"It's going to be 'checkmate' if you don't pay attention," Jack teased.

Again, Seamus pointed. Finally, Jack looked behind him. He jumped to his feet, and the others followed suit. "Maggie?"

She didn't speak.

"But—why? How?"

"We heard you were wounded." Emotion flashed in her pale blue eyes as she glared at her brothers. "And no one wrote." She paused. "And so I came to fetch you home. To care for you myself."

Jack held up his bandaged hand. "For this? I lost a finger. It's not that serious."

Color flooded her cheeks. "So I see. So the sergeant told me."

Jack looked at Colt, who explained, "She means Captain Quinn."

Miss Malone looked over at him. "He's a captain?"

Colt nodded.

"That's better than a sergeant, isn't it?"

The men burst out laughing. "By several ranks," Jack said.

She lifted her chin. "Well, he didn't correct me. How was I to know?"

"He was too amazed by the way you corralled his dog," Colt said, and grinned at Jack. "One word from your sister and Hero was transfigured into an angelic version of himself."

"She tamed the demon-dog?" One of the other men spoke up—Ashby, Colt thought. When Colt relayed what had happened, Ashby put his hand over his heart. "Please, Miss Malone. Stay and be our guardian angel."

Another man nodded. "Stay and be our cook."

"I'll pay you to mend my shirt," another said, displaying a jagged tear in one sleeve. "A minié ball. Barely missed me."

Seamus looked over at him. "You caught it on a bramble harvesting gooseberries last night."

The soldier was unrepentant. "Well, it needs mending just the same." He looked hopefully at Maggie.

"She's our sister, not a maid," Jack said, "and I'll thank you to show some respect."

Miss Malone glowered at him. "Aren't you the one to be talking of respect? A man who can't even write to say he isn't anywhere near death's door, the image of which has kept his sister awake, lo these many nights." She turned to Seamus. "How is it, Seamus, that neither of you thought to let us know that there was no need to borrow money and set off downriver; no need to ignore the broken windows and the ruined garden; no need to wait to put things to rights?"

Apparently, she was angry enough to ignore the tears spilling down her cheeks as she gave her brothers the finest noncursing tongue-lashing Colt had ever witnessed. She was amazing—anger and hurt spilled out of her in a raging torrent, and yet she never descended into anything approaching female hysteria. She was, in a word, magnificent.

In the wake of Miss Malone's tirade, Ashby and the others drifted away. Finally, it was just Colt and Miss Malone, Jack and Seamus standing in front of an empty tent, the forgotten game of chess waiting on the tree stump behind them.

At some point, Jack reached out, grabbed one of sister's hands, and gave it a tug. "Wait. What do you mean, 'broken windows'? The garden's ruined? And *bushwhackers*? What's happened? What have they done?"

Miss Malone jerked her hand away. "What haven't they done?" She described the state of things on the Malone farm.

"But how—how'd it happen?" Seamus asked.

She'd been hunting, she said. She'd interrupted the attack. When she mentioned that their Uncle Paddy had been hurt, Jack began to swear. "He's mending," his sister said, then pointed at Jack's hand. "Hurt worse than you, though. Broken ribs. A fractured collarbone. Bruises—such a beating they gave him. One eye swelled shut. The color got worse before it began to fade, and then we thought he had pneumonia. We've lost the cow and her calf...the boar...maybe the shoats." She paused. "And one of them had a burlap sack full of my chickens tied to the saddle when he turned tail and ran."

Seamus broke in, suggesting they all sit down.

Miss Malone bent to pick up her satchel. "Don't think I'm finished being angry with you," she said. She sank onto the single camp chair just outside the tent.

He should probably leave them to talk things through, just the three of them, but Colt didn't want to leave. Not yet, at least. Besides, Captain Quinn would likely want a full accounting of what had ensued. An awkward silence reigned for a moment after they'd all settled around the chessboard.

Seamus was the first to speak. "Thank God you weren't hurt. It's amazing, what you did."

Miss Malone shrugged. "Kerry-boy distracted them. Gave me time to load the old rifle and get off a couple of volleys."

"You must be quite a good shot," Colt said.

Seamus grinned. "She's better than me, and almost as good as Jack."

Miss Malone opened the satchel at her feet and motioned for Jack to show her his hand. "I brought some of our medicine with me. If you don't think your fancy doctors would object, I can help it heal."

Jack nodded and held out his hand. He looked over at Colt. "Our Da taught Maggie some of the old ways. She could see to that arm. It'll heal faster."

Miss Malone glanced over at Colt. "If you like."

Seamus said something about fetching fresh water. Grabbing his and Jack's canteens, he hurried off toward the creek at the bottom of the grassy hill where Company D had pitched its tents. Colt offered to get fresh bandages from the surgeon, but Miss Malone shook her head.

"No need," she said, and withdrew a roll of bandages from her satchel, along with a cotton bag of what looked to Colt like dried weeds. Shrugging out of the blue cape she'd been wearing, she draped it over the back of the camp chair.

In the next half hour, Miss Malone tended both Jack and Colt's wounds. She moved with a quiet confidence acquired, Colt assumed, from years of tending the various and probably common injuries and illnesses her men encountered as a normal part of farm life. She didn't flinch at the first sight of the place where her brother's little finger had once been attached to his hand. She didn't go pale as she cleaned and then rewrapped it in a way that held a mix of dried herbs directly on the wound.

When it was Colt's turn, she untied the sling and laid it over the back of the camp chair where she'd hung her blue cape, waiting while he removed his belt and cartridge pouch and then setting them on the camp seat as well. He felt foolish wincing over the simple task of unbuttoning a row of gilt buttons, but apparently the muscles above a man's elbow helped the hand manage even simple tasks, for as he worked, the wound began to burn. When she'd helped him wrestle his way out of his uniform jacket, he fumbled with rolling up his shirt sleeve.

"Let me get that," she said, and took up the task as matter-of-factly as had the surgeon's assistant just yesterday when he'd checked the wound and pronounced it to be healing. "The angels must have been watchin' over you," she said when she saw the gouge the bullet had carved out. She glanced at Jack. "And you."

While Miss Malone tended Colt's arm, he recounted the story of his horse, Blue's, charge across the open field and Jack's marksmanship. "Of course, we both looked like darned fools in the end—celebrating victory a second too soon. I waved a thanks and Jack signaled back. I wouldn't be surprised if the same bullet got us both." Miss Malone glanced up at him. He couldn't read the expression on her face, but he was grateful not to be on the receiving end of another scolding like the one she'd given her brothers moments ago.

"Blue sounds like a fine horse," she said.

Colt was just about to offer to walk her over to the line of tethered horses so that she could see his pride and joy when Captain Quinn came into view, Hero trotting along at his side.

Miss Malone kept working as he approached, as if it were the most normal thing in the world for a woman to be tending the men of Company D. She rolled his sleeve down and buttoned the cuff, then reached for Colt's jacket and held it up while he put it back on. As soon as the captain was within the sound of her voice, she said, "I called you the wrong thing. I am sorry, *Captain* Quinn." She smoothed Colt's coat into place across his shoulders, then reached for his cartridge pouch and handed it over. She tapped one of the shoulder straps. "I don't know how to read all of this." She looked over at the captain and put her hand to one of her own shoulders. "But I should have seen that it's not the same as Sergeant Coulter's."

The captain waved her words away. "There is no need to apologize. I've sent someone into town to find proper accommodations for you," he said. "There's not another packet headed upriver until tomorrow. I wonder if you would consider dining with me this evening." He glanced at the three men. "We'll invite these three to join us as well."

Colt thought it a fine plan, but Miss Malone never had a chance to respond, because just then a courier ran up. While the captain scanned the contents of the message he'd just been handed, Hero padded over to Miss Malone and sat beside her.

The courier left, and Captain Quinn said quietly, "Gentlemen, we've received orders. We're to move out immediately in the direction of Carthage, in hopes that we can catch up with the retreating State Guard, which—according to all reports—is growing in numbers with every passing day." He turned to Maggie. "It has been a pleasure to meet you, Miss Malone. Sergeant Coulter will escort you back into Boonville. Unfortunately, in light of this recent information, I think it best for you to remain in the city, at least until the safety of river travel between here and Littleton can be guaranteed."

After promising Miss Malone he wouldn't be long, Colt hurried off in the wake of the captain, wondering how his arm would fare when it came to saddling Blue—and what Miss Malone would have to say to her brothers, now that their failure to write was about to leave her stranded miles from home.

Chapter 8

The meaning of stripes on sleeves and bars on shoulders wasn't the only thing Maggie didn't understand about the army. There was obviously a language to the bugles and drums sounding throughout the camp—a language spoken by everyone but her.

First there was a four-note call, and all around them, men rose to their feet. "That just means 'heads up,'" Seamus explained. In a minute—and before he could say the words, another call sounded. "And that's 'The General.' It means we're to pack up. I'm sorry, Maggie—about everything." Seamus handed her the leather satchel and joined the other men in striking the tent.

Maggie stood, satchel in hand, feeling strangely isolated, even though she was standing in the middle of a camp full of busy men. The captain's ordering her to stay in Boonville had happened so quickly she'd hardly had a chance to react. Not that he'd given her the chance. He'd barked the order, assumed it would be obeyed, and left. Which, she supposed was what captains were supposed to do. Their men probably trusted that they could make the right decisions and make them quickly. And of course it was Sergeant Coulter's duty to follow those orders. Jack's and Seamus's and everyone else's, too. But as she stood quietly in the midst of the chaos around her, Maggie rebelled against the idea of being ordered away.

Why couldn't she march at least part of the way with her boys? Even a day with them would give her more good news for Uncle Paddy. All they were doing was walking. What could it hurt for her to walk with them? Captain Quinn didn't think the river was safe, but surely she'd be safe with an entire brigade of soldiers. How many was a brigade, anyway? From the looks of things, at least a few hundred.

Gazing about, she saw plenty of opportunities to make herself useful, and in spite of scattered protests, she set the satchel down and began to help. Anyone could roll up a blanket or extinguish a campfire. There was nothing to striking a tent. As she worked, protests died down. When she returned from filling the men's canteens in the creek and handed one to Ashby, she remembered the torn sleeve he'd asked her to mend. She could do that when they made camp this evening. In fact, she could do a lot of mending in the course of an evening.

Another bugle call sounded, and Seamus spoke up. "That's the order to fall in, Maggie. It's time for you to go."

Maggie pointed at the men working to hitch mules to what she assumed were supply wagons. "Can't I walk alongside a wagon? You know I won't be any trouble. Just for a day. You won't exactly be marching past our front door, but it'll be close enough to get me home, won't it?"

Jack shook his head. "You heard Captain Quinn. Things are changing too fast. You need to stay here—at least until the army's sure it's safe to travel the river."

"Stay here? With Paddy hurt and the farm undefended?"

"You said that Paddy's at the Feenys'. They'll keep him in town with them." He paused. "In any case, you and Paddy can't expect to defend the farm. He'll be safe in Littleton, and you'll be safe in Boonville. You can telegraph word that all is well."

Maggie snorted. "And who's to say bushwhackers won't set fire to *Boonville* tonight?"

"Not likely," Seamus said. "Company A—that's a hundred men—has been ordered to stay behind to defend the town. You have to stay and we have to go." He kissed Maggie on the cheek. "I'll write. I promise." He hurried off.

Jack promised, too. "We'll send our letters in care of Company A. They'll find you."

"Why would they bother?"

"John Coulter isn't the only man in this army who owes his well-being to my marksmanship. Remember the name *Donald Ryan*, and if he comes looking for you, have a kind word. He'll be bringin' your mail." He seemed about to say something else, but Maggie preempted it.

The last thing Jack needed to carry away with him was the memory of a willful sister—at least the kind of willfulness that made them fight. As if she was going to blow him a kiss, she bussed the tips of her fingers, then carried the kiss to his cheek with a little pat. "God keep you and Seamus," she said. Her voice broke, and so she picked up her satchel and began marching away in the general direction the captain and Sergeant Coulter had gone.

She'd taken only a few steps when hoofbeats sounded behind her. Wherever or however he had done it, Sergeant Coulter had circled around and caught up with Jack. Whatever he said, Jack turned about and walked with him to where Maggie stood waiting. The hope that had flickered about the captain changing his mind and her being allowed to stay with the men died as soon as they reached her side.

The sergeant patted his sling. "I'm afraid you'll have to hold on to the satchel. Do you think you can do it? We aren't that far from Boonville."

As if she didn't know that. As if she hadn't walked through the town just hours ago. She was perfectly able to walk, but she supposed this wasn't the time to argue about it. With a deep sigh, she set the satchel down and let Jack lift her up to sit just behind the sergeant's saddle. Jack handed the satchel up, and with a final good-bye and yet another promise that they'd write, he hurried off to take his place in the ranks.

Feeling sure she would slide off the tall gray horse at any moment, Maggie grasped the edge of Sergeant Coulter's saddle with her free hand. At least the horse was blessed with a broad back. Still, Maggie couldn't help but wonder how a lady managed to control a horse while she was seated with both legs off to one side. The way perching atop a side-saddle twisted a woman's spine, it was a wonder Serena Ellerbe and Elizabeth Blair weren't permanently deformed. It was unnatural—and if Sergeant Coulter's horse made any sudden movements, Maggie wasn't going to be able to stay aboard.

The sergeant urged his horse forward, even as a soldier bearing a green silk flag decorated with the gold harp of Erin took his place next to the Stars and Stripes. So that was the flag Jack had told her about. Sure, and it was a beautiful thing. The flag bearer looked like a child as he waved the flag back and forth and shouted "*Fág an Bealach*" at the top of his lungs. When the columns of men answered with a rousing cheer, Maggie's blinked unwelcome tears away. What if this was the last time she saw her boys? *Don't dare even think such a thing. It's bad luck.* She shifted to praying. *Heavenly Father, keep them safe. Bring them home soon.*

She scanned the rows of men, looking in vain for Seamus and Jack. "They don't match," she said aloud.

"Ma'am?" Sergeant Coulter spoke over his shoulder.

"The uniforms. I thought—I hadn't noticed, but they don't match. They aren't really uniforms at all."

"Production problems," the sergeant said. "It must take miles of blue wool and thousands of hours. Think of all the buttons. Can you imagine the logistics? You should have heard Fish swear when he got word that only one of the three regiments in the Irish Brigade would be outfitted before we left St. Louis."

"*Fish*," Maggie said. "That's such an odd name."

"Not as odd as his real name." Without Maggie's asking, Coulter recited it. All Maggie heard was *Marquis* and a couple of other syllables that made no sense at all. He chuckled. "So you can see why we're all grateful he answers to *Fish*. He's an interesting man. A professional warrior, from what I can tell. Fought under Napoleon. I don't really know much about how he ended up here—other than he came upriver from New Orleans and joined up, literally the day after President Lincoln made the first call for volunteers."

While the sergeant talked, his horse, Blue, was carrying them across the camp and through the tangle of supply wagons and mule teams. Maggie clutched the satchel to her, using her free hand to grip the back of the sergeant's saddle and concentrating on the wagons and the mules and Sergeant Coulter's story about the soldier they all called Fish. Anything to keep her thoughts away from the sight of the boys marching away from her—again.

The dark wool cloth stretched taut across Sergeant Coulter's shoulders was certainly fine. Apparently *he* hadn't had any problems procuring a uniform. That made sense, now that she thought about it. He rode a fine horse, too. Fine cloth, a fine horse, and a fine-looking man—surely taking a moment to notice was a harmless distraction.

More distractions came in the form of a couple of ribald comments uttered as Maggie and Sergeant Coulter rode past. "Hey, Fish! Colt's caught himself a female!"

The strangely outfitted Fish popped into view from the opposite side of a supply wagon. "Mind your tongue, O'Malley, and get those mules in harness." With a flourish, Fish clicked his heels and bowed at Maggie. The movement made the tassel attached to the tip of the man's red wool cap sway back and forth.

Maggie was musing on the challenges of outfitting thousands of men and the "production problems" Sergeant Coulter had mentioned when someone screamed a warning. There was a flash of white, a crash, and a sharp yelp. Blue tossed his head and danced sideways. Despite a frantic attempt to stay aboard, Maggie slid off. She almost managed to land on her feet. In the end, though, the satchel threw her off balance, and with a very unladylike grunt, she landed in a tangle of blue calico skirts and white petticoats.

"Are you all right? Ma'am! Are you hurt?"

In her haste to right things, Maggie hadn't even seen Sergeant Coulter dismount, but here he was. He'd dropped to one knee beside her, his handsome face clouded with concern. For her. She must have had the wind knocked out of her, for she couldn't summon a response. *What an idgit, falling off the man's horse.* She smoothed her skirt and finally managed a not-very-convincing, "I—I'm fine." She moved to get up. Sergeant Coulter reached out to help her, but she pretended not to notice and got up herself—with no grace at all and yet another grunt.

Thankfully, the sergeant looked away in time to save her further embarrassment from the fact that she was blushing. But it wasn't good manners that made him look away.

It was the rapid-fire, albeit unintelligible, words streaming from Fish's mouth as he shoved his way past the circle of men standing around a broken crate—and something just beyond the crate that Maggie could not quite see.

Sergeant Coulter groaned, "Oh, no," dropped the reins, and hurried away.

With a glance at Blue, who had calmed down and was standing as if tied to a hitching post, Maggie followed, horrified when she saw what everyone was looking at. The captain's dog lay on its side next to a splintered crate. Blood oozed out of a wound just above one ear, staining the dog's white coat pink. But the cut wasn't the worst problem. The worst problem was that front paw.

"The miserable cur nearly bowled me over," a soldier protested. "Lost my balance. Lucky *I'm* not the one with a broken foot." When no one seemed to agree, he raised his voice, adding colorful epithets to his defense. The animal shouldn't have been given free rein to roam about the camp, he said. Something like this was bound to happen.

As the burly and distinctly aromatic soldier defended himself, Maggie brushed past Sergeant Coulter and knelt beside the dog. Speaking in a low, calm voice, she tucked her fingers into her palm and held the loose fist out to him. When Hero bared his teeth, she didn't waver. "Here, now," she said, "you remember me, now don't you? I'm Maggie, and I'm going to help you."

A low growl sounded, and one of the men in the circle muttered, "It'll take your hand off. Always did have a nasty temper. Anyone can see that the leg is broken. Best to put it out of its misery."

Ignoring the comment, Maggie continued to speak words of comfort to the dog.

While Maggie talked, Hero had rolled onto his belly and begun to lick the paw that lay at such an odd angle. Even if it was fractured, the bone hadn't broken the skin. Maggie slid her hand across the earth and extended her fingers. She didn't touch the wounded leg, but at some point as she talked to soothe the dog, Hero nudged her fingers with his snout and swiped them with his tongue.

"Never saw a wounded animal do that," someone said.

Maggie looked up at the men gathered 'round. "Anyone have whiskey?"

They looked at each other and then back at her. Shook their heads.

"A fine lot of Irishmen you are," she scolded.

Hero's ears came up. He let out a pathetic yelp. His tail thumped the ground. Maggie turned to see Captain Quinn headed their way. One look at his dog and he let loose a stream of invective. "Who's responsible for this!" He glared at the men standing in the circle. They stared at the ground. The captain knelt beside the dog. When he passed his hand over the animal's head, Hero whined and licked his hand. Taking a deep breath, he said quietly, "Well, old man...we had a good run." He reached for his revolver.

Fish uttered a protest, and Maggie stayed the captain's hand. "My Kerry-boy had a similar mishap when he was a pup. Aside from a bit of a limp when the weather's changin', he's fine." The captain hesitated. Maggie looked into the man's dark eyes. "I'll see to him. I'll stitch the ear and bind the leg and tend him until he's better."

"He won't let you."

Maggie smiled, forcing herself to sound more confident than she really felt. "Of course he will." She looked down at the dog. "We've an understandin', don't we, old man?"

The tail slapped the earth. Only once, but it was all the captain needed to see. Hope glimmered. He nodded. "All right, but it'll have to be done quickly."

Maggie opened her satchel and took out her sewing kit. "Won't take but a moment." She glanced at Fish. "We really do need a bit of whiskey. And someone strong enough to hold him down."

"I can do that." John Coulter knelt beside her.

"I'll get the whiskey," Fish said.

The captain allowed a little smile as he said, "I'll pay you, Miss Malone. Have the sergeant bring you up the line before you leave us."

The words came out before Maggie had time to weigh them. "I won't take your money. Just let me walk with the supply wagons. I'll see to your dog along the way. And take myself home the minute I've worn out my welcome."

Fish took up her cause. "I will carry the dog in my wagon." He smiled at Maggie. "As to *mademoiselle* . . . she is most welcome to march with the supply train."

Maggie spoke before the captain could say no. "I'm good with animals," she said. "Ask my brothers if you doubt it. I'll feed Hero with my own hand, and he'll be better in a week or so. By then you'll have cleared the rebels out of the county—if there's even any clearing to do." Surely the Wildwood Guard was headed south by now to join the rebels the Irish Brigade had helped roust out of Boonville. "It'll be safe by then, and I'll go home."

The captain resisted the idea of her staying with the regiment. "It's just not possible."

"Well, of course it is, if only you'll change your mind." She paused. "I can be useful, and you don't need to worry a bit about me keeping up. I've two strong legs. I can march as well as any man." Fish said something Maggie didn't understand, although his tone of voice made her think it was something good. She pulled Da's pistol out of her pocket. "I've faced bushwhackers alone, and I can't think of a safer way to travel than in the wake of nearly a thousand of the bravest men in the land."

"*Bravo, mademoiselle.*" Fish stifled a laugh by swiping his palm across his mouth. When Captain Quinn glared at him, he shrugged. "*C'est vrai, n'est-ce pas?*"

The captain sighed. Again, he addressed Fish. "You'll accept responsibility for her?"

Again, the tassel danced. Fish nodded. "I do not think that the lady wishes someone else to take such responsibility." He winked at Maggie. "She seems quite capable, does she not?"

The captain looked down at his dog. For a very long moment. Finally, he said, "All right, Miss Malone. You win." A steamboat whistle sounded in the distance. "That would be the *McDowell* telling me she's ready to shove off." There was another sharp screech. He frowned. "And that would mean there's a problem." He hesitated for a moment and turned to Maggie. "Do you really think you can mend Hero's leg?"

"It's up to the good Lord to do the mending, sir. My job will be to keep the dog from worrying the wound. That, sir, I can do."

He almost smiled. "All right." He hesitated, then said, "If you hear shots fired, I want you to take cover under the nearest wagon."

"Yes, sir."

He nodded at the pistol. "Once you've taken cover, you take that pistol out of your pocket and get ready to fire it. And then you stay put until Fish or Sergeant Coulter tells you it's safe to come out."

"Yes, sir."

"And don't hesitate to pull the trigger if Johnny Reb comes to call."

"I won't, sir."

The captain grimaced. "You say that now, but you'll find it's not quite so easy to pull a trigger when you're looking a man in the eye."

Maggie allowed a little smile. "I don't doubt that, sir, but if it's all the same to you, I won't let Johnny get that close before I defend myself."

The captain barely managed to camouflage a short, barking laugh. "All right, then." He gave Hero a quick pat on the head before nodding at Fish. "I'm leaving these two with you, Sergeant."

Fish saluted.

The captain turned to Sergeant Coulter. "A word, Sergeant." Together, the two men mounted up and rode away.

Chapter 9

When Captain Quinn's horse stepped out, Blue took the bit and tried to make it a race. Newly aware of the fact that his arm was nowhere near healed, Colt struggled to keep control of a big horse with a mind of its own. He won the battle, but barely. Blue snorted and half reared before settling into an easy lope alongside the captain's buckskin.

When the men dismounted at the edge of the levee and Blue danced away, the captain chuckled. "Somebody's been in camp too long." He nodded at Colt's sling. "How long do you have to wear that thing?"

"The surgeon recommended another week." With a grimace, Colt eased his arm out of the sling and flexed it. "He might have been overly cautious, though." He pulled off the sling and tucked it in his saddlebag.

The steamboat pilot hurried up the levee. "You have to see this," he huffed, trying to catch his breath as he pointed toward the *McDowell*. He called out to a rail-thin mulatto boy who was standing at the river's edge, skipping rocks. "You there! Noah! Mind the horses and I'll have Cook give you some corn bread."

The boy looked the pilot's way from beneath the brim of a beat-up straw hat. "And molasses?"

"Don't push it!" With a shrug, the boy shoved his hands in his pockets and began to amble away. Swearing, the pilot agreed to molasses. The boy grinned and trotted up the levee to where Colt and the captain waited.

The captain handed over his horse's reins without a word, but Colt sounded a warning when he saw that the boy was barefoot. "Blue has a mind of his own today. Be careful he doesn't step on you."

When the boy took the reins and put his hand on Blue's muzzle, Blue lowered his head. The boy muttered something, and the captain's horse nosed his way into the moment. Whatever his story, Noah seemed to have a way with horses. Colt hurried on board and across the freight deck to where the pilot and Captain Quinn stood, staring down at what, according to the label stenciled on the side, had been a crate of "hardware."

"Mose over there"—the pilot pointed to a muscular Negro standing with the deckhands by the boiler—"stumbled and knocked it off the top of this pile. When it broke open—well. You can see."

Captain Quinn picked up one of the dozen or so rifles that had spilled onto the deck. He ran his gloved hand over the polished stock, inspected the barrel, then glanced over at Colt. "Don't think it's ever been fired." He scanned the stacks of crates. "Where's it all headed?"

"Littleton," the pilot said, then corrected himself. "Well, not Littleton exactly. There's a planter between Littleton and Lexington—has a private landing. Name of Walker Blair." The pilot motioned to three-man-high stacks of crates, all of them bearing labels for the kinds of goods needed on every plantation in Little Dixie. "These are all for Wildwood Grove."

The captain swore softly. "And from there, south to General Price."

Colt frowned. "What kind of man tries to smuggle arms

for the rebellion on board a steamboat equipped with a Union Army howitzer?"

"A desperate one," Quinn said. Then he tilted his head. "Or...maybe a really smart one. After all, who would suspect it?"

The pilot held up both hands like a criminal signaling surrender. "I'm not in league with any gun smugglers. The minute I saw this, I blew that whistle to get you down here." He went on to curse the "low-life Johnny Reb" who had the "unmitigated gall" to try to sneak "arms for the blank-blank enemy" on board his packet. The man's profane vocabulary was astonishing, his delivery so vociferous that it had caught the attention of his deckhands, several of whom were standing by the boiler smiling with admiration—until the pilot left off cursing the enemy and turned his invective on them. He waved the tall one over and began peppering him with questions.

Half an hour later, Captain Quinn was none the wiser as to who might have helped the smugglers. He asked the pilot to guard the shipment for a few minutes, then motioned for Colt to follow him back onshore. As the two men walked toward their horses, the captain charged Colt with overseeing the opening of every crate on the steamboat's freight deck. "We're going to need a couple of wagons to haul those Henrys. Expect to find ammunition, too. And there's simply no way I'm going to leave perfectly good weapons sitting here in Boonville." He smiled. "Besides, there's a certain sense of justice in the idea of using guns intended *for* Johnny Reb *against* him." He gazed off up the street and into town. "I'll see what I can do about requisitioning a couple of farm wagons, then send a squadron to load it all and catch up with us. You'll be in charge."

"There's two good wagons out behind Saxton's Livery." The boy who'd been holding the horses was just out of sight— sitting on a rock behind a tall stand of grass.

"Eavesdropping could get you in a passel of trouble," the captain scolded. "How do I know you aren't a spy for the enemy?"

"Wasn't eavesdropping," the boy said, scowling. "I was taking a breather while I waited for my corn bread." He squinted up at the captain. "Saxton's got two wagons out behind his livery. But he's only got one decent pair of mules for sale. Big ears with a notch cut in 'em. Don't take the other pair. They look better, but they're mean as dirt and they don't pull for nothing."

"And I suppose you know where I could requisition a better pair?"

"I might." The boy shoved his hands in his pockets.

"Well?"

He shrugged. Took the battered hat off his head and pretended to inspect the edge of the brim. "Sure is a fine day. Day like this, a feller can't help but think on the delights of penny candy."

Barely managing to hide a smile, Colt fished a coin out of his pocket. When the boy reached for it, Colt closed his palm. "The other team?"

"Brewster's Farm Implements," the boy said. "Two streets over from Saxton's. Took 'em as partial payment for a plow."

Captain Quinn spoke up. "And how do I know they aren't just as worthless as the ones you told me to avoid at Saxton's? You getting a finder's fee for steering me their way?"

"*Finer-fee?*" the boy asked. "I'm just a little boy. I don't know nothin' 'bout no 'finer-fee.'"

"I'm inclined to think otherwise," Captain Quinn said. "And so I ask again, how do I know I can trust your advice about mules?"

The boy shrugged his bony shoulders. "Guess you don't. But I used to visit 'em on a farm east of here." The boy pointed east. "There's a good fishin' hole on the place. I go there sometimes, and I've seen those mules pull. That farmer nearly cried when he had to turn 'em over to Brewster." He put the hat back on and tugged on the brim. "That's what I know. Take it or leave it."

"You seem to know a lot about people's affairs in Boonville," Captain Quinn said.

"Pays to keep apprised of things." He looked up at Cole. "Can I have that penny now?" He glowered at the steamboat. "Don't look like I'm gettin' corn bread and molasses, after all."

Colt opened his hand. The boy snatched the coin and took off up the street like he'd been shot from a cannon.

"I'll arrange for the wagons," Captain Quinn said, and nodded back toward the *McDowell*. "Think your arm can handle prying all those crates open?"

"I'll manage."

"Work quickly, but be thorough. And stay alert. Someone had to know they weren't hauling coffee and crackers aboard that steamboat." He looked toward the *McDowell*. "Now that I think of it, I wonder if that Negro really did lose his balance. Maybe knocking that crate down wasn't really an accident."

"He'd never admit such a thing," Colt said.

"And who could blame him?" The captain stared at the steamboat for a moment. Whatever he was thinking, he didn't see his way to sharing it. After a moment, he mounted up and rode off to arrange for the wagons.

Colt had just walked up the street and begun to hitch Blue outside a freshly whitewashed mercantile when the boy emerged from between the alley that ran between the mercantile and a saloon. From the evident bulge of one cheek, he'd wasted no time in the matter of the penny candy.

He took his hat off and pretended to mop sweat off his brow. "It's going to take you a while to check all that freight," he said. "I could see to your horse. Water and a shady spot to graze. Watch him all day if you want."

"How much?"

The boy seemed to consider. "Tell you what." He patted Blue's neck. "Normally I'd want at least a dime. But I like this horse. I'll do it for a nickel."

"Where's this shade you're talking about?"

The boy scowled. "I ain't gonna steal your horse, mister." He waved a hand downriver. "See that big ole chestnut tree right there along the river? You'll be able to see him the whole time. But it's better'n bein' tied up to a hitchin' post for hours and hours."

"What's your mama gonna say about you being gone all day?"

"She dead," the boy said. "But she'd be glad to see me earnin' my way."

Dead. The word was shocking, coming so quickly, spoken so matter-of-factly. Colt wanted to know more, but just when he'd opened his mouth to ask another question, the wagons Captain Quinn had requisitioned rattled into view and, just behind them, the squadron he'd sent from the brigade.

"Tell you what," Colt said. "I'll pay you the dime, just not until I'm ready to ride out."

The boy smiled. Nodded. "Right smart of you, Sergeant." He took Blue's reins and, with a practiced cluck of his tongue, trotted away.

                                                                     ~

Maggie had intended to spend the first night camping with the Irish Brigade wrapped in the blanket she'd brought with her and leaning against a wagon wheel, but when Fish realized what she was doing, he produced an extra blanket and insisted she take shelter beneath his wagon. She didn't know how far they'd marched, but it didn't seem all that much farther than she might have walked on an overnight hunting excursion.

The next day—Friday—passed without incident. Reveille sounded before dawn. Maggie smiled to herself when she recognized the call that meant "fall in." She was learning. Other than Seamus and Jack and Fish, the men gave Maggie a wide berth, except for Private Ashby, who trotted up in the middle of the afternoon and offered to pay her a nickel if she'd mend a new tear in his shirt.

"Encounter another minié ball?" Maggie teased.

A blush climbed from beneath the collar on the private's sack coat jacket and up his neck, eventually spreading across his cheeks. "I didn't mean anything by that. I was just..." He didn't finish the sentence.

Maggie smiled. "Bring it to me after we've made camp. I'll see what I can do."

"I'll expect to pay you," Ashby said. "Wouldn't want your brothers to think I'm taking advantage."

Maggie considered for a moment. Nodded. "All right. The next time you're scavenging about, bring me a cup full of gooseberries, and I'll mark your account paid in full. Does that suit?"

"Yes, ma'am, it sure does." Ashby touched two fingers to the brim of his forage cap by way of salute and then trotted off.

As the day wore on, Maggie began to suspect that no one gave a man grief if he stepped away from the column for a moment or two. When Maggie asked Fish about it later, he didn't seem to know what to say. Finally, he used Hero as an example and Maggie understood. Bugle calls told the men when to march, when to halt, and when to rest. Apparently there was no specific bugle call for "take to the woods and do what's necessary." The thought made her chuckle.

Hero spent most of the day curled up on a makeshift bed Fish had created by stuffing three empty burlap bags inside a fourth. He barely whimpered when Maggie took him to "do the necessary." Still, knowing the dog was in pain and seeing him limp tore at Maggie's heart. Her feelings of fondness appeared to be mutual, for when Maggie gathered Hero up at the end of the second day and carried him with her to settle beside Fish's campfire, the dog thanked her with a pink tongue applied to the back of her hand. Heating a chunk of pork fat over the campfire, she dropped two squares of hardtack into the resulting grease. Once the hardtack had soaked up the grease, she took it off the fire. It had cooled down and she was hand feeding bits of it to Hero when Jack and Seamus joined her.

"You're spoiling him," Jack said.

Seamus joined in, peering over at Jack and whining, "She never treated us like that when *we* were sick."

Maggie gave it right back. "I don't know what to tell you boys. There's just something irresistible about a man who obeys me and then wags his tail as if I've done him a favor."

Just as she said it, Hero's ears came up. He struggled to sit up, trembling from the effort of supporting the weight of his front quarters on his uninjured front leg. Maggie swept him into her arms and stood up just in time to see Sergeant Coulter and two wagons escorted by a squadron of men come into view.

News of the discovery on board the *August McDowell* had made its way throughout the company, but while Jack and Seamus hurried to join the gathering group of soldiers, Maggie held back. Something about seeing Sergeant Coulter made her feel awkward. Why just seeing him would evoke such a response made no sense. He'd been nothing but kind. Maybe she was nervous for him. He wasn't wearing the sling, and he'd said the surgeons wanted him to keep it on for at least another week. That was probably it.

Seamus returned with confirmation of the story that had spread through the men. A deckhand had upset a pile of crates and one broke open, leading to the discovery of smuggled Henry rifles. "Captain Quinn say's they'll be distributed to those of us using older muskets from home."

"One thing we hadn't heard," Jack added, "is where the shipment was headed." He paused. "Wildwood Grove."

At mention of smuggled arms and the plantation, Maggie told the boys about the *Clara* stopping at the Wildwood Grove levee. She told them about the amount of freight that had been offloaded there, and how surprised she'd been to see the uniformed Wildwood Guard there to receive it.

Jack glared at her. "And you didn't think to mention it until now?"

"And when would I have done that," Maggie snapped. "Before or after your fine captain ordered me out of camp?

And if you'll recall, I had other things on my mind—like a brother who, for all I knew, lay dying in the military hospital in St. Louis."

They all just stood there looking at each other for half a beat, and then Jack said, "All right. I'm sorry. But—Blair's mansion overlooks the river. It's a perfect vantage point. Why, a man could stand up on that second-floor balcony and see what's coming from a long way off."

Seamus chimed in. "Maybe Blair is bringing in weapons to defend the plantation."

Jack nodded. "To arm his own private militia, so they can keep the county for the Confederacy. With Wildwood Grove as the headquarters for the entire operation, and a private levee for receiving supplies."

"We should talk to Sergeant Coulter," Seamus said. "If we're right, it could completely change our orders."

Maggie spoke up. "Could what happened at the farm be connected to such a plan in some way?"

"I don't see how," Jack said, frowning.

"Could it have been some kind of...experiment...to see if there'd be any kind of unified response to an attack on a place owned by Union sympathizers?"

"I'd hate to think it was anything like that."

"I don't want to think it, either," Maggie said. "But Sheriff Green never did a thing about it. He made promises, and then he resigned. He's *Major* Isham Green now, and when I left home, Littleton still didn't have a sheriff." She told the boys about meeting Blair and his overseer and the newly out-fitted Major Green on the road to the farm. "I've never been able to shake the notion that he knew what had happened and why. That all three of them did." The notion was enough to make her wish for more than a pocket pistol the next time she encountered a rebel.

"It doesn't sound all that far-fetched," Jack said. "Especially with a militia organizing at Wildwood Grove." He glanced at Seamus. "You're right. We've got to talk to—"

A shout went up from the soldiers gathered around the newly arrived wagons, just as a ragged mulatto boy scrambled across the cargo while a red-faced Fish gestured and shouted at the driver. Maggie recognized the boy from the Boonville levee. Together she, Jack, and Seamus inched closer to hear what was happening.

"I didn't know!" the driver insisted. "He must have caught up to us and slipped under the cover when no one was looking."

As for the boy, he didn't seem in the least bit cowed by the vitriol directed at him. In fact, he hardly paid attention. He was, instead, standing on tiptoe, looking out over the gathering of soldiers. When he caught Maggie's eye, he grinned, scampered over the wagon seat and onto the tongue, skittered between the two mules hitched to it, and finally stopped next to Maggie.

"Please, ma'am," he pleaded. "I helped you find the Irish, and I didn't even charge for it. Please don't let them send me back."

Chapter 10

Ever since the officers of the Wildwood Guard had taken up residence at the house, Walker had made it clear that he expected Libbie to reign over meals as if she were already the leading lady of Missouri society. Five course dinners served on the good china had become *de rigueur*, and so it was on a fine June evening that Libbie was seated at her dressing table when she heard booted feet charge in the front door and clomp into Walker's private office.

The fact that whoever it was hadn't waited to be let in was reason enough to know there was trouble—without the shouts and cursing that echoed into the hall and up the stairs and through Libbie's closed bedroom door. Libbie glanced at Ora Lee's reflection in the mirror. The girl grimaced.

"Mr. Blair breathin' fire about somethin'," she said, and continued putting the final touches on the complex combination of braids and twists that would keep Libbie's abundant dark hair under control during the supper hour.

Picking up her silver hand mirror, Libbie turned about to survey Ora Lee's work. "I don't know how you do that," she said, touching the strand of pearls the girl had woven into the arrangement. "You're an artist when it comes to arrangin' hair."

Ora Lee, who had stepped back when Libbie took up the mirror, stood quietly, her hands clasped behind her back.

"Thank you, Miss Libbie. I enjoys it and I am glad you are pleased."

Annabelle had said that Ora Lee would be grateful for the chance to escape the quarters, and she'd been right. The girl had done everything Libbie asked with quiet efficiency. She wasn't Mariah, but it wasn't hard to imagine that Ora Lee and a young Mariah would probably have had much in common.

More noise from down below made Libbie set the mirror down and cross the carpeted floor to open her bedroom door. Her room opened onto the wide hall that split the house into two equal halves. Exterior doors at each end of the hall opened onto balconies, the front looking out over the river, the back over the kitchen garden and the fields beyond. A small sitting area opposite the stairs provided a place to take refuge on hot, rainy days—and to hopefully capture any breeze that might waft up from the river.

While the four doors opening onto the upstairs hall admitted inhabitants to bedrooms, the downstairs hall separated the formal parlor and family sitting room on the west side of the house from Walker's office and the dining room on the east. The painted wood floor did nothing to deaden the sound, and Libbie could hear nearly every word spilling from Walker's office.

She was careful to remain out of sight. She'd learned very early on that Walker saw trouble, no matter how slight, as a personal affront—evidence of failure on his part—and if Libbie personally witnessed her brother's failure, things did not go well for her. She'd teased him once about that ribbon of masculine pride. Only once. Walker had not one sliver of a sense of humor when it came to his personal failings. The evidence of his turning his rage on her was only bruises, and while he profusely apologized for causing them, Libbie had ever after made it her business not to know Walker's.

In the case of whatever was going on downstairs right now, had the cause of Walker's unhappiness been something to do with the running of the plantation, it would be easy enough to stay here in her room and mind her own business. But with officers staying at the house and Walker expecting a nice supper, Libbie couldn't do that. The question was what she should do—and how.

War had come to Lafayette County. The veneer of gracious living had already cracked, and one only had to look out the back door of the house at the dozens of tents pitched in the field beyond the kitchen garden to know it. Even the servants had sensed the change. Oh, they were as deferential as ever, but there was something new in the way they behaved. The frequency with which they glanced at the horizon. The expression on their faces when they looked at the river— expressions that changed the instant they realized Libbie had taken notice. She didn't ask the obvious question, because she knew they wouldn't answer truthfully. Still, she could not help but think it. *Federals are camped just down the river at Boonville. Why don't you run?*

At the sound of the front door slamming, Libbie jumped. She glanced at Ora Lee, who was still standing by the dressing table. Libbie held up one finger, signaling. *Wait just a minute.* Ora Lee nodded understanding, and Libbie stepped out into the hall. As soundlessly as possible, she moved to the head of the stairs. Careful to stand where her hooped skirt would remain out of sight, she listened.

"Discovered?" Walker roared. "That's the second shipment!" He pounded something—with his fist, Libbie thought from the sound of it. "I want to know the name of every single—"

Walker broke off. Another voice—calmer, quieter—murmured something Libbie couldn't make out. Walker yelled a response.

"Well, now *Major* Green—" He emphasized the rank, his tone mocking. "They *weren't* reliable, were they? If they'd been *reliable*, the men camped in my backyard would have brand-new Henrys! There'd be a battery mounted at the top of that rock wall. We'd be talking *cavalry* instead of trying to figure out how to arm the men camped in my pasture!"

Another voice from below sounded, and Walker interrupted.

" 'These things happen'? Don't tell me 'these things happen'! Do you have any idea how expensive it is to purchase silence? How much it costs to find pilots willing to take their chances on that river? And what do we have to show for it? Nothing!" Walker laughed—an ugly sound. "The Wildwood Guard, armed with hunting rifles and muskets. Without so much as one cannon. We'll be the laugh of the county. And God help us if the Federals march on us with the *McDowell*'s howitzer to back them up. Don't tell me 'these things happen'!"

Libbie stepped back, her heart racing. Ora Lee had come to the bedroom door. When Libbie motioned for her to leave by way of the servants' stairs, Ora Lee hesitated, casting a concerned look Libbie's way. Libbie forced a smile. Nodded. *I'll be all right.* She pressed her hands together, closed her eyes, and pantomimed going to sleep. *I won't need you again until bedtime.*

Ora Lee still hesitated, but when Libbie made a shooing motion, the girl finally obeyed. On the one hand, it was wonderful to finally have someone like Mariah—someone who could practically read her mind and who seemed to care about her well-being. On the other, it was a burden. Ora Lee noticed every hidden bruise, and there had been more than the usual number of late.

Walker's skill at inflicting pain never ceased to amaze Libbie. It was as if he'd made a study of just where and how to hurt someone with the least effort possible. Walker could manage it with Isham Green standing right next to them, and Green never suspected what was happening. Or maybe he did and just pretended not to notice.

Tiptoeing toward the door at the opposite end of the hall, Libbie stepped out onto the balcony that afforded a view of the river. The peaceful river, its surface gleaming in the golden light of yet another sunset. Walker had chosen this land because of that river. Every year, it transported thousands of miles of the rope created from the plantation's hemp to St. Louis and beyond. From imported cigars to fine wool and silk to whale oil for the lamps, the river delivered everything a man needed to create a life of ease. And yet, for all the fine things Walker Blair had had transported upriver to his plantation...he was not satisfied. Would he ever be satisfied?

She didn't know anything about war, but lately, Libbie had begun to fantasize about Yankees using the river to descend on Wildwood Grove and put an end to Walker's dreams of greatness. If he'd only let go of his frantic ambition, maybe they could somehow manage a reasonably happy life. Better yet, maybe he'd let her go. The idea of leaving Wildwood Grove hadn't developed into a plan yet, but it had begun a persistent fluttering along the fringes of her consciousness. Maybe the river could help her flee. Did she have the courage to make it possible? She would need money. How much would it take to buy her own freedom? How much would be enough?

Enough. Walker didn't seem to know the meaning of the

word. Discontent raged through the man like a wildfire. If the hemp crop was good, he wished they'd planted more acres to hemp. If it rained, he was gloomy. If the sun shone, he complained it was too hot. If Annabelle made a good supper, Walker wished he'd invited someone powerful to share it.

Annabelle. Annabelle thanked God for all kinds of things. Simple things, like sunshine and rain. Libbie had heard her and Betty both singing hymns as they went about their work. *Praise, sister, praise God, I praise my Lord until I die... Praise, sister, praise God, and reach your heavenly home.* Ora Lee was thankful, too. That very first day when Malachi brought her up from the quarters to help clean out the spinning room, Libbie had recognized the tune Ora Lee hummed while she worked. *Praise God, I praise my Lord until I die...*

How odd, Libbie thought, as a gentle breeze wafted up from the river, that while his slaves thanked God, Walker Blair complained. About everything. How was it possible, Libbie wondered, for a man with everything to be so unhappy? He even complained about the house—the finest house in the county. The downstairs hall had been painted to look like a black-and-white checkerboard. It was the latest style, and every lady who saw it—including Serena Ellerbe, who normally would rather choke than give a compliment— oohed and aahed. But for some reason Libbie could not suss out, Walker decided he hated it. Trying to please him, Libbie oversaw the creation of an oilcloth floor covering. Walker stared at it with a frown and complained of the cost. And now... now someone had come stomping in the back door and there was even more chaos downstairs.

Libbie glanced behind her. Walker wouldn't want her down there, but the sun was sinking fast. What would he want her to do about supper? Should she go down and ask, or let things calm down a bit? If she served at the usual hour and Walker hadn't solved the problem yet, he'd grumble about "foolish women who think the world revolves around their entertaining." If she delayed the meal and one of his guests said something about being hungry, he'd blame her for the delay. And Lord help Annabelle if the meal wasn't perfect. Things dried out when you tried to hold them... didn't they?

The truth was, there was just no way to please Walker. Even the fact that she'd followed his instructions and put up with Isham Green hadn't won her brother's approval. If he'd noticed, he hadn't said a word. Libbie sighed. Ah, well. She would go down to the kitchen and see what Annabelle thought. Could the meal be delayed without ruining it? As quietly as possible, Libbie descended to the first floor and slipped out the back door. For a moment, she hesitated, looking off toward the stables with a twinge of regret. It had only been a few days since she'd been forbidden to ride, but it felt like a month.

Malachi had let Pilot out into the small pasture dotted with burr oak trees. Of course, the horse had found the one spot of bare earth in that pasture, and was determinedly rolling in it, grinding dust into his coat, his hoofs pawing the air. With a sad smile and a sigh, Libbie stepped off the porch— just as Walker barged out the back door behind her.

He let the screen door slam. "If you weren't so all-fired taken up with standing out here daydreaming, you'd know we have guests waiting to be fed."

Libbie turned to face him, folding her hands before her, doing her best to seem relaxed. "I was just going to check in with Annabelle to see if—"

"To see if what? If she's cooking anything?"

"Well, of course she's cooking. I was just...I didn't know when you'd want to have it served."

He glowered at her. "And you think Annabelle is the one to answer that question?" He sneered as he said, "By all means, let us consult the slave to see what might accommodate her schedule."

"That's not what I meant." Libbie glanced past him at the house. "I didn't think you would want to be disturbed until—"

"Until what? Until my guests started complaining of hunger?"

Libbie swallowed. Forcing a calm she did not feel into her voice, she said, "I didn't think you'd want me interrupting." She clenched her hands behind her, hoping against hope that her calm demeanor would help quench the wildfire that was Walker's temper.

"What I want," he snapped, "is for at least one tiny little part of this cursed week to go according to plan. Is that asking too much, Elizabeth? To at least have meals served on time?"

"I'm sorry, Walker. I—"

"Don't apologize! Just—see to it. For once in your life, see that something at Wildwood Grove gets done properly without my having to personally oversee it!" He reached out and yanked on the edge of her sleeve. "Now—stop daydreaming about that worthless horse and do your job. Lord knows you've cost me a fortune. Gowns and shawls and bonnets and high-stepping horses. And what do I have to show for it? Very little." He looked past her to the encampment and muttered, "An entire regiment eager to fight, and their weapons have fallen into enemy hands." He glared back at her. "And all your precious Isham has to say is, 'These things happen.'"

My...precious...? He'd demanded she walk with a preening fool she could scarcely tolerate, and she'd obeyed. How dare he use her obedience as a weapon? How dare he blame her—for anything? "*My* Isham? He's not *my* Isham. May I remind you, dear brother, that *you're* the one who insisted that I—"

She didn't even see it coming. Had no time to step back. No chance to make it a glancing blow. It happened so quickly that Libbie barely remembered Walker's palm making contact with her cheek. One second she was correcting him about why she'd deigned to walk in the moonlight with Isham Green, and the next she was standing with her own palm to her face, her eyes watering from a combination of shame and pain.

Walker's anger disintegrated. He reached for her hand—the one she held to her face. When she flinched and pulled away, he bowed his head. "My God, Libbie. Forgive me. I—I didn't mean—"

Out of nowhere, Libbie heard Ora Lee call out, "That's all right, Mr. Walker. I'll see to her. You go on inside, now. Supper be served before you know it."

She must have been watching. From where, Libbie wasn't certain, but here she was, taking Libbie's arm—much as you would an old woman's—and leading her away, assuring Walker that "little bit of ice, and Miss Libbie be good as new. She be in in just a few minutes to call the gentlemens to da table."

Annabelle called out from the kitchen door. "Twenty minutes, Mastah Blair. And you best be hungry. I done roasted a ham just the way you like it. Sweet potato pie, too. Those gentlemens never gonna want to leave Wildwood Grove."

Libbie let herself be led away. When they reached the kitchen door, she glanced behind her just in time to see Walker go back into the house. Ora Lee guided her to the nanny rocker by the window. Libbie sat while the girl leaned down and examined her face. Shame coursed through her. Why would they be kind to her?

"Get some ice on it," Annabelle said. "She got supper to preside over." She glanced over at Libbie. "Don't think it'll show until tomorrow, and I suppose you can be 'sick.'"

Libbie frowned. She'd never pretended illness a day in her life.

"You gonna have a black eye," Annabelle said. "It already swelling up. Ice will keep it so's they don't notice. Not by candlelight. And this here dinner ain't gonna be ready until after sundown. Can't be helped. I burned the taters."

Libbie looked over at the perfect mound of mashed potatoes. Then she looked up at Annabelle. And then...then she let herself cry.

Chapter 11

When Sergeant Coulter dismounted and strode after him, the boy stepped behind Maggie, effectively using her as a shield. Maggie edged away. She'd waged many a war against vermin on the farm, and didn't want a personal encounter with head lice ever again. The boy probably couldn't help it, but still—before she spent much time with him, she'd want to see him deloused.

Coulter reached around Maggie and hauled the boy away from her, but his tone was almost gentle as he said, "You can't stay with the army, Noah."

"Why not?" He struggled to free himself.

"Promise me you'll stay put," Coulter said, "and I'll let go."

The boy nodded. When Coulter released him, he pointed at Maggie. "I can march as good as any woman," he said. "Why—there's drummer boys younger than me."

"If we needed one—which we do not—would you want to be a drummer boy?"

The boy smiled, exposing a gap in his upper row of teeth. "Would I get a uniform? 'Cause I could use some new trousers." He bent one of his legs, exposing a knobby knee through a gaping hole. When Coulter asked if he knew how to play a drum, the boy didn't answer. He pointed at Blue. "I could take care of your horse some more. We get along. I can gather firewood, too. Repair harness. Haul feed. I helped you get those wagons and the mules, and ain't they good teams? I can do all kinds of things. You should give me a try."

When Coulter said nothing, the boy spoke to Maggie. "Don't you miss havin' help? Let me stay. I'll be better'n any of your other servants."

Maggie sputtered, "I—what?"

"Servants," the boy repeated. "Don't you miss 'em?" He looked up at Sergeant Coulter. "You should have let her bring at least one. The army lets wives bring servants. I've seen 'em headed west to fight Indians. Steamboats full of soldiers and wagons and wives and servants. Pets, too. Whole families."

Maggie felt her face heating up. "I'm not anyone's wife."

The boy blinked. "Well, I—I'm sorry. I just thought—" He shrugged. "Don't make no difference to me if you're married or not, ma'am. I'll still help ya. 'Judge not.' That's what the Good Book says, and I think it's right good advice."

Jack grabbed a handful of shirt and gave the boy a little shake. "Miss Malone is my sister, and you'll keep your filthy ideas to yourself, or I'll give your mouth a good cleaning out with soap."

Maggie blanched. The boy thought she was a camp follower? There was no time to finish either the thought or the conversation, for just at that moment the woods to the north erupted with a barrage of terrifying, high-pitched yells. Shots rang out. A shower of splinters erupted from the edge of the wagon just to the right of where Maggie was standing. Mules brayed. Blue screamed. In the chaos, a hand closed about Maggie's wrist like a vise. Sergeant Coulter pulled her beneath a wagon. She landed with a thud next to the boy, who'd somehow managed to collect Hero before taking cover beneath the wagon.

"Get that pistol out and stay put," Coulter said, and then

he was gone, racing to untie Blue and send the horse fleeing into the woods and away from the gunfire. Next, he darted around to the back of the wagon, lowered the tailgate, and scuttled into the wagon bed next to one of the crates of rifles.

Maggie stared after him in disbelief. *He made sure I was safe.* As she watched the sergeant work to open one of the crates in the wagon, she realized what he had in mind. At least two dozen men lay on their bellies beneath the wagons, with only their side arms as weapons—and only if they were already loaded, which was doubtful. Coulter was going to try to arm them with the Henrys—but that would only help if they had ammunition, and the boxes of cartridges were in the wagon right above her head.

Yelling at Noah to stay put, she crept to the back end of the wagon. Her heart pounding, she popped up to lower the tailgate. Her first attempt failed, but on the second try she succeeded. She could see the ammunition boxes, but they were out of reach. She was going to have to scramble into the wagon bed. She'd just grabbed a fistful of skirt and petticoat when Noah slipped past her and did just that. Keeping low, he shoved an ammunition box off the end of the wagon. It landed with a thud, and paper-wrapped cartridges spilled out. A second box landed beside the first, and then the boy jumped down, grabbed two fists full of cartridges, and set out for the men lying beneath the closest wagon.

Maggie focused on the one that was farthest away. A flash of a bandaged hand identified Jack. Fish was there, too. That red hat—didn't he realize it made a perfect target? Taking her revolver out of her pocket, she stuffed both pockets with cartridge packets. Uttering a panicked prayer, she cocked the revolver and charged out from between the two supply wagons. It seemed to take a century to cross the open field.

The weapon only fired .31 caliber balls and was of little use beyond close range. Still, just pulling the trigger made her feel better. She'd only gotten off two shots before she arrived at the wagon and threw herself beneath it. She tossed cartridge packages to the men with both hands. While they loaded, she flopped onto her stomach, and emptied the revolver's remaining three chambers in the direction of the trees.

It was over in moments. As soon as the men began to return fire with the Henrys, whoever had ambushed them retreated. A few minutes of silence, and the men began to crawl out from beneath the wagons. Maggie followed suit, her hands shaking so badly it took three tries before she managed to get Da's gun back in her pocket.

Jack grabbed her in a bear hug and spun her about. "I should scold you until I'm hoarse, Mary Margaret. What were you thinking?"

"That you needed cartridges."

"You're a blessed fool," Seamus said, wrapping his arms about her and lifting her off the ground. "And may the dear Lord bless you for it."

Fish handed her a kepi. "You are more soldier than you realize, mademoiselle. Wear it in good health."

Maggie's hand went to her bare head. What had happened to her bonnet?

"I don't think you'll be wearing it again, Maggie-girl," Seamus said, and reached over to pull what looked like a rag dangling from a nail protruding from the bottom board of the wagon they'd all sheltered under. "You must have snagged it when you dove for cover."

The poor old thing was shredded beyond repair. Maggie looked at the kepi.

"Go on, then," Seamus said. Taking the blue cap out of

her hands, he plopped it on her head, then stood back, arms folded to inspect it. "All you need is a bit of braid on the cape, and you'll look a proper soldier—better than most of us, in fact, ragged lot that we are."

Maggie just shook her head. She glanced back at the wagon where she and Noah had been when everything started. He was busy returning unused cartridge packets to the ammunition boxes. "I should help him. And see to Hero."

The dog had crept out from beneath the wagon and was none the worse for being dragged unceremoniously from beneath Fish's wagon seat. "You're a brave little man, aren't you?" Maggie said, scratching him behind the ears and happy to accept a couple of swipes from the pink tongue.

"He's not the only one."

Maggie turned around just as Sergeant Coulter strode up with Blue in tow. She nodded at the horse. "Glad to see he didn't go far."

"So was I." When he smiled and Maggie realized he was looking at the forage cap on her head, she reached up to take it off, but he stilled her hand. "It suits you. You were very brave."

"Not all that brave," Maggie said. "If I'd stopped to think about it, I'd probably still be cowering beneath a wagon."

"Who's a coward?" the boy protested. "Neither one of us, if you ask me."

"Neither one," Fish said, and plopped a forage cap on Noah's head.

Noah's eyes shone as he took the cap off and inspected it. "Had me a good straw hat," he said, "but it fell off when I was climbing into that wagon. Sure hated to lose it." He put the cap back on, lifted his chin, and saluted. "This is better, though."

"Finish packing those cartridges," Fish said. "Then come and eat."

"Yes, sir!" Noah hurried to obey the order.

Maggie peered into the woods. "How did they get past the pickets?"

"Untrained recruits," Coulter said. "Those first shots that sounded so far away? The pickets thought they should investigate. They chased a handful of rebels halfway to the river, and by the time they realized that drawing them away was exactly the enemy's plan, all they could do was circle around and hope not to get killed by friendly fire."

"I thought Captain Quinn said the armed rebels were in the southwestern part of the state."

Coulter shrugged. "It's no surprise that they'd want to recover those rifles."

"Were they really intended for Wildwood Grove?"

"It looks that way."

Quickly, Jack told the sergeant about Maggie's seeing freight delivered to the private Wildwood levee on her way to Boonville.

"I should have said something," Maggie said. "I just—I didn't give it all that much thought. I was too worried about Jack. The packet stopped three or four times, taking on freight, putting passengers off."

"Think back to it," Sergeant Coulter said. "Tell me everything you can remember. Every detail."

He wanted to know the number and sizes of the crates. He asked if Maggie had noticed any markings. How many men did she see on the levee? Were they all in uniform? And what, exactly, did she know about Walker Blair and his Wildwood Guard? Maggie told him everything she could remember, right down to the fact that Major Green rode a big white horse. "I—I'm sorry I didn't say anything before now. I just—I didn't think. Even though Dr. Feeny explained how important control of the river is—and how that particular plantation is well located for that purpose—" She shook her head. "I didn't think."

Coulter looked surprised. "Did you just say *Feeny*?"

"Yes...why?"

He shook his head. "Another time. It's just—it's an interesting coincidence." He turned to Jack and Seamus. "How well do you know this Wildwood Grove?"

"Jack knows more than either Maggie or me," Seamus said, batting his eyelids and lifting one shoulder as he pretended to fan himself and gave forth the worst imitation of a Southern accent Maggie could have imagined. "Oh, Jack eye-uh just cain't tell yuh how mah little hahrt races when y'all come ne-ah."

Jack pounded Seamus's shoulder with a none-too-gentle fist as he explained to the sergeant. "I did a little harmless flirting from time to time when the planters' daughters came to town, but Elizabeth Blair never took part in the game." He abruptly changed the subject, telling the sergeant about the conversation he and Seamus and Maggie had had just prior to the skirmish.

"And you know the layout of the place?" Coulter asked.

Jack nodded, and a slow smile crept over his face. "If Captain Quinn was of a mind to authorize it, we could do a fine job of reconnoitering."

Seamus agreed. "Jack and I know every hill and valley near that place—and most of the plantation itself. Officially, of course, we never dared trespass on Walker Blair's private property. Not unless we wanted to risk a night in the Littleton jail."

"Really?" Coulter sounded surprised. "Blair was that intent on keeping people away?"

Jack grunted. "And now that I think about—" He glanced at Maggie. "You wondered if there might be a connection between the Wildwood Guard and what happened at the farm? Without anyone living on our farm, there'd be less chance of Union sympathizers noticing something going on at the plantation."

Sergeant Coulter motioned for Seamus and Jack to come with him. "Let's see what Captain Quinn thinks about it all."

~~~

After the boys and Sergeant Coulter went to find Captain Quinn, Maggie busied herself in camp. She tended to Hero, made coffee, and ended the day with more mending. Ashby had apparently shown his mended shirt to someone, and the word had spread that the woman in camp was not only a good shot—she was willing to sew. Most men offered to pay her for her efforts, but beyond teasing Ashby about paying her in gooseberries, Maggie refused their money. She liked the idea of helping them out. In fact, at least insofar as she'd experienced it, there was a lot to like about camp life. If it weren't for Paddy, she'd be trying to find a way to stay with the Irish a bit longer. *Paddy*. She must write to him again tonight—and avoid the topic of the skirmish.

The moon had risen over the Irish Brigade encampment before Jack, Seamus, and Sergeant Coulter returned from their meeting with Captain Quinn—and, Maggie assumed, the brigade commander. Coulter nodded at Maggie as he walked past, but instead of lingering, he said something about seeing to Blue and headed off to where the horses were picketed. The boys settled by the campfire, strangely silent.

Maggie finally asked. "Well?"

"The usual." The way Seamus spat out the words made Maggie look up. He was angry.

Jack took a deep breath. "I'm going to get my mess kit," he said to Seamus. "Want me to bring yours?" He made a show of leaning over the campfire and inhaling. "The coffee smells good."

Seamus grumbled a reply, and Jack went to retrieve their mugs.

"Are you going to tell me what's happened, or am I to beg?"

Seamus harrumphed. "What's happened is the captain is sending Jack and Colt off and—as usual—I'll have no part in the adventure."

"What kind of adventure?"

"To Wildwood Grove to see what Walker Blair is up to."

Maggie waited a moment before saying quietly, "Wildwood Grove being a few days' march from where we are now, I don't suppose they'll be going on foot."

Seamus didn't answer. Instead, he lay back with his arms behind his head, staring up at the stars. Finally, he muttered, "You're right, of course. Jack isn't the best rider, either—but he's far better than me. I'd only slow them down. Likely break my neck trying to ride some half-broke army nag." He sat up. "But I don't have to like it."

Maggie did her best to keep from smiling. "You mean it's no fun being the one left behind? Hard not knowing what's happening?"

Seamus shrugged, pulled his fife out of its case, and began to play a mournful tune. When Jack returned, Sergeant Coulter was with him. Seamus put his fife away and poured himself a mug of coffee. No one said anything for a while, until Coulter finally flexed his left arm and said to Maggie, "I don't know what was in those herbs you packed against that bullet trail across my arm, but they've done wonders."

Maggie was glad for the low light to hide her self-conscious blush as she said, "I'm glad to hear it, but didn't you say the surgeons wanted you to keep it in the sling for a while longer? I wouldn't want to be blamed for your going against their orders."

The golden light of the campfire illuminated a beautiful smile as Coulter said, "If anything, they should ask what you used to speed up the healing." He paused. "And as for your leaving camp—you can't."

Jack cleared his throat. "What the sergeant means, Maggiegirl, is that Captain Quinn thinks it would be better for you to stay with the brigade until we have a better idea of what's going on in Lafayette County."

Maggie suppressed a smile. Jack knew better than to say *you can't* to her. "I don't mind being told I can't leave," she said. "I've at least a dozen shirts to mend, and if Fish can be convinced to allow it, I'll help with the cleaning of those rifles we fired earlier today."

"It shouldn't be for too long," the sergeant said. "Jack and I will be moving as quickly as we can—learning as much as we can in as short a time as possible."

Jack mentioned sneaking into Littleton as part of the assignment. "I'll let Paddy know you're safe so that he doesn't worry."

Maggie let a note of sarcasm drip into her voice. "Thoughtful of you, Jack. Not wanting him to worry."

"Thoughtful as can be," Seamus said. "Especially when it means he'll get to visit Bridget Feeny."

"*Feeny*," Sergeant Coulter said. "You mentioned a Feeny earlier. Brick house on a corner? Not far from the newspaper office?" He paused. "I don't remember a Bridget, though. It was just the good doctor and his wife, the last I knew."

Seamus spoke up. "How do you know the Feenys? I thought you were from St. Louis."

Coulter reached out to pet Hero, who was curled up close to the campfire. "I'm not from anyplace, really. I was in St. Louis when I joined the army, and that's as good a place as any to call home. As to the Feenys, I only know of them. We've never met. My grandparents lived in Littleton when I was a boy. I spent quite a bit of time with them—until the spring after I turned twelve. That's when an uncle talked Grandpop into letting me come on board his steamboat. Told them he'd make me his cub pilot." He took a long, slow breath, and with a last stroke of Hero's sleek coat, said, "Uncle and I eventually agreed that steamboating wasn't for me."

There was more to the story than the sergeant wanted to reveal. Some long-ago hurt lay behind the man's words. Maggie was sure of it. Remembering how Seamus had cried when they laid Da to rest in the churchyard made her wish she could somehow soothe the hurt Sergeant Coulter was feeling as he spoke of losing his grandparents—and their home.

"At any rate," he continued, "during the time I was working for my uncle, my grandparents passed on, and Uncle sold their house. I remembered the name *Feeny* from a 'discussion' he and I had about the matter."

A *discussion*. Maggie could just imagine. All these years later, Sergeant Coulter still felt the emotion of what must have been a fight. It sounded in his voice—just a wee thread of anger.

The sergeant let out a low grunt. "A heated discussion."

Ah. She was right, then. The man had cared deeply for his grandparents and their home. For some reason, the home had been wrested from him, and the memory still caused him pain.

"But all of that aside," Coulter said, and his voice took on a lighter tone. "I have good memories of Littleton." He looked over at Maggie. "That all happened back in...'49. I don't remember any Malones. And I do think I'd remember you."

Thankfully, Seamus spoke into the awkward silence Maggie had no idea how to fill.

"Maggie was only eleven when Da moved us all to Littleton," Seamus said. "That would have been...1850?" He glanced over at Jack, who nodded.

"Then I was right," Coulter said. "We wouldn't have crossed paths. With my grandparents gone and their home sold to the Feenys, there hasn't been a reason to go back." A slow smile replaced the sadness on his face. "I remember when they were building the courthouse. It was the talk of the county."

"Littleton's quite the metropolis now," Maggie said. "You'll be surprised when you see it."

A bugle sounded "Lights Out," and Sergeant Coulter stood and said good night. Seamus and Jack doused the campfire, while Maggie moved Hero's bed from beneath the wagon seat to beside the blanket she spread out in the shelter of Fish's wagon. When she called to him, Hero whined a protest, but then he rose and limped over. "Good boy," Maggie said, and gave him a pat. "Very good boy."

Sheltered beneath the wagon, she took down her hair and did her best to work a comb through it. Once she had it braided, she lay back, petting Hero and trying not to think about Jack and Sergeant Coulter spying on Walker Blair and whoever else might be gathered at Blair's plantation. Thinking instead about a young boy learning that his grandparents had died and being told that the home where he'd grown up was sold. How that must have hurt.

Reaching into her pocket, she pulled out the square of lavender soap. When Hero whined, Maggie looked over at him. The dog's eyes were fixed on the bit of soap. He thumped his tail. Maggie chuckled. "You little beggar." She let him take a sniff. He sneezed and then, with a deep sigh, flopped onto his side and closed his eyes.

"Good idea," Maggie murmured. Wrapping herself in her blanket, she settled down, Paddy's satchel for a pillow. Eventually, the low rumble of men's voices faded away, and there was only the sawing of cicadas in the trees, and the image of Sergeant John Coulter speaking about his past and then smiling at her, his handsome face illuminated by the firelight. There was a sadness to the man...even when he smiled. As she stared at the dying campfire, she whispered a prayer. *Dear Lord in heaven, I know that it's askin' a great deal, but I'm askin' it anyway. Make my boys invisible to the eyes of the enemy... Seamus and Jack...and John Coulter, too. Keep them safe. As for Noah, I don't know what to ask. Just—be mindful of him, as you are of us all. And if it's all the same to you, dear Lord...I wouldn't mind stayin' on for a bit.*

Chapter 12

⟨ ⟩

The familiar sound of Ora Lee's humming woke Libbie on Sunday morning. It had been a restless night, and now she heard rather than saw Ora Lee open the shutters and raise the window. When the warmth of the morning sun splashed across her face, she turned her head toward the window and took a deep breath. And realized that she couldn't open her left eye all the way.

Ora Lee stopped humming. "I'm gonna fetch some ice," she said, and slipped out of the room.

Libbie sat up in bed, exploring the left side of her face with her fingertips. It wasn't terribly sore. That had to be good—didn't it? Taking a deep breath, she slipped out of bed and crossed to her dressing table. She leaned down to look in the mirror. *Oh, my.* Sitting down abruptly, she gazed out the window toward the river, listening to the song of a red bird that must have been nesting somewhere in the trees just beyond the carefully tended lawn. She looked back in the mirror. Annabelle had been right. She was going to have a black eye. Bruises got worse over the first couple of days.

She was still sitting at the dressing table when Ora Lee returned, accompanied by Annabelle, who took one look at Libbie and sighed. "Lord, have mercy." She handed Libbie the cold compress she'd brought with her.

"It doesn't hurt," Libbie said, closing her eyes as she applied the compress to her swollen cheekbone.

"No headache?" Annabelle asked.

Libbie shook her head. "I'm actually surprised it looks as bad as it does." She held the compress away and prodded a little more energetically with the fingertips of her free hand. "Is there anything I can do? I mean—I can't be seen like this. Walker would kill—I mean. He wouldn't want anyone to know."

Annabelle's grunt spoke the words she didn't dare speak.

Libbie swallowed. "He apologized. He didn't mean to hurt me."

Again Annabelle grunted. Then she asked, "You sure your head don't hurt? Can you see clear?"

"I can see just fine, out of my right eye, anyway."

With a sigh, Annabelle turned to go. "I'll send your breakfast up here. Got some salve might help a bit."

Ora Lee opened the door to Libbie's wardrobe, but then she hesitated. "What you want me to pull outta here, Miss Libbie? Mastah Blair be expectin' you for the church service."

A knock sounded at the bedroom door, and Walker spoke Libbie's name—barely loud enough for her to hear it. He rarely gave her more than half a minute to come to the door before barging in. Today, though, he waited. Libbie called out for him to wait a moment while she "made herself decent."

"The church service begins in half an hour," he said quietly. "Seein' a beautiful woman is good for the men. It reminds 'em of what they are fightin' for."

Libbie hadn't really minded the ritual of walking the grounds at Walker's side while he basked in the salutes and the greetings of the men in "his" regiment. The idea that he was displaying her like a possession rankled, but her resentment paled when she concentrated on the smiles of the men who populated the Wildwood Guard. As far as the church service was concerned, Walker had selected a chaplain known for short sermons, and when it came time to sing, the men did so with enthusiasm. Libbie enjoyed hearing all those masculine voices. It made her feel safe. Or it had. Now that she knew there was a problem arming them... *dear Lord*. Knowing Walker's true reason for organizing a regiment had made it all seem like a game. She hadn't let herself think about the idea that some of them might die. Soon.

"Will you come? Please, Libbie. I—the men. Will you come for them?"

"I can't," Libbie said as she opened the door. She lowered the compress and showed him the bruised side of her face.

Walker stared. For once, he didn't seem to know what to say. Voices sounded behind him. Men were coming out of their rooms. Walker pressed against the door, intending to step into her room. When Libbie blocked the door with her foot, he turned away and pulled it closed behind him. She heard him greet the men. "I believe there is coffee waiting in the dining room. I'll join you directly."

Footsteps sounded as the men walked past Walker and descended to the main floor. He rattled the doorknob. "Please. Libbie. Open the door."

Again, Libbie cracked it open. Again, she blocked his entrance with her foot.

"Isn't there some way to—can't you do something? A bonnet?" He paused. "Surely there's a way to hide—"

"If there is, I don't know it," Libbie said. "You'll have to think of some excuse." She closed the door. Firmly. And leaned against it, her heart pounding. Walker had never let her have the key. If he wanted to force the issue, she wouldn't be able to keep him out. But he didn't. She could sense him just standing there on the other side of the door. She practically held her breath while she waited to see what he would do. Finally, he retreated. She heard him descend the stairs.

She spoke to Ora Lee. "Annabelle said something about breakfast. Could you go down and get it? I'm hungrier than a bear coming out of hibernation." After Ora Lee left, Libbie sat at her dressing table, staring at her swollen face. Making a plan.

Nowhere to go. That was the real problem, Libbie realized. Even if she wanted to leave Wildwood Grove, she had nowhere to go. Serena Ellerbe might be willing to take her in, but her father, Mason, was one of the men Walker was trusting to further his political career once the fighting ended. Libbie could just imagine the conversation that would take place if she should arrive on the Ellerbes' doorstep looking like this. Walker would never forgive her.

Walker. Maybe she should hate him, but she didn't. After all, he was all she had. She couldn't just walk away and never look back. And yet…she needed a refuge. Needed to feel that she was back in control of at least some part of her life beyond deciding menus and reading the latest issue of *Godey's* and being paraded about on Isham Green's arm.

Standing at her bedroom window, she looked toward the river. *I've got peace like a river…in my soul.* Annabelle sang those words all the time. How Libbie wished she could somehow know peace…in her soul. She needed to think. To calm her jangled nerves. To find the same kind of peace that river symbolized as it rolled on by, never stopping. Powerful. Strong.

The river. She needed time by the river. She took a deep breath. Everyone on the place was preoccupied with the church service this morning. Even the slaves would be down there, clustered along the garden fence, visible testimony to Walker Blair's power over his possessions. Walker would count heads. He'd know Malachi and Ora Lee and Annabelle were all there as expected. If Libbie took a ride this morning, Walker wouldn't be able to blame anyone but her. And if he tried to hit her again—well. That wouldn't happen. Not ever again. But she needed to think.

Hurrying to dress, Libbie left her room. At the bottom of the stairs, she hesitated. She wanted—needed—the key to her bedroom door. Would it be in Walker's office? She intended to make the search a quick one, but was brought up short at the sight of a map of some kind atop a rustic table that had been dragged in from somewhere. She lingered over it a moment, reading words that sent a chill down her spine. Someone had written *earthworks* just beyond the row of log cabins where the field hands lived. *Battery* at the top of a ridge—the very ridge above her hideout, if she was reading the map correctly.

It didn't take a military education to know what it all meant. Someone expected there to be a battle. Here. At Wildwood Grove. The notion made her tremble. How could she have been so willfully ignorant? She hadn't set foot in this room since the officers arrived. Hadn't wanted to, really. It was enough that she had to be charming every evening. Enough that she had to walk with Isham Green after dinner.

Looking at the map of the plantation, Libbie wondered at Walker's true motivation for forbidding her to ride. If earthworks were being dug along the quarters, she'd see them if she went riding. Did Walker want to hide things from her because he didn't want to frighten her—or because he didn't trust her? Maybe his injunction was less about her personal safety and more about keeping his plans from her. Now that she thought about it, she'd seen Walker hastily fold the map up one evening when she and Sheriff Green returned from a walk via the front door.

What else might Walker be hiding from her? She didn't know, but the notion that he had secrets made her want to find her door key more than ever. Moving quickly, she checked every drawer in the room. No keys. When footsteps sounded in the hall, Libbie spun about, her heart pounding, but it was only Ora Lee. Libbie frowned. "Aren't you supposed to be at church? Walker will know you weren't there. He counts heads."

"He axed me to come see to you. Said to stay with you."

There it was again—a new suspicion about Walker's keeping things from her. Assigning Ora Lee to watch her. "I was thinking I might saddle Pilot and go for a ride," Libbie said. "It won't get Malachi into trouble if I go while he's at church."

"But it'll get you into trouble. Plenty of trouble."

Libbie shrugged. "I don't care." She looked about her at the room. "Well—I won't care so much if I can find the key to my bedroom door."

Ora Lee's soft grunt reminded Libbie of the way Annabelle had found to comment or disagree without actually saying anything. But Ora Lee had something to say. "Seems to me it'd take more than a key to keep Mr. Blair from doing something, once he put his mind to it."

Libbie raised her palm to her face. She didn't dare go riding now. Walker would take everything out on Ora Lee. Tears gathered, but she blinked them away. "You're right. He'd just take it out on you."

Ora Lee seemed to ponder the idea for a moment. Finally, with a glance in the direction of the back door, she said, "I could just go back to hear the rest of the sermon. If he asks, I could say you was sleeping." She nodded. "Yes'm. You was sleeping and so I thought I'd come back and hear the rest of the sermon. He'll like that. Mastah has that preacher readin' about how slaves is to obey they masters. He'll like it if I come back in time to hear the sermon. Won't be nobody in trouble—'cept you." She hesitated. "You sure you want to do this, Miss Libbie?"

Libbie nodded. "I do. More than anything. Never mind about the key." She took a step toward the door.

Ora Lee turned to go, but then she paused in the doorway. "I don't know 'bout keys, Miss Libbie, but I do remember Betty sayin' that Robert knows a lot about this here room Mastah Blair wishes he didn't. Betty like to boast about it." As she turned to go, she pretended to stumble on the threshold and put her hand out to catch herself. Something clicked. "Would you listen to that," she said. "Creaky old house. *Secrets*, Betty said. This house got all kinda secrets." She patted the panel where'd she caught herself and headed back outside.

After Ora Lee was gone, Libbie pressed on the spot where the girl had placed her hand. A decorative panel popped open to reveal several keys of varying sizes hanging on nails pounded into the lathe. Cobwebs thick with dust clung to the slats and to the keys. What on earth—what were they all for? She reached for one, but then hesitated. If one of these was to her bedroom door, and if she ever actually used it— Libbie shuddered to think what Walker would do to Robert. To every single house slave, until one of them told him what he wanted to know. With a trembling hand, she closed the false panel. She felt more trapped than ever, as if the house itself were in league against her. She had to get away. If only for a little while, she had to be free.

Her heart pounding, Libbie hurried out the front door and alongside the house, using a hedge to shield her movements.

It was probably her imagination, but Pilot seemed glad to see her. He whickered low when she opened the stall door, and stood quietly while she saddled him. He took the bit without any of his usual tossing of the head and dancing about, and remained still while she mounted. Once she was in the saddle, though, he let it be known that he was ready to run. She would have to let him have a bit of a chase. They headed up the road first, keeping the house and buildings between them and the worship service. Once she was certain they were out of sight, she gave Pilot his head. They would run for a bit, and then she would settle him and ride along the river. They'd take the path that led away from the landing and through the woods. She might even brave a return to the old lookout for a few minutes.

As for the rest of the day...as Pilot cantered down the road, Libbie realized that the ride could give her an excuse for her bruised and swollen face. *Pilot was so frisky—why, a little ole leaf blew across the road and that crazy horse shied. He nearly threw me, but I managed to stay on. I'd just about righted myself when the top of Pilot's head slammed against my cheek. Lord have mercy, I saw stars. Can you believe what a ninny I am? I should-a been payin' better attention.* If anything, Walker would be relieved that she'd come up with an excuse for her bruises that would enable her to be seen in public. And she would be seen. Seen and heard.

Upon her return, she would visit the encampment to encourage the men and perhaps see what she might do to provide a special meal for them later in the week. It had taken everyone's considered effort to keep them fed—even with the neighbors helping and supplies arriving down at the river landing. The Ellerbe ladies would help her organize something. Perhaps they'd even have a social of some kind. She'd ask Sheriff—no, it was *Major* Green and she must remember that—she'd ask *Major* Green to escort her to the Ellerbes' this afternoon. She'd hang on his every word over the evening meal, and wrangle an invitation to walk after dinner. As for the moment when she'd be most vulnerable to Walker's anger—when she retired after supper, she would block her bedroom door with a piece of furniture. And if she wanted to take a ride by the river tomorrow, she would do it.

Reining Pilot in, Libbie let him pick his way down to the path by the river and headed for her lookout, humming as she went. *I've got peace like a river...*

⁂

With a last look toward the plantation house in the distance, Colt dropped out of sight behind the ridge. He lay still for a moment. Listening. He glanced over at Jack, who was positioned on the same ridge a few yards away. After a moment, the men nodded, sliding backward across the grass on their bellies, making as little noise as possible, ever aware that pickets or lookouts or militia or snipers could, at any moment, detect their presence.

They'd just reached the bottom of the hill when they heard singing—men's voices carrying from the outdoor church service taking place just this side of one of the brick outbuildings behind the two-story house. For a moment the two of them sat still, listening. *Am I a soldier of the cross...* Colt recognized the tune...*must I be carried to the skies on flow'ry beds of ease...while others fought to win the prize and sailed through bloody seas...*

How odd it was to hear rebels singing a hymn he'd heard

in his grandparents' home church; men he might have to kill before the month was out. The thought made the hair on the back of his neck stand up. *Don't think about that. Think about—* the earthworks up along the road; the obvious signs that the plantation owner was involved in a lot more than just smuggling arms to the rebels gathering in southwestern Missouri. Everything pointed to the Confederates in Lafayette County preparing for action right here in their own part of the state. There might even be a larger plan in play that, if executed properly, could put the Irish Brigade in the untenable position of having to fight Confederate forces on *two* fronts.

Captain Quinn had said something about a message from the editor of the newspaper in nearby Littleton; something about rebel militia patrolling the streets of town. But he'd said nothing about an encampment at a nearby plantation. Was it possible he didn't know the scope of what was going on just a few miles away? Jack seemed to think so. Colt supposed anything was possible these days. Nothing was sure in Missouri. Not anymore. A neighbor might be harboring the enemy, and the definition of that word, *enemy*, could change with the crossing of a property line.

Colt and Jack hunkered together at the bottom of the hill, water lapping at the riverbank just a few feet away. They'd spent much of yesterday gathering information before rolling up in their blankets for a long night on a ledge overlooking the river—a hideout Jack had known about. This morning, they'd watched the plantation's private landing, which was now guarded by a dozen militia who'd created what looked like a semipermanent camp there. It was a perfect place for steamboats to slip in and unload weapons. Troops. Horses. Supplies. The men guarding it had dug in and were obviously expecting to stay for a while.

Jack said that no fewer than half a dozen steamboats landed at the Littleton levee on most days. It didn't take any imagination at all to expect that more than just that one shipment of Henrys they'd discovered at Boonville was expected at Wildwood Grove. His sister had witnessed one. None had arrived since Jack and Colt had been watching, but they were going to have to leave soon. Captain Quinn and the rest of command needed to know about the encampment here.

It was the common belief that most of the rebel troops were in the southwestern part of the state, biding their time until enough troops had amassed there to launch a major campaign to move back north and recapture the river that traversed the entire state in a rough east-to-west line. Now, though, it looked like something more might be going on. It was hard to know for certain. Jack seemed to think the plantation owner was a lot more interested in protecting his personal property than in actually fighting for "the cause." If that was the case, then the troops camped here might be only defensive. If the fight came to them, they'd be ready.

Walker Blair had political aspirations, Jack said, and Colt knew there was nothing like a uniform and a few medals to win votes. More than one politician had crowed about his involvement in the War of 1812 to curry the favor of voters. As for what was going on here at Wildwood Grove, it was hard to know for sure. It certainly seemed like more troops were gathered than a man would need to defend one plantation. It would be up to command to interpret what they reported. All Colt and Jack could do was provide the information.

The hymn singing ended, bringing Colt back to the moment. As he and Jack sat hidden beneath the arched branches of a blackberry thicket, he looked to Jack for confirmation of what they'd learned so far. "Three...four hundred?"

Jack nodded. "At least."

"No artillery, though."

"Not yet."

Colt pointed toward the river. "Probably on its way."

Jack nodded.

"Wish we knew when."

Jack thought for a moment. He smiled. "Too bad we didn't bring Maggie with us. She'd be free to nose about in town without raising anyone's suspicion."

Maggie. The more Colt was around her, the more the woman fascinated him. Who would ever expect a woman to run through gunfire to supply men with ammunition? She hadn't hesitated, and once things calmed down, she'd settled back as if nothing had happened. A lesser woman would have fainted dead away. Colt looked over at Jack. "Your sister." He paused. "Is she—I mean—is anyone courting her?"

"Maggie?"

It didn't take a genius to understand the meaning behind the way Jack said the name.

Colt frowned. "She may be your sister, but—she's also a fascinating woman."

"*Fascinating*? Maggie? You're joking, right?"

"If I were," Colt snapped, "I'd expect you to be doubling up your fist right now to teach me some respect—whether I'm your superior officer or not."

Jack frowned. He looked over at Colt, clearly mystified. "Maggie." He spoke the name, but then he said nothing for a moment. When he did, his tone was...careful. "Maggie's... different. Unique. She's...strong. Not delicate." He swallowed. "She's just not the kind of woman men notice. In the way you mean. Men who are looking for someone to court, I mean."

Colt grunted and looked away, struggling to hide just

how happy he was to learn that Miss Maggie Malone was unattached. He scratched the back of his neck. Brushed an imaginary bit of dirt off his sleeve. "Guess you answered my question. No Irish farmers plighting their troth, then."

"None." He paused. "On the subject of troths and such—do you think we should try to sneak into town after dark and talk to some folks? Dr. Feeny can be trusted. So can the man who runs the biggest mercantile in town. Both of them are in the perfect position to learn what people are seeing and hearing. Ed Markum can be trusted as well. He's editor at the *Leader*."

Colt pondered for a moment. "We need to report what we already know. We don't know that they mean to do it, but if the troops camped here march south within the next few days, they'll intercept the Irish. Our men could end up being caught in the middle."

"You're right," Jack said. "The thing is, if we do a little reconnoitering in Littleton, we'll be able to give a more complete report."

Colt nodded. Finally, he pointed toward the overhang where they'd left their horses tethered out of sight against a concave rock wall. "Let's tuck in up there. After dark, I'll head east to tell the captain what we've already seen. You sneak into town and see if you can learn anything more." Jack nodded, and set off for the overhang.

Colt waited, listening for the signal that he'd reached the horses and all was well. The cry of a hawk meant it was safe to head that way. If a crow cackled, he'd slide into the river and float downstream. Jack would do his best to spook Blue and send him tearing off into the woods along the water. After that, it would be up to Colt.

Chapter 13

—⟨≈⟩—

I've got joy like a—whoa. Libbie stopped mid-sentence and pulled back on the reins. Pilot stopped. There was a man crouched by the spring. Libbie was just about to make a run for it when Pilot whickered. The man jumped up, spun about, and snatched the forage cap off his head.

"Wait. Miss Blair." The words wouldn't have carried much farther than the trail, but the tone was urgent. Pleading.

Libbie hesitated. Pilot took another step, and a gray horse came into view, standing broadside to the rock wall jutting out of the hillside. She glanced up to the top of the ridge. Clever. No one would see the gray from up above. *Or the bay behind him.* Two horses, standing nose-to-tail. Where was the other rider?

"It's Jack Malone, Miss Blair." The soldier stood still, his cap in his hands, the expression on his handsome face wary. "Please don't scream. I was just getting a drink here at the spring. You nearly scared me to death. The last thing I expected..."

While Jack Malone rambled, Libbie looked past him toward the horses. The gray was a fine animal. She couldn't remember ever seeing a Malone astride a horse, though. What was going on? Something crackled just behind her on the trail. Pilot danced sideways, and another soldier stepped up. He must have been up above them. Had she ridden right past him without seeing him? He moved quickly, and before Libbie had time to react, he'd pulled her out of the saddle and clamped a filthy hand over her mouth.

She struggled against him. Pilot threw a fit. Jack Malone grabbed the reins, barely preventing the horse from bolting. Grabbing the bridle, he backed Pilot up until his hind quarters were practically touching the wall of rock, trying to calm him down. The soldier who was holding Libbie forced her into the shadow of the rocky ledge.

Pilot settled down, but Malone kept hold of the horse's reins while he spoke to her. "Don't scream. We aren't going to hurt you, but we can't let you sound an alarm."

Libbie grunted a response. Struggled some more.

"If the sergeant lets you go, promise me you won't raise the alarm."

Libbie stopped fighting. Nodded. The hand came away from her mouth. She tried to pull free. "I'm not going to holler," she hissed. "Just. Let me *go*!" The man must have been looking at Malone, for when the Irishman nodded, the soldier released his grip.

Libbie whirled about. She glared up at him, but she kept her voice low as she spoke. "Who in tarnation are you?" She looked over at Jack. "And what do you think you're doin'? Don't you know there's men guarding the landing not half a mile upriver? You could get yourselves killed roamin' around Wildwood Grove." She looked toward the river. "Where'd you come from, anyway?"

Malone and the other soldier—a sergeant, Malone had said—exchanged glances, and Libbie realized. *Lord have mercy. They were spyin' on the Guard.* She noticed Malone's bandaged hand. "You're hurt."

Malone looked down at his hand and then back up at her.

Something flickered in his blue eyes. He tilted his head. "So are you."

Libbie's gloved hand cupped the left side of her face. "I—uh—I fell." Now why couldn't she remember the story she'd already concocted? She swallowed, suddenly aware of being thirsty. She cleared her throat. Nodded at the bubbling spring. "All right with you if I get a drink?"

Malone handed Pilot's reins to the stranger and retrieved a tin cup from the saddlebags on the other horse—the one half hidden behind the gray. Libbie looked over at the sergeant. "I don't recall ever seein' the Malones ride. Is the gray yours?" He didn't answer. She shrugged. "He's a beauty." Malone dipped his cup into the spring and then handed it to her. While she drank, the silent sergeant led Pilot over and let him drink, too. Libbie handed the cup back to Jack Malone and thanked him.

She looked over her shoulder at the river, then back at Malone. "I heard what happened at your farm. I'm sorry." She glanced at the silent sergeant. "I truly mean it."

The words were out before she realized that Jack Malone might not know about it, but he must have read her expression, for he said, "Thank you." He held up his bandaged hand. "When I was reported as wounded, Maggie tracked us down. Came all the way to Boonville." One corner of his mouth curled up as he said, "She told us about the farm in the middle of giving both Seamus and me a very thorough scolding for not writing to tell her I was all right." He paused. "I hadn't stopped to think there'd be a list of the wounded in the paper."

"Well, I'm glad you're all right," Libbie said, and she truly meant that, too. She supposed it might seem strange for a Southerner to say such a thing about neighbors who'd decided to stand with the Union, but how could anyone wish ill on hard-working people like the Malones? As for considering them her enemies, she didn't think she could.

Maybe she'd feel differently if Walker or someone else she cared for had been hurt.

She hadn't witnessed the scene in town when news came that some of the local boys had been wounded, but she'd heard about it from Serena Ellerbe. Serena's beau had fought at Boonville, too. Unlike Sheriff Green and Asa James's brothers, William Dunn escaped the battle without injury. William would have a chance for "greater glory." That was how Serena put it when she talked about it. It was, in fact, how many of the men talked about the upcoming battles. Fighting was a matter of honor. Not just a duty, but a privilege. Libbie didn't understand the way they felt. Sometimes, the glittering fervor with which they spoke of fighting frightened her. Especially when she wondered if men on the other side of things felt the same way. Did the two standing here with her right now feel just as passionately about keeping the thirty-four states united under one flag as Walker and the Wildwood Guard felt about being part of an independent Confederacy? Best not to think too much about that right now.

Libbie focused once again on the Malones. "It's good that your sister knows you're all right. As to what happened on your farm, I am sad to say that I doubt you'll be able to count on Sheriff Green to do much about finding whoever did all the damage. He's resigned to join the Guard."

"We heard," Malone said. "To tell the truth, I wouldn't have expected him to do much anyway. After all, we're Irish."

Libbie tried to suppress a sigh. Yes. She knew. As far as Walker was concerned, in the hierarchy of humanity, the Irish were barely above the Negroes—and only because they had white skin. She imagined Isham Green shared Walker's opinion on the matter. "The sheriff's *Major* Green now." She looked from Malone to the sergeant and back again. "I suppose that's why you're here. The Guard." Malone didn't answer. He didn't have to. With a little nod, Libbie asked again, "So. What are you goin' to do with me?"

"That depends," Malone said. "What are you 'goin' to do' about *us*?"

Libbie considered. She wasn't inclined to raise the alarm. The Malones were good people.

At the sound of a steamboat whistle screeching its approach, Libbie started. Time was passing. "If I don't get back to the house, Walker *will* send someone after me. As it is, I'm not supposed to be out ridin'. He'll have my hide." She gazed up toward the top of the ridge. "He knows this place. Knows I like to come here."

Something flickered in Jack Malone's blue eyes. He was looking at the bruises on her face. "You mean he'll hurt you. Again."

A combination of the look on his face and the tone of voice made Libbie tremble—for Walker. She lifted her chin and forced conviction into her voice as she said, "He won't. Not ever again." Just saying the words made her feel stronger. Not brave yet...but getting there. "Before you ask for more information, I'll tell you truly that I have made it my considered duty to mind my own business when it comes to my brother's affairs. I already told you all I know about the military. I saw earthworks along the road as Pilot and I came this way." She took a deep breath. "And so I ask again, what are you two gentlemen goin' to do with me?"

When Malone's gaze flicked to the other soldier and then down to the river, Libbie realized that the stranger was the problem. Jack Malone might trust her to keep the peace, but the sergeant never would. She looked over at him. "I don't suppose you'd do me the honor of introducin' yourself."

"No ma'am. You already know more than you should."

Libbie sighed. "Well, what amazin' bit of information do you think I might reveal? Even if I said anything, all I could say was I saw a couple of raggedy-lookin' men camped by the river. Deserters, to my way of thinking. How's that gonna do anybody any good?" She tilted her head. Studied the stranger's handsome face. "The truth is, there's somethin' familiar about you. As if I've seen you before." She waved the thought away as if it were a pesky fly. "No matter."

She looked off toward the river. Toward the landing. And just like that, she knew what to do. She gave the sergeant the most charming smile she could muster. "I'll ride with you gentlemen a ways. Far enough and long enough that even if I did raise the alarm, you'd be long gone. Why, you can even lead Pilot until you decide to let me go." She reached into her pocket and pulled out a white handkerchief. "Here. Gag me so I can't holler."

Jack Malone spoke up. "You won't holler." Doubt flickered. "Will you?"

"If I was inclined to holler, don't you think I would-a done it?" The soldier who wouldn't tell her his name still looked doubtful. Libbie waved the white handkerchief at Malone. "Your friend doesn't believe me." She turned around so that he could tie the gag in place. "Go ahead," she said. "I'm waitin'."

Malone touched her shoulder and turned her back around. "Just don't try to run for it," he said, and smiled. "It wouldn't do you any good anyway. Sergeant Coulter's a first-class rider, and that horse of his—"

"Don't I know it," Libbie said. "That big fellah could likely give Pilot a run for his money." She looked at the blue-eyed sergeant.

He said nothing. Instead, in one fluid movement, he mounted the gray horse. So. The man with the fine horse was also a fine horseman. When he nudged his gray horse close enough to reach Pilot's reins, the two horses snorted and made a show, but Coulter wasn't rattled. He simply grabbed Pilot's reins and waited for the two geldings to make peace.

When Malone laced his fingers together to make a platform to boost her into the saddle, Libbie hesitated. "I don't want to hurt that bandaged hand." Malone took her hesitation for permission to pick her up, and before she quite knew what had happened, he'd lifted her into the saddle. She clutched Pilot's mane as Coulter nudged his horse toward the trail that would take them away from Wildwood Grove.

Pilot tried to resist, but when Libbie urged him forward, he settled down and followed the big gray gelding. She glanced behind her just as Jack Malone mounted the bay. It was clear that that horse and rider weren't used to each other. Thinking about Malone's poor horsemanship reminded her of the fine team of Belgians the family owned—the ones Walker had tried and failed to buy.

What would Walker think if he could see her letting herself be led along the river between Sergeant Coulter and Jack Malone? What would he call her if he knew she'd been the one to suggest a brief "kidnapping"? The thought made her shudder. He'd call her a traitor, or worse. But as Libbie and the two Yankees made their way along the trail, Libbie realized that she didn't feel like a traitor. She felt like a woman who was beginning to find her way to her own ideas about honor and duty, loyalty and strength.

As the three horses picked their way along the river's edge, Libbie thought back to the night she'd heard more about Maggie Malone's encounter with the bushwhackers. Miss Malone had to be a brave woman to have defended her uncle the way she did. It had been the talk of the dinner table one evening right after it happened. Walker's friends had said some very unkind things about "a woman who behaved in such a manner," but Libbie knew that while they might be horrified on the surface, they were flat out amazed by what Miss Malone had done that day. They'd be even more amazed if they knew about Miss Malone's having set out into a battle zone in search of her brothers. Where did a woman get that kind of courage? Libbie supposed it came from having to do things for oneself—having to depend on oneself.

What would that be like? Libbie had always had either parents or Walker to take care of her. Or servants. And then it hit her. The servants! What would happen to Ora Lee and Annabelle and the rest of the slaves if—no, not if—*when* war came to Wildwood Grove? They'd be defenseless, unless they ran. Maybe even then. With war all around, where would a slave go? She twisted about in her saddle. Jack Malone nudged his bay and came up alongside Pilot.

"What is it?"

"I was just thinkin'. If you're coming to fight the Guard, what'll happen to the Negroes?"

The sergeant reined his gray horse around. "We're not having a tea party here, and you need to keep your voice down. And for the record, no one's received orders to fight the men camped on your plantation."

Libbie snorted. "First of all, no one in the Guard is hidin' in these woods. I happen to know they're plannin' to start patrolling tomorrow, so as long as I don't scream to high heaven, y'all are safe. As to fightin', there's earthworks along the road. I'm no fool. Someone's expecting a fight." She paused. "Which is a special cause for concern for me as the mistress of the plantation. Walker will never let Negroes have weapons." She glared at the sergeant. "I don't suppose the Yankees will, either, will they?"

The sergeant was quiet for a moment. Finally, he asked, "How many slaves are you talking about—not in the county, just at Wildwood Grove?"

Maybe he was just trying to do more spying, but for that moment Libbie cared more about Ora Lee and Annabelle, Malachi and Robert, Betty and Cooper—and the others— than she did about anything else. "Twenty down in the quarters and six at the house." She paused. Tilted her head. "Malachi and Annabelle—that's our driver and the cook—I suppose they'd be safe if I sent them into town. They have family there, who work for the doctor."

"You mean Dix and Sally?" Malone sounded surprised.

"You didn't know? Dix bought himself and Sally from the Ellerbes. He's tried to get Malachi and Annabelle away from the Grove—Annabelle and Sally are sisters—but Walker won't hear of it." Her voice wavered. She touched the side of her face. "Walker doesn't let his possessions go. Not as long as they can do him any good."

There was an awkward silence, and then Malone said, "It's never been truly safe for anyone to harbor runaways, but right now, with things the way they are, it'd be even worse for free Negroes if they were caught doing such a thing. If you send anyone to Dix and Sally, they'll all have to run for their lives."

Of course that made sense, but it didn't solve the matter of how to keep the Wildwood Grove slaves safe in the midst of a battle right here in Lafayette County. Libbie glanced over at the sergeant. "If I wanted to protect my people, how long do you think I'd have to figure a way to do it?" The sergeant looked at Malone. Libbie might not be raising the alarm, but the two Yankees weren't about to trust her with any more information. And who could blame them?

"Y'all aren't goin' ta answer that. Don't reckon I blame you." Libbie smiled. "If it's all the same to you two gentlemen, I think we're far enough away now that you might let me go. Even if I was inclined to raise the alarm—which I am not, although I don't expect you'll believe that—you'd be clean into the next county and then some before anyone could give chase."

Chapter 14

The sergeant and Jack Malone had taken cover in a stand of pines just as Libbie rode away. She could feel them watching her as she cued Pilot into a canter and headed home. She spent much of the ride back to the stable practicing the story she would tell to explain the bruising and swelling about her eye. Once she had that ready, she moved on to the problem of the slaves. What would happen to them when the Yankees came? *What will happen to me?* For all the drilling and target practice that had been going on in recent days, she hadn't really considered what it all might mean for her beyond... something different. She was presiding over more meals and Sheriff—*Major* Green was ever about, but beyond that... what would happen to her? She'd thought of the war and battles in the sense of something that happened somewhere else. To someone else. But now...she pulled Pilot up, and as he stood in the road, she tried to imagine the landscape around her. How would it change? What did a battle do to fields of hemp and hedgerows, to houses and barns?

She thought of the Malones' farm—the empty house, the ruined garden. That wouldn't happen to Wildwood Grove—would it? Swallowing, she turned about and looked behind her. An army might soon be marching up that road; an army bent on forcing every man in the Wildwood Guard to surrender; an army willing to kill the ones who refused.

Libbie had known fear before. She'd been afraid when the steamboat that brought her to live with Walker landed and she made her way across the gangplank and up the levee. She'd been afraid the first time she performed her duties as Walker's hostess. And she was always afraid of his anger. But this new fear was something else. Forces beyond her control were coming to attack the way of life that had sustained her since the day she was born. *Neighbors* were willing to fight to destroy it. To kill Walker, and Isham Green, and every man who had smiled at her in recent days. *Will they be willing... will they want...to kill me?* Cold fear and dread washed over her as she wondered.

She hadn't been afraid once she realized the men at the spring were Jack Malone and a friend. Her appearance had been a problem for them, but they'd been kind. After those first few seconds when the sergeant was afraid she might scream, she hadn't felt threatened or in danger. But now, as she thought about what they were after and what they would do with what they learned, she shivered at the idea of how things might have gone if it had been two other Yankee soldiers spying.

Libbie was less than a mile from the stable at home when a white horse appeared on the road up ahead. When Isham Green caught sight of her, he slowed his horse to a walk and waited for her to come alongside. Libbie slowed Pilot to a walk and called out to him. "Is the service already over, then?"

"Long since," Green said. His expression changed when she got close enough for him to see her bruised face. "What's happened? Walker said you were indisposed." He frowned. "You shouldn't have taken the horse out alone."

Libbie did her best to sound lighthearted as she said, "Nothing's really hurt but my pride." She told the well-rehearsed story about Pilot's shying and nearly unseating her, hoping God would forgive the lie. "I was feeling a bit peaked earlier, but I just couldn't stand being cooped up in that house one more second. Which leads me to a question I been ponderin'. Is there any chance you'd drive me over to the Ellerbes' after lunch? I want to plan something special for the Guard. A social—maybe a calico ball. Would you be willing to help?"

Doubt and displeasure gave way to a smile. The major gave a little bow. "I would be truly honored, Miss Libbie."

"I knew I could count on you, Major Green." Libbie batted her eyelashes at him. "Now if you'll only be my gallant defender in the matter of Walker. Sometimes I don't think he remembers what it was like to be young. But you know how desperately I love riding. This morning when I woke up, I was feeling so blue I didn't even want to come down to breakfast. But then I thought that maybe if I took the air—I know it was impetuous, but I just up and did it. Will you be my savior and help me make Walker understand?"

Green was lapping it up, preening with every compliment. And so Libbie kept talking, barely giving the sheriff a chance to speak until finally, they were back at the stables. The major had just helped Libbie dismount when Walker strode up with an expression on his face that made her tremble. Thankfully, Isham spoke for her.

"Here she is, safe and sound, just as I predicted—although she's had a little mishap."

Libbie picked up where the sheriff had left off. "Now, I know what you're gonna say, Walker, but Pilot didn't mean it. A gopher or some other creature darted out onto the road. When Pilot shied, I just wasn't ready for it. I lost my seat— just for an instant, mind you—and Pilot's head came up and mine went down and—well—" She turned her head to the side, making a show of displaying the result. "As you can see, I suffered the brunt of it. Who would have thought a horse's head was that hard?"

Walker stepped right into the role. "I suppose I must forgive you for the worry you've caused us, now that you're safe at home." Malachi walked up from the direction of the kitchen, and Walker ordered him to tend Pilot before saying to Libbie, "But you must come inside now. We have important things to discuss." He took a step toward the house. When Libbie hesitated, he looked back. "I said come along inside, Elizabeth."

Libbie stood her ground. "I'll be there directly. First, though, I'm gonna help Malachi see to Pilot." She reached up and tugged on the horse's dark mane. "Just so he knows there's no hard feelin's about the bruises."

Walker studied her face. She met his gaze and held it for a long, tense moment. Finally, he relented. With a shrug he muttered, "Suit yourself," and retreated toward the house.

A thrill of victory surged through her for a moment. And then, her courage wavered. A shiver crept up her spine. Sweat broke out on her forehead. Had she really just defied Walker, in front of Isham Green and Malachi? What price would she pay later? She closed her eyes, remembering what she'd said to Jack Malone. *Never again.* Malachi led Pilot away without a word.

Libbie reached in her pocket and dabbed at her forehead with the white handkerchief—smiling at the memory of how she'd offered it to Jack Malone and how he'd waved it away. *You won't raise the alarm—will you?* She looked about her at the house, the kitchen, the gardens. Why hadn't she hollered? And just now—why hadn't she told Walker about the Federals? She wasn't sure.

Pilot whickered and Libbie turned about. Malachi had

already hitched him to the ring just outside his stall and was carrying the saddle into the tack room. Libbie followed him through the door. Hanging her riding crop on a hook, she grabbed up the bucket of grooming tools and carried it to where Pilot waited in the passageway. While Malachi worked with the hoof pick, Libbie brushed the chestnut's coat until it gleamed.

∞

Maggie was sitting beside Fish's wagon stitching up what felt like the hundredth rip in the hundredth soldier's uniform when Hero lifted his head and growled. She glanced up at Seamus and smiled, and he settled beside her—away from the dog.

"The mutt's feelin' better, I see," Seamus said. He nodded at the shirt in her lap. "You're becoming somethin' of a darlin' to the troops, Maggie-girl. In less than two weeks you've got them calling you 'Miss Maggie' to your face and 'our warrior-seamstress' behind your back."

Maggie snorted as she took a backstitch and then overcast the seam to reinforce it. "What nonsense."

Seamus reached over to tug on the brim of her forage cap. "It's not nonsense. A man might well have gotten a promotion for supplying his brothers with cartridges the way you did when those rebels attacked the wagon train."

"The boys just like having a seamstress at their beck and call."

"They're all 'the boys' now, are they?"

"Not all," Maggie said and patted the pile of shirts on the ground beside her, thinking of a few soldiers she made it her business to avoid as much as possible. "Besides, there's only so much daylight for mending. It won't be long and some of 'em will be disappointed in my ability to stitch or cook or something I haven't even thought about yet that might be of use but that I just don't have enough time to do."

Seamus grinned. "If word gets around that you know how to clean a gun, you'll be in real trouble." He nodded at the pile of mending. "As for that, you could refuse, ya know."

"Why would I refuse? I don't really mind." Maggie looked out over the men lounging about campfires reading, playing cards, or napping. "Any one of their mothers or sisters or wives would do the same if only they could be here."

"Not many would care to be here," Seamus said, and he nudged her arm. "You were raised to cope with a quartet of scurvy dogs," he teased. "What's a hundred more? Not many women who could sleep on the ground and eat hardtack day in and day out and not complain."

"As it happens, I've been hearing stories to the contrary," Maggie said. "Even Captain Quinn admits to knowing of women traveling with this or that regiment—good women, not the other kind. They work as laundresses and such. And according to Fish, there was a tradition in Napoleon's army— I can't say the French word for them, but they were regular members of the regiment. They carried the colors on parade, tended the men after battle—they even had uniforms that matched their soldiers."

Seamus sputtered disbelief about the uniforms.

"Don't be daft," Maggie said. "Fish says they dressed like ladies in every way—although some of 'em shortened their hems a bit to make it easier to move about. But them that did such wore trousers beneath. They weren't flashin' their ankles like a bunch of heathen strumpets."

Seamus was quiet for a moment. When he finally spoke, it was to comment on the idea of a woman in uniform. "You're about there, Maggie-girl, what with the forage cap and the blue cape."

"I won't be donning trousers anytime soon, Seamus Malone. But I won't deny being glad to hear that the boys don't see my presence as a burden."

"From what I know, most will be sad to see you go."

Maggie concentrated on taking the last few stitches, knotted the thread, and snipped it off. Truth be told, she didn't really want to think about it herself. Careful to tuck her needle away in the roll-up sewing kit the soldiers called a "housewife," she folded the shirt and sat back. "Dr. Feeny told me that you would all be spending more time in camp than actually fighting. I thought he was telling tales by way of keeping me from worrying. Fish said something to that effect the first night I was here. I thought he was trying to make me feel better, too, but—"

"Fish likes you, but he wouldn't lie just to make you feel better." Seamus grinned. "Besides, he says you're a better soldier than some of the men who've volunteered."

"Just what a woman wants to hear." Maggie laughed.

"It's a compliment and not one to be taken lightly. According to Captain Quinn, Monsieur-with-the-name-longer-than-my-arm is descended from a long line of warriors. 'Tis no small thing to impress Fish."

Maggie only shrugged. She liked the idea of being in the quartermaster's good graces, but to have a man admire her because she was good at manly things—she wasn't sure how she felt about that.

Seamus scratched at his patchy beard. "I'm glad you haven't been terrified every moment you've been with us," he said, and then gave a low laugh. "Do you realize that, when it comes right down to it, you've been in battle longer than either Jack or me?"

Maggie snorted in disbelief.

"'Tis true. From what you said about that day at the farm, that was more of a fight than Boonville. From first shot to last, we were only in it for about twenty minutes. I barely had a chance to fire my weapon."

"I'd think you'd be grateful."

"Oh, I am. It's just—I didn't volunteer to sit around a campfire playing my fife and honing my chess game. All the waiting makes for long days and longer nights. A man starts to worry that he's missing the best of the action."

"And again I say, it isn't easy being the one who gets left behind, is it?"

"It isn't easy bein' 'not Jack,' either."

"What are you talking about—'not Jack'?"

Seamus sighed. "It's nothing. I just—I thought soldiering would be my chance."

"Your chance for what?"

"To find something in the whole of God's wide world that I might do better than Jack."

Maggie frowned. "You do many things better than Jack."

"Really? Name something." When Maggie was quiet, he nodded. "That's all right. I didn't expect an answer. Don't misunderstand. I love my brother. It's just—he casts a big shadow. I thought the army might give me a way out from under it." He shrugged. "I should have known better. Jack's the best shot. The fastest runner. The one Sergeant Coulter wants doing reconnaissance with him. The hero everyone looks up to." At the sound of his name, Hero lifted his head and looked over at Seamus, who chuckled and pulled his fife out of the fringed leather bag hanging from his belt. "I'm sorry. I sound like a regular fool, whinin' about me own brother."

Maggie reached over and tapped the fife. "Jack may well be all those things you just said, but he has no music in him. He'd never have thought to give me that fire grate you had the blacksmith make for my Christmas that year."

"He said it was a terrible gift," Seamus muttered. "'You never make a gift of something connected to a woman's work,'" he said.

Maggie nudged his shoulder again. "Don't you know what his making fun means?"

"It means exactly what he said," Seamus muttered. "That I don't know a thing about women."

Maggie shook her head. "Not at all. It means that you, Seamus Malone, think of ways to make life better for the people you love. It means that you take the time to notice things Jack doesn't. Any man can wander into a mercantile and buy a gift. *You* cared enough to do something special. And the woman who is blessed enough to share your life one day will thank the Lord for that part of you."

Seamus grunted his disbelief. "That's kind of you to say, but Jack's the better man when it comes to the ladies, too. Bridget Feeny thinks he lifts the sun above the horizon every morning."

Maggie looked over at him. For a moment she studied his expression. When he raised the pipe to his lips to play, she grabbed his arm. "Seamus Malone. Have you been pining for Bridget while she pines after Jack?" Seamus shrugged. Maggie sputtered, "Jack has no more interest in Bridget Feeny than Hero has in playing your fife. He teases her, is all."

"And she blushes and hangs on his every word."

"Have you ever once let her know how you feel?"

"When would I ever get the chance to do that, with Jack about all the time?"

Maggie got to her feet. "Wait right there. I'm going to take this shirt to Private Murphy. After that, I'm going to find the quartermaster, and when I get back, I'll have an answer to that question. And you'd better still be sitting right here." She looked at Hero. "See that he stays put."

Maggie bustled off. Once she'd given Private Murphy his newly mended shirt, she sought out Fish. "Where might I find a sheaf of paper?"

"Writin' a love letter?" The unwelcome question came from just past a supply wagon, where a half-dozen soldiers were playing a card game—and not a particularly friendly one, from the stack of coins in the center of the game.

Fish scolded the soldier who'd spoken. "I'll thank you to show respect for the lady." He thought for a moment, then shook his head. "I sincerely regret, mademoiselle, that I do not—"

"I can get you some." Noah ducked out from beneath the wagon.

With a stream of French that Maggie didn't understand, Fish scolded the boy, who responded as if he'd understood every word. "You don't have to yell, mon-sir. I wasn't eavesdropping. I was sitting right here under this wagon having a perfectly good nap when you yelled at Private O'Malley and woke me up." He grinned at Maggie. "I can get paper. You need a pencil, too? What about an envelope and a stamp?"

Fish shook his head. "He is impossible, zis boy."

"How much?" Maggie asked.

"I can get you everything you need for a nickel." Noah looked up at Fish. "And I ain't gonna steal it, so don't ask. I'll pay for it, soon as Miss Maggie pays me."

Fish glowered at him. "And how much profit will you make from the transaction?"

Noah grinned. "What's it matter, as long as all parties are happy?" He trotted away.

Fish shook his head. "That boy."

Maggie smiled. "Have you been able to learn anything about him?"

Fish pursed his lips. "Sometimes, when he sleeps…he dreams. And he cries. There is water. He calls for his *maman* to 'hang on.'" He sighed. "She must not have done so." He paused, thinking. "He never speaks of his father. Perhaps he does not know who he was." Again, he sighed. But then he said, "I think it is why Sergeant Coulter takes ze boy under his wing and pleads his case with the captain."

"He—what?"

Fish leaned close and, with a conspiratorial smile said, "The sergeant is a very good man. He says to our captain that he knows something of the life this boy has had, and he wishes to see better things for him."

"B-But," Maggie said, frowning. "Haven't I heard the sergeant tell Noah he can't stay with the army?"

Fish shrugged. "Perhaps. And it might have been so, until the sergeant offers to pay for the boy's rations, if only the captain will let him remain with the Irish." He lowered his voice. "Of course, he does not want others to know. Not even the boy himself."

"But you're telling me," Maggie said.

"*Oui.*" Fish nodded. "This is because you are not just 'anyone,' mademoiselle."

Maggie didn't quite know what to make of it. "Well…the secret's safe with me."

"As I knew it would be," Fish said. "And now you know a

little bit more about what a fine man is Sergeant *Jean* Coulter, eh?" And he winked.

Thankfully, Noah trotted up and, with a little flourish, presented Maggie with a sheaf of paper. It was folded in half with a stamped envelope tucked inside. The boy pulled a freshly sharpened pencil from where he'd had it tucked over his left ear. "Five cents, please. I promised the original owner I'd pay him right away." He leaned close. "He's losing badly at dominoes on the far side of the camp."

"How does a man lose money playing dominoes?" Maggie would never understand the passion with which soldiers gambled. Noah looked over at Fish, and they both laughed. "Never mind," Maggie groused. "Come with me and I'll get your nickel." They crossed the camp. At the sight of Noah, Hero wagged his tail and gave a little yip of welcome.

"That dog likes everyone but me," Seamus said.

"Not true," Maggie said. She dug a coin out of Paddy's battered leather satchel and paid Noah, who scampered off. "But Noah pulled him to safety beneath the wagon the other day." She bent down to scratch the dog behind the ears. "He never forgets a favor." She looked over at Seamus and smiled. "Now that I think about it, Hero only *objects* to you. He *hates* Jack. So there's something else you're better at, 'not Jack.'"

Seamus smirked. He looked over at Hero. "You hate me less than you hate Jack. Do I have that right?" The dog chuffed. Seamus laughed.

Maggie handed him the paper and the pencil. "And here's something else you're about to be better at than your big brother."

"Writing? Writing what?"

"Not what. Who."

"Who am I writing to?"

Maggie sighed. "If you don't know the answer to that, Seamus Malone, you deserve to die a lonely old man."

Both eyebrows went up as Seamus realized what Maggie was suggesting. "You think she'll answer?"

"There's only one way to discover the answer to that question, boy-o." She settled beside him and reached for another shirt waiting to be mended. "Personally, I don't think she'll be able to resist. Not if you write even a wee bit of the music that's in your heart."

Seamus positioned the paper on his knee. *Dear*—he hesitated. Looked over at Maggie. "Music, you say?"

Maggie smiled. "There's not a woman in the land who wouldn't like to be serenaded by a handsome man."

Seamus added *e-s-t* to the first word.

Maggie pretended to concentrate on threading a needle while she stole a peek at the letter. She smiled. *Dearest Bridget*... The boy had music in his heart, all right.

Chapter 15

———— ❧ ————

At midday on the eighth day after Jack and Sergeant John Coulter had ridden out of camp—not that she was counting—Maggie had followed a limping Hero to the edge of the woods to do his business when a flash of gray made her look up. Sergeant Coulter astride Blue. The horse was moving toward her at an easy lope, and when Coulter saw Maggie, he raised his hand in greeting, almost as if he was looking for her.

To hide the fact that she was blushing, Maggie turned away and scolded Hero. "I'm not taking a stroll for my health. Get on with it." The dog sat down, whined, and lifted his bandaged paw. "You're a pathetic little beggar. You'll want to get out of the wagon not fifty feet up the road." With a sigh of frustration, she turned about and nearly plowed into the sergeant—made more disconcerting than ever because she wasn't quite used to being that close to a man who was that much taller than her. It made her feel...womanly. Until, that is, Coulter muttered *whoa, there*—as if she were a horse.

"Captain Quinn sent me to explain what's happened so you wouldn't worry about Jack as soon as you saw me. It's only me back with Company D, but Jack's fine. We split up so that I could head back here to report what we've learned. Jack was going to do some more looking about in Littleton."

Maggie nodded. "Thank you." And then she frowned, because the column was coming to a halt. "What's happening?"

"Colonel Kelley has ordered us to make camp while he relays information to General Fremont in St. Louis. We're to stay put until he receives new orders."

New orders. "Rumors have been flying," Maggie said. "I know not to believe them all, but it's only logical that Jackson's army in the south would be growing. Whatever the exact numbers, it has to be thousands."

Coulter nodded. "Between five and ten thousand, according to what I just heard."

The idea that he trusted her with news he'd just received in a meeting with the command was gratifying—but the news itself terrified her. "But if there's only the Irish to face them…how many are we? Surely not nearly so many." She barely managed to stifle a horrified shudder.

"Colonel Sigel's regiment has been sent out from St. Louis."

A regiment. Another thousand men. Still not enough. If they were forced into a confrontation, Maggie couldn't think of any way her boys could win. She couldn't—wouldn't—allow herself to imagine the aftermath of such a battle. *And in the aftermath, who would care for them?* To mask her fear, she went to Hero and crouched down to pet him.

The sergeant followed suit. His voice was gentle as he said, "Don't be afraid. We'll be in camp at least until Jack reports in. Then there will be more relaying of messages back and forth. Don't borrow tomorrow's troubles."

Maggie forced a smile as she stood back up. "You sounded a bit like Private Ashby there at the last."

"Ashby quotes the Bible?"

"That he does," Maggie said. "Carries a prayer book in his breast pocket. He doesn't read it. I don't think he needs to read it. Seems to have it memorized."

"The few phrases I remember," Coulter said, "are remnants of Sabbath School training. My grandparents were quite devout."

"I never knew mine," Maggie said. "Nor my Mam, who died when I was just a wee child, may the good Lord rest her soul."

"I didn't really know my father. But my grandparents were good people. Very good people."

Was he avoiding mention of his mother? "At least you have your uncle," Maggie said. "I imagine you've heard about our Uncle Paddy from the boys."

Coulter ignored the mention of his uncle. "Anyone who heard you talk about your family would think you were at least a dozen years older than Jack and Seamus. The way you call them 'boys'—the way you mother them."

Maggie shrugged. "I haven't really thought about it. 'Twas only natural for me to step into the role, I suppose." She hesitated. "As it happens, I'm the youngest of us three." She looked down at her hands. "But I see why you wouldn't think it." Feeling self-conscious, she reached down for Hero and swept him into her arms.

"The youngest," Coulter murmured as he reached out to pat Hero on the head. "Well, you certainly don't act it—and I mean that as a compliment." He smiled. "I think I missed a great blessing by not having a sister."

He was standing so close. So very close. She laughed and made a joke. "There's been times over the years when you could have easily had one. Me brothers would have gladly given me away more times than I care to admit." She glanced off in the direction of home. "Jack went into Littleton, then?"

"We decided he was the best choice. Blue's faster than the

bay Jack was riding, so I could get back here faster. And Jack knows the people in town. I doubt there's anyone still there who'd remember me. They'll be more likely to trust Jack with information." He touched her arm. "I'll carry Hero back to Fish's wagon for you, if you'll lead Blue for me." He didn't wait for Maggie to respond, just handed her the reins, and reached for the dog.

Maggie walked beside him, wondering what painful truths lay behind Colt's reluctance to speak of his uncle—or to even mention his own mother. When they got to Fish's wagon, Maggie pulled the burlap bed out from beneath the wagon seat and settled it just beneath the wagon. As Colt bent to set the dog down, she said, "So you discovered troops at Wildwood Grove, after all."

Colt made a show of smoothing Hero's bed before standing up. Still, he took a moment to answer. "Why would you think such a thing?"

She patted Blue's neck as she said, "Well, something inspired a fast ride back here to report, while Jack stayed behind. And now we've been ordered to hold our position in the middle of nowhere, while the command considers what's to be done. The most obvious reason would be that you found an unexpected number of Confederates in or around Littleton 'fixin' to fight,'" as our Southern neighbors would put it."

Colt was quiet for a moment. Finally, he gave a low laugh. "That's some powerful deducing, Miss Maggie."

Maggie looked up at him, studying his grim expression, trying to read it. Colt took Blue's reins back in hand. And yet, he lingered.

She made another mental leap. "Captain Quinn doesn't need to worry about me. You can tell him—" She broke off. "Never mind. I'll tell him myself, next time I see him. It was thoughtful of him to send you to tell me why Jack wasn't with you. It was a kindness I won't forget."

Colt took his hat off, held it in the same hand as Blue's reins, and raked his fingers through his long, blond hair. "Well, actually...it was my idea to come looking for you—although if I'd given him a minute, I'm sure Captain Quinn would have thought of it. He likes you. Apart from what you've done for Hero, I mean. He says you've been good for morale."

Maggie allowed a little smile. "That's very nice to hear. I hope he knows that if there's to be a fight before I can find my way home, he doesn't have to worry about me. I'll do what I'm told, and afterwards, I'll help. I'll carry water, wrap bandages." She touched the sleeve that covered the place where he'd been wounded. "You know I can manage it."

Again, that smile. And something in those blue eyes that made her feel—strange. "I suspect, Miss Maggie, that you could manage anything you put your mind to. And I'm fairly certain that not only Captain Quinn but also every man in this brigade knows it."

He'd called her *Miss Maggie* twice now. Did he realize how it made her feel to hear her given name spoken with such—well, not tenderness, of course. But something more than courtesy. At least it seemed that way to her. Then again, what did she know of such things? She sputtered disbelief. "There's no need to flatter me, John Coulter."

"It isn't flattery. Both the colonel and the captain have heard half a dozen versions of what happened in that skirmish when I brought those Henrys into camp. Every single version has one thing in common—an extraordinary woman who kept her head and did the very thing that was most needed at the exact moment it was needed—at great risk to her own life."

Blue shook his head. When Colt put his hand on the horse's neck, Blue whickered and stamped his foot. Colt chuckled. "All right, old man. You've been patient, and now I'll give you the attention you deserve." He smiled at Maggie. "May I call on you this evening, Miss Maggie?" He leaned close. "Noah tells me he's come into some honest-to-goodness coffee instead of that roasted barley we've had lately, and there's another rumor in camp that you make the best coffee in the state."

Maggie smiled. "If Noah really does have coffee, you're welcome to share it—as long as he approves, of course."

"I'll convince him," Colt said.

"I can't imagine where he would have found coffee. We're miles from the nearest town."

Colt chuckled as he mounted Blue. Once in the saddle, he said, "I think that when it comes to young Noah, it's probably best not to ask too many questions." Before he rode away, though, he asked, "Is it all right, then, my calling you *Miss Maggie?*"

"That's my name."

He nodded. "All right, then." He put his hat on. "And I'm *John*," he said. "Or *Colt*, if you prefer." When Maggie didn't respond, he chuckled. "Just think about it, Miss Maggie. Please. And I'll be around for coffee later."

⁓

As soon as Maggie had gathered wood and started a campfire, Noah walked up, talking about how much he was looking forward to "a nice cup of coffee and a good cigar."

Maggie thought he was joking about the cigar until the boy pulled one out of the inside pocket of his stained vest. "Give me that," Maggie ordered, and held out her hand.

"Why should I?"

"Because some things are not meant for boys of a certain age."

"What age is that?"

"Whatever age you are," Maggie said.

"What if I don't know—exactly?"

"Doesn't matter," Maggie said. "You're exactly too young to be smoking cigars."

Noah handed the cigar over. "You'll keep it for me—until I can sell it?"

"I won't destroy it."

A slow smile spread across the boy's face. The missing-tooth smile that never failed to weaken Maggie's resolve to be strict with the boy. "*You* could buy it," he said, "and give it to Sergeant Coulter when he comes for coffee later."

"I don't even know if he smokes," Maggie said. Why would the boy think she'd have any interest in giving John Coulter a gift? Not something she would ask aloud, for fear of the answer.

"Well, of course he smokes. Every self-respecting officer smokes. Or chews. Or takes snuff. Or something." He paused, twisting his mouth up as if it hurt him to think. "Could be he'd prefer a pipe, though."

Maggie changed the subject. "Where's this amazing coffee you've been boasting about?"

Noah made a show of walking over to Fish's wagon, reaching over the side, and pulling out a small brown bag, which he rattled. "Just waiting for your magic touch, Miss Maggie." He took a deep breath. "Can I ply my wares while you roast the beans?"

"Can you what?"

"Sell the cigar. Or at least try."

"Look at me, Noah."

"Ma'am?"

"Look me in the eye." Finally, Noah met her gaze. "Promise me that you will not smoke this cigar."

"Why would I? I can prob'ly get a dime for it. I'm saving up."

"For what?"

Noah shrugged. He looked away. "Something good."

With a sigh, Maggie handed him the cigar. "Keep your promise."

"Didn't promise, exactly. But I ain't gonna smoke it. Smoking makes me sick." He grinned. "Be back for coffee."

Maggie didn't want to know how the boy had learned that smoking didn't agree with him. For the next few minutes, she busied herself roasting coffee beans over a campfire. She'd just taken the whole beans off the fire when Colt walked up, coffee grinder in hand.

"Courtesy of Captain Quinn," he said. "With one caveat. We have to save him a cup. He'll be along directly." He settled comfortably by the campfire, and patted the ground beside him. "Come sit here, Miss Maggie. I've permission to tell you everything Jack and I discovered. With the understanding, of course, that you won't encourage any of the gossip flying through the camp." He held the coffee grinder out to her. "I assured him that you are about the farthest thing from a gossip I've ever seen in the female contingent."

"Thank you. I think." Maggie poured beans into the grinder, braced it against her hipbone, and began to turn the crank.

Colt closed his eyes and inhaled. "I'd say we're in for some great coffee." He waited until Maggie had settled the coffeepot over the coals and sat down beside him before proceeding. "We counted at least three hundred camped at the plantation. We didn't see any artillery, but that doesn't mean they aren't at this very minute rolling a couple of 12-pounders up from that levee. Based on some things Miss Blair said, we're suspecting—"

Maggie interrupted him. "Miss Blair?"

Colt nodded, and told her a fantastical story about how he and Jack had been hidden at an overhang near a spring when Miss Blair found them.

"And she didn't raise the alarm?"

Colt shook his head. "Quite the opposite. She actually suggested we kidnap her." He described how Jack had lifted her into the saddle and then he'd taken the horse's reins and led them all away from Wildwood Grove, with Miss Blair and her horse between him and Jack.

"She said there'd been plenty of steamboat landings in recent days. More than usual. She hadn't really paid all that much attention to the numbers or the details, so for all we know, more than one shipment has gotten through since we intercepted the Henrys on the *McDowell*. There could even be artillery hidden somewhere, just waiting to be rolled into place."

"And you trust what she said?" Maggie didn't recognize the emotion that flared up at the idea of John Coulter leading Miss Blair's horse along through the woods at first. When she did, she scolded herself. Jealousy was not only a sin but, in this case, patently ridiculous.

"We didn't have to trust her," Colt was saying. "It made sense that she wouldn't know about the arms. She said her brother has never wanted her to know his business." He frowned. "She had...bruising. A swollen eye." Colt brushed a hand across his left brow. "Jack thinks her brother did it."

"No!" Maggie said the word before she thought. After all, she might not like Walker Blair, but she didn't want to think he was *that* sort of man. She thought back to that day in the mercantile. Something between Miss Blair and her brother had made her uncomfortable, but she'd been too distracted by how Serena Ellerbe and the others had been laughing at her from behind their fans to pay much attention to it.

Colt was watching her. He tilted his head. "No," he said, "but...maybe?"

Maggie told him about that day in the mercantile. "It was barely a flicker of something. I told myself I was imagining things."

"She didn't admit it, so perhaps we all are."

"But you don't think so."

He shook his head. "She told us the officers of the Wildwood Guard have been staying at the plantation house, but that her brother has kept her very close to home. In fact, she claimed she hadn't realized they were digging earthworks until the day we saw her."

Maggie looked about them at the camp teeming with soldiers cleaning rifles, writing letters, drinking coffee, playing cards. What would it be like to be responsible for feeding a few hundred of them? She couldn't imagine. If Miss Blair could do that, there had to be more to her than a tiny waist and pretty gowns.

"It was actually her idea to ride with us," Colt said. "She suggested we keep her long enough that even if she did tell someone about us, they wouldn't be able to catch us."

Maggie didn't hide her surprise. "Is she a secret Yankee, or something?"

Colt chuckled. "I don't think so. I think she's like a lot of people who didn't see the war coming and then found themselves caught up in it."

Maggie could certainly understand that. "So you *did* trust her, after all."

Colt shrugged. "Maybe a little. We certainly weren't about to gag her. If she'd been inclined to raise the alarm, she would have done that right away. Still, Jack waited to head for Littleton until she was well out of sight and on her way back home—and he took…shall we say…an *indirect* route."

"I suspect I know the one," Maggie said. She sighed. "He'll come over the hill behind our place and get a panoramic view of the farm—what's left of it."

Colt looked over at her. "That bad?"

His sympathy made her throat constrict. She shrugged and stood up abruptly, but she told him about the scorched floor and the ruined garden—and everything else—as she made a show of checking on the coffee. She took up a rag to use as a hot pad, lifted the coffeepot off the fire, and leaning over, inhaled the aroma of the coffee. Finished talking, she concentrated on pouring it into the two waiting tin mugs, careful not to waste a drop. And as she returned the coffeepot to the coals to keep the contents warm, Colt bent down to take up the two coffee mugs. When he handed hers over, he held on to it until she'd looked up at him.

"I am so sorry, Maggie. So sorry you had to endure that—alone."

She didn't dare trust her voice, and so she merely nodded and held on to the mug until he let go. She swiped at the tear that had escaped. "Well, that's enough of that. Uncle Paddy is on the mend, and we'll deal with the farm when we must. Right now, all I have to deal with is whether or not this coffee passes muster." She waited for Colt to taste it.

He blew across the surface before taking a sip. "Jack

wished we'd taken you along. He thought you'd have made the perfect spy to send into Littleton."

Maggie shook her head. "I've never been any good at pretending. I say what I mean and I mean what I say."

"That's exactly what I told him," Colt said. "In fact, now that I think about it, if you'd been in Miss Blair's place, I don't think you'd have offered to let us kidnap you."

"It was a fairly smart thing to do—if she wasn't inclined to scream or faint."

Colt considered. "I don't think she's the fainting kind."

Again, the little bit of jealousy raised its ugly head.

"You aren't, either, of course," he said.

"So what do you think I'd have done?"

He laughed. "I think you would have pulled that pistol out of your pocket and made a run for it."

He was likely right. Maggie wondered if he thought that a good thing... or a manly thing. But she didn't ask. Instead, she sat down next to him, content to sip coffee and think about the Wildwood Guard and Littleton, steamboats and smuggled arms—all of it keeping the Irish in camp. Out of battle. *Safe*, at least for a few more days.

"Good coffee, Miss Maggie," Colt muttered.

Maggie nodded. "Thank you, Sergeant Coulter."

"Still Sergeant? Not... Colt, at least?"

They were treading far too close to a line that Maggie was wary of crossing. "Did the captain really say that I'm good for morale?"

"He did."

"That means a great deal, coming from a man who ordered you to haul me off to town that first day. I won't be inclined to do or say anything that would tempt him to change his mind." She cleared her throat. "Such as...behaving in a way that's a little too..."

"All right. I understand." He grinned. "I suppose I even respect it, Miss Malone."

"The boys call me *Miss Maggie*. No reason you shouldn't." She grinned at him. "They *don't* call you 'Colt.'"

He nodded. "Will you at least *think* 'Colt'?"

"I'll not be sharing my thoughts with you, Sergeant Coulter."

"And here I thought I was making progress." He settled back to drink his coffee.

Strangely enough, the silence that ensued didn't feel strained. Maggie and Colt—for she did think of him that way—sat in comfortable silence for a while, sipping coffee, wondering aloud at what was keeping Noah so long and hoping that Jack would bring useful information back from Littleton. Maggie said she was looking forward to hearing news from Paddy.

"See, now?" Colt teased. "You did share a thought, after all."

Maggie teased back. "Turnabout is fair play, Sergeant Coulter."

He considered for a moment, and then grew serious. "After my grandparents died and my uncle sold their house, I never thought I'd want to see Littleton again. I thought it would only remind me of everything I'd held dear and lost." His blue eyes held something that made Maggie go still when he said, "I don't feel that way anymore." He gestured around them. "After this is over, I think I'd like to go back."

Maggie took a gulp of coffee. "Will you—what did you—I mean—you said you didn't care for steamboating. I've always thought it would be a romantic life, standing in that house of glass and ruling over everything beneath your feet."

Colt grunted. Shook his head. "It's the river that rules, not the pilot." He took a deep breath. "I suppose it does seem romantic from a distance. But there's a very ugly side to it—just beneath the veneer of the 'floating palace' advertisements." He paused. "Now that I think about it, it's not unlike the genteel portrait of life on a plantation."

"You mean the slaves," Maggie said.

"Not just the slaves. At least not if Jack was right about where Miss Blair got those bruises we saw." He shook his head. "Is anything as it seems in this world?" He turned to look at her. "When I first saw Miss Blair, for example, I made certain assumptions." He went on to tell Maggie about the woman's concern for the twenty-odd slaves on her plantation. "That surprised me. I mean—I didn't expect her to care." He shook his head. "She knows she's looking into the face of a battle, and she's worried about her servants. Who would have expected that?"

She's looking into the face of battle? Suddenly, everything fell into place, like dominoes set up to amuse a child and then falling according to a preordained pattern. Maggie swallowed and took a deep breath. "Once Jack comes back with more information, we're going to be ordered to move back north, aren't we? It isn't really a matter of *where* we'll be going— it's a matter of how many companies it will take to defeat the Wildwood Guard. They have to be stopped so they can't move south to join up with the rest of the Confederates—and so they can't trap us between the Guard and Price's army to the south." Almost without knowing what she was doing, she put her hand into her pocket and grasped Da's pistol.

Colt didn't say anything at first. He did, however, put one

warm hand to the small of her back as he murmured, "Don't be afraid, Miss Maggie. It's going to be all right."

She didn't dare look at him. She stared into the fire and drank her coffee. It tasted bitter now. Fish and Seamus and Ashby stepped out from behind one of the supply wagons and headed toward the campfire. Colt only dropped his hand when she moved to get up and pour their coffee. But before she stood, she looked over at him and murmured, "I'm going to need one of those Henrys."

Chapter 16

As she rode through the encampment with Major Green on a cloudy Wednesday morning, Libbie detected something different about the Guard. The men greeted her as always, but their smiles quickly faded. And there was no music. She'd grown accustomed to the sounds of mouth harps and fifes. One gray-haired man she'd heard others call *Pops* even had a violin. Today, Pops was nowhere in sight.

When Libbie mentioned it on the way back to the stable, Major Green simply shrugged and said, "Weather rolling in." Back at the stable, Green dismounted quickly, handed the reins of his white horse off to a waiting Malachi, and took his leave—with a muttered apology for "desertin' her."

Libbie rather preferred tending Pilot at her own pace and without the need to keep up conversation with Isham Green, but as she brushed Pilot's coat and combed his mane, she couldn't shake the sense of—something. Perhaps it was just the weather. Clouds had rolled in, and the sky was that unnatural color that usually preceded a high wind and a downpour. She supposed that could be it. And then there was the idea that there would be no Fourth of July celebration tomorrow. She supposed that might have cast something of a pall over the camp.

Ah, well. Finishing with Pilot and turning him into his stall, Libbie made her way to the kitchen to tell Annabelle that, as expected, Walker had declared that no one at Wildwood Grove was to have anything to do with the "Yankees' Independence Day."

Annabelle barely looked up when Libbie said it. "No surprise, Miss Libbie."

"It's less work for you," Libbie said.

"Yes'm," Annabelle said. "And it gives me more time to bake the pies for the calico ball."

Annabelle wasn't complaining. She was just stating fact. Skipping an Independence Celebration really hadn't changed her workload all that much. This coming Saturday the Ellerbes and all the other planters' families in the county were coming to the Grove to help stage a barbeque and a calico ball. And so while Annabelle and the other cooks might not be in the throes of planning for a party tomorrow, there would still be hours and hours of extra work in coming days. Hours and hours of work added to the already heavy load created by the men who'd been invited to be Walker's guests.

"Should we call some more help up from the quarters?" she asked.

"Nobody left down there I want in my kitchen," Annabelle said quickly. "Betty said she'd give me a hand if it comes to it. I'll be all right, Miss Libbie. Didn't mean to complain."

"I didn't think you were," Libbie said. "Tell you what. How about I see if Susan Ellerbe will lend us Mavis and Doll?"

Annabelle glanced up. Smiled. "That'd be mighty nice of you. Those girls know what it means to work hard. I could turn all the piecrusts over to Mavis and never give it another thought. Be free to tend to other things."

Free. Hearing Annabelle use the term so casually made Libbie want to do more than just call in some more slaves. Could she do more? "I'll see to it," she said, and turned away.

Stepping outside, she looked off toward the encampment, shivering as a cool wind blew up from the river. Rain was coming. She could feel it. She imagined she could even smell it. Just a hint of damp on the breeze. Oh, she hoped it didn't rain on Saturday. The men needed something to take their mind off a July 4 devoid of celebration.

Independence Day. Libbie glanced back toward the kitchen, and then wandered toward the front of the house and the view of the clouds gathering toward the west. What did Annabelle and the others think every year in July, when their masters celebrated by reciting the Declaration of Independence and the Preamble to the United States Constitution? *All men are created equal...* She'd never considered the irony before. But now—now that she was wondering and worrying over what would happen to Ora Lee and Annabelle and the others, should the fight come to Walnut Grove, the term *Independence Day* made her uncomfortable.

As she rounded the back corner of the house and made her way past Walker's office windows, she could hear the rumble of men's voices. Another meeting. More plans. Wishing she had her shawl, she continued on past the colonnaded porch and then toward the edge of the lawn and the drop-off, where brambles and tangled underbrush obscured the earth at the base of the trees growing on the steep hillside all the way down to the water's edge. The distant clang of a steamboat bell drew her attention upriver, but she couldn't see the packet yet. Perhaps it was at the Littleton landing a few miles away.

She glanced back toward the house, wondering if the men inside were planning for more shipments of weapons. Or would they be gathered about that map strategizing? What were they planning anyway? Surely they weren't going to spend the war here at the Grove. What was going to happen? How foolish she felt for getting caught up in something as inconsequential as a calico ball. Walker said such things helped the men. He said that just seeing a beautiful woman reminded them of what they were fighting for. She didn't like the idea of men fighting for her.

A lot of things made her uncomfortable these days. Wondering about Robert's knowing more about the house than he probably should. Imagining Jack Malone and that sergeant who wouldn't tell her his name taking aim at the men camped in view of the house. Noticing how young Cooper had grown recently and thinking about what it must be like to have a child and not know if you would get to see him grow to manhood. Why hadn't that ever bothered her before? Walker had advertised "Negro Boys at Auction" in the past. No faces came to mind when she thought about them. How could she not have cared?

She had just turned away from the river to go back up to the house when Ora Lee came trotting into view from the direction of the kitchen. "You best be comin' in, Miss Libbie. Mastah Blair fit to be tied. He say you got to come pack."

"Pack?" Libbie frowned.

"Yes'm. He packing, too."

"But—why? What's he packing?"

"Seem like everything," Ora Lee said as she hurried alongside Libbie. "Don't know why. He sent me to get you. I heard him tell Robert and Malachi to bring down your trunk."

Ora Lee hurried around back. She would mount the steep, narrow servants' stairs to the second floor and enter Libbie's room by way of an unfinished room at the back of the house. Libbie, on the other hand, hurried up the sweeping front steps, crossed the veranda, and entered through the front door, just in time to see Isham Green clomp down the stairs with Cooper in tow, the latter bearing two huge carpet-bags. Green and Cooper were followed closely by Mason Ellerbe and his private servant, the latter burdened with the two monstrous valises Ellerbe had brought with him when he moved over from Hickory Hill.

"Ah, there you are." Walker stepped outside his office door just as Robert and Malachi rounded the corner from the servants' entrance, a large trunk between them. "That's the one," Walker said, motioning for them to take the trunk into the library. "Retrieve the other two while I speak with Miss Libbie. Just line them up along the fireplace wall." He motioned for Libbie to follow him across the hall and into the formal parlor. "We'll talk in here." He seemed to be in a hurry, but as soon as he'd closed the door, it was as if he didn't know what to say. He crossed to the window and stood, staring out toward the river. Finally, with a deep sigh, he turned to face her.

Libbie hadn't noticed it, but in the gray light she realized that Walker had aged in recent days. He looked almost haggard.

"The officers are joining their men in the field," he said.

"So I assumed," Libbie said. "But Ora Lee said that you're packing up the whole house. I thought she was exaggerating, but now it seems that there's at least some truth to what she said."

Walker nodded. "Our... *activity* here at the Grove has been detected by the enemy. Plans had been laid down carefully, but based on some new information that's just been received, those plans must now change." He paused. Looked about them. "When I formed the Guard, I never expected— well. I don't suppose that matters now." Again, he hesitated.

"I suppose you've been aware of the fact that it isn't just food-stuffs and blankets that we've been unloading off the packets that have been stopping at our landing."

She didn't quite know what to say. After all, Walker had gone out of his way to keep her from knowing very much at all. "I haven't really paid very much attention. I thought that was the way you wanted it." Without her really thinking about it, her hand went to the place where he'd struck her.

His expression changed to something resembling sadness as he studied her face. Finally, he said, "You're almost healed up." He brushed his own hand across the side of his face.

"Yes. It's fine."

He nodded, and looked back out the window, just as thunder sounded. "It's goin' to pour rain any minute." With a deep sigh, he finally turned to face her again. "Why'd you come up with that story about you and Pilot colliding? Why'd you protect me?"

Lightning crackled, and the flash of light made Libbie start. "I wasn't protecting you. I was trying to avoid being locked in my room until the bruises faded." The rain began. She motioned toward the window, although she did not move closer to Walker. "We should close the windows so it doesn't rain in."

"It's falling straight down," Walker said. Again, he swiped across his forehead, and then he looked about him, almost as if he were seeing the room for the first time in a long while. He sighed. "I am very sorry for what happened that day. Truly sorry."

Was he waiting for her to say that she forgave him? She hadn't. Maybe she would one day, but right now ... no. Something deep inside her had changed since that day. Not only on that day, but also on the day when she'd suggested that

Jack Malone and his sergeant lead her horse along with them until they felt safe. She wasn't certain what that meant, but she did know that she'd begun to change. For one thing, she was stronger now. She supposed at least some of the strength was fueled by anger, but whatever it was, it had been useful. It made her remember to be wary of Walker and what he might do. She'd stopped taking her position in this house for granted. She'd begun to think for herself, and to question things. She didn't know where any of it would take her, but she wasn't going back to the way things had been between them. And she wasn't going to brush off what Walker had done, as if it didn't matter.

Walker cleared his throat. "A couple of the shipments of arms were intercepted by the enemy. Apparently that caused someone to look more closely into what might be going on, both here at Wildwood Grove and in Littleton with the militia. The details aren't really important. The way it affects us now—today—is that there is at least part of a brigade marching toward us. That means that Wildwood Grove is to become a battleground."

This time when thunder rolled, Libbie's hand went to her throat. Were the heavens providing them all with a preview of what it would sound like...here...in coming days?

"You needn't be afraid, Elizabeth. I have made plans to protect you—and our home."

There was a knock at the door. Libbie stepped aside as Walker went to answer it. Robert said something about keys. Walker started to answer, but then he glanced over at Libbie. Instead of answering Robert's question, he mentioned newspapers in the attic. "Begin wrapping the books," he said. "Wrap each one separately. There are some valuable volumes on those shelves. I'll be out directly."

Robert murmured, "Yes sir," and Walker closed the door and turned back to Libbie. "I have done the only thing I could think of to save our home in light of these changes. Wildwood Grove is to become a field hospital. We'll fly a white flag beginning tomorrow. The Yankees will honor a flag that designates a hospital."

So this was why Walker was in such a state. Libbie's mind began to race as she looked about her. "We can have all the furniture moved into the hall. If we roll up the carpets and open the pocket doors"—she motioned to the doors separating the formal from the family parlor—"if we do that, this side of the house can be an infirmary. Ora Lee and I can bring down the feather beds, while the men move the furniture."

Walker frowned. "What in the Sam Hill are you talkin' about, carrying feather beds down?"

"For the wounded. We can't have them lying about on the bare floors." She brightened. "And if you let Malachi drive me into town tomorrow—a farm wagon, not the carriage—I can go door to door collecting blankets. More feather beds. I'm sure people will want to help." She was rambling on when Walker interrupted her.

"Elizabeth. I am not draggin' my feather bed down here so that some sharecropper can bleed all over it. As for your going into town, no one is askin' you to organize a ladies aid. All I want you to do is go upstairs and pack your own things. It's all arranged. The *Nebraska* will stop here tomorrow evening. I've booked passage for you and Ora Lee to Omaha. You'll have rooms in the Herndon House there. I'm told it's the finest hotel in the city. You'll be comfortable—and safe—until this"—he gestured about them—"until this is nothing but a terrible memory." He forced a smile. "And when you return, I'll give you a very impressive budget with which to redecorate. Lord knows the place will need it." He hurried on. "I'm going into town first thing in the morning to make a withdrawal from the bank—"

Libbie interrupted him. "But, Walker—I don't know anyone in Omaha." It was a stupid thing to say, even if it was the truth.

Walker paid her no mind. "Wait here just a moment. I'll be right back."

While he was gone, Libbie moved to the window. The rain had stopped, but the clouds moving in were thick and obviously heavy with still more rain. The break in the storm wouldn't last long.

Walker returned with a square metal box in hand. He set it on the marble-topped table in the center of the room. "You can use this as a strongbox when you travel. I've already put some important papers in it—things that must not fall into enemy hands." He paused. "Now. As I was sayin', I'll be making a withdrawal, and you'll have all the money you need to live quite comfortably for several weeks. I don't expect it to take that long to settle the matter of Missouri, but should it last longer, I'll send more. Barrett Dunning knows trustworthy bankers in Omaha, and he's sending a letter of introduction so that should there be some unforeseen difficulty, you will have contacts. Which answers the worry about knowing anyone. I'll ask Barrett to give you a personal letter of introduction to a few of his friends. You'll be fine."

"I don't want to go."

"You must," Walker said. He reached for her then, and grasped her upper arm—gently. Almost fondly. "I really do care about you, Elizabeth, in my own way." He let go. "I wasn't at all happy with the idea of taking you on when you first arrived. I suppose that comes as no secret to you. I can be a rather—abrupt man. But you've proven yourself to be a lovely—well—an asset, really. You're a delightful hostess. Major Green and the others have all been quite taken with you. You're also managed the servants very well, especially in recent days when we've needed so much more help here at the house—and on such short notice. But you won't be needed now. Dr. Johnson and his two assistants will be moving in tomorrow evening. I offered to leave one of the guest rooms set up for him, but he seems to think he'll need every room for patients. I hope to God he's wrong about that, but if he wants to sleep under canvas in the yard or out in the stable, I suppose that is his prerogative."

Libbie barely heard what Walker said about the surgeon. Had he really just called her *an asset*? Indeed. "I could be useful here," she said. "You're still going to need someone to run the house. I know the servants and they know me. They don't know Dr. Johnson. What's to become of them?"

"That is not your concern," Walker said. He picked up the metal box and thrust it at her just before opening the door and striding out into the hall. Then he turned back. "After you've packed," he said, "would you help Betty with the china?"

Libbie nodded. She had to think. Her heart hammered in her chest as she headed for the stairs. She was halfway up when Betty called to her and hurried to catch up with her.

"Mastah Blair say you put the key to that box on this. Wear it around your neck."

Libbie took the chain.

"What's gonna happen to us, Miss Libbie?" Betty asked. She looked behind her toward the library, obviously making sure that Walker didn't see her.

"I don't know," Libbie said. "But I'll try to think of something. Just—I'll be back down directly to help with the china. Try not to worry."

The words felt empty. They were empty. *God help me. Please. Help me.* All the way up the stairs she thought of Annabelle and Betty singing while they worked. Singing about peace. Thanking God. And she felt ashamed.

Chapter 17

———⁂———

Libbie paused in the doorway to her bedroom. Ora Lee had been hard at work, lighting lamps to overcome the gray light of the stormy day, selecting some gowns to pack, spreading them across the bed for Libbie's approval, and collecting the small mountain of unmentionables that would be required to accommodate a fashionable journey and introduction to Omaha society. Libbie's trunk stood open by the window, the removable top tray waiting on the window seat beside the carpetbag she'd carried from home all those years ago. Her traveling case sat on the dressing table. Libbie slid the black metal box Walker had given her onto the bed next to the footboard, crossed the room, and raised the lid of the leather-clad case.

"Prettiest thing I ever seen," Ora Lee said as Libbie took out one of the crystal jars.

"I squealed with delight when I first saw it. I can still hear Mama's voice sayin', 'Every lady needs a proper traveling case, dear.' She'd been to Nashville, meaning to bring it home and give it to me when I'd finished at Miss Robeson's School. But then she couldn't wait to give it to me." Two center trays lifted out, and the bottom one revealed a set of ivory-handled sewing tools nestled in a rose-colored silk-lined tray. The thimble was gold, its border engraved with the initials *ECB*. *Elizabeth Chestnut Blair*. Mama had been a Chestnut, a member of a proud Alabama family.

Libbie put the thimble on the middle finger of her right hand, wondering for the first time about Mama's cousins in Mobile and how they would fare if the war didn't end quickly...if the battle came to them. None of the Chestnuts had stepped forward to offer to take Libbie in when the cholera left her alone. Given a choice, Libbie would have probably gone to them rather than coming to Missouri, if nothing else but for the fact that their manner of life would have been more like what she'd always known. Folks in Alabama would be standing together against the Yankees right now. They probably didn't give a moment's thought to what Walker called "that viper's nest of abolitionists that meet at Turner Hall" or "that traitor of a newspaper editor." She didn't imagine anyone in Alabama had neighbors like the Malones who'd openly taken the side of the Union.

"How come you never use it when you sew?" Ora Lee asked, nodding at the thimble.

Why had she left it to be stored away? At first, it had been too painful to remember everything she'd lost. Libbie sighed. "I'll use it now," she said. "I suppose I'll have all kinds of time for fancy stitching once we're in Omaha." The idea filled her with dread. Hours in some hotel room in a foreign land... wondering. Worrying. Waiting for word.

"You do make a fine stitch, Miss Libbie," Ora Lee mumbled.

And who cared about gold thimbles and fine stitching in the face of war? Willing her bleak thoughts away, Libbie looked over to the bed, where Ora Lee had laid out four simple day dresses and the related undergarments needed to create the proper silhouette for each one.

"You want the ball gowns? We'll need another trunk if you do."

Another peal of thunder and a crack of lightning made

Libbie jump. She began to think about traveling into a storm and leaving Wildwood Grove and what would happen to Annabelle and Malachi and the others if she was gone...and tears welled up.

"We gonna be all right," Ora Lee said. "Mastah Blair, he say we gonna be fine."

Libbie didn't answer. Instead, she reached for the metal box, took the key out of the lock, and put it on the chain. "Walker says I should wear it around my neck," she said, and sat down on the dressing table bench, waiting while Ora Lee undid the clasp, lowered it over her head, then fastened it. Libbie felt it fall into place beneath her chemise as she rose and crossed the room to close the door. When she turned back around, she blurted out a question.

"Do you *want* to go to Omaha, Ora Lee?"

The girl didn't answer for a moment. "Mastah Blair sending us, ain't he?" She clasped her hands before her and looked down at the floor, unmoving.

"But do you *want* to go?"

Ora Lee's expression was instantly unreadable. She actually took a step back. "I don't understand, Miss Libbie. Ain't I been takin' good care of you? I thought you was pleased with me." She glanced up then, just for a second. "You sayin' you leavin' me here? They all wonderin' what's gonna happen. I don't want you to leave me behind."

"That's not—no. That's not what I mean." Her voice wavered. She thought back to that day when she'd come upon Jack Malone and the sergeant at the spring. She'd asked them what would happen to the slaves. They didn't have an answer. Of course, she couldn't tell Ora Lee about that. She took a deep breath and tried to compose herself. Tried to look as kind as possible as she lowered her voice. "I've thought about what's to happen, Ora Lee. I've thought and thought about it, and all that happens is the mountain of things I don't understand keeps growing." Finally, she blurted out the question. "But of all the things I don't understand, the one I think about the most is this: Why don't you run?" She'd said it quietly, and yet it felt like the words were hanging in the air, a visible banner between them.

Ora Lee stood so still for so long that Libbie wasn't certain she was going to say anything at all. Finally, though, in a very quiet voice, the girl asked, "Where to, Miss Libbie?"

Libbie gazed out the window at the rain that had once again begun to fall. "Anywhere." She nodded toward the river. "We're surrounded by states that have outlawed slavery."

Ora Lee shrugged. She studied the carpet. She rubbed her nose with the back of one hand. Looked out the window. Rubbed her forehead. And remained silent. Finally, she glanced up at Libbie. "But I don't know those places."

"You could learn about them. You're a very smart girl. You could learn and take responsibility for yourself. Make your own decisions about where you want to live. What you want to do. Think how quickly you learned all of Betty's recipes for starch and—all sorts of things. You came up from the quarters, and it wasn't even a week and it was as if you'd grown up in this house."

A door slammed down on the first floor, and Ora Lee started. "I'm grateful you brung me up, Miss Libbie. You been kind and I thank you."

Libbie sighed. "I wasn't trying to get you to thank me. I just—I'm worried."

"Yes'm." Ora Lee glanced up at her. When Libbie met her gaze, the girl looked away, but still she asked, "You scared about goin' to that Omaha?"

"A little," Libbie admitted. "I don't know anyone there. Littleton is the farthest west I've ever been."

Ora Lee nodded. "That's how it be for me if I was to think on going anyplace else." She looked away and out the window. "Suppose I was to go to one of them free places. What happen when I get thirsty? What I gonna do when I get hungry—I mean at first, before I learn my way. Here, I just go out to the garden and help myself. Long as I don't take too much, Mastah Blair don't mind one bit. But if I in one of them free places and I take something out a white man's garden, they likely to kill me." She visibly shuddered. "Mastah Blair is a hard man, but if we do what he say, we know things be mostly all right. Men is men wherever they lives, Miss Libbie. Here, I knows who is safe and who isn't." The girl shook her head. "Wandering around, afraid all the time. Hungry. Thirsty. That ain't no kind of freedom I want."

Libbie knew that Ora Lee was giving her an amazing gift, and it was not one that she was likely ever to receive again. To have a Negro trust her with such truths... *Mastah Blair a hard man, but if we do what he say, we know things be mostly all right... Men is men wherever they live... That ain't no kind of freedom I want.* The full meaning behind the words made Libbie ashamed. Compared to Ora Lee, she knew nothing of the world. Nothing of life. She gazed about her at the gowns lying on the bed—purchased by Walker. At the traveling case—a gift from Mama. At the fine furniture—provided by Walker. Walker, who had promised a generous budget once the war was over so that she could redecorate the house. Walker, who would put cash in the black metal box before they left and provide a safe haven for her and even include letters of introduction to people in Omaha and bring her home when the war was over.

As the gray light faded toward sundown and the lamps flickered, shame swept over her. *Elizabeth Chestnut Blair.* Who did she think she was, talking to Ora Lee about freedom and "taking responsibility for herself"? As if she knew anything about it. Anything at all.

☙

Waiting. From what Maggie had experienced the past couple of days, the men in the army weren't any better at it than she'd been after Jack and Seamus left her at home. Fish said that over the course of a long conflict, boredom could be as much an enemy as the enemy. Even with camp life regulated by the bugle announcing roll call and drill, sick call and fatigue call, inspection and meals, the men still had enough free time on their hands for troublemakers to cause trouble. A weapon could only be cleaned so many times before a man felt foolish doing it again—before his tent mates started to think he might be nervous about the coming fight—and no one would admit to that if they could help it. It would just invite more troublemakers to make trouble.

On the evening before Independence Day, the holiday itself was reason enough for the men's spirits to lag, and the fact that storm clouds were gathering in the west didn't help their moods, as they reminisced about past celebrations and apple pie and parades and fireworks displays. There would be no apple pie on the morrow, no parades with beautiful women waving their kerchiefs to cheer them on, no fireworks displays, no flag-waving, no fancy speeches. Oh, the chaplain could be counted on to try, but he was given to stammering even on his best days. It wouldn't be the same.

As clouds began to gather and obscure the blue sky, Maggie tried to think what she might do to cheer the boys up.

Finally, she decided that music might serve as a remedy, and so she made her way across camp to where Seamus and his tent mates—minus Jack, who still hadn't returned from his foray into Littleton—had pitched their tent beneath an ancient pine tree.

"Let's have us a song," she said. Seamus played a couple of old Irish tunes, but no one seemed particularly interested in joining in until Maggie talked Private Ashby into singing along. When the quiet, unassuming boy turned out to have much more than a serviceable singing voice, his tent mates appeared to be just as surprised as Maggie.

"Yer a pure nightingale," one of them said. Ashby tried to wave the compliment away, but his tent mate was serious. "I mean it, man," he said. "It's good to hear it."

The nods around the campfire encouraged Ashby, and before long Maggie had stopped singing, content to listen to a voice that was better than any she'd ever heard. As it happened, Private Ashby really was a "pure nightingale." When someone requested an old hymn that Seamus didn't know, Ashby launched into it on his own. By the second verse, Seamus had picked it up and was playing along. More men gathered about to listen. Some joined in, harmonizing.

When Maggie noticed that Hero had gotten to his feet and was watching the proceedings with interest, she retreated to Fish's wagon, collected him, and carried him over. He squirmed, wanting to be put down, and when Maggie set him down at her feet, he limped away—intending to greet Colt, as it turned out.

Colt crouched down to pet the dog before saying, "The captain sent me to see if his dog might be up to paying a visit while we're camped."

"He's nearly well," Maggie said. "The cut's entirely healed, and he's begun taking it upon himself to limp about the campfire these warm summer evenings. He's not ready to march yet, but he's nearly mended."

Colt picked the dog up. "Walk with me?" he asked, and Maggie did. Gladly.

At the captain's tent, Hero limped over to his usual place just beneath the captain's cot and lay down with a sigh that made Maggie chuckle. "There's no place like home, eh?" She smiled up at Colt. "He wants to stay. I'll fetch his water bowl."

"I'll come with you."

"There's no need."

"I know," Colt said. "I'll come with you."

Well. She could not deny that it gave her pleasure to walk beside him as the day died away and the sun broke through a bank of clouds in the west. When she retrieved the chipped enamelware bowl she'd been using for Hero and reached for a canteen, Colt took it up.

"If we're going to beat the rain, we'd better hurry," he said, and without waiting for a reply, he led the way to the swift-running creek at the bottom of a cleft in the surface of the earth.

Maggie peered over the edge, content to wait while Colt picked his way down the steep bank. When he climbed back up, he was red-faced and panting. "I'm surprised you allowed me to do it for you," he said, "but I'm grateful. Carrying you back up would have been difficult. Enjoyable…but difficult."

Was he flirting with her? *Are you out of your mind?* Feeling awkward and unsettled, Maggie said nothing, just followed Colt back to the captain's tent, with a stop along the way to retrieve a clean bandage roll from her satchel. Hero came out from his old haunt beneath the captain's cot with great reluctance, but once Maggie sank to the earth and patted her lap, he finally limped over and allowed her to re-dress his injured paw. The captain walked up just as she'd finished.

He crouched down beside her to pet his dog. "How long before he can hold his own without being carried about?"

"I can't say. It's really up to him."

The captain spoke to the dog. "What say you, Hero, are you ready to soldier again—or would you rather remain in the company of the lady?"

Maggie laughed and shook her head. "The lady already has more dog than she sometimes knows how to handle back at home. Hero'll be fit as a fiddle soon enough."

The captain smiled. "I wish there were some way to thank you for all you've done for him."

Maggie looked off toward home and then back at the captain. "You can tell me what more I can do to help the boys. There's something...different in the air since we've camped here. I know the date on the calendar is part of it, but there's more to it. They're going through the same motions, and yet...it isn't the same. Or am I just a foolish woman imagining things?"

The captain shook his head. "You aren't imagining—and from what I know of you, Miss Malone, there's no foolishness in you. You've been with the brigade long enough to know the boys and to sense their moods. Waiting is sometimes the hardest part of being a soldier. They've signed on willing to do their duty, but while they wait to do it, they have time to think—and worry. Oh, they'll pretend it's just another night like all the others, but they know it isn't. This time next week they'll have fought another battle. There's not a man

among them who isn't wondering if he'll still be here...still
be whole." He broke off. "I apologize if I've frightened you."

"I'm not frightened. Not in the way you mean. I just—I
wish I could help them. Somehow."

"You help them by smiling."

"It isn't enough."

The captain nodded. "You're a good woman, Miss Maggie
Malone. I am proud to have met you. You'll be missed when
you're gone."

Then don't send me away. She almost wanted to raise the
idea of the women Fish had talked about in other armies.
Women who carried water to their boys in the aftermath of a
battle; who helped the wounded until they could be carried
from the field; who sometimes even wore uniforms designed
to match their regiment. Fish said they were welcomed;
treated like daughters and sisters. It was of course a ridiculous
notion, and yet she'd begun to think about it. She hadn't been
tested in battle, of course—except for the skirmish, which
was probably nothing to compare to a real battle. And yet, as
she thought back on that event, she hadn't been afraid. She'd
been too busy doing what was needed. She couldn't imagine going back to the farm now, staying there with Paddy and
waiting for news. She didn't think she could do it.

All of this raced through her mind as Captain Quinn pet-
ted his dog and the sun made a last effort at pouring splashes
of gold onto the earth through the trees. Finally, though, the
clouds took over the sky and thunder sounded in the distance.
The captain picked the dog up and said, "As much as I'd like
to keep you here, you'll be safer with Miss Maggie until you
can run like your old self."

Colt offered to take Hero, but Quinn shook his head and

smiled at Maggie. "May we both have the honor of seeing you home, Miss Maggie?"

Maggie forced a smile, and the three of them walked back to the quartermaster's part of the camp in silence. When the captain went to set Hero in the wagon box, Maggie asked him to put the dog down by the campfire instead. "The boys like having him about." She smiled. Shrugged. "It's another way to pretend it's just another night in camp."

Captain Quinn nodded and set Hero down. The dog limped over to a grassy spot beside Fish's wagon, circled a few times, and then lay down. Before he left, the captain said, "Sergeant Coulter tells me you've mentioned wanting a better weapon."

Maggie glanced at Colt, then back to the captain. "As my Da used to say, 'Nothing ventured, nothing gained.'"

"I thought your father came over from Ireland."

"We all did, sir, me brothers and Da and our Uncle Paddy. In 1847, aboard the *Arabia*. From Dublin to New Orleans and up the river to St. Louis."

"But he quoted Benjamin Franklin?"

Maggie grinned. "Well, to hear Da tell it, Ben Franklin's *Poor Richard* was Irish."

The captain laughed. Bending down to give Hero a last pat on the head, he said good night and took his leave. Colt, on the other hand, settled beside Hero, as if he belonged by her campfire. Which, Maggie thought, he most certainly could for as long as he desired it.

The men gathered near Seamus's tent were still singing, and Maggie and Colt talked about Ashby's fine voice and Seamus's fife playing, and before she realized what she was doing, Maggie was telling Colt about growing up in a man's world and how much she loved working alongside the boys and Paddy and how God had blessed them with such a fine home, and Colt was listening as if every word she said was of great importance. As if he wanted to know the details of her life.

She was feeling dangerously close to falling into something approaching love with John Coulter when Noah turned up and, thankfully, saved her from making a fool of herself over a man. The bag slung over Noah's shoulder proved to contain a small ham, a pile of fresh green beans, and half a dozen huge turnips. He spilled it all on the ground beside her with all the pride of a contestant who'd won a ribbon at the county fair.

When Maggie scolded him for thieving, Noah was unrepentant. "The farmer was a Union man," he said. "He's probably glad we're here to chase the Rebels off."

"And how do you know he's a Union man? I suppose he told you that just before he *gave* you all of this."

"Well..." Noah pondered for a moment. "For one thing, he didn't have a row of cabins down by the cornfield."

"It isn't quite as simple as that to know where a Missouri farmer's loyalties lie," Maggie said. "Not every Southern sympathizer in Little Dixie owns slaves. In fact, there's probably more who don't than do—but the ones who don't might be just as rabid about states' rights and such as an old Louisiana family." She almost laughed at herself, then. She sounded like Uncle Paddy, going on about the political stew that made Missouri a slave state but had, thus far at least, kept it from seceding from the Union and joining the Confederacy.

Noah was unimpressed by the lecture. He merely shrugged. "Guess maybe I could be mistaken." He grinned. "But I can't exactly take it all back. It's getting dark. A man hears someone rustling around in his garden at night, he's likely to shoot first and ask 'who goes there' later. How'd you feel if I got shot because you made me return a few turnips?"

Maggie just shook her head as she pointed at the green beans. "Start snapping the stems off. I'll be back after I find something besides a skillet to cook with. And if you run off, I'm liable to feed your portion to the dog, so you stay put."

Noah looked over at Hero. "He don't eat turnips and green beans."

"I wouldn't be too sure," Maggie said. "I plan to put that ham hock you brought in the pot right along with the beans."

"And we all plan to help you eat it." It was Seamus, who'd apparently caught sight of Noah headed this way with the bag over his shoulder and come to investigate.

The rain held off, and while the stew pot boiled, Seamus and Ashby and Colt and Noah and a few other homesick soldiers sat around Maggie's campfire listening to Noah's aggrandized version of how he'd foraged for what they were eating, telling their own boyhood stories, and laughing. And for those hours Maggie thought that there was no more beautiful sight in the world than a soldier's smile and nothing more important in the world than doing what a woman could to make it appear.

Chapter 18

Libbie stood at the top of the well-worn path to the levee, afraid to take a step. A night of rain had turned it into little more than a mudslide. Just as Ora Lee muttered, *Lord, have mercy*, a gust of wind swept up the hill and snatched the ivory-handled umbrella out of Libbie's hand, carrying it halfway to the house. Libbie looked after it in time to see Walker hurrying out the front door. The same fierce wind that had stolen her umbrella nearly snatched the screen door out of his hand. Keeping the door on its hinges meant losing his hat, and it sailed away in the direction of the umbrella, both of them tumbling end over end, first toward the kitchen wing and then toward the necessaries at the far edge of the lawn.

The early morning hours had been gloomy, but dry. Now the overcast sky and the wind kept their promise. With a flicker of lightning and a rumble that barely gave warning, it began to pour. Grabbing Ora Lee by the hand, Libbie shouted, "Come on!" and ran for the shelter of the front porch. Walker had gone after his hat. And, Libbie thought, perhaps the umbrella. Or perhaps not. She was not going to risk getting drenched chasing after an umbrella. And so she led Ora Lee back inside, where their footsteps echoed in the bare hall, for the red-and-white oilcloth had been rolled up and stored in the basement along with much of the rest of the furniture and all of the finer things that had made up the Blairs' lives at Wildwood Grove.

Walker came in the front door without his hat. "It's a good bet the *Nebraska* will have tied up somewhere downriver," he said. "There's not much point in trying to get down to the levee this morning."

"Did you see the mud?" Libbie asked. "We'd likely break our necks trying."

Walker nodded. For a moment, he said nothing, but then his expression changed. "Come with me," he said to both women, and led the way down the hall and out the back door where the three of them stood beneath the overhang created by the upstairs balcony. The kitchen door was closed against the storm, but there was a lamp in the window, and Libbie imagined Annabelle and Malachi inside, warm and dry, enjoying breakfast together at the little table crowded against the wall opposite the door.

When Walker finally spoke, he'd come up with a plan. He sent Ora Lee to fetch Malachi and Robert and then directed Libbie to "run to the stable" as soon as the rain let up. "I'm going to have the men retrieve your trunks from the levee. We'll load up, and Malachi can drive us to Littleton in the old phaeton. You and the girl can take shelter at the Littleton Arms until I learn where the *Nebraska* is and when it's expected at Littleton. I'll telegraph the captain of the steamboat about our change in plans. Once it's all settled and we know more, I'll leave you to wait while I return to the Grove to join my men. I should have known to make other plans as soon as the weather turned yesterday. That trail never has been worth much. I should have improved it last year." He nodded. "Yes. That's what we'll do. Littleton. And then the path. When everything's settled, I mean. Perhaps a new load-ing dock as well." He broke off and looked off to the field where hundreds of tents reflected the pale light.

Libbie imagined the men huddled inside, in a vain attempt to stay dry. Would they be forced to drill in the rain? Did wars go on in the midst of a downpour? It would be impossible—wouldn't it? She couldn't imagine loading a musket with wet hands. And wet powder—the thought of what would hap-pen to the men camped off in that field, should the Yankees mount a surprise attack in the middle of this storm—but then, they'd be just as drenched as the Guard. Surely nothing would happen today.

"And that field," Walker was saying. "Something will have to be done. They've destroyed it. Never should have let them camp so close to the house."

From the subject of the encampment and the condition of the pasture, Walker took another detour and mentioned a long list of things that needed to be done at Wildwood Grove. Libbie supposed they did, but it was a strange time for Walker to be thinking about painting fences. Goodness, since the Guard had been camped here, many of the fences had dis-appeared into campfires. Why was Walker babbling on about fence lines and grading the road to encourage runoff?

The combination of his rambling speech, his flushed face, and the wild expression in his eyes frightened her. She'd learned to deal with many of Walker's moods over the years, but this—whatever it was—this mood almost seemed to be bordering on madness. He returned to the topic of her leav-ing. "The key," he finally said to her. "You have the key, right? And the money box. And the papers I told you about. You must keep the papers safe."

"Yes, Walker." She tried to keep her tone calm. Assured.

"Everything's in order. The money box is right here in my satchel. Do you want to see it?" She held the satchel up.

Walker stayed her hand. "No, no. That's all right. I just—" Again he broke off. "Ah, here they are."

Malachi and Robert exited the kitchen and stepped up onto the porch, and Walker told them what he wanted. "Miss Libbie will be waiting down at the stables for you," he said to Malachi. "Waste no time in hitching up the phaeton. Take her to the Archer Arms."

"But—aren't you coming?" Libbie looked up at him.

"Yes, yes. Of course. I'll come. I just—I need to be with the men. The situation has changed. It's all—everything—" He looked behind him at the house. "Everything's changed." He barked at Malachi and Robert to hurry up and do what they were told. The two men turned their collars up against the rain and headed for the levee.

Movement in the kitchen window drew Libbie's attention, and at sight of Annabelle peering out, she found herself longing to step into the warm, dry kitchen, with its familiar aromas of spices and yeast bread. To hear Annabelle humming about peace and God.

Walker kept talking. Talking. Talking. About ruined crops and saving the house and hiding the silver. About the servants and how they'd probably all run off before much longer. The rain let up, and he nudged her. "Time to go."

And Libbie stood her ground and said *no*.

⚘

Maggie woke with a start. It was still dark, but the rain had stopped, and where once its incessant drumming on the rubber sheeting stretched over the wagon bed above her had kept her awake, now the cessation of the sound did the same thing.

She lay still for a moment, listening, and when she realized that Hero had risen to his feet and was standing, his ears alert, looking out into the night, she sat up and whispered, "What is it, boy?"

The dog glanced at her, whined softly, and peered back into the night. Feeling the prickle of danger climb up the back of her neck, Maggie slipped her hand into her pocket, grateful that she'd just last night cleaned and reloaded the revolver. She put her thumb on the hammer, ready to cock it. When a low growl sounded in Hero's throat, she took the pistol out and aimed it in the direction the dog seemed to think danger lurked. Her heart thumped.

"If you've got that pistol out of your pocket, Maggie-girl, you can put it away."

Jack. Relief flooded through her. Maggie put the pistol away. She kept her voice low, even as she climbed out from beneath the wagon and whispered a scolding. "Yer a blessed fool, Jack Malone." He stirred up the campfire, and as the flames flickered and she caught sight of him, relieved tears sprang to her eyes. Home safe, thank the good Lord. At least as close to home as she'd be able to drag him for a bit. And as safe as she could keep him.

She didn't bother to pin up her hair, but let the long braid trail down her back as she administered a fierce hug. Expecting to smell a week's worth of filth and sweat, she was surprised to find him clean-shaven and sporting a new shirt. "What's this?" She tugged on the kerchief tied about his neck.

"Bridget Feeny," he said. "She wouldn't take no for an answer. Sent the same for Seamus—along with enough notepaper for the boy to write her a book, if he's of a mind to do it." He took a deep breath and settled back, poking aimlessly at the fire.

"I'll make you coffee. I'm afraid rations have been a bit scarce, so I can't offer much in the way of anything else—unless you've a taste for hardtack soaked in a bit of grease."

"You're a dear, but the captain sent his aide after feeding me when I first came in an hour or so ago," he said. "I wouldn't say no to coffee, though."

So. He'd had time to dry out while he told the command what he'd learned sneaking about Littleton. And he likely had news, but he didn't seem inclined to share it yet. All right. She wouldn't ask about anything but family matters. "I've a bit of roasted grounds left from last night." She emptied water from her canteen into the pot Fish had entrusted to her. "So tell me, now. How is Uncle Paddy?"

"Back at the farm," Jack said. He gave her the look she'd come to recognize as his way of scolding. It didn't need words, which was just as well, since Jack wasn't one to expend more than a few. "You didn't really tell it true, Maggie-girl."

She snapped a reply. "Don't you be calling me a liar, Jack Malone."

"You know what I mean. The garden. The house. The stock. It's all so much worse than what you said."

"I said it was bad. That seemed enough."

Jack thought for a moment. "You should have made me see it," he said. "Should have told me you needed me to come home."

Maggie harrumphed. "And what good would that have done but to make me look like a mewling weakling? You aren't coming home anytime soon, so where's the good in whining about it? You and Seamus have a bigger task at hand and I'll not be weighing you down with worries over broken fences and missing shoats."

He smiled, then. "The shoats are back. All save two. Paddy

claimed that walking the miles it took to round them up was good for him." He shrugged. "Maybe it was."

"He's on the mend, then?"

Jack nodded. "Nearly mended. And singing your praises every chance he gets. I told him you'd taken to soldiering as if you were one of us." He grinned. "If it weren't for the fact that you've managed not to stink so bad as the rest of the boys— and the skirt, of course—there'd be little difference when it comes down to it." He glanced up at her. "I meant that by way of a compliment. I don't suppose it's a very good one."

Maggie ignored what almost seemed an apology while she fetched a couple of tin mugs. Fish had helped her collect a dozen or so and told her to keep them at hand. He'd said that the boys who spent time around her campfire seemed to be better for it, and he'd do what he could to encourage what he called her "regimental tea parties."

"And how are things in the town?" she asked as she served the weak but very hot amber liquid. "Did you learn anything to help the brigade?" She handed him a mug. "It's weak, but it's the best we've got until the supply train catches up to us in a couple of days."

Jack sipped coffee and stared into the fire. "I learned a good deal. It was right that Sergeant Coulter had me stay behind."

"I'm not asking you to reveal any secrets," Maggie said. "If you can't tell me—"

"Everyone will know soon enough," Jack said. And just as he opened his mouth to speak, reveille sounded.

"Seems early," Maggie said as the sounds of an encampment of men waking up carried on the clear, night air.

"It is," Jack said. "The wait's over, Maggie-girl. Half the regiment is to split off and march northwest to intercept the Wildwood Guard and the Ellerbe Militia."

"The—what?"

Jack nodded. "I learned about it in town—courtesy of an article in the *Littleton Leader*. Walker Blair wasn't the only planter bent on funding his own private army. The Guard is at least three hundred strong, and Ellerbe raised another couple hundred to join them. The thing is, the militia aren't green recruits. They're mostly General Price's men, encouraged to stay up north after Boonville." Jack finished his coffee and stood up. "We're going to make them regret that decision."

"What about Paddy? You said he's back on the farm? Alone?"

"Not to worry, dearie. He'll be driving the wagon back into town today or tomorrow, and he promised me he'd stay there until the Irish parade through Littleton to the cheers of the Union loyal." He winked at her. "I told him to keep an eye out for you—that you'd be home within the week." He reached for the haversack he'd dumped beside the fire. "Now I've got a package to deliver to me brother—who seems to have stolen a girl's heart right from beneath my crooked Irish nose, and with *poetry*, of all things." He chuckled. "To think that I told Seamus he didn't know anything about women."

"You don't—mind, do you—about Bridget?"

"If Bridget wants a poet, she'd be miserable with the likes of me. Besides that, my brain's been rattling on about someone else, ever since the sergeant and I—" He stopped in mid-sentence.

"Ever since...what?"

Jack shook his head. "Never mind. It's foolishness anyway." And then he smiled at her. "Speaking of the sergeant, he asked me if you were being courted."

Maggie sputtered disbelief. "He did not."

"Oh, but he did. Of course, I put a stop to that nonsense

right away," Jack said. "I told him you're duty-bound to keep house for your two bachelor brothers and your uncle."

Maggie laughed. "Since I'm quite certain that none of this really happened, I'll play along. What did the handsome Sergeant Coulter say to that?"

"You think he's handsome, then."

"I think," Maggie said, glancing around her at the activity in the now fully awake and bustling camp, "that you likely have better things to do than tease your poor sister, and if I only had a dishrag in my hand, I'd be snapping it to encourage you to get to it."

"But I'm not teasing you—oh, all right, maybe I am a little. But he really did ask after you. Right before he said, and I quote, 'She's a fascinating woman.' "

Maggie busied herself with drinking the rest of the weak coffee. Taking a last gulp, she said, "Go on, then. Take Seamus his new shirt and let him know you've done with poor Bridget Feeny." Jack left, and for just a fleeting moment, Maggie basked in the idea that John Coulter had apparently thought it possible that a man might choose to court her. *Her.* And then she pondered the word *fascinating.*

Chapter 19

———◈———

As the supply train topped a ridge on the third day of the march toward what the boys were already calling the Battle of Wildwood Grove, Maggie looked down to see that they would camp just beyond a bridge that afforded passage across a ravine intersecting the pasture from south to north. The recent rain had turned what was probably a meandering little brook into a swift-running creek. As she walked alongside the supply train toward the bridge, Maggie could hear the rushing water above the noise of creaking harness and plodding mules. When it was her turn to cross the bridge, she did so in the company of Noah, his bare feet nearly soundless, while her own heavy boots clomped as loudly as any soldier's.

"We getting close to your farm?" Noah asked as they stepped onto damp earth on the opposite side of the bridge.

"Fifteen miles or so up that road," Maggie said, nodding toward what old-timers in the area said had once been an Indian trail. "Wildwood Grove stands between us and the farm, and then Littleton is another five miles or so beyond that."

"You could be back home by sundown easy," Noah said.

"I could, but I'm not going. Not yet."

As the supply wagon came to a stop and Fish jumped down to unhitch the mules, Noah trailed after Maggie and helped her gather wood for the campfire. As they walked back toward the wagons, he asked, "How many slaves you figure they got on that plantation?"

Maggie looked up from stacking the kindling. "I don't know," she said. "Why?"

Noah shrugged. "If they got slaves, they got at least one overseer. Smart for me to keep that in mind before I go to foraging anywhere hereabouts. Might be more dangerous for a fella than usual."

Maggie hadn't thought about Noah in the context of where they were—or what would happen in the next couple of days. The realization shamed her. Of course he was afraid. He'd probably lingered at the waterfront in Boonville because he knew where to run, where he could hide, and who was and was not to be counted on in a crisis. She wondered if stowing away in a wagon had been a boy's impetuous decision. Did he regret it now? She hadn't really thought about the idea that the Irish were about to do battle with slave owners. Hadn't thought about the slaves at Wildwood Grove, either. What would happen to them? On impulse, Maggie reached over to grasp Noah's thin forearm. When he looked over at her, she smiled. "Might be better if you gave up foraging for a few days."

Noah seemed to be considering the advice, although he made no promises.

"I mean it."

The boy flashed a smile. "I know you do, Miss Maggie, and I appreciate it."

"Does that mean you'll stay close by?"

"Soon as I see to a few things." He trotted off before Maggie could protest.

He was headed in the general direction of the river, Maggie thought. She glanced off toward the north where, according to Colt, the *McDowell* with its howitzer was tied up, just waiting to provide battle support. *Nothing you can do about the boy right now.* For the next couple of hours, Maggie busied herself with starting the fire, retrieving the coffeepot from the supply wagon, lifting Hero down from his spot on the wagon seat, and generally making camp. In the matter of Noah, she tried to comfort herself with the notion that the boy had proven himself to be resourceful and wily. He would be all right, she told herself, but still, she worried. About so many things.

Tonight's encampment would be the last one before the Irish saw action again. No one would be pitching tents tonight. They'd roll up in a blanket and sleep on the ground, and tomorrow...ah...tomorrow. What Maggie eventually thought of as "controlled anxiety" hovered over the men as they went about their duties. A few of the boys were louder than usual at first—nerves, Maggie suspected—but over the course of the evening, things quieted down. The men spoke in low tones, and they settled beside campfires early to clean their weapons.

Noah finally turned up at sundown with two rabbits he'd managed to kill with the slingshot he carried in his back pocket. Feeling a bit guilty about eating something as good as fresh rabbit when all around her hundreds of men were dining on army rations, Maggie assuaged her personal guilt by assigning Noah the task of deciding who would share the rabbit stew. "Just be sure you let Fish know about it," she said. Noah returned with Jack and Seamus and their tent mates in tow—and John Coulter. And so, as the setting sun splashed the sky with crimson and purple, a handful of soldiers gathered around her campfire, tin mugs in hand, while Maggie dished up rabbit stew.

She waited until the men were seated around the campfire before she served herself, but the moment she'd done so, the men all shifted to make room for her next to Colt, as if an unspoken agreement existed between them all. She slipped into the space, relieved when no one seemed inclined to comment about the current status of this particular "tea party." When she finally looked up, Fish caught her eye and winked. If he was trying to get her to blush, he succeeded.

Wash Thomas murmured appreciation for Maggie's cooking. "The only thing missing is my mama's corn bread."

"She make it sweet?" Ashby asked.

Thomas shook his head. "Corn bread wasn't meant to be sweet."

"Unless you pour molasses over it," Jim Jackson said.

Thomas agreed, but then Ashby said that honey was better than molasses.

"Yeah," Jackson said, "but a man's got to be willing to get stung a hundred times to get at it. Don't get stung making molasses."

Ashby nodded. "Guess you got me there, Jim. Anyway, Miss Maggie. This is the best meal we've had since Noah scavenged those turnips and such last week. Thank you." One by one, the men finished eating and wandered off to rinse their dishes. As night fell and the fire died down, Noah settled beneath the supply wagon. The boy was half asleep before Hero limped over to where he lay, but when the dog nudged him, Noah held out one arm to create an opening in his blanket just large enough for the dog to tunnel into. Fish wandered off, muttering something about checking on one of his mules. Finally, it was just Maggie and Colt—who did not seem inclined to turn in.

Maggie busied herself rinsing the cooking pot, inverting it

so that it would air dry, ever conscious of Colt's presence and wondering how a man could call a woman who spent most of her time performing such mundane chores as making camp, cooking, and mending *fascinating.* When she'd finally run out of anything to do, Maggie sat back down, consciously putting a little extra distance between herself and Colt.

For a while, Colt commandeered the usual amount of small talk. About a particularly evil mule who'd taken to biting when the men tried to harness the creature to a wagon. Hero's healing. The clear night sky. The mournful sound of a mouth harp floating from somewhere on the far side of the camp to where they were sitting, staring into the dying coals of the campfire. Anything, it seemed, to avoid the subject of the coming battle. Finally, Colt took a long, slow breath, and said quietly, "I've something to ask you, Miss Maggie."

Maggie tried to sound lighthearted. "You want the recipe for my rabbit stew?"

He sighed audibly. "Why do you do that?"

"Do what?"

"Make light of everything I say."

"I don't."

"Well, it's either that or you do something else to make certain there's—space—between you and me." He reached over and touched the back of her hand. She pulled away. "There. Like that."

Maggie clenched her hands in her lap. "It's only proper. As I've already said, I'll not be giving the boys or anyone else the idea that I'm the kind of camp follower Captain Quinn seemed to think me that first day we met."

"No one would ever think that of you." He paused. "I was hoping for a bit of a serious talk—in light of tomorrow."

Just the word made her stomach hurt. She'd done her best

not to think on it, but it was here now, and she couldn't bear the thought of what might happen to men she'd grown to care for. More than Jack and Seamus now. So many more. She took a deep breath. She could sense Colt watching her, and that only made things worse. He reached out and caught her hand. Moved closer. When she tried to pull free, he wouldn't let go. She sat, her fingers curled into a fist, his grip about her wrist. She couldn't pull free without the risk of making a scene. The camp was quiet, but plenty of men were still seated around nearby campfires. Near enough anyway. And who was to say whether Noah was asleep or not? As long as she could help it, none of her boys would see Maggie Malone acting the fool over a man. And so she sat quietly, the fact that Colt was holding on to her obscured by her apron.

"If I let go, will you stay for a moment? No one would ever think evil of you. You're an honorable woman, and we all know it. In fact, I think it's fair to say that, down to a man, these soldiers you call your 'boys' would fight anyone who suggested otherwise."

Maggie looked over at him. "I doubt Philem O'Malley would concern himself with my honor."

Colt grunted. "Well, now, you don't think of him as one of 'your boys,' do you?"

He was right. She didn't. Not in the same way. "I don't— understand men like him."

"That's because you've chosen differently than men like him. He's chosen anger and bitterness and to blame everyone else for whatever it is that set him on the road to perdition— which is where he will end unless he makes a different choice. You, on the other hand, give of yourself every day. You find a way to make coffee out of anything you can roast and grind— and it's usually good. You must have mended dozens of shirts by now. You've bound wounds and written letters. You never complain, and you *listen*." He paused, and his voice warmed as he said, "Do you know what a gift you give a man just by *listening?*"

Maggie shook her head. "It's not a *gift* to be silent because you can't think of anything worth saying."

"I disagree," Colt said. "It takes a smart woman to know that. Most of the women I've known don't even consider the idea. They gossip and babble and talk about nothing and call it 'entertaining the gentlemen.'"

Maggie hadn't spent all that much time in the company of other women, but what Colt had just said made her think of Bridget Feeny—and then made her feel guilty about thinking it. After all, Bridget had been more than kind in the matter of the farm and Uncle Paddy's injuries. And besides that, Colt was giving her more credit than she deserved. She wasn't silent because she was smart. Again, she resisted his compliment. "I've never thought it a particular boon to be tongue-tied."

"You've probably never thought it a particular boon to be as physically strong as you are, either. Or to be a better shot than your brother. But look where we'd all be if you weren't."

Don't look at him. You won't see what you long for. This isn't—that. It's just a man facing battle who wants a moment of tenderness, and you're the only woman for miles about. She shoved her hands into her pockets. Da's pistol on the right. The lavender soap on the left. "You said you had something to ask of me."

Colt reached inside his frock coat and pulled out an envelope. "I'd like to ask you to give your word that if anything should happen—"

She leaned away from him, shaking her head. "Don't. Don't say it. 'Tis bad luck."

"I don't believe in luck," he said. "I believe in a man making his plans and the Lord directing his steps. God holds my tomorrow. Whatever happens has nothing to do with 'luck.'"

"I agree with what you're saying," Maggie said, "but you're going to make me cry if you keep—" She broke off.

"Would you cry for me then, Maggie-girl?"

She swallowed and willed the tears away. "I won't be crying for you or any other of my boys, John Coulter, because every single one of you is going to be sitting around my campfire this time tomorrow night, and that's all there is to be said about it."

"Agreed. But I'm still asking you to promise that if I can't deliver it personally, you will."

Maggie took the envelope and looked down at it. *Almina Coulter.*

"My mother," Colt said.

"But I thought—your grandparents. You said they raised you. And you didn't really know your father."

"But I didn't mention my mother, did I? And you didn't pry. Thank you for that." He paused. "I've never told anyone about it."

"And you don't have to now," Maggie said. "Just—tell me what you need me to do. I'll do it."

He took a deep breath. "My father died when I was only five years old. He'd been gone less than six months when one of his friends joined us for a Sunday afternoon meal. And then a Friday evening. And before I knew it, he was taking every evening meal with us. You can imagine my reaction. I was confused and frightened, and I acted out. Told the man I hated him. After that, I dined in the kitchen. Mother became Mrs. Wilbur Babcock before the year anniversary of my father's death. Her friends were scandalized, but she didn't care. As for Babcock, he had no use for a rebellious boy who resented his presence."

"And so you came to Littleton," Maggie said.

Colt nodded. "Mother sent me to live with her parents—who were inclined to think her hasty marriage in poor taste—at the very least." He smiled. "They spoiled me for a glorious few years."

"But then they sent you away, too?"

Colt shook his head. "Oh, no. Going onto my uncle's steamboat was my idea, and they fought it. But they weren't any good at denying me what I wanted, and as young boys will be, I was taken with what I saw as a glamorous life of adventure. Eventually, they let me go." He paused again. "They knew my uncle wasn't exactly a gentleman, but they didn't know the half of it. He was—a violent man. Cruel. In less than a month, I was trying to think of a way to get off that boat. I was afraid to run away, but I was counting the days until we landed at Littleton and I could go back to my grandparents. And then...word arrived of their deaths."

"Oh, John," Maggie said, and put her hand on his arm. He covered it with his own and gave it a squeeze before continuing.

"To this day I'm not certain how my uncle rigged things so that he could sell the house. My anger over that gave me the courage to run away. I volunteered with the army. And somewhere in the fog of grief, I realized that I didn't want to lose anyone else I loved. And so I wrote a letter. Mother answered. I wrote again. And so on. I haven't visited her yet, but—"

"Because of Mr. Babcock?"

Colt shook his head. "No. He's been good to her. They're happy. I just—I've let the army keep me away. Until now." He reached out and tapped the letter. "There are things in there that I mean to tell her face-to-face, but if that isn't possible . . . please, Maggie. Say you'll do it. For me."

"Of course I will."

"And you'll deliver it personally?"

"Yes, but—I don't understand why that's important."

"You really don't?" He smiled. "I want her to meet you, Maggie-girl."

Her heart pounded. Her throat went dry. "But—why?"

"Because I want her to know that you weren't a figment of my imagination." He reached over, took the letter out of her hand, set it between them, and took her hand. "I've already written about you. 'Dear Mother,' I said. 'I suppose you'll doubt my sanity to say it, but it's true. I met the woman I'm going to marry today. She strode into camp looking for her wounded brother. She'd seen his name on a list of wounded, but neither he nor his perfectly healthy brother had written a single letter home. So she came looking for them. You should have been there to see her striding into camp. She scolded Captain Quinn, ordered Hero to behave—which he did—and then, when she'd found her brothers (the wound was slight), gave them both the finest dressing down I've ever witnessed. Her name is Maggie Malone and she is, in a word, *magnificent*.'"

Something must be wrong with her hearing. John Coulter was still talking, but Maggie's ears were buzzing with two words only. The last words on earth she would ever have expected such a man to pronounce in a sentence about her. *Marry*, he'd said. *Magnificent*, he'd called her.

"As I said, I want her to meet you."

Maggie looked down at the letter. This couldn't be happening. Not to her. John Coulter couldn't be interested in her *as a woman*. It was a pretty speech, but that's all it was. Desperation made men say all kinds of things they didn't really mean, and who could be more desperate than a soldier facing battle? And so she sat, staring down at the letter, saying nothing.

"You don't believe me. Why not?"

She shrugged. "Because there's no logic in it."

He sounded upset. "I'm not talking about logic, Maggie-girl. I've just told you things about myself that I've never told anyone. And now I'm telling you what's in my heart—as plainly as I know how to say it."

Perhaps it was good that he was going to make her say it—*plainly*, to use his word. Maybe it would help, somehow, to remember how much it hurt to be forced to speak the words. She took a deep breath, and while she did not look him in the face, she did turn her head a bit so that she could see his fine hands and a bit of the fine blue coat that fit him so well. The well-tailored trousers with the dark stripe. The scuffed toe of his expensive leather boots. All of it in stark contrast to Maggie's well-worn calico skirt.

She pointed then, first to him and then back at the faded skirt. "Men who look like you do not fall in love with women who look like me, John Coulter. They do not marry farm girls with calluses on their hands and filth beneath their nails. Women who've grown tanned from working outside and who'd rather hunt rabbits than go to town. Women who don't know the first thing about cotillions—and that's just as well, for they'd never be asked to one anyway." She was so angry, so hurt, that she didn't think she was going to win out over the threatening tears, and so she pulled Mam's wedding handkerchief out of her pocket. The square of lavender soap came with it and plopped onto the grass.

Colt snatched it up before she could. He inhaled the

aroma. "Lavender," he said, before reaching out and placing it in her palm. Closing her fingers about it, he brushed his lips across her fingertips. He leaned so close that she could feel his warm breath at her ear. "I'm going to make you believe me."

She stuffed the bit of soap back into her pocket.

"What else do you keep in that pocket?"

"The broken bits of my mother's rosary."

"The bushwhackers destroyed even that?"

She nodded.

"And I say it again. I am so sorry, Maggie-girl."

"Stop it, now. I won't be turned into a crying fool, here in the middle of camp."

"Mary Margaret Malone is no fool." He chuckled. "All those M's... *magnificent* goes right along."

She looked over at him.

"You are magnificent," he insisted. "And you are loved."

"And you, John Coulter, are daft."

"You'll have to get used to it." He leaned close again and murmured, "What I want to know this night is... am *I* loved?"

Now where was a witty reply when a woman most needed it? A hurricane of emotion raging through her and not a single word would come to mind save one.

Yes.

She didn't know when it had happened. Only that it was true.

John took his leave, and Maggie watched his retreat until the darkness gathered him in. *John.* The intimacy of even thinking the name made her heart pound. After tucking his letter into her satchel, she pulled her blanket about her and lay back on the earth, staring up at the night sky and trying to remember every word that had just been spoken. He'd written to his mother about her. His mother, for heaven's sake. He'd called her magnificent. She would store the memory up against the future.

Admire her as he would, once the battles were over... well. He might think her magnificent to the end of his days, but he would inevitably come to his senses in the matter of marrying. She lay staring up at the stars replaying their conversation over and over in her mind until she fell asleep.

Chapter 20

———— ❧ ————

It was still dark when a general murmuring rolled across the camp. Rising to see what was happening, Maggie caught her breath at the sight of the fire in the distance. Noah climbed out of his bedroll beneath the wagon and came to stand beside her. "Jack was right," he said. "They burned the barn."

"But—why?"

"Jack said it was a perfect place for sharpshooters to hide and pick off the Irish as they marched toward Wildwood Grove. Command must have agreed and given the order to burn it dow—" A horrific blast sent Noah ducking for cover. In the space of a moment, a screeching grew louder and louder and then, the sound of splitting wood on the hill above them—complete with the crash of trees being felled.

Maggie had joined Noah beneath the wagon, and now she peered toward the hill in the direction of the noise. "Wh-what was that?" Noah didn't answer, but someone in the camp hollered about a "12-pounder."

"Guess the rebels didn't appreciate the burning barn," Noah said when it seemed they were safe and the soldiers settled back in their tents.

Maggie rolled up her blanket and tucked it into Fish's wagon before luring Hero out and encouraging him to walk to the tall grass to attend to necessary things. As dawn lit the eastern sky, Noah pointed to three dark sentinels standing on the hill where trees had once been in the path of the cannon-ball. Nothing remained but bare trunks a few feet tall and, scattered about them, the shattered remains of branches and leaves. Maggie shivered. For a moment she thought she might be sick. If a cannon ball could do that to an oak tree...

Bugle calls sounded and the camp came alive. The men ate quickly, many of them not even bothering to sit down in their hurry to get on with the day, strapping on newly filled cartridge pouches, filling the cap pouches hanging from their equipment belts, slinging canteens over their heads, piling knapsacks and haversacks into the supply wagons that would stay at the rear during the battle.

Ashby came trotting up just as assembly sounded. He was carrying a scrap of paper, which he handed to her. "I meant to ask you last night, but then Sergeant Coulter—I didn't want to interrupt, but—would you put my name down?"

"Of course, but—"

"It's Leander, Miss Maggie. Leander Ashby. Mount Sterling, Missouri." He patted the pocket where he kept the little testament he read every night. "Want to tuck it in—just in case—well, you know. I'd want my people to know if I was to—you know."

Maggie retrieved her pencil and wrote the name—ashamed that her hand trembled.

"I got a girl," Ashby said as he watched her write. "Name's Molly. Molly Darnell. If it happens—would you make sure she gets word? And my prayer book. She gave it to me, and I want her to know I kept it close. Looked at it every day. Will you tell her so she knows I died a Christian?"

Maggie nodded. "Of course I will, but, Ashby, it would

have meant so much more to her if you'd written something yourself. When you have a chance, you should write and tell her in your own words."

Ashby shrugged. Looked about, as if making sure no one could hear them. "Yes'm, I know. The thing is—I was ashamed to admit it, after all the boys made fun. You know—about me reading the testament so much."

"Don't let anyone make fun of your faith, Ashby. It's to be admired, no matter what the heathens say."

"I know that. The thing is—" He cleared his throat. "I ain't really reading it. I'm just sort of...pretending." He blushed. "I never quite learned." He tucked the paper with his name on it into his pocket. "You won't tell, will you, Miss Maggie?"

"Not a word."

"Thank you, Miss Maggie. And—God bless you."

Maggie croaked, "You're welcome," and turned away. She put the pencil in her pocket and busied herself with trifles, thinking all the while of Leander Ashby marching into battle, the name he couldn't write himself tucked into his pocket along with a testament he couldn't read.

Ordered to stay in the rear, Maggie watched as her boys moved away from camp as one dark, moving mass, their polished guns gleaming in the sunlight, banners waving, drums beating, the men stepping out in cadence. It seemed to Maggie that every able-bodied man in Little Dixie must be stretched out before her, even though she knew that just as many awaited them less than two miles away.

Word was that once they realized they would have to fight their way south, the Guard and the Ellerbe Militia had dug trenches in a wide arc, their position designed not only to protect the plantation house but also to prevent the enemy from approaching Littleton. Whoever won the battle would also win control of a long stretch of the Missouri River.

As the wagons trundled along through the clouds of dust raised by the marching men, it was all Maggie could do not to run ahead in search of Jack and Seamus. She could see John Coulter in the distance, riding alongside Captain Quinn. How could the sky be blue, the birds be singing, the air be clean and fresh on a day that would soon take them all into— what, she didn't know. It was all she could do to keep walking.

As she moved along, Maggie thrust her left hand into her pocket and touched the beads of Mam's broken rosary. She'd never really seen the point to reciting the same rote prayers over and over again, but she'd cherished the rosary as a connection to Mam. Today, as she fingered a bead, she spoke a name. Ashby and Thomas. Seamus and Jack. John and Fish. Captain Quinn. Private Murphy. And yes, even Philem O'Malley, who might not be the best sort of man but who should have a chance today. A chance to survive. A chance to change. When she ran out of beads, she began again, reciting more names, praying for each one. *Let them do their duty. Let them be brave. Let them survive.*

She thought of the stack of letters in her satchel. John's had only been the first. Other men had come to her this morning. Because of Ashby, she wondered if they were carrying something with them that would tell others who they were. As she scanned the column of men, she regretted the names she didn't know. Why hadn't the army addressed the matter? Perhaps they had, and Ashby had misplaced his. When the battle was over, she would ask Captain Quinn. She would find a way to help keep track of her boys.

As her thoughts settled onto the ways she might be of use, Maggie wondered if she should have offered to help roll bandages. Did the surgeons have enough? And canteens—if she could get to that spring Jack had talked about on the plantation, she could fill and refill canteens so the boys didn't go thirsty. A man could fight when he was hungry, but thirst—thirst had a way of cutting a man down. She'd seen that happen in the fields. But she had not seen war. Had not seen the aftermath of battle.

You can do nothing about that now. Think on what you can do to help them. And so Maggie prayed, reciting the names of her Irish Brigade boys, holding them up for the Almighty's notice. What was it John had said about God? That God had numbered his days and would see that he received every single one. She had not thought on it all that much, but a God who could create a world in seven days could number a man's days. Didn't the Bible say that God noticed when a blackbird fell? No—not a blackbird. A sparrow. That was it.

She thought back to the day when she'd watched Jack and Seamus leave home. A day when there was no John Coulter in her life. She'd thought her heart was breaking that day. She hadn't known the half of it.

Holy Father in heaven. Please help us. Remember us…let us live another day. Make me brave. Make me strong. Show me what needs doing and help me do it. Our Father who art in heaven, hallowed be thy name. Thy kingdom come. Thy will be done on earth…

❧

It was not yet light out, when a thunderous blast shook the house. Ora Lee shrieked. Libbie bolted out of bed and ran to the second-floor hall windows and saw—nothing unusual. Campfires glowing in the darkness. A few tents illuminated by lamps someone had taken inside. The familiar golden light spilling out of the kitchen window that said that Annabelle had awakened and descended the exterior stairs to begin her day in the kitchen. A pale light in the eastern sky.

As Libbie stood at the railing, Annabelle stepped into view in the kitchen doorway and looked in the direction of the awful sound. "Did you hear it?" Libbie called down.

When Annabelle looked up, the light from the kitchen illuminated her strong jaw, her broad shoulders. Libbie could not quite make out the older woman's face, and yet she could imagine the expression in Annabelle's amber eyes as she said, "The saints at rest in the Littleton cemetery heard that, Miss Libbie."

A voice sounded in the night from the direction of the stable. "Just a little welcome for the boys in blue."

Libbie recognized Isham Green's voice before he stepped into the pool of light spilling out of the kitchen. He swept the plumed hat off his head and nodded up at her. "You have nothing to fear, Miss Libbie. Five hundred men will give their lives today rather than see you harmed."

The very idea made her go cold. Wrapping her arms about herself, Libbie stepped back from the railing. She didn't *want* five hundred men to give their lives. She wanted them all to go home. If the Yankees wanted to free the slaves, let them. If the editorials in the *Littleton Leader* were any indication, much of the state of Missouri agreed with her. Walker and his compatriots hadn't even been able to get the resolution passed to secede from the Union. The Guard should all just go home. If the South wanted to fight a war, let them, but leave Missouri out of it.

All of that and more ran through Libbie's mind as she

stood barefoot in the dark, looking down at Isham Green. But she said none of it, lest Major Green scold her for not taking "the cause" seriously. She was taking things quite seriously— just not the same things as Major Green and Walker. They spoke of states' rights and political agendas. Libbie cared about what was going to happen right here at Wildwood Grove when the Federals engaged the Guard. She'd seen Surgeon Johnson's medical equipment when he laid it out in the upstairs bedroom late yesterday, and it didn't take any imagination to know that the doctor was expecting horrible things to happen in that room. The prospect terrified her.

The eastern sky was growing light. A golden glow was visible just above the roofline of the stables. Had something exploded? She asked Major Green, and he laughed. "I sincerely hope so. We wouldn't want to think that Major Lusk's battery just wasted a 12-pounder."

"Looks like it set fire to something," Libbie said, and just then one of the other officers came hurrying up and in a low voice, obviously designed to keep Libbie from hearing what was being said, reported something to Major Green, who did not take care to lower his voice as he swore about whatever it was he'd just heard.

"I must go," he called up to Libbie and headed off into the night.

Libbie retreated back inside. Her refusing to leave had thrown Walker into a momentary tizzy. He reminded her that all of her furniture had been broken down and put in storage. Libbie said that she and Ora Lee could camp in the back room. It wasn't possible, Walker said. Well, of course it was, Libbie replied, and proceeded to prove him wrong. She and Ora Lee descended to the basement and dragged Libbie's feather bed and another mattress back up the stairs along with enough bedding to be serviceable, and before all was said and done, Libbie was comfortably "camping" in the back room.

As soon as she was dressed, she descended to the kitchen, just as Annabelle pulled a loaf of fresh-baked bread out of the oven. Libbie closed her eyes and inhaled. Her mouth watered as she envisioned a generous slab of butter and a dollop of Annabelle's blackberry preserves painted across a slice of that bread. But that would have to wait. First—*Robert*.

"Robert's down at the encampment," Betty said as soon as Libbie asked about him. "Mastah Blair said all the officers travel with at least one slave."

"You want I should take a message down?" Malachi had been sitting at the small kitchen table when Libbie first came in. Now he rose, hat in hand, ready to do Libbie's bidding. Libbie hesitated. "I don't—know. I thought we should have a plan of some kind. Walker assured me that there was no need for concern, what with the white flag designating us a hospital, but—"

Cooper came hurrying in. "Yankees coming," he said. "I was up to the quarters and I heard the cannon. Climbed that tree just off Overseer James's outhouse. I could see 'em, flags and all. Heard 'em, too. The drums."

A chill swept over her and Libbie said, "I want you all to come into the house. We'll go down to the basement, where the furniture is stored." No one said a word, but Libbie pressed on. "We should haul some buckets of water down there. Food, too."

"This house a hospital, Miss Libbie," Betty said. "No one gonna fire on a hospital."

The words were barely out of her mouth when Isham Green came loping across the yard with four soldiers in tow and bounded into the house. Maybe she was worried for no reason. With armed men in place—but just then, the upstairs windows opened and Green could be heard giving the men orders to "make every shot count."

Malachi spoke up. "Sharpshooters."

Libbie frowned. "But—that means the enemy will—"

"Yes'm." Malachi nodded. "Soon as they catch on, the Yankees will fire on the house to put a stop to it."

Libbie looked at the people in the room. "So. Unless you're planning on leaving—and I don't blame you if you are, but— if you're staying, we need a plan. Now. And the only one I can think of is to take shelter in the basement, because you won't be allowed weapons."

Annabelle harrumphed. "Ain't no freedom-lovin' Yankee chasin' me outta the only home I've ever known." She reached for a basket. "I be gatherin' up what I can soon as my bread comes out the oven. Then I'll head for the basement."

Betty spoke next, and she sounded almost hopeful. "Robert says we be safe right here in the house." She glanced at Libbie and then away. "Wouldn't mind if you was to get the key, though, Miss Libbie—now that Robert got to be with Mastah Blair."

Annabelle let out a huff. It sounded suspiciously like she was trying to silence Betty, but when Libbie looked her way, Annabelle said nothing.

"Is anyone going to tell me what's going on? I'm concerned for more than just you—us. I was hoping Robert or Malachi would somehow get word to the field hands, too. Tell them we'll do our best to shelter them if they want to come to the house. That'll be nearly thirty people, and from what I know of the basement, we'll be hard pressed to keep that many safe, what with all the furniture and half the things that were in the attic filling it up now. I know I should have said something—or done something—before now, but—well, I was afraid of what Walker might say. Or do." She felt foolish when she realized that she'd just raised her hand to touch the place where he'd struck her. She sensed rather than heard or saw communication passing among the people in the room.

Malachi was the one who finally spoke, and what he said was directed at Ora Lee. "Tell Miss Libbie about them keys," he said.

"She know they there," Ora Lee responded.

Libbie frowned. "Are you talking about the row of keys in Walker's office? Behind that panel?" It was a stupid question. "If I retrieve them—does someone know what they open?"

"Robert knows about all of 'em," Betty said. "But he won't say. He never dared." She took a wavering breath. "Don't want nothing to happen to my two mens. Don't think I'd live through it if Mastah Blair was to take a notion to sell 'em, and if he find out we been talkin' about them keys, he do it, sure."

"I'll get the keys," Libbie said. "As it happens, I already knew about them. What I don't quite understand is how they'll keep us all safe." She glanced at Malachi. "But I expect I'm about to find out." She nodded to Betty and Ora Lee. "You two see what you can do about getting us some water." She glanced outside, wondering how long they would all be trapped in the basement. How many wounded would be brought to the house? How much blood would spill onto the polished wood floor in that upstairs bedroom? She shuddered.

Malachi took a step. Libbie looked up just in time to see the exchange of knowing looks between the old man and his wife. An imperceptible nod from Annabelle, and Malachi spoke to Betty. "You tend to the water, like Miss Libbie says. Then see about breakfast for the surgeon and his men. I'll show her what she needs to see." He hesitated before asking Libbie, "You sure you want to invite the field hands up here from quarters?"

Annabelle muttered something about "no-account field hands," but when Malachi put his hand on her shoulder, she stopped. "I know, old man, I know. The Lord don't like it and I am willing to change how I feel, but that's how I feel now."

"You can stand it if you have to," Malachi said.

"Reckon I can," Annabelle muttered. "Reckon I will. Don't mean I got to like it."

Libbie took a deep breath. "They deserve a chance," she said.

Malachi nodded. "Yes ma'am." He glanced over at Cooper. "You run down there, tell them Miss Libbie say if they want to stay on the place, they come to the stable. Wait for Malachi." He glanced at Libbie. "I am sorry, Miss Libbie, but they're not likely to trust you. Best they come to me. I'll bring them in—the ones that want to come."

It made sense. Why would any of them trust her? Why would anyone, when it came down to it? What had she ever done to show herself worthy of trust? She thanked Malachi, and together they went inside. She could hear men in the upstairs hall. The surgeon and Major Green were having a heated debate about the presence of the sharpshooters. Libbie hurried into Walker's office, pressed on the false panel, and collected the keys—which were no longer covered with dust and cobwebs. Someone had used them.

Annabelle met them at the servants' entrance at the back of the house. She'd lit two small kerosene lamps—the kind that everyone used for middle-of-the-night visits to the necessary at the edge of the woods. Handing one to Libbie and one to Malachi, the cook said something about warm bread and hot coffee and retreated to the kitchen.

The stairs to the basement had always been steep. Libbie descended slowly, grateful for the whitewashed walls to reflect the light. At the bottom of the stairs, she realized that early morning light was spilling through the narrow basement windows on the eastern side of the house.

She was about to extinguish the lamp when Malachi said, "No'm. You be needing that directly." He motioned for Libbie to proceed into the half of the basement where the furniture had been stored.

All the bedding in the house had been required to drape things to Walker's satisfaction, and things had been arranged in the four corners of the room depending on what room they would be returned to one day. At one time, he'd almost had a second kitchen added down here, and even had paneled walls installed. But then a fire at another house where the owner had installed an oven in the basement convinced Walker that the plan was unwise. Libbie had never questioned the story and never paid the wood paneling any mind. But as she stood with Malachi, watching the old man survey a portion of one paneled wall, Libbie realized there was more to the way the furniture was stacked in the room than where things belonged upstairs.

Malachi was running his calloused hands across those boards, obviously looking for something. *Ah.* A loose board. When he dislodged it and pulled it away from what should be the rough stone foundation to the house, a key hole came into view. Next, Malachi counted a few boards over from the key hole and removed two more loose boards. *Hinges*. He ran his hand over the rest of the boards. "This here the foundation wall of the house, Miss Libbie. Whatever's on the other side of this door is under the yard. A good place to be safe, if a body was to need one."

Libbie had just tried the first key when she heard booted feet clomping down the stairs.

Chapter 21

Deafening rebel yells and smoke, thundering cannon, and a constant barrage of rapid fire from the trenches. Blue reared up and tried to bolt, but Colt held him in, and the Irish kept going, a solid line responding to the drums as the cadence quickened until finally, with the order to charge, what had once been a few acres of farmland was transformed. Slouch hats and kepis, flannel shirts and frock coats all blended together as the men of the Irish Brigade surged forward to meet the Wildwood Guard and the Ellerbe Militia.

When Colt first saw the flash of pale green calico and realized what it was, his blood ran cold. The din of battle folded in on itself as he focused on a lone figure crouching over a fallen man. Still astride Blue, Colt charged behind the lines and dropped to the earth, screaming at Maggie. "What d'ya think you're doing!"

She was carrying a canteen—no, four. And two haversacks. While Colt watched, she opened one haversack, pulled out a roll of bandages, and quickly fashioned a tourniquet about the man's upper leg. She was pale, but she worked quickly, leaning close and saying something to the soldier, who lay back, his expression one of agony—and no wonder. The leg was mangled.

Colt yelled at her. "You have to move back! You're to stay in the rear!"

Wild-eyed and red-faced, Maggie refused. She pushed him away, screaming, "Go on with ya! Win the blessed battle before anyone else dies!" On the far side of the field, another man went down, and before Colt could prevent it, Maggie was off and running, her skirt tucked into her belt, her feet flying, her back hunched—as if by bending low she could protect herself from the virtual hail of minié balls peppering the Irish.

❧

Libbie had handed Malachi the keys and stepped in front of him before Major Green appeared in the doorway. No acting ability was required to make her voice tremble when she spoke. "I—I thought—" She bit her lower lip and put her hands to her temples. "I'm goin' ta bring the house servants down here," she said. "I'll go mad if I have to listen to it." Just then a cannon blasted away in the distance. Libbie let out a little screech. "I saw you bring those men in here. They're sharpshooters, aren't they? That means the Yankees will fire on the house!"

Major Green looked back up the stairs and then at her. "I was just coming to find you," he said. "To tell you to do this very thing." He motioned around them and then looked at Malachi. "Have your woman bring some provisions down here and y'all stay put until this thing is over, y'hear?"

"Yes sir," Malachi said. "We do that, sir. And thank you, sir."

Would he see the boards they'd removed? Did he know about whatever was behind the hidden door? If so, Green gave no indication, but they couldn't afford for him to stay down here any longer. Libbie hurried to his side. "I should have gone to Omaha," she said. "I don't know what I was thinkin'." She put her hand on the major's forearm.

He covered it with his own and gave it a pat. "I'll send

some of my own men to guard the stairs if it'll give you peace of mind."

"You mustn't do that," Libbie said quickly. "You need every able body in the camp to get rid of the infernal Yankees." She glanced back toward where Malachi stood, positioned in a way that mostly hid the boards he'd removed and leaned against the wall. "We'll be all right," she said. "Just—" She gave his arm a little squeeze, hoping he would take her inability to finish the sentence as evidence of a heart filled with emotion. It would not do for him to witness Libbie's discovering one of Walker's secrets—with the help of a slave.

Green cleared his throat and spoke to Malachi. "You take good care of Miss Libbie, and you will be well rewarded."

"I will, sir." Malachi nodded. "Ain't no reward necessary, Mastah Green. We all loves Miss Libbie. We won't let nothin' happen to her."

Finally, Green turned and headed back up the stairs.

In minutes, Libbie had discovered the right key. The door opened, revealing another room, this one empty. Set into the far stone wall was yet another door. Libbie hurried over to it. Once the right key was inserted into the old lock, Malachi pulled it open. A gust of damp, dusty air blew past thick cobwebs trailing down from the moldy ceiling. With a shudder, Libbie backed away. Tilted her head. Peered into the darkness, and saw . . . a circle of light at the far end of what had to be a tunnel leading down to the river.

⚬≈≈⚬

Colt was about to run after Maggie and carry her bodily back to the rear, when the odd angle of a muzzle flash made him look toward the brick plantation house. They were flying a white flag—marking it a hospital and, therefore, not to be a target, but when yet another flash emerged from the second-story window, Colt realized it was only subterfuge. They might be planning on using the house for a hospital at some point, but right now it was providing cover for at least two rebel sharpshooters. Unless someone stopped them, they'd have free rein to fire on the Irish.

Leaping back into the saddle, Colt urged Blue forward. He charged past Maggie, who was kneeling beside yet another fallen soldier in a vain attempt to stanch the flow of blood from a neck wound. "Go back, Maggie! Go back!" he screamed, and then he was gone, flattening himself against Blue's neck and charging into the fray.

He couldn't do it alone. *Dear God, show me.* He slid off Blue, slapped the horse's haunches, and sent him running, then hesitated, grateful when he caught sight of Jack Malone with a squad moving toward the river. An attempt to flank the enemy, come up behind the battery, and eliminate the threat of those cannons.

Catching up with the squad, Colt charged after Jack, slapping him on the shoulder, pointing at the house, and yelling "Sharpshooters!"

The squad slid down the steep hillside toward the river, moving from tree to tree, taking cover, catching their breath, and finally making it to the rock wall. A blast from the howitzer aboard the *McDowell* hit the rock and sent them all ducking for cover. Jack slapped one man on the back and sent him scrambling up into one of the trees, from where he'd use a mirror to help the howitzer operator on board the steamboat hone in on the enemy battery. Those cannons had to be put out of commission.

Another squad was coming up behind them, and when they arrived, Colt gave orders that would provide cover for the man going up the tree. Pointing at Ashby and Thomas, Seamus and Jack, and motioning for them to come with him, Colt set off up the river in the general direction of the house.

They would have to clear out the rebels guarding the levee to reach the house—unless they could creep past unnoticed. They almost made it, but not quite. Ferocious fire broke out between the two squads. The rebels took shelter behind a six-foot wall of hemp bales stacked on the levee, and for what felt like hours, Colt and his men used the trees for cover, ducking out to take shots that had no more effect on the rebels behind the hemp bales than a child tossing pebbles to destroy a rock wall.

Feeling helpless, Colt looked past the bales of hemp and toward the hillside beyond where a narrow path led up to the house. He was just about to order all of the squad except Jack to fire at will and create cover for a desperate charge toward that narrow trail when a Negro boy skittered into view. He seemed to have emerged from the hillside itself. Another man appeared next to him, and together the two launched something at the bales of hemp. They disappeared from view—but not before Colt realized what they'd done. They'd thrown oil lamps—lighted lamps—at the hemp.

When the hemp began to burn, the rebels who'd been using it for cover scattered, some up the very path Colt wanted to follow to the house, others upriver along the water's edge, and still others actually into the river itself. Colt signaled Seamus and the others to defend their current position. Then, firing their pistols, Jack and Colt charged past the flaming bales of hemp and after the men who'd run up the trail. A massive explosion sounded from the direction of the battery. Apparently the howitzer had finally done its work and eliminated that threat.

Together, Jack and Colt chased up the trail. Four rebels waited at the top of the trail, determined to keep them from reaching the house. Spinning away, Jack and Colt dove for cover beneath a tangle of vines while shots peppered the earth around them. Colt had just about managed to reload when a loud pop sounded. Whoever was out there was coming after them. Plunging out from beneath the cover, Colt wielded his rifle like a club. The butt hit the soldier just below the ear and he went down like a felled tree, but not before a minié ball cut a path through one sideburn and clipped Colt's ear. His hand went to the side of his head. It came back red with blood. He staggered and almost went down. Jack took aim and fired. The rebel fell at the top of the trail, and together the men charged up the last few feet, broke into the open, and raced across the lawn to the house.

They took shelter behind the hedges flanking the steps, catching their breath and taking stock. Jack checked Colt's ear. "Just a nick, but it's bleeding bad." He untied the kerchief about his neck and handed it over. Colt took his hat off, tied the bandanna around his head and over the torn ear, and pulled the hat back on.

"You think there's really wounded men inside?" Jack asked.

"Hard to tell," Colt replied. "Haven't seen them carry anyone off the field, but that doesn't mean much."

"Has to be a surgeon and a couple of assistants at least inside."

"They're supposed to be noncombatants."

"Right. And this is supposed to be a hospital, not a nest of sharpshooters."

"How many?"

"Two, at least."

"Wouldn't mind having a couple more of our boys with us."

"Wouldn't mind it," Jack agreed. "Don't have it."

Colt nodded, and together the men crept up the steps and onto the porch. They hunkered down so they wouldn't be visible through the narrow windows on either side of the door. Jack popped up quickly to take stock and whispered, "The hall's empty."

"What about Miss Blair?" Colt asked.

Jack shook his head. "Bridget heard she was being sent to Omaha."

Colt nodded. That was good. Slowly, he turned the knob and opened the screen door just far enough for Jack to do the same with the main door. The door wasn't locked. They both took a deep breath. Exchanged glances. Nodded. And burst through the door.

❧

Libbie stood at the base of the basement stairs, trembling—listening. Only moments ago, Malachi had brought half a dozen of the field hands up from the stable. Now the four women and two men crouched in a corner of the safe room clinging to one another and seemingly afraid to accept so much as a drink of water, even from Annabelle's hand. One of the women had been crying since the moment they arrived. She didn't make a sound, but tears streamed down her face in spite of attempts to comfort her from the younger of the two men.

"Only six?" Libbie had said after the half dozen had passed by her and settled in a corner on the opposite side of the room from the house servants.

"Six is better than none," Malachi said.

Libbie supposed he was right. Still, she was disappointed. If Malachi knew what had become of the rest of the field hands, he wasn't saying. Perhaps they'd run off as soon as they could get away without being noticed. As for the six who braved a glance her way every once in a while, who could blame them if they didn't trust her? She'd never done anything for them. Never paid them any mind.

Shots rang out from up above, and Libbie's heart began to pound. It was hard to believe that Walker would have agreed to the stationing of sharpshooters on the second floor of the house. He'd done everything he could to protect the place. But where was Walker? Libbie had expected him to check in with her at first light. She'd asked Isham Green about him, but Green had merely shrugged and said that he and Walker were acting "independently" today—whatever that meant. Walker wasn't a soldier. Where was he? Maybe they'd argued about the sharpshooters. Was that what Green had meant about their "acting independently"?

Ora Lee was the first one to cross the room and speak to the newcomers. Taking up a loaf of bread, she offered it to the youngest of the four women, who took it, tore a bit off, and then passed it to the next person. Betty brought a bucket of water and a dipper over. The youngest woman said thank you, took a drink, and passed the dipper.

Cooper came to Malachi's side and said something. Malachi brought the boy's concern to Libbie. "Might be we should talk," he said, clearly wanting to have a word in private.

Libbie led the way into the storage room. "What is it?"

"Might be we should think on what we'd do if the house don't hold. Them Yankees get mad enough, they're likely to use some mighty big guns to stop them men up on the second floor."

Shouts and curses sounded from up above. A thud and then an odd sound just outside the narrow basement window as if gravel were falling from the sky.

"Somethin' hit the house," Malachi said. "Back wall. They've seen the sharpshooters."

A chill coursed through Libbie, and she looked past the stairs and at the door to the tunnel. "But even if we run to the river, what then? It can't be any safer than an underground room."

"Likely be just fine right where we are," Malachi agreed. "But we'd be safer if it was up to us who we opened doors to and who we kept out. At least until it's all settled."

He thought they should hide in the secret room. Maybe he was right. Libbie nodded. "All right. Let's move everyone in, but—we won't be able to lock it from inside."

Malachi knew what to do. In a few moments, they'd moved all the food and water into the secret room—along with the candles Annabelle had brought with her. Both doors opened into the room, and they used furniture that had been put in storage to bar the one that connected to the house, but Libbie wanted to know more about the tunnel, and so she and Malachi and Cooper went into the tunnel with the small kerosene lamps to light the way.

Libbie shivered as cobwebs swept across her face and shuddered at the imagined sounds of creatures scuttling away from them. Halfway down the tunnel, they stumbled over an odd collection of crates and boxes. When shouts and gunshots echoed up the tunnel from the direction of the river, Malachi and Cooper put the lamps out. They stood in the dark, listening. Something was going on down at the levee. The Yankees must have gotten past the trenches and come up along the river. Thinking on it reminded Libbie of the day she'd caught Jack Malone and John Coulter doing just that.

Malachi muttered something about seeing what was happening, and although Libbie protested, he paid her no mind, but crept away. His hulking form almost obliterated the light at the far end of the tunnel where it must open just above the river—not far from the levee. A smaller form was following Malachi; Cooper was going after him.

Minutes passed. Suddenly, there was an odd flash of light and a shout and more gunfire, and suddenly Malachi and Cooper were hurrying back toward her. They were only halfway to her side when they both stopped. Waited. And then, for whatever reason, they seemed to think it safe to move again and they came to her side. They smelled of kerosene, but when Libbie wanted them to light one of the lamps again, they didn't have them. Cooper slipped away and was back in a moment with a candle, which flickered dangerously low but gave enough light for Libbie to look over the crates. They were nailed shut.

"Leave them," Libbie said, and together they returned to the secret room. They didn't completely bar the door that opened onto the tunnel. Instead, they cracked the door to let air flow into the room, and to listen to the distant sound of the battle. Things were quiet on the levee now as far as Libbie could tell, but she knew that what sounded like distant thunder was nothing so harmless as a summer storm.

"What gonna happen to us, Miss Libbie?"

In the gray light, Libbie had no idea who'd asked the question. And no idea how to answer it.

Chapter 22

Bursting in the front door of the plantation house, Colt and Jack darted past the rooms on the main floor and charged to the stairs. They hadn't reached the top when two rebels ran to the railing. Gunfire erupted, bits of plaster flying, as Colt and Jack fought their way up to the second floor. One rebel fell in the hall while the other one ducked into a back room. Jack charged after him.

More gunfire, and Jack appeared in the doorway and shouted, "Room's clear!"

Together, he and Colt moved toward the rooms opening onto the far end of the hall.

"We're medical personnel in here," a voice called out. "Three of us. Surgeon Johnson and two assistants. Only wounded men in the room across the hall."

There was a moment of silence, with Colt wondering what to do next, and then hades itself came charging in the back door down on the main floor in the guise of a squad of the Wildwood Guard. One of them hit the bottom step just as Colt glanced over the railing. He fell back, shot by one of Colt's squad, who were just now pouring into the house through the front door. Colt and Jack ducked out of the line of fire and into the room where three men stood in a corner, their hands raised above their heads.

Colt motioned for the three men to sit down. They obeyed. When he'd determined that the rebels were indeed unarmed, he and Jack crossed to the other room, where, as the surgeon had said, half a dozen wounded men lay on makeshift cots on the floor.

They waited, listening as the conflict below disintegrated into shouts and a few shots punctuated, finally, with a profane declaration of surrender that was not at all complementary to the United States Army. Jack stepped out of the room, and someone shot through the floor, barely missing him.

"Hold your fire!" he yelled.

"Who goes there?"

"Seamus, is that you? It's Jack, and you darned near shot my foot off."

Colt went to the top of the stairs, where Seamus could see him. "Two dead, three unarmed, six wounded up here."

Jack motioned for the surgeon and his assistants to come out, sending them down the stairs ahead of him and Colt.

Wallpaper that had once depicted a pastoral scene with willow trees mirrored in a lake was now peppered with blotches of brown and white where the plaster and lathe showed through. Strangely, the brass light with crystal shades hanging from the center of the ceiling had survived the indoor skirmish unscathed. Three wounded rebels leaned against one wall—and each other.

The surgeon spoke up. "May I attend to the wounded?"

Colt nodded, and the doctor went to work. He was kneeling beside the first patient when he looked up and said, "Now that the house really is nothing more than a hospital, you might wish to inform the lady in the basement that it's safe for her and her Negroes to come out."

Maggie didn't know how long it had been since John had screamed at her to go back to safety in the rear. He'd been astride Blue and he'd kept going, tearing across the battlefield, finally dismounting and disappearing into the fray. She'd watched with a horrible kind of fascination as Blue galloped away, willing both horse and rider to somehow fill only the spaces between the bullets. And then, when Colt dropped out of sight, she'd looked down at the boy she was tending and was jerked back to another terrible reality.

She could not stop the bleeding, and when she raised her hand from the neck wound and saw why, her heart lurched. She could smell the blood. Bile rose to her mouth. The boy was staring up at her with panic in his eyes, and with everything that was in her, Maggie mustered kindness and an expression that she desperately willed to feign hope. He was barely old enough to grow a beard. The patchy blond stubble served only to make him look like a child trying to be a man. He was going to die, and she would have to watch, for she would not let him die alone. She hunkered down beside him. "Tell me your name."

One hand fluttered toward his chest. He gurgled something about a message in his pocket.

"Don't worry," Maggie said. "I'll see to it." She put her hand over his and stared into his pale eyes. "Look at me, Private. You aren't alone. The Good Lord is here and so is Maggie Malone. Neither of us is leaving you." She had just begun to recite the Our Father when the light in his pale eyes flickered and went out.

Not far away, a shell burst. A horse screamed. Thinking of Blue, Maggie spun about, but the victim was a bay, and both horse and rider had gone down, the horse landing on its side and never moving. Maggie left the boy she'd just seen off and ran to the rider. Already gone. Nothing to do. She inched her way up the horse's carcass and peered out over the field, not wanting to believe what was before her. It was impossible to tell who might yet be alive. For a moment all she could think of was that she would be safe here, beside the animal's carcass. Hunkered down, nothing would harm her.

A yell made her look toward a copse of low bushes and a wounded man trying to drag himself beneath them. The same instincts drove them both. Find shelter. Get away. Swallowing, Maggie closed her eyes. *Our Father... help me!* Before she could think another word, she ran for the soldier. He'd passed out—or so she thought.

When she sank down beside him, he groaned. He opened his eyes and, with a look of horror, begged, "Help me. Please. Just—I'm sorry. Don't let me die."

A rebel. No uniform to identify him as such, but there was no mistaking that drawl. *Somebody's brother-son-father.* She could not cry out to God for help and then turn away from the first man He brought her way.

"You're not dying today," she snapped. "Not if I can help it." She ripped the blood-soaked shirt open and saw it. Not the wound, but a filthy length of braided string fashioned into a kind of necklace threaded with beads and shells. *And a coin.* A battered, ancient coin from Ireland. Her mother's coin.

The bushwhacker grabbed her hand, croaked another plea, and either lost consciousness or died. Maggie wasn't sure which at first, and she wasn't sure she cared, for rage and anger threatened to dissolve compassion. For a moment, she sat frozen, the bandage roll clenched so tightly in her palm that her hand went numb. She closed her eyes. Swallowed. And went back to work. What she'd thought to be blood from a gut wound had actually spread from the bushwhacker's arm. He must have cradled it against himself as he scrambled off the field. He would lose the arm, but thanks to Maggie, he wouldn't bleed to death.

Lord have mercy. Help me. Help me. Help. A scream brought her back into the battle. As if waking from a nightmare, she ran to the next fallen man. And then the next. And the next. Crawling when she had to. Crouching. Running. Praying. *Our Father... help. Father... help.* As all around her, boys lay dying.

❧

After what felt like hours of waiting, Libbie convinced Malachi to come with her to the far end of the tunnel. Just to listen, she said. To try and understand what was happening. If it might be safe to venture out. The room echoed with the sound as they slid the crates they'd used to bar the door out of the way and slowly opened it. They decided not to take candles this time. They knew about the crates off to the left. If they stayed to the right and moved toward the light, nothing would impede their progress.

Grateful for the weeds and the tangle of vines that undoubtedly obscured the narrow tunnel opening from any casual observer, Libbie paused, listening for the battle. Hearing nothing. Frowning she looked over at Malachi. "Could it be finished already?"

When she moved as if to step into the sunlight, Malachi touched her arm. "Sorry, Miss Libbie, but—you best be sure."

And so they waited. And waited. And finally retreated back to the hidden room. After a few moments, they opened the door into the basement. Only a few inches at first. Libbie was afraid to go farther. There might be silence down by the river, but men were fighting inside the house. Gunshots. Yells. And the faint smell of burned gunpowder, even here in the basement. Who was up there? Friend or enemy? Libbie stepped back into the safe room and pulled the door closed behind her. After another few moments, she decided that she couldn't stand to wait any longer. "I'm going to go out through the tunnel and see what I can learn."

There was a murmur of dissent. Annabelle spoke up. "Not by yourself you ain't. I ain't fed you all these years to have you shot by some fool shooting first and looking later."

"I'll come, too," Ora Lee said.

Annabelle nodded. "Be good if you come with us." She glanced over at her husband. "Stay with these field hands and don't let 'em get in any trouble. We be back directly and see to y'all." She spoke to the field hands. "Just don't be runnin' off. You be safe and you won't go hungry if you stay put with the rest of us." Annabelle gestured at the door to the tunnel. "Best be getting on with it, Miss Libbie. I got a bad feeling about leavin' my kitchen to whosoever might take a notion to inspect the premises. Sooner I get back to it, better I'll feel."

Libbie suspected it was mostly bravado, but somehow Annabelle's speech and attitude gave her courage, and so she led the way back up the tunnel. Once again, she paused to listen, and once again she heard nothing to warn her away from ducking into the light to take stock of things.

The first thing she saw was the burned hemp and, at the base of the hemp, shattered glass and a broken lantern. The fire had sputtered out, but most of the bales were badly damaged. Stepping carefully, Libbie made her way past the levee. She saw the first body—and clamped both hands over her mouth to keep from screaming. When she took a step back, Annabelle reached from behind to grasp her forearms and to turn her toward the trail that led up the hill to the house. She could hear drums and a bugle, but no accompanying gunfire. What did the drums mean? The bugle?

The three women picked their way along the edge of the woods growing up the hillside from the river, pausing when the roof of the kitchen came into view. And then the main floor windows. They crept up the hill, past the necessary, to the back wall of the kitchen and the one window on this side that faced the river. It was open, and they could hear someone inside.

Annabelle took a peek, and practically growled, "You better *get* your no-account Yankee hands off them preserves!"

Before Libbie could hold her back, Annabelle hurried away. The three women rounded the corner just as a Yankee soldier stepped through the door, cradling two jars of preserves in one arm.

The man quickly rearranged his expression of surprise into a not-very-convincing smile. "Lookee here, Mammy—I think I earned the right—"

"I ain't your Mammy," Annabelle snapped, and she grabbed the preserves. "And these here is Miss Libbie's. She say you can have some, you can have 'em. Until then—they belong to her and Mastah Blair."

If Annabelle expected the soldier to pale beneath her diatribe, she was disappointed, for the man growled an epithet and took a step forward. Annabelle stood her ground. Libbie was just about to invite him to help himself to anything in the kitchen he wanted when a voice sounded from the back door of the house.

"Private O'Malley. I don't believe your orders included a stop at the kitchen."

Libbie had never seen insolence salute, but she saw it

now, although the man's sneer faded when he turned to face the man giving the order. "No sir. Just doing a little—reconnoitering, sir. Making sure there wasn't some rebel coward hiding in one of the outbuildings."

Relief flooded through her when Libbie recognized Jack Malone. Malone met her gaze and gave a little nod before glaring back at the private. "Don't see a single coward. Do you?"

The private hurried off in the general direction of the garden and what had been the Wildwood Guard encampment. Libbie watched him go. And then she saw the battlefield. A sea of men... wounded... or dead? Surely not all of them dead. Horses. Shattered caissons. Splintered trees. Ruin.

"Lord have mercy."

Ora Lee said it. Annabelle echoed it. Libbie whispered it, even as she staggered forward toward the garden, unbelieving, her hand at her mouth. She paused beside the well, staring across the field to the row of cabins in the distance that had been the quarters. Avoiding the sight of the men on the field, she looked back at the stable. Something had blown away the far end of the roof. The corner beneath that part of the roof had dissolved into red brick rubble. Libbie swallowed, remembering the fit she'd thrown when Walker insisted they take Pilot and the carriage horse into town and board them there. Now she was grateful he'd done it.

Malone had come to stand beside her. "Part of the intelligence I gathered in Littleton indicated that your brother had sent you to Omaha."

Libbie shrugged. "He tried. I refused." She gazed back out at the battlefield. Where was Walker in all of this? "Do you know—have you seen my brother?"

"I'm sorry, no." Malone gestured toward the battlefield. "It could be a while before we know much. Some of the Ellerbe

Militia hightailed it toward Littleton—probably planning to take a stand there. I doubt it'll be more than a skirmish."

"More fighting," Libbie said. "In Littleton." She took a deep breath.

Malone must have thought she might faint, for he reached out to take her arm. "Where—I mean how—where'd you come from?" he asked. "The surgeon told me there was a woman in the basement, but we searched. There was no sign of anyone."

For a moment, Libbie hesitated to explain. Would she perhaps need that secret room again? But then she gazed back at the house and noticed the pockmarks in the brick walls, the broken windows, the screen door ripped from its hinges and lying in the grass. The white flag tied to the upstairs balcony, fluttering in the breeze. It was over—at least for Wildwood Grove. The battle was over and they had lost, and what did it matter if Jack Malone knew about Walker's secret room?

The warmth of Malone's hand on her arm steadied her. "I am very glad to see that you are all right," he said. He looked past her at Annabelle and Ora Lee. "I'm glad you're all safe."

Annabelle eyed him for a moment before asking, "Yankees eat corn pone?"

Malone smiled. "These days, Yankees are grateful for anything that's offered, ma'am."

Ma'am. Annabelle narrowed her gaze. "Don't you be 'ma'am-in'' me. Name's Annabelle."

"Yes, ma—Annabelle." Malone nodded.

"Can't feed the whole army," Annabelle said, "but I'll see what I can rustle up for you and the doctors in the house. They be workin' all through the night, I expect."

Malone sighed audibly. Nodded.

Libbie reached into her pocket and took out the keys.

"Come with me," she said. "I'll show you." She took a step toward the house, then turned back. "Ora Lee. You stay and help Annabelle. I'll be back directly with Betty and the others. Then we'll—" She glanced at Jack Malone. "Maybe we'll know what we should do."

Malachi and Cooper showed no fear and seemed to recognize Jack when he and Libbie stepped into the basement. As far as Libbie knew, Betty had never seen Jack Malone, but she followed Malachi and Cooper's lead. The field hands, however, shrank back into the corner they'd first occupied a few hours ago.

Malone tried to reassure them, but it wasn't until Malachi spoke up that they seemed to relax a little. "This here Mr. Jack Malone. He and his brother own a farm just past the Grove. They good people. You be all right if you do what Mr. Malone say."

The taller of the two men who hadn't run off stood a little straighter. "We got to go back to the quarters, Miss Libbie?"

Libbie didn't know. When she hesitated, Malone spoke up, and before long the field hands followed him upstairs and back outside in search of the quartermaster. Jack said he would welcome their help and see that they shared army rations in return for their work. Libbie heard one of the women say that that was just fine but the Yankees would have to make arrangements with Mastah Blair once the mastah returned to the Grove.

Everyone carried a water bucket and one of the baskets of food they'd brought down with them as they made their way back up the stairs and outside. A buggy was driving in from the direction of town. Libbie recognized Dr. Feeny.

In the time it had taken for her to lead Jack Malone down

to the basement, a dozen wounded men had made their way to the yard. They were seated near one another in the shade of one of the oldest apple trees on the place. The only apple tree in the yard. Another wagon pulled up in the drive, this one pulled by mules. Jack Malone hurried to it, and as Libbie watched, two of the field hands took litters from the wagon bed and headed for the battlefield. Jack led the women toward Dr. Feeny. Apparently they would become nurses, at least for the next few hours.

Libbie handed the basket she'd carried up from the basement to Betty. Water bucket in hand, she stood staring out at the battlefield. This must be what it was like to live inside a nightmare. She caught a glimpse of someone trotting across the field in the distance. A woman. A woman? Whoever she was, she knelt beside a man...tending him, it seemed. As Libbie watched, another man lifted his hand. The woman moved to him, bending low, obviously comforting him. And again Libbie wondered. Was Walker out there somewhere?

The image of Walker lying on the battlefield, alone and wounded, somehow pierced the fog that had shrouded her mind since she'd seen the slain soldier down by the levee. And the burned hemp...and everything else. Since then, she'd been reacting to whatever happened. Not really thinking so much as scrambling just to stay ahead of the immediate. Now, she rallied.

If Walker was out there, it was her duty to find him. To see that he was cared for. She refused the other possibility. Forced the word *death* out of her thoughts. She wouldn't think about that now. Now...she needed to move. But first, the men beneath the apple tree. She set her own water bucket down and stepped to the kitchen. "Ora Lee. Betty. I'm going to take this water and go look for my brother. There's wounded men

out here in the yard. Get some more buckets and start hauling water. When you've seen to these men, I want you to go
inside the house and ask the surgeon if you can help him."
She glanced over at the men. They weren't so badly hurt that
they wouldn't welcome a bit of food. "Offer the bread we had
downstairs to anyone here in the yard who wants it. Small
pieces. Make it go as far as you can."

Betty spoke up. "They Yankees. Maybe they kilt Mastah
Blair." Her eyes filled with tears as she croaked, "Maybe they
kilt my Robert."

Betty was right, of course. Perhaps they had. But as Libbie
looked about her, all she could think was that she didn't want
any part in killing or, for that matter, in causing still more
suffering by withholding help.

"If you don't want to do it," she snapped, "then don't. But
if someone I loved was hurt in some Yankee town, I'd hope
there'd be kind women there who'd look past the uniform
and see a man who needed help." She glanced over at Ora
Lee. "Will you do it?"

"Yes'm," she said.

"Thank you." In the kitchen, Libbie retrieved a dipper, and
picking up the water bucket, she headed for the battlefield.

Chapter 23

———— ⌇ ————

Closing her eyes, Maggie listened. To silence. Blessed silence, at last. The din of battle stilled. The killing over, at least for now. She'd emptied the last of the four canteens she carried with her moments ago, dribbling the last few drops across the parched lips of a dying man. She could hear shouts in the distance. The creak of wagon wheels and then...a bark. She opened her eyes, and here came Hero. He was barely limping as he made his way, first to one man and then the next. What was he doing? Maggie didn't know. Finally, though, the dog sat down next to a soldier and began to bark. Wondering what he was up to, Maggie rose and trotted over, and her heart sank.

She hadn't seen any of the boys she knew by name since John and her brothers had disappeared in the thick of the battle. She had no idea where they'd gone, and she hadn't let herself think on it, knowing that if she let herself wallow in worry, she'd be of little use here where she was most needed. Now a new challenge, as she put a trembling hand to Ashby's forehead and willed him to be alive.

At her touch, Ashby's eyelids fluttered. He groaned. "It's Maggie, Private."

He opened his eyes, but there was no recognition in them. Hero came alongside. Whining, he began to lick Ashby's face, but the soldier didn't respond. Maggie scanned his still form.

No blood, anywhere that she could see. But then she saw a dark stain at the back of his collar. *Oh no.* Moving him as little as possible, she slipped her hand beneath him. Sticky. Her heart lurched. He'd been shot in the head. But he was still alive.

Clearing her throat, she willed her voice not to wobble. "I'm going to help you, Ashby," she said, praying that it might be true. Hero yipped just as a shadow fell across Ashby's face. Maggie had time only to register the yellow skirt before a woman set a bucket of water on the earth and knelt down beside them.

"Tell me what to do," she said.

Hearing the Southern drawl, Maggie frowned as she glanced over and recognized Miss Blair. Still lovely, in spite of the terror in her eyes. Tears spilled down her pale cheeks as she waited for Maggie to answer.

When Maggie said nothing, Miss Blair filled a dipper with water and held it out. Maggie took it. First, she drank half of it herself. She was grateful for the water, but if all the woman could do was tremble and cry, Maggie wished she would just go away. She turned back to Ashby, moistening Mam's wedding handkerchief and pressing it against the boy's lips, rejoicing when he responded with a flick of his swollen tongue.

"That's it," she said. This time she dipped the handkerchief into the bucket, squeezed it out, and dripped water into Ashby's mouth. She wanted to shout with joy when he parted his lips to accept the offering.

Miss Blair withdrew her own handkerchief from her pocket. Moistening it, she folded the kerchief and swiped at the filth on Ashby's forehead.

"Don't waste the water," Maggie warned.

"There's a spring not far away. I'll bring you as much as you want."

Quickly, Maggie shrugged out of the four now-empty canteens she'd been carrying with her. Perhaps Miss Blair would be of some use, after all. If Maggie could just stop being so irritated by the sound of the woman's voice.

Ashby groaned. Hero yipped and swiped at his forehead with a pink tongue.

Was it her imagination, or had one side of Ashby's mouth curled up? Was he trying to smile at being licked by the captain's dog? That had to mean there was hope, didn't it? She needed to see the wound. "Can you roll onto your side, Ashby? Let me see what's happened?"

She watched his face, and perhaps it was only her imagination, but it seemed a furrow appeared just above his brow. "All right," she said. "I'll do it for you. Just—it may hurt, and I'm sorry, but I have to see it." Bracing herself as best she could, Maggie managed to roll him onto his side. What she saw first made her flinch, but then she thought that perhaps the boy's longish hair all tangled in the wound was making it look worse than it was. She bound it as best she could, and she'd just finished when Miss Blair spoke. Maggie was surprised the woman was still there.

"If this man's canteen's empty," she said, "I could fill it for him." She glanced about them. "I could take ever' one we find...fill 'em at the spring and bring 'em back. That'd help—wouldn't it?"

"You came out here to be a water girl?" Maggie let the doubt sound in her voice. She couldn't help it. She'd never seen anything to indicate that any of these Southern ladies were worth much when it came to real work.

Miss Blair arched one eyebrow. Anger flickered in her dark

eyes. "I came out here to be a help. And to look for my brother. If the water isn't what y'all need, then tell me what is."

Her brother. Of course. Maggie glanced about them. Men bearing litters were beginning to fan out across the battlefield, assessing the need, carrying the wounded up toward the mansion. Hero had nosed up next to Ashby, clearly intending to stay put. Across the way, a wounded man was struggling to sit up. Calling for help. Maggie relented. "All right then. Bring water. And if you see anything we can tear into strips for bandages—I just wrapped the last of mine about Private Ashby's head." Inspiration struck. *Her petticoat.* She'd have to untuck her skirt from her belt, but—she began to work at the side seam of the petticoat, dismayed by how filthy it was. Still, it was better than nothing.

Miss Blair's eyes opened wide, but then, with a glance about them, she followed suit, talking as she ripped. "It won't be enough. What about the sheets at the house? I could—"

Maggie interrupted her. "The water's more important." She looked about them. "Some of these boys have been out here for hours by now." She spoke to Ashby. "But don't you worry, Ashby. I'm getting the litter bearers over here as fast as I can."

Miss Blair frowned. She glanced at Ashby. "You know him?"

Maggie nodded. Her voice faltered. "He's one of mine." And then she looked out across the field. They were all hers in a way, weren't they? They all held part of her heart.

"How do ya—stand it?"

"They need me," Maggie said, impatient. Irritated. And then angry. "If you can't stand it," she snapped, "then be gone with ya." She grabbed the bucket. "But leave me the bucket. And the canteens."

The change was almost imperceptible, but it was there,

as Miss Blair lifted her chin and narrowed her gaze. "Tell me what to do."

Maggie swallowed. Her throat was parched. She took another drink. "Stop caring so much. If you care too much, you'll be of no use to them. Wipe your tears. Hide your horror. And do the next thing." And with that, she picked the bucket up and hurried off toward the man who'd been calling for help.

⊛

Libbie watched Miss Malone hurry away, thinking that the bucket was, after all, a rather clumsy way to bring water to the men. One by one, she slung the empty canteens Miss Malone had left in the dirt over her own thin shoulders. She couldn't just leave the suffering man without a word, and so she bent down and said, "You hold on, y'hear, Mr. Ashby?" When her voice threatened to wobble, she stopped. Swallowed. And said as clearly as she could, "Help is comin' directly. You hold on."

She headed for the spring. Someone had dropped a canteen a few feet away, but when Libbie picked it up, there was a hole in it. She began to look about her for more canteens, wondering how many she could carry once they were filled with water. With a shudder, she bent over a dead soldier. "I am sorry," she whispered as she peeled the canteen away. "May you rest in peace."

With the five canteens, she hurried to the spring, slipping and sliding down the trail, filling them as quickly as possible, pausing only to splash her own face with cold water before heading back to Miss Malone, who continued moving from one soldier to the next. Details of uniformed Yankees were now combing the battlefield as well. Some transported the wounded up to the house on litters. Libbie caught sight of her two field hands and realized they weren't rescuing the wounded anymore. They were adding to the row of bodies lined up near the road.

With every trip to the spring, Libbie traversed a different part of the battlefield, always on the lookout for Walker. Finally, she saw a wagon coming up the road from the direction of Littleton and realized that the men in the back were part of the Ellerbe Militia. The militia had decided to set themselves apart from the Wildwood Guard by attaching a red cockade to the crown of their slouch hats, and as the wagon trundled onto the battlefield, the cockades glowed in the afternoon sun. The skirmish in Littleton must be over. The militia was here to gather the dead—accompanied by mounted Yankees keeping watch. Men she might know were now prisoners of war.

There was something familiar about the man who was driving the wagon. He seemed older, and Libbie's heart thudded, thinking it might be Walker. But it wasn't. When the man took his hat off, wildly curly hair sprung to life, and Libbie recognized Mason Ellerbe. What would happen to him, she wondered. To Serena and her mother?

On Libbie's fourth trip to the spring for water, she was filling the last canteen when a twig snapped just above her. She started, looked up, and saw Robert. He was limping and hugging one arm to his body as if it might be broken. Blood trickled down the side of his face.

"Thank the Lord Almighty," he said as he limped toward Libbie. "I been hiding down by the river, wondering what to do. Couldn't let any of the Guard see me for fear they'd shoot me just out of spite. Afraid of the Yankees. Got so thirsty I thought I'd surely die. Finally told myself to brave the spring—" He broke off then, and while he wasn't crying audibly, tears began to stream down his cheeks.

Libbie handed him a canteen, but he waved it away. "Don't think them soldiers care for a Negro drinking outta their canteens, miss." He crouched down at the spring and lapped up water.

"Sure is good to see you, Miss Libbie. Everybody all right?"

Libbie nodded. "We were safe in that secret room."

"Glad you found it. Betty told you?"

"Not exactly. It isn't important. She'll be so happy to know you're all right."

There was an awkward silence, with Libby somehow reluctant to ask the obvious question and Robert not seeming to want to raise the subject. Finally, he cleared his throat. "I am sorry about Mastah Blair, Miss Libbie."

"You know where he is?"

"Yes'm. I can take you."

When Robert refused to meet her gaze, Libbie knew with certainty. She looked away for a moment. *Remember what Miss Malone said. Wipe your tears. Do the next thing.* She took a deep breath. "I need to carry these canteens to Miss Malone first. She's up there helping her boys. That's what she calls them. *Her* boys."

Robert extended his good arm. "I'll help."

"No. You're hurt. Come with me, though." Libbie scrambled back up the hillside, hesitating at the top of the trail to watch the groups of soldiers. They seemed to be more methodical now. Did that mean all the survivors had been identified? She glanced toward the house. It was hard to tell from this far away, but it looked as if the yard was a sea of wounded men. Annabelle would be beside herself at the prospect of feeding so many. Surely the army would have supplies. Wouldn't they? Behind her, a steamboat whistle sounded, and while she and Robert watched, a packet named the *McDowell* churned its way upriver. Maybe the Yankees were bringing supplies to the Wildwood Grove landing. Someone could have telegraphed from Littleton.

Together, she and Robert hurried to Miss Malone, who was standing at the edge of the battlefield near the quarters. Libbie handed the first canteen to her. "Have you had anything to eat all day?"

Miss Malone shrugged. "Hardtack in my haversack. I'm fine."

"You're done in," Libbie said.

"They need me."

"But they won't *have* you if you make yourself sick."

Miss Malone looked over at Robert. "You're hurt."

"This is my brother's man, Robert," Libbie said. "He found me at the spring." She turned to Robert. "Tell Miss Malone how you were hurt."

"Slipped and fell is all," Robert said. "Hit my head."

Miss Malone looked at his head first. "Needs sewing up," she said. "I can do it, but I've used up all my thread."

Was it Libbie's imagination, or was the exhausted woman about to cry because she'd run out of thread? "What about the arm?" she asked.

Miss Malone grasped Robert by the wrist and slowly rotated it. Robert winced. "I don't think it's broken," she said. "A sling would be the best we can do until you see one of the doctors up at the house."

"I'll be all right," Robert said.

Libbie began to take the rest of the canteens off. "I—um— I need to go with Robert for a minute. He knows where—I mean—he can take me to Walker."

Miss Malone nodded. "He's all right, then?"

Libbie hesitated, and in hesitation said what she could not quite say aloud just yet.

"I'll come with you," Miss Malone said, and picked up the canteens.

"You don't have to."

"But I want to. If it was Jack or Seamus—" Her voice wavered. *Or John. Oh . . . dear Lord.* She cleared her throat.

Libbie huffed regret. "Heaven forgive me, I thought you'd know—but then, how would you?" She told Miss Malone about encountering Jack up at the house. "I'm sorry that I didn't think to ask about Seamus."

A brief smile flickered. "How would you know that I was the madwoman out here on the battlefield? Jack's all right. I'm thankful to know it." *And Seamus and John will be all right, too. And Noah. Surely Noah would have managed to stay safe.* For she could not imagine her life without them.

⌘

Maggie felt guilty, smiling at Miss Blair's news of Jack when the poor woman's own brother was dead. But a few moments later, as she stood gazing down at Walker Blair's remains, Maggie realized that whatever feeling Libbie Blair had for her brother, it was nothing like the furious love Maggie felt for her brothers. She had expected wailing and perhaps fainting. After all, the Southern ladies in town got the vapors over the slightest thing. But Miss Blair stood quietly, looking down an incline so steep a man would have had to be mad to try what Walker Blair had tried, listening quietly while "her brother's man" told the story as he knew it. With careful wording, Maggie thought, designed to spare Miss Blair the shame attached to a death without honor.

The rebels on the battlefield behind them could claim honor. They'd died defending something they believed in, and even if what they believed in was wrong, Maggie could allow them an honorable death. She'd tended a few of them today, and found it impossible to hate any of them. That both surprised and confused her. But there was nothing confusing about what had happened to Walker Blair. He'd been running.

The top of the ridge where he'd fallen was trampled—as if the horse hadn't wanted to plunge over. But Blair had won out. Had he felt a few seconds of relief as the horse carried him over the ridge, into the air, and away from the battle? That had to be what he'd been doing, for the only thing beyond this ridge was the river. But the horse hadn't cleared the narrow strip of land. Hadn't made it to the water. Neither had Walker Blair, who'd fallen off his horse and, from the position of the body, broken his neck.

Maggie looked over at Miss Blair. "I am so sorry," she said, and in an uncharacteristic show of femininity, she grasped the other woman's hand. They stood together for a moment and then, with a little shudder, Miss Blair said to Robert, "Miss Malone and I are going to return to helping the living," she said. "I would appreciate it greatly if before you go up to the house to get that arm attended to, you would take word to the Guard's men out here on the field so that they can retrieve the body. They can tell me later what arrangements have been made."

Robert hesitated. "You want me to move him first? I mean—bring him up here?" He paused. "The horse could have bolted, Miss Libbie. Everybody knows that animal had a wild streak in him."

Miss Blair thought for a moment. She shook her head. "God bless you, Robert, but I wouldn't dream of asking you to do such a thing."

"Might be something important in those saddlebags," Robert said.

It might only be her imagination, but it seemed to Maggie

that Walker Blair's man was trying to say something important without actually saying it. Was that the way slaves communicated to their owners, or was it just that Robert didn't trust the Irishwoman? Either way, Miss Blair apparently shouldn't leave her brother's belongings at the bottom of this ridge. And so Maggie spoke up. "Let me climb down there," she said. "I mean—someone might misunderstand Robert carrying saddlebags and—whatever else." She felt awkward bringing it up, but a Negro who seemed to have taken something off a dead soldier risked being shot if anyone saw him.

"That's not necessary," Libbie said. "I know a way down there that doesn't require anyone to scale a cliff." She hesitated and asked Robert, "You're certain this is necessary?"

"Yes'm. I think so."

With a sigh, Libbie turned to Maggie. "Please. Go back to your men. I'll see to this—matter—as quickly as possible." She paused. "And I'll bring you something to eat—and more thread—when I return."

Maggie considered insisting that she go along again, but the initial shock regarding Walker Blair's fate was over, and it was clear that Robert didn't want a stranger involved in the matter of his master's personal effects. So be it. "I'll watch for you," she said. And then she thought of the wounded men who'd begged her for something to eat while she tended them. "Bring as much food as you can," she said. "We can share it with the boys."

Chapter 24

It was nearly sundown before Maggie and Libbie staggered into the yard behind the plantation house. By then they were calling one another by their given names, for at some point as they worked alongside one another, each woman had shed her preconceived ideas about the other. Maggie had realized that Miss Blair was no empty-headed, tiny-waisted Southern belle interested only in being served. There was, in fact, a prodigious amount of gentle strength beneath that refined exterior. As for Libbie, she'd quickly realized that Jack Malone's sister used her size and a slightly mannish manner to hide an uncommon capacity for tenderness that, for reasons Libbie did not understand, seemed to embarrass her.

Numb from all she'd seen and done that day, Maggie sank down beside Libbie, grateful to finally be done with the battlefield, and yet newly aware of just how much there remained to do. The yard was filled with the less seriously wounded, and if this many men were still in the yard, Maggie couldn't imagine what it was like inside the house, where Dr. Feeny and two other doctors who'd driven in from Littleton were caring for the worst cases.

When Libbie had been up at the house retrieving two baskets of bread—and thread, as promised—she'd learned that the confederate surgeon and his assistant would oversee the transfer of their rebel patients to Hickory Hill, the Ellerbes' plantation. It was farther upriver near Lexington, she said. The Ellerbes had offered a corner of the family burial plot for the "heroic dead" of the Guard and the Militia.

Heroes. Rebels. Invaders. Defenders. Still more words with different meanings, depending on who spoke them. Maggie stirred. "That first boy you helped me tend," she said. "I need to find him." *And John. I have to find John. And Seamus. And Noah.*

"I'll come with you," Libbie said. This time, when the women rose to their feet, there was a stir among the men seated around a campfire over by the garden.

"That you, Miss Maggie?"

It was Noah. Relief flooded through her as the boy emerged from the kitchen behind them. "Barely." Maggie forced herself to make a joke, lest she cry with joy.

"It's Miss Maggie, boys," a nearby soldier called, and all around them, one by one, men struggled to their feet. Scattered applause was broken by a call to "Give her a cheer, boys!" And voices filled the night. "Hurrah for the ladies! Hurrah for Miss Maggie! Hurrah for Miss Libbie!"

Grateful for the lengthening shadows, Maggie put one hand to her heart. The other, she extended out over the yard, returning the emotion and then trying in vain to quiet them. "Go on, now, that's enough!" she cried, but the din went on.

Jack and Seamus emerged from the shadows, standing beside the two women like sentinels. *Seamus. Alive. Whole.* Seeing her brothers broke through Maggie's resolve. She'd managed to hold her emotions in check all the day long, but the combination of being cheered by the ragged, hurting men in the yard and seeing Jack and Seamus unharmed burst the dam. Tears flowed as Maggie and Libbie made their way to the back door of the house.

With a little wave at the cheering men, Libbie stepped inside. Jack and Seamus followed her, but Maggie stood for a moment in the doorway, letting the men see how much their accolades meant to her before finally swiping her tears away and ducking out of sight. Her joy was short-lived, for here in the house the suffering was palpable. Libbie was waiting by the doorway tucked beneath the sweeping front stairs, talking to Jack and Seamus. Two slaves were moving among the men in the hall, wiping foreheads and giving drinks of water.

"You can come with us," Seamus said.

"Wh-what?" Maggie rubbed her forehead and tried to remember what they'd been talking about.

"To Littleton tomorrow," Libbie said. "It seems so long ago that it happened, but when Walker first told me about the Guard and offering the house as a hospital, I wanted to take the farm wagon into town and collect feather beds and blankets. He made fun." She nodded toward the wounded men lying on the bare hallway floor. "Now I wish I'd done it anyway."

"We're going to get permission to do it tomorrow," Jack said, then glanced down at Libbie. "And I'll drive."

Seamus looked over at Maggie. "He should let me drive. I could see Bridget."

Dr. Feeny strode up. "Did someone mention Bridget?"

"Yes, sir," Seamus said. "Is she well?"

"Quite well, thank you."

"She must have been terrified," Seamus said.

"Thankfully the fighting never got that close to our home," the doctor replied. And then he smiled. "I had to practically tie your Uncle Paddy down to keep him from heading into the fray."

"That would be Uncle Paddy," Maggie said.

"Once the rebels cleared out—there really wasn't much in the way of a battle in Littleton—a few chases through this garden or that, but it was all over very quickly. At any rate—I've offered the house as the colonel's headquarters for as long as he requires it." He paused. "And I was amazed to meet a young man who says he spent a great deal of time there as a child. Apparently his grandparents nearly raised him."

Jack nudged Maggie, who was in no mood to be teased about John Coulter. She barely managed to croak the name. "He's all right then? John—I mean *Sergeant* Coulter?" And when Dr. Feeny said *yes*, relief surged through her—and something else, too; an emotion so strong that she feared her knees would go weak. And so she asked about Leander Ashby. Immediately, Dr. Feeny's expression sobered.

"He is clinging to life, but I cannot think why. Short of a miracle..." He shook his head.

"May I see him?"

"Miss Malone, after what you've done today, you never need ask that question. He'll be very glad to see you. When I asked him who'd tended the wound, he said something about an angel."

"He was barely conscious," Maggie said, and then she remembered Hero. "Maybe it was the white dog." She looked over at Jack.

"The dog's still with him." At Maggie's look of surprise, Dr. Feeny nodded. "Refused to stay outside."

Maggie remembered the stories about Hero and Fish and how Hero had an uncanny talent for seeking out "his" wounded and guarding them on the battlefield. If Hero was with Ashby, did that mean that Ashby was the only one from Company D who'd been badly hurt? *May it be.*

Jack and Seamus said something about "corn pone," and

with a low laugh, Libbie offered to escort them to the "dining room."

Maggie said she'd be along directly, but first she wanted to see Ashby. *Directly.* An afternoon with a Southerner, and she was beginning to sound like one. Taking a deep breath, she picked her way through the crowded hallway of what had obviously been a beautiful mansion. It seemed little more than a battered shell now. Thinking back to her own emotions when she'd stood in the doorway looking at what the bushwhackers had done to her home, Maggie wondered if Libbie had felt similarly dismayed moments ago. If so, she hadn't shown it. In fact, the first words out of her mouth had been about rounding up mattresses and feather beds for the wounded. Yet another surprise. Maggie grunted. If she wasn't careful, she was going to end up wanting to be friends with the woman.

Ashby was in one of the front rooms off the main hall. He lay unmoving, the rising and falling of his chest the only sign that he was alive. When Hero caught sight of Maggie, he gave a little snort. The tail thumped. Once.

Ashby opened his eyes, but they didn't seem to focus.

Maggie sank down beside him and took his hand.

"Molly?" He moistened his lips.

Maggie squeezed his hand. "'Tis Maggie Malone, Ashby."

With his free hand, Ashby tried to pull something out of his pocket. *The testament.* Maggie did it for him. "I've the testament here in my hand. Would you like me to read to you, Leander?"

"Lee," he said, so quietly that she could barely hear it.

"Would you like me to read to you, Lee?"

Ashby squeezed her hand.

Maggie looked down at the little booklet. She'd need a

lamp if she was going to read. "I'll get a lamp and be right back." Before Maggie could get up, a slave woman was there, lamp in hand. She opened the shutters and raised the window and set the lamp on the windowsill, where it would spill down onto Ashby's face—and the booklet, if Maggie held it just right.

The pamphlet wasn't a testament, after all. *The Soldier's Prayer Book* contained page after page of prayers; prayers for congress and the president; prayers before a battle; finally, one that spoke to the moment. A prayer for a sick person. Maggie read.

> O Father of mercies and God of all comfort, our only help in time of need; Look down from heaven, we humbly beseech thee, behold, visit, and relieve thy sick servant, for whom our prayers are desired. Look upon him with the eyes of thy mercy; comfort him with a sense of thy goodness; preserve him from the temptations of the enemy; give him patience under his affliction; and, in thy good time, restore him to health, and enable him to lead the residue of his life in thy fear, and to thy glory. Give him grace that, after this painful life is ended, he may dwell with thee in life everlasting; through Jesus Christ our Lord. *Amen.*

A nice enough prayer, Maggie thought, thinking back to the pages of Mam's prayer book, and feeling guilty that she'd never really read it. She paged past more prayers and paused at the one the seemed the best of all. *The Soldier's Prayer.*

> O GOD our Father! Wash us from all our sins in the Saviour's blood, and we shall be whiter than snow. Create in

us a clean heart, and fill us with the Holy Ghost, that we may never be ashamed to confess the faith of Christ crucified, and manfully to fight under His banner, against sin, the world, and the devil; looking to Jesus the great Captain of our salvation. We ask it all, because He lived, died, rose again, and ever liveth to make intercession for us. *Amen.*

Now that was a wonderful prayer. Who wouldn't like the idea of Jesus as the Captain of salvation? Maggie couldn't help but smile a bit, wondering why the Protestants who'd written the prayer book hadn't called the dear Lord by the highest rank in the army. Maybe they were just as ignorant as she'd been at first, when it came to ranks and titles. Then again, she didn't suppose the Lord Jesus minded, as long as a man called upon him for all the things mentioned in that beautiful prayer.

Ashby stirred. "More," he said.

The prayers gave way to Psalms and hymns. Maggie kept reading, aware that a new stillness had settled over the men in the room with them. Were they listening, too? Finding comfort in the words? If it gave them comfort, she would read all night long. And she meant to. But after a while, the flickering light and the sounds in the night conspired against her. The day took its toll, and Maggie fell asleep, right where she sat.

⁓

As the sun dipped behind the western horizon, Captain Quinn ordered Colt to ride to Wildwood Grove at the head of a squad the colonel was sending out with various orders connected to the occupation of the county. Apparently the Irish Brigade would be in Lafayette County for at least a few days.

Colt was to select a burial detail and oversee the transporting of the deceased to be buried with honors in the churchyard. Headboards were being made for each of the graves, and the colonel was already at work gathering the details of each man's sacrifice to share with families and loved ones. He'd charged Colt with the unhappy but necessary duty of making certain that identities were accurately recorded and personal effects collected for return to the grieving families.

As a result of helping locate homes willing to house the colonel and his staff, Colt had met the doctor who'd purchased his grandparents' home, and consequently, Paddy Malone—and Kerry-boy, who snuffled Colt up one side and down the other, sneezed, and then ignored him. When Malone realized that Colt was the man who'd been sent with Jack to spy on the rebels, it took very little to encourage a retelling of Maggie's encounter with the bushwhackers.

"I shouldn't be surprised," Colt said. "The woman's a wonder," and he told Maggie's uncle about the way she'd run onto the battlefield to tend "her boys." "I would have had to carry her bodily off the field to stop her," he said. "And then she'd only have waited for me to ride away before she went right back to it." He paused. "There's no stopping her when she puts her mind to something, is there."

Paddy Devlin laughed. "That's our Maggie-girl."

Perhaps it was only his imagination, but as Colt rode out of Littleton in the direction of Wildwood Grove, it seemed to him that Paddy Malone had taken a sudden interest in learning more about Colt's background after Colt praised Maggie. Which was fine with him. If he could get Paddy Malone on his side—and win Kerry-boy over—perhaps it would help convince Maggie to lower her guard. With the day's duties behind him, he could think of little else but Maggie. She might be magnificent, but she was also hardheaded. And brave. Stubborn. And tireless. Headstrong. And fearless. Willful. And still fascinating. Heaven help him, he loved her. Couldn't imagine life without her.

⊱✦⊰

Hands on her shoulders brought Maggie instantly awake. Her first thought was for Ashby. He lay still. But...yes. Praise be to God, he was still breathing. Hero was sitting up. Looking at her. Wagging his tail. But he didn't make a sound.

"Come and rest, Maggie-girl. You've done all you can do for him."

John crouched down beside her. Reaching for her hand, he drew her to her feet alongside him. She stifled a groan as her weary muscles protested. Saints preserve us, but she was stiff. She'd been sleeping so soundly she was drooling. It was a wonder she hadn't toppled over.

John led her out of the room and through the front door, but once they were out on the porch, she pulled away from him and looked back into the house. "Do you know where Libbie is? And Noah—what about Noah—is he—"

"Noah and—Cooper, I think his name is—Noah and he volunteered as waterboys for the men out on the lawn. Dr. Feeny said he ordered Miss Blair to bed about an hour ago." He smiled. "Is it Libbie, then?"

"And if it is?"

"I'd say there's hope for the nation, if a Southern rebel and an Irish Federal can be friends."

He was teasing, but she wasn't in the mood. "Don't make light of it."

"All right."

"And don't scold me for yesterday."

"All right."

"And don't treat me like I'm a child."

"I won't."

"You're doing it right now," she snapped. "Agreeing with everything I say."

He gave a soft grunt. "Have you seen Seamus and Jack?"

"Jack's already charmed Libbie's cook to the point she's talking about baking him a gooseberry pie tomorrow, and Seamus can't speak of anything but getting into town to see Bridget Feeny. They're going to drive a wagon in and try to collect mattresses for the boys." By the time she said the next words, she was choking back unspent tears. "We're—all—j-just—f-fine."

John reached for her.

She pulled away.

"Let me hold you."

She shook her head. "I'm fine."

"No," he said, "you're not." Before she could duck away, he wrapped her in his arms and held on. "And if you were, I'd think you were daft. Dear Maggie Malone, you're a wonder. But you're still only human, and the things you've seen—the things you've done—"

She shuddered. Couldn't hold it back. "S-So many d-died," she said. "I tried to keep them alive, but I couldn't. There was this boy—he was barely old enough to grow a beard. And I was looking in his eyes and the light just—went. There was nothing I could do."

"You were there," John said. "He didn't die alone."

"But others did," she sobbed. "I couldn't—h-help—them all." He held on. He didn't try to tell her not to feel the way she felt. He just held on. She'd been standing with her arms at her sides, but now she wrapped them about his waist. She felt the strength in him, and for the first time in her young life, Maggie didn't have to be strong for herself. John was there and he would be strong enough for them both. It was all right to feel what she felt. It was even all right to cry a little. John held her until the moment passed and she realized how she must smell and how she must look and she stiffened and pulled away.

"I must look like a witch—and I reek."

"You're beautiful," he said. "As for the smell...we could both use a bit of that lavender soap." He gave a dramatic sigh. "If only you'd married me the first time I asked." And then he frowned. "But wait—I don't think I did ask, did I?"

"You're safe, John Coulter. You didn't ask."

He grimaced. "You still doubt me."

She shrugged. "A little less perhaps. It's the best I can do."

"Then it will have to be enough. For now." He paused. "I met your Uncle Paddy. And that monster you call a dog. Your uncle agreed with me that you're a wonder. I should probably tell you that I'm determined to win the dog over and to enlist Paddy's support to win your heart."

Maggie just shook her head. Didn't he know that he already had her heart? Couldn't he see? She looked down at her filthy, faded skirt. Thought of the petticoat that hung in shreds because she'd torn strips away to make bandages. She couldn't speak of love dressed like this. She put her hands in her pockets. And for some reason, the gesture made Colt swear.

"What's this?" He pointed to a frayed spot near the pocket. "And this?" He crouched down.

Maggie looked down. What was he talking about? And then she saw them. Only three. No, there was another one. All right. Four.

John took his hat off and stepped away to the edge of the porch. He slapped the hat against his thigh like a man trying to rid it of dust, but he didn't put it back on. Finally, he turned about. "Bullet holes! Your skirt is riddled with bullet holes." His eyes glimmered in the moonlight. Tears?

"Well, as you can see, John Coulter, I'm fine."

"That you are." He dropped his hat and pulled her into his arms.

The first kiss was sweet enough to fill a year's worth of dreams. She kept her guard up all the while, willing herself to memorize the moment for the future when she would need the memory.

Somehow John must have read her thoughts, for he pulled away. His voice was gruff as he said, "Kiss me back. I love you. I won't hurt you and I'll never leave you. Now kiss me back."

She'd never been kissed before, but apparently she was getting the hang of it, for the second kiss left them both more than a little breathless. The third took them dangerously close to the edge of a cliff Maggie had never suspected she would ever approach.

John ended that kiss, put his hands to her waist, and drew her close. "As long as I live, I'll never love anyone else, Maggie Malone. Say you'll marry me."

Somehow the fact that she could whisper made it easier. "I do love you, John Coulter. But I'm afraid."

He leaned away, just enough to look into her eyes. "You're the bravest woman I've ever known. How can you be afraid of love? Of me?"

"I just—am," Maggie murmured. "I can't help it."

He sighed. "I don't understand you, but I don't suppose I have to. I love you. I'll wait." With a sweet hug, he stepped away and retrieved his hat. "Be forewarned. The proposals will continue until you say 'yes.'" He put the hat on and offered his arm. "May I have the honor of seeing you home?"

They walked around the side of the house to the servants' steps at the back. Libbie had said that Malachi and Cooper would bring a mattress up from the basement. Maggie was to share Libbie and Ora Lee's room as long as she was here at Wildwood Grove.

John wished her good night with a kiss on the cheek. She might be his sister for all the passion in it. The flicker of doubt raised its head again. Until John leaned close and muttered something about lavender soap that made her blush.

Chapter 25

It was mid-morning before Maggie and Libbie awoke, and when Libbie scolded Ora Lee for letting them sleep, the poor girl actually got tears in her eyes.

"All your mens said we was to let you sleep," she said.

Maggie and Libbie exchanged looks.

Libbie asked the question, "And who, pray tell, are 'all our mens'?"

"Well…" Ora Lee extended a finger with each name. "Dr. Feeny said you was both close to exhaustion and you'd get sick if you didn't rest. Then, when I went down early this morning to help Annabelle with the breakfast, there was a new boy, name of Noah, eating with Mr. Malone—that be Jack Malone—and they both say to let you sleep as long as you like. And the other Malone agreed. I don't remember his name. He got red hair."

"That's my brother Seamus," Maggie said.

Ora Lee nodded. "Yep. That the one." She extended another finger. "Then another Irishman come looking for you"—she glanced at Maggie—"and when he heard you was sleeping, he said to tell you Uncle Paddy come out from town but he know you needs your rest. By then that handsome Sergeant Coulter was eating breakfas' with Mr. Jack and he agreed with all the other mens that it was good you was both still asleep." Ora Lee looked down at her hands. "So that's six or seven men ordered us all to leave you be. I lost count, but don't be yellin' at me 'cause I done what I was told."

Libbie just shook her head. "All right. I won't yell." She started to get up, groaned, rubbed her back, and sat back. Sniffed. Looked up at Ora Lee. "Is that *me* I smell?"

When the girl didn't respond, Libbie nodded. "All right. Do you have time to haul a pail of water up here so I can wash up?"

"Two pails," Maggie said, and forced herself to stand up. "I'll help get it." She glanced over at Libbie. "I have to see if I can find Fish and retrieve my satchel. I've a change of clothes tucked in it." Mention of the satchel reminded her of the letters that had been entrusted to her.

Mention of a change of clothes seemed to attract Libbie's attention to the holes in Maggie's skirt. "Are those—*bullet holes?*"

Maggie looked down at them. "I suppose so."

Libbie shuddered.

Ora Lee spoke up. "You must-a had a angel running with you yesterday, Miss Maggie. You stay right here. I get the water for you both." She hesitated. "Who that Fish man you need to find?"

Maggie chuckled. "Fish is the quartermaster. His real name is something so long and French that no one can say it. But part of his name means 'fish,' so that's what everyone calls him. Anyway, he keeps track of the supplies. Hands out the food, distributes letters—now that I think about it, Fish seems to run everything that isn't associated with guns and cannon."

"He wear a funny red hat?"

"He does."

"He set up down by the levee. Seem like maybe the Yankees expecting a steamboat sometime today. Anyway, I'll send Cooper to find him and get your satchel. Send Betty up with some biscuits and coffee. Anything else you need?"

Maggie protested. "You don't have to do all that."

"What if I want to?" Ora Lee appealed to Libbie. "You tell her, Miss Libbie. You wasn't orderin' me around—except with the water, and I'm used to haulin' water for a full bathtub. Two buckets ain't nothin'. Anyway, tell Miss Maggie to let us help."

"Ora Lee wants to help," Libbie said. "Let her."

Maggie gave up, although she made a face as she said, "Coffee and clothes and breakfast, if you please. And thank you."

Ora Lee smiled. "Comin' up." She ducked out of the room, then ducked back in. "Oh. And that Mr. Ashby doin' better this morning. Dr. Feeny say to tell you."

❧

Half an hour after Ora Lee hauled the two pails of cold well water up to the glorified closet that Libbie and Maggie now shared, the two women had let down their hair, scrubbed themselves clean, and donned fresh unmentionables—albeit Maggie's were decidedly less fresh than Libbie's, having suffered from the extended travel with the Irish.

"I couldn't exactly hang my drawers out to dry in full view of the boys," she said, blushing at the thought. She put up only the faintest protest when Libbie summoned Betty and requested that she tailor a fresh chemise and petticoat for Miss Maggie. How Betty was going to accomplish such a miracle with anything that would fit Libbie Blair was beyond Maggie's ability to understand, but she wasn't about to insult Betty's skills by declaring it impossible. And so she waited, and by the time she'd eaten breakfast and managed to comb out the disaster that was her hair, Betty was back.

Maggie slipped the petticoat over her head and buttoned

it at her waist. "It's wonderful. Thank you. How's Robert this morning?"

Betty smiled. "He fine, Miss Maggie. Thank you for asking. He told me how you tended him."

"I didn't, really. I was out of thread. And I didn't have any way to make a sling."

"But you was willing," Betty said. "That was very kind of you." She glanced over at Libbie and said that she'd send Ora Lee up to finish her hair.

Libbie stretched again, her arms lifted above her head. "It is amazin'," she said, "that hot coffee, cold water, and clean clothes can make a woman feel like she just might be human again." She stood up and looked out the window toward the river. "It seems strange, though—to hear birds singing. It's almost as if the world hasn't really noticed what happened here yesterday."

Maggie didn't know whether she should say something or not, but when Libbie's shoulders began to shake a bit and Maggie realized the woman was crying, she went to her side and put a hand on her shoulder. "I—um—I don't really know how to be—I mean, I've never been around women much. I grew up with my brothers and my uncle. So if this is all wrong—but—if you need a friend—I'll try. I probably won't be any good at it, but I'll try." When Libbie said nothing, but only cried harder, Maggie looked about her, feeling panic. She grabbed up the towel that Libbie had used to dry off and handed it to her. Libbie took it, blew her nose, and handed it back.

"Oh—I'm sorry." She snatched it away. "I'm not really sure how friendship works, either."

Maggie frowned. "But you—I mean—all those other belles. You were always with a group of them when I saw you in town."

"You mean the ones who made fools of themselves over your brother?"

Maggie nodded. "You never did that, but still—I mean—you were with them."

"We aren't really friends. They'd all known each other for years before I was forced on 'em."

"Forced on them?" Maggie asked. "What's that mean?"

Libbie told her. About her parents dying and her coming to live with her only brother. Who didn't really want her, until he realized there was something to be said for having a "gracious hostess." "Don't misunderstand. Walker gave me many beautiful things. I even think he loved me, in his own way. But we never really knew one another. I always felt a little like a guest in the home of a stranger."

Maggie couldn't imagine something so horrible. She had never for one moment doubted that Jack and Seamus and Uncle Paddy loved her. They drove her to madness sometimes with their teasing, but she also knew they'd die for her, and she for them. She might have been lonely growing up, but it was nothing like what Libbie had experienced. And she said so. "I'm sorry for you," Maggie said. "Sorry for what's happened. To you and your brother and your home. I was wondering about it last night, when you saw all the damage—thinking that you must feel horrible. And angry. No one would blame you."

Libbie crossed the room and ran her hands over the bullet holes peppering the wall. "I'm not sure what I feel. In the six years I've lived here, there have been times when I honestly wished this house would fall down." She touched the left side of her face. "Walker was so caught up in making an impression on just the right people. I always thought this house was beautiful, but he was never satisfied with it. Or me. Now...I should feel terrible, but I don't." She grunted. "After all his strutting and all the talk and all the plans, he deserted the Guard. He *ran*."

Maggie didn't know what to say. The men she knew weren't blinded by fear. They trembled, but they did their duty anyway. Libbie would have to find a way to live with awful news about her only brother. Maggie couldn't imagine it. She blurted out the question. "What will you do now?"

"I have no idea. I can't seem to suss it out." She lifted the corner of her mattress and pulled out an envelope. "This was in Walker's saddlebags." She pointed to the words Blair had scrawled across the envelope. *For Libbie.* "He never called me 'Libbie.' Well—almost never."

"You haven't read it?"

She shook her head. "I suppose I'll be caught in some kind of limbo until I do, but whatever it says...he *ran*."

"You're angry."

"I'm furious. All those beautiful boys who died. And more who are hurting over at the Ellerbes. And Walker ran?" She shuddered. "I'm not ready to hear from him." She put the letter back beneath the mattress, and then she asked Maggie, "What are you goin' to do?"

"Stay with the Irish, if they'll have me."

"Even when they move on?"

Maggie nodded.

"You'd want to? After everything that happened yesterday?"

"It's *because* of everything that's happened," Maggie said, and she realized she wasn't talking about John Coulter. Oh, he was part of it, of course. But not all of it. Not even most of it. "I did some good, and that felt wonderful. Do you think it's odd for me to feel good about it?"

Libbie sighed. "If it is, then we're both odd." She paused. "I don't think I'll ever be the same. I dread going downstairs, and yet I look forward to it—to doing something beyond sitting at the head of a dinner table and fluttering my eyelashes at a man who needs to be reassured about his rightful position as the ruler of his kingdom." She grimaced. "I sound like a spoiled brat. Let's find 'our mens,' as Ora Lee calls them, and see what we can do to help them today."

⁓

Sometimes the thing that helped a man the most was the thing a woman least wanted to do. And yet it was necessary. Perhaps even hallowed, in some way, Libbie thought, when Sergeant Coulter asked for their help identifying the dead and recovering their personal effects before they were taken into Littleton for burial.

"The day will be warm," the sergeant said. "We must act quickly." He looked over at Maggie. "If you think you can bear it—"

"I can," Maggie said. "It's important."

Libbie wasn't certain she could bear it, but she didn't admit it, and once she got past the first few moments and realized that Maggie was right—it was important, and it would help the living—she was able to bear it.

Maggie came up with the idea of writing each man's identity and a note about how they died along with the personal effects that had been found with them, and then to seal it in a jar that would be buried with each man. The goal was to provide still more certainty as to identities. After all, headboards would weather and fade. If families decided to reclaim the bodies, there should be no doubt as to the identity and no doubt that the men were treated with honor and respect.

Libbie served as Sergeant Coulter's secretary, completing four columns on several sheets of paper, noting each soldier's name including his rank, his regimental affiliation, any personal effects found with him, and the exact location of his grave. Jack Malone saw to the personal effects, stowing them in sugar sacks or flour sacks, tying them closed, and then affixing a shipping tag to each bag that duplicated the information on Libbie's list. The bags would be crated and shipped downriver to St. Louis, where they would be held at headquarters until claimed by the families.

It took most of the morning to accomplish the sad duty, and more than once Libbie had to blink away tears as lockets displaying children's faces, locks of hair, and other sentimental relics were removed from pockets and hiding places. Many of the dead had written letters the night before the battle. Some were bloodstained. They were treated with special reverence.

The bodies were transported to town as quickly as identifications were completed, and as the last wagon trundled away with its tragic cargo, Sergeant Coulter touched Maggie's arm in a way that communicated more than he'd likely intended. "Are you all right?" he asked.

Maggie shook her head. "No. But I will be." And she turned to Libbie. "We can collect the bedding in town this afternoon. I'd like—a cup of coffee." She shrugged. "Or whiskey. I can't decide which."

Together, the women trudged to the kitchen. Something about seeing all those letters reminded Libbie of the letter waiting beneath her mattress. She was still angry with Walker, but there didn't seem to be any point to ignoring his letter. She was only hurting herself by refusing to face it. She would read it tonight.

When it came time to make the drive into Littleton to gather bedding, Libbie held back, suddenly afraid of what the citizens might say to her. When she finally told Maggie the real reason for her reluctance—she was afraid that Union supporters would slam the door in her face—Maggie understood. "Don't worry about it," she said. "Paddy and I will go."

"Would you mind if I rode as far as the livery? I'd like to bring Pilot home. I'm hoping the owner will just take the carriage horse in payment for the board."

Jack Malone spoke up, offering to borrow a mount and ride alongside the wagon so that he could escort Libbie back to the Grove.

The livery owner seemed delighted to accept the carriage horse, who really was a fine animal, as payment for Pilot's board. "Wish I had a dozen like him," he said, and then, with a glance Jack Malone's way, he lowered his voice and said, "I thought you'd want to know, Miss Libbie, that I happen to know that our former sheriff is on his way to join up with General Price."

Libbie frowned. "Isham was—here?"

The livery owner nodded. "He'd actually left his own horse here at the livery. Rode one of Ellerbe's Thoroughbreds into the fray." He snorted. "Said the fool horse went crazy when the first shots were fired. Arrived here on foot, saddled that big white gelding of his, and hightailed it south."

"I see. Well... thank you."

Pilot must have heard her, for he thrust his head over the half door to his stall and whickered. As soon as Libbie was near enough, the horse nuzzled her shoulder.

"Seems happy to see you," Malone said.

Libbie smiled and nodded.

"And you're happy to see him."

She leaned into the horse's neck to hide her tears. As they headed out of town, Pilot danced and pranced, and Jack Malone seemed truly concerned that Libbie might be thrown. "I've been riding since before I could walk, Private Malone," she said. "He's just happy to have me back," and she patted Pilot's broad neck.

"It's good to see you smile," Malone said.

Libbie did her best to settle Pilot so they could talk. "I appreciate your being so kind to me."

He frowned. "Have some of the boys been *un*kind? Because if they have—"

"No, no, of course they haven't. But I'll admit to being surprised by the fact. Me being—who I am."

"You mean you being the woman who's worked tirelessly to feed and nurse them and do her part to see that the dead are properly buried?"

"You know what I mean. My brother and all. And then after what happened at your farm. It *was* Southerners who did that."

"You had nothing to do with it," Malone said. They hadn't ridden far when he asked, "Not that it's any of my particular business, but—have you decided what you'll do now? Will you leave Missouri?"

"And go where?"

"To family?"

"Walker was my only family—unless you count distant cousins in Alabama who forced Walker to take me in because they didn't want me. And I choose not to. Count them, that is." She looked over at him. "You're very fortunate, you know, to have such a loving family."

Malone grinned. "I am blessed. Although we drive each other nearly to madness at times."

"But at all times, you'd die for each other." Libbie said it before she thought, and then she thought of Walker—again— and that he hadn't been willing to die for anything but himself. Feeling weepy, she urged Pilot to a trot and pulled away from Malone a bit. She needed to gather herself. She heard a yelp and looked back and Malone was sitting on the ground looking surprised. The raggedy bay that had thrown him was nearby, grazing.

Libbie hurried back to him. "Are you hurt?"

"Only my Irish pride," Malone said, picking himself up and slapping the dust off his backside. He retrieved the horse and remounted. "As you might have guessed, I'm not a very good rider." When the horse tossed its head, Malone pretended to address the animal. "All right, all right. I'm a terrible rider. We've only the Belgians on the farm and I've precious little experience in the saddle. But in my defense, you're not exactly the best-behaved horse in the army, either."

Libbie laughed. "Then I must thank you for being so kind as to agree to escort Pilot and me home."

"Oh, that wasn't kindness. That was hoping for a chance to ask if you might call me *Jack*. And allow me to write, once we've received our marching orders."

Libbie stared at him in disbelief.

"Will you at least think about it?"

She would. She rather liked the idea, in fact. Of the writing, at least. She didn't know if she was quite ready to be so familiar as to use his given name, though. Not until she'd thought about it some more. For the rest of the day anyway. Or until she'd tended to Pilot and turned him into his stall at home. Or at least until they reached the turn into the yard.

Chapter 26

Libbie sat with her back against the wall, staring down at Walker's letter. The afternoon had been busy, with Maggie and her uncle driving in with a wagonload of bedding to be distributed throughout the house, and the various companies and squads receiving orders as to where they should camp. Once again, the field beyond the garden was a sea of soldiers' tents, and as the evening wore on, the sound of mouth harps and pipes floated on the night air.

Libbie had spent most of the afternoon in the house, completing the same kind of form that she'd worked with earlier that morning, only this time she was recording the names of the living. Dr. Feeny had had the idea after finding a note that one of the more serious cases had written before enduring the surgery that required the amputation of his right arm. *I am Private James O'Reilly of St. Louis, Missouri. I am a patient at the hospital that was formerly the Wildwood Grove Plantation near Littleton, Missouri. I write this so that in the event I am unable to provide the information after surgery, my family can be notified of my condition.*

"He's right-handed," Dr. Feeny said.

Libbie nodded. "Is he conscious?"

"He is. But feverish."

Libbie spent the afternoon with the patients in Private

O'Reilly's part of the house, and before supper, O'Reilly had dictated letters to a younger brother and to his mother. He'd also flirted with Libbie so outrageously that he made her blush. As good a sign as any that the private would recover.

And now here she sat, staring down at Walker's letter and once again hesitating to read it.

Maggie came in, saw the letter, and excused herself.

"No," Libbie said. "Don't go. I'd rather not be alone when I read it."

Maggie sat down opposite her.

Taking a deep breath, Libbie opened the envelope. "Two pages," she said. Walker had had a lot to say.

Monday evening, July 8, 1861

Dear sister,

If you are reading this letter, I am gone. I do not know how I will have left you. I hope the circumstances will be such that you can say that it was a good death. I fear that my skills do not extend to the battlefield. I fear leaving you alone. I fear that our plans to ascend to political office will fail. I fear being weak. And I fear that, once all is said and done, you will be unable to forgive me for the countless times I have disappointed you, and for the times I have caused you pain. Even now, in what I fear may be my final hours of life on this mortal plane, I fear asking forgiveness, for I can think of no reason for you to extend it.

In my fear, I have done something that, should you read this letter, will at least provide for your future. Knowing men as I do, I suspect that part of the battle for Littleton will include a battle for the funds housed in the vault at the bank. Our brothers will want to protect it from the thieving Federals, and the latter will want to protect it from furthering the Cause. And so I have taken steps to secure it in a place where no government will ever find it.

You are my only heir, Elizabeth. The papers I was so concerned about your keeping track of—the papers in the black metal box—include a copy of my will. If it is somehow stolen from you or if you lose it, Mason Ellerbe has a copy. He also knows my wishes in regards to our home, and should anyone attempt to fight your inheritance, he will come to your aid.

And now to the end of the matter. Robert knows the location of some keys. Have him get them for you, but under no circumstances are you to have him with you when you use them. Robert already knows too much, and it is never healthy for a man's slaves to know all his secrets. There is a false door behind the paneling in the basement room where we stored the furniture. As you stand in the doorway looking into the room, count from the left-hand corner. The twenty-first board is loose. Remove it and you will find a hidden door. The hinges are ten boards to the right of the lock.

Behind that room there is a tunnel, and halfway down the tunnel, there is a pile of crates. They hold some things of interest, intended only to distract looters. There is a significant amount of Confederate money in one of the metal boxes. I doubt that by the time you read this letter it will have much value. If it makes me a traitor to say it, then call me a traitor. I write what I believe.

What came out of the vault is buried beneath those crates. Once you have located all 1250, you have everything. Take extreme care not to reveal the location. Take extreme care in the use of the funds. Do nothing to garner unwanted attention, and please remember that you are a beautiful woman and there will always be men seeking to prey on the lonely.

I have loved you in my own way, Elizabeth. The 1250 are the only proof I can offer you now. I would hope that if I'd had another chance, I would have behaved more honorably. That is all. Good-bye.

Libbie read the letter three times. She didn't cry, and yet she couldn't help but think that Walker's letter was one of the most tragic things she'd ever encountered. He sounded so desperately alone. Frightened, but unable to share it—or show it. Caring for his sister, and yet so woefully incapable of expressing it. Ambitious, and yet unable to truly enjoy anything he'd accomplished. Desperately unhappy, knowing it, and powerless to rectify it. She bowed her head. *Lord God in heaven, please save me from making the same mistakes.*

Maggie hadn't said a word. When Libbie finally looked over at her, concern shone in her expression. "Is there anything I can do?"

Libbie held out the letter. "Read it. Please." She shivered. So many warnings. He'd said so many things designed to build a hedge around her. To protect her, he said. But if being protected meant that she had to keep secrets...had to be alone...she'd been alone long enough.

Maggie handed the letter back. "He did care for you," she said.

"Too late," Libbie said. "Too late for it to do either of us any good." She swiped at the tears. "I suppose I can answer yours and Jack's question about what I'm going to do now." She looked about her. "I'll be staying here. Not that I ever thought I'd leave."

"But you own it now," Maggie said. "You can do what you want with it."

Whatever I want. What did she want? She didn't know the first thing about running a plantation.

Maggie reached over and squeezed her hand. "Don't be afraid."

"I'd be a fool if I weren't. I don't know the first thing about running a plantation. I don't know much of anything about things that matter."

"You'll learn," Maggie said.

"I'd better learn in a hurry. I have to tell the slaves about this. Make out their papers. And if Annabelle and Malachi decide to leave—I'll starve, for one thing. I've never cooked a thing in my life."

"I can't imagine Annabelle leaving," Maggie said. "She seems truly fond of you. Offer her a position. Head cook. Kitchen boss. Whatever suits her. She knows you need her."

"Simple as that?"

"Well, no," Maggie said. "I doubt anything will be quite as simple as that, but we've hired help before on the farm. I don't see any reason you can't. How many acres do you have?"

"I don't know."

"Someone knows," Maggie said. "What about Asa James?"

Libbie shuddered. "He's gone with the Guard and I don't want him back. Ever."

"You'll find someone."

"Now *I'm* the one who's afraid." She looked back at the letter. "And what's he talking about...twelve hundred fifty? Twelve hundred and fifty what?"

"Easy enough to find out," Maggie said.

"Come with me."

Maggie shook her head. "He expressly ordered you not to let anyone else know."

"If it's twelve hundred and fifty dollars," Libbie said, "are you going to hit me over the head and run off with it?"

Maggie snorted. "Of course not. I'll smother you in your sleep and pretend to be distraught when you don't wake up tomorrow."

"Not very creative," Libbie said and got to her feet. She lit one of the small lamps used for after-dark visits to the outhouse. "At least we don't have our nightgowns on yet," she said. "Come on. Neither of us will be able to sleep until we dig it up—whatever it is."

Maggie shook her head. "I mean it. I don't want to know."

"But I trust you."

"Then trust that I'm doing the right thing. Whatever you find in that tunnel, I don't want you to speak of it. I wish I'd never heard of it. Whatever it is, move it. Don't tell me where, just move it and let that be the end of it."

"But—why? You're my friend. I know I can trust you."

"You're the only true friend I've ever had, Libbie Blair. I don't care if it's the pot of gold at the end of the Irish rainbow, I don't want to hear about it." She handed Libbie the letter. "Take this with you. I wish I'd never read it."

❧

United States of America. Twenty D. An eagle on one side, Lady Liberty on the other. Libbie stared down at the two rows in disbelief. Walker had left her one thousand two hundred and fifty twenty-dollar gold coins. *How much was it?* Her index finger wrote the numbers in the air as she worked the problem. She worked it again. And yet again, for she couldn't believe it.

She'd always thought their parents were wealthy, and Walker had inherited it all, but he always worried about money. The man had twenty-five thousand dollars in gold in a bank vault and he'd never taken any joy in it.

Libbie didn't know whether to be angry at him—again—or weep for him. Weeping won out. And with the tears came a jolt of fear. Her mind reeled. *Move it. Don't tell anyone.* And then, finally, *do only good.* She could do a lot of good. And she would start with Maggie Malone, who was going to be trekking about the country with her boys. She would need at least a couple of skirts without bullet holes in them. Betty would know what to buy and how to make them.

By the time Libbie locked the doors behind her and padded back up the stairs, she was smiling. With God's help, she would see to it that Walker's fortune gave only joy. Anonymously.

Stepping out of the back door and looking up at the night sky, Libbie felt the cloud that had hung over her future dissipate. Wildwood Grove had been many things, but it had never been her home. That was about to change.

❧

Two weeks after the Battle of Wildwood Grove, the Irish Brigade was ordered to the Missouri-Kansas border, where a guerilla named Quantrill was wreaking havoc. The brigade was to be transported to Kansas City by steamboat, but not before they treated the city of Littleton to a full dress parade. The men spent the better part of two days polishing boots, trimming beards, cleaning weapons, and grooming horses and mules.

Maggie watched it all with a growing sense of desperation. She'd requested a private meeting with Captain Quinn to plead her case, but either he didn't get the message or he didn't want to see her. It was as if he'd forgotten what she'd done for Hero—who was happily ensconced at the Feenys'.

Jack and Seamus had been given leave to do some of the cleanup at the farm, and much to Maggie's surprise, when Paddy mentioned the possibility of young Noah staying on to help with chores, Noah said he would do it. He hadn't ever had a home away from the river, he said, and he liked the idea of giving it a try. Not to mention, he and Kerry-boy had taken to each other so much that the pair had become inseparable. When Paddy expressed doubts as to his own ability to raise a boy, Noah said that he was mostly raised and that wouldn't be a problem. Maggie suspected the two would have their share of arguments, but then the Malones had always been inclined to show affection by the way they reconciled after a good fight.

She didn't want to go home. She'd made a home with the Irish. She'd fallen in love with a soldier. The men had applauded her. But now they seemed bent on marching away without her. They were all acting strange as the day approached when they would leave. It was as if they were watching her. As if they hadn't gotten to know her. Even Ashby, who was, praise be to God, on the mend, was different when she came around. He seemed to favor Libbie now. And while it was true that Libbie was teaching him to read, Maggie didn't see that that was any reason for Ashby to switch loyalties quite so completely.

John Coulter was no comfort, either. Just when Maggie thought she'd say yes the next time he proposed marriage, he seemed to give up on her. They'd all given up on her, it seemed.

"Don't be silly," Libbie said. "Nothing's changed. Your boys still love you and so does John. They're just busy getting ready to move out. That's all it is. They don't mean anything by it."

The morning that Libbie and Betty presented Maggie with two completely new ensembles and the requisite unmentionables, Maggie cried—not because she was touched, which of course she was, but because she didn't think she needed to be "outfitted for the march," as Libbie said.

"Captain Quinn won't speak to me about it," she said. "And John refuses to plead my case."

"And since when does Maggie Malone need permission to join the army?" Libbie teased. "You waded right in the last time."

But something in Maggie had changed. She cared what the boys thought of her now. She wanted them to want her. She didn't want to force herself upon them. What had she done wrong? Were they really going to leave her behind?

The morning of July 23 was beautiful. Absolutely perfect for a day's march. When Maggie made the point to John, he gave her a lukewarm hug and said, "Have faith, Maggie-girl. Captain Quinn hasn't forgotten you, nor have the boys. They never will." And then he teased her about the lavender soap. "Still have it in your pocket?"

"Does it matter?" Maggie snapped.

John smiled. "Would I ask if it didn't?" He kissed her on the cheek, mounted Blue, and rode away.

It would be a glorious day, and Maggie was miserable. Couldn't John see that her heart was breaking? She needed more than a hastily whispered "Have faith." He wasn't even going to accompany her into town. Fish was stuck with her.

"May I offer you a ride, mademoiselle?" Fish called, patting the wagon seat and flashing a smile. "We are to form the parade just outside of town. You will have to walk only a short distance. Miss Feeny says you will watch with her, is that correct?"

Maggie supposed it was. The Feeny home was right across

the street from the small park where all the speeches would be given. The regimental band would play and then the boys would march away, drums beating, fifes playing, all the way to the levee and on board the two steamboats waiting to take them to Kansas City.

Libbie was riding Pilot to town, thereby leaving the carriage for Malachi and Annabelle, Betty, Robert, and Ora Lee. The field hands would follow in one of the smaller farm wagons. Captain Quinn had even arranged for some of the wounded men who'd been camping in the yard to be taken to town by wagons so that they wouldn't miss the speeches. Maggie envisioned that it would be almost as inspiring as Independence Day. Without the fireworks, of course.

Fish whistled and hummed all the way to Littleton, admiring the Malone farm as they drove past. It did look nice, Maggie had to admit. Paddy had replanted the garden, and repaired the broken windows. No one would ever suspect what it had looked like back in June.

There were worse things than being sent home, she supposed. *Much worse things. Stop feeling sorry for yourself.*

Fish practically kicked her out of the wagon at the edge of town and sent her off to the Feenys'. She was only halfway there when Libbie rode up. Hopping down, she walked the rest of the way, with her beautiful chestnut gelding prancing beside them.

Littleton had dressed for the day. Nearly every home along the parade route was flying the Stars and Stripes. Before long, the townspeople began to filter out of their homes and line the parade route. Red, white, and blue bunting festooned the newspaper office and several other businesses. Maggie had noticed flowers on every soldier's grave in the churchyard.

The sound of drums in the distance was met by the cheers of the crowd. Here came the colors, the golden harp glistening against the solid green silk, the Stars and Stripes rippling in the wind. Fifes played, and then the sound of marching. First, the colonel and his staff. Then the men. Captain Quinn and John Coulter riding side by side. Was it her imagination, or had Captain Quinn nodded as he rode past? John had definitely winked at her. Saints above, she did love him. *Let him ask me again. Just once more, Father. I'll say yes with my whole heart.*

The regiment marched past, and somewhere in the midst of her broken heart Maggie let the pride shine through. She was proud of every one of them. Even Philem O'Malley had taken a turn for the better, she thought. President Lincoln should be here. It would have been worth the trip all the way from Washington to see such loyal men, willing to give their very lives for things that truly mattered.

The troops moved along, and Bridget and Libbie each grabbed one of Maggie's hands and dragged her across the street and into the park. "We have to get closer," they insisted. "We don't want to miss a word."

The colonel spoke and the mayor of Littleton spoke. The new sheriff—a Union man. Captain Quinn said a few words, as did each of the company captains. It was all fine and flowery, but the crowd was becoming restive and Maggie wanted time with John before he left. The dignitaries rambled, and finally it seemed that everyone who could possibly have anything to say had said it. But then the colonel waved for everyone to be quiet "for just a moment longer—if you please, ladies and gentlemen. We have a bit of business to conduct."

The crowd quieted. The colonel reached behind him and draped what looked like a blue blanket over one arm.

"There is a tradition," he said, "that I am told began in Napoleon's army. Now, while we who fight for freedom have no desire to follow the example of an emperor, Americans have always been known for taking the best of everything and purposing it for the cause of liberty. And so we wish to do this day." He paused. "If you would be so kind, Miss Maggie Malone, would you make your way to the podium?"

Maggie frowned. She glanced over at Libbie.

Libbie gave her a little nudge. "You heard him. Go on."

Bridget clasped her hands together and giggled.

Fish appeared, seemingly out of nowhere, bowed, and offered his arm. The crowd parted as they made their way to the podium.

"Ah, here she is." The colonel nodded. He looked across the crowd, and then he spoke to Maggie. "We took a vote, Miss Malone. It was unanimous." He held up the blue blanket—which was not a blanket at all, but her blue wool cape, adorned with gold buttons and red braid. "The Irish Brigade begs the honor of serving alongside you, Miss Malone. Will you accept the title of Daughter of the Regiment? Will you march with us?"

Cheering began. The boys hooted and stomped and hurrahed.

Maggie couldn't speak. She could only nod. The colonel draped the cape over her shoulders. She looked down at the three rows of gilt buttons, the red braid. Fish had teased her about it so many times, and here it was. The finest moment of her life.

Except that it wasn't, for John Coulter was approaching the stage, and while the boys continued to holler and hoot, he was getting down on one knee and asking her to marry him.

The colonel leaned in. "As I understand it, Miss Malone,

Daughters of the Regiment are generally married to an officer. *Lieutenant* Coulter offered to satisfy that requirement. He actually said he'd been trying to satisfy it for some time now, but that he couldn't get you to accept."

"I accept," Maggie said. But John couldn't hear her. In fact, she hadn't really heard the proposal. And so she leaned down. "Did you want to ask me something?"

He took her hand at the same time that he nuzzled her ear. "Will you marry me?"

"When?"

That surprised him. "Today?"

She would.

And she did.

AFTERWORD

As the Daughter of her Regiment, **Mary Margaret Malone Coulter** served her boys faithfully. She was with them when they operated against William Quantrill and his Missouri Guerillas, with them in Tennessee, and with them during the siege of Vicksburg. When Colonel and Mrs. John Coulter were mustered out in December 1864, they returned to Littleton, where they raised prize-winning Belgians (with the help of Paddy Devlin), Irish wolfhounds, and tall children.

Libbie Blair and Jack Malone corresponded for three years and were married in 1864. After the war, Major and Mrs. Jack Malone remained in the Littleton area and enjoyed a long and happy married life as partners in a horse-breeding venture that produced some of the finest saddle horses in America. Like the Coulters, the Malones also raised children: six of their own, four siblings who'd been orphaned by the war, and an unknown number of not exactly orphaned but desperately needy children. At their sixtieth wedding anniversary, nearly one hundred of those in attendance claimed familial ties.

Seamus Malone romanced Bridget Feeny through the mail until she agreed to marry him, in November 1862. The couple were married in December and welcomed their first child nine months later and their second exactly nine months after Seamus's second furlough. He endured the endless jokes by the men of Company D with good grace, and after the war, Captain and Mrs. Seamus Malone lived happily ever after on the Malone family farm.

Malachi and Annabelle Blair stayed on at Wildwood Grove, with Malachi as head caretaker and gardener and Annabelle reigning over a kitchen staff that produced some of the best food in the state. Along with Dix and Sally Little, the Blairs were founding members of Littleton's African Methodist Episcopal Church. In 1875, the church welcomed Reverend Noah Devlin as head pastor. Reverend Devlin celebrated his golden anniversary at the Littleton AME Church in 1900— with an impressive number of local Irish in attendance.

Rumors regarding buried treasure at the plantation Miss Blair inherited from her brother were never substantiated, although no one was ever able to determine the exact source of the wealth that enabled the newly married Mrs. Malone to renovate her brick mansion and donate it to the Littleton Memorial Society as a home for destitute soldiers. For as long as they lived, no member of the Irish Brigade, the Wildwood Guard, or the Ellerbe Militia who came to the Grove seeking help was turned away.

AUTHOR'S NOTE

Dear Reader,

This book is a result of highway signs intended to lure travelers driving across Missouri on Interstate 70 to visit the site of the Battle of Lexington and a Confederate cemetery. Confederates in Missouri? A plantation worked by slaves less than fifty miles from Kansas City? Congratulations, Missouri Department of Tourism. You got me. I visited. I read. I researched.

The State of Missouri holds a unique place in Civil War history. Its citizenry represented passionate abolitionists such as Elijah Lovejoy of St. Louis and equally passionate slaveholders whose plantations dotted the countryside of what was then called Little Dixie. For a brief time in 1861, Missouri actually had two state governments, each one equally determined to see that citizens followed its laws and upheld its beliefs.

At some point during my research journey, I "met" a woman named Kady Brownell. She introduced me to the topic of Civil War Daughters of the Regiment. I read about Irish Biddy (Bridget Divers of the 1st Michigan) and many others. I visited the Oliver C. Anderson house in Lexington, Missouri, and wandered the Confederate Cemetery at Higginsville, Missouri. I read. And read. And read. Slowly, an idea for a book formed, and when Christina Boys of Faith-Words agreed that it was a story worth telling, I began to write.

The subject was immense—overwhelming, in many ways. My life as a novelist grew directly out of a passionate interest in history and the lives of the individual women who lived through momentous events. It's not an exaggeration to say that, for me, when it comes to my writing life, the history comes first. Each one of my twenty-plus novels has been inspired by actual events and real women. There is historic precedent for every aspect of every story. That being said, I'm not teaching history. My primary job as a novelist is to entertain, and even though I embrace that purpose, there is still sometimes a kind of "creative dissonance," wherein the historian and the storyteller are forced to resolve conflict.

The conflict between Whitson, the historian, and Stephanie Grace, the storyteller, has never been a greater challenge for me than it has been as I worked on the book you hold in your hands. Scholars dedicate their lives to interpreting and understanding the myriad aspects of the Civil War in America. Thousands of contemporary reenactors dedicate themselves to authenticity. And here I am, seeking to add my voice to the mix. I do so with humility and with appreciation for the immensity of the task I've taken on.

This book is more "fiction" than any of my other novels to this point. Why? Because, out of profound respect for the people who actually lived those turbulent years of war (the heroes and heroines who fought and those who served in countless other ways), I decided that the most respectful thing I could do was to acknowledge my inability to adequately replicate real battles and real brigades in their proper political and geographical context.

As far as my research has shown, there were no official "daughters" attached to Missouri regiments during the American Civil War, but the Daughters of the Regiment mentioned in the dedication were very real. You can read about them in Elizabeth D. Leonard's fascinating and scholarly work *All the Daring of the Soldier* and see the uniform that inspired Maggie's cape pictured on the cover of this book by visiting the Smithsonian Institution's website. The Irish Brigade that fights the Battle of Wildwood Grove is my own creation (inspired by Missouri's Irish Seventh). I invented the Battle of Wildwood Grove (inspired by the Battle of Lexington). This is how I work. I seek out historic precedent, strive for as much accuracy in historical detail as possible, and then I tell the best story I know how to tell.

There is a well-known epitaph that reads, "She hath done what she could." The phrase could easily be applied to this book. I have done the best I can to create a story that pays tribute to the friendships won and lost, the wartime love stories, and the profound changes that the Civil War wrought in society.

I set out to sing the praises of the Daughters of the Regiment. And now, it's up to you to decide if I succeeded.

Stephanie Grace Whitson
March 2014
Stephanie@stephaniewhitson.com
www.stephaniewhitson.com

The Daughter of the Regiment

Who with the soldiers was stanch danger-sharer,—
Marched in the ranks through the shriek of the shell?
Who was their comrade, their brave color-bearer?
Who but the resolute Kady Brownell!

Over the marshland and over the highland,
Where'er the columns wound, meadow or dell,
Fared she, this daughter of little Rhode Island,—
She, the intrepid one, Kady Brownell!

While the mad rout at Manassas was surging,
When those around her fled wildly, or fell,
And the bold Beauregard onward was urging,
Who so undaunted as Kady Brownell!

When gallant Burnside made dash upon Newberne,
Sailing the Neuse 'gainst the sweep of the swell,
Watching the flag on the heaven's broad blue burn,
Who higher hearted than Kady Brownell!

In the deep slough of the springtide debarking,
Toiling o'er leagues that are weary to tell,
Time with the sturdiest soldiery marking,
Forward, straight forward, strode Kady Brownell.

Reaching the lines where the army was forming,
Forming to charge on those ramparts of hell,
When from the wood came her regiment swarming,
What did she see there—this Kady Brownell?

—*Clinton Scollard*

DISCUSSION QUESTIONS

- What made you want to read *Daughter of the Regiment*? To which character did you relate most? What was it about that character that spoke to you?
- Both Maggie and Libbie are guilty of making assumptions about others based on externals. Both women are also victims of the same tendency in others. Have you ever experienced similar situations? How can healing occur when relationships have been broken by false assumptions? If you were either woman's confidante, how would you counsel her? What Scripture would you use?
- Both Maggie and Libbie have to deal with deep disappointment and fear. What is similar about their reactions? What is different? Why do you think the differences exist?
- Discuss Libbie's relationship with Ora Lee and Annabelle. How did each woman benefit from knowing the others? How do you think their relationship will change in the years after the book ends?
- What would you say was the most difficult decision Maggie had to make over the course of the story? What about Libbie? If you were in their shoes, do you think you would have decided differently? Why or why not?
- Did you already know about the Daughters of the Regiment who served during the Civil War before reading this

book? If so, did you learn anything new? What did you admire most about their service as portrayed in the novel? What would have been the most difficult part of being a Daughter?

- Based on your family heritage (e.g., where your ancestors lived in 1861), what "side" of the Civil War would you have been on? Would you have experienced some of the same neighbor vs. neighbor tensions depicted in the book? Would different members of your family have been loyal to opposing sides? How would you have coped? How would you have served?

- Who was your favorite minor character (and yes, the dogs could be considered minor characters)? Why?

- Do you agree with how the author presented the future in the Afterword? If not, what would you change? How?

- You are the casting director for the film version of *Daughter of the Regiment*. Who would you cast to play Maggie Malone? Libbie Blair? What about John Coulter? Other characters?

ABOUT THE AUTHOR

STEPHANIE GRACE WHITSON is the bestselling author of over twenty inspirational novels and two works of nonfiction. A lifelong learner, she received a master of arts degree in history in 2012 and has a passionate interest in pioneer women's history. When she isn't writing, speaking, or trying to keep up with her five grown children and perfect grandchildren, Stephanie enjoys long-distance rides aboard her Honda Magna motorcycle named Kitty. Her church and the International Quilt Study Center and Museum in Lincoln, Nebraska, take up the rest of her free time. Visit her website at www.stephaniewhitson.com.

ALSO BY
STEPHANIE GRACE WHITSON

A Captain for Laura Rose

Laura Rose White's late father taught her everything he knew about piloting a Missouri River steamboat and even named their boat after her. Still, it seems that Laura will forever be a "cub pilot" to her brother Joe, because in 1867, a female riverboat captain is unheard of. That is, until tragedy strikes and Laura must make the two-month journey from St. Louis to Fort Benton and back in order to save her family's legacy, her home, and the only life she's ever known.

The only way for her to overcome the nearly insurmountable odds is with the help of her brother's disreputable friend Finn MacKnight, a skilled pilot with a terrible reputation. Laura loathes having to accept MacKnight as her copilot, especially when she learns she must also provide passage for his two sisters. Straitlaced Fiona has a fear of water, and unpredictable Adele seems much too comfortable with the idea of life in the rough and tumble environment of the untamed river and the men who ply it. Though they are thrown together by necessity, this historic journey may lead Laura and the MacKnights to far more than they ever expected.

Available in trade paperback and ebook formats from FaithWords wherever books are sold.